KARL BAKKE

FADE TO BLACK

D1707288

The currency of life is time,
not money,
spend it well.
KB

Arctic Night Publishing
A division of Arctic Night Productions, INC.

This is a work of fiction. Names, characters, organizations, places, events,
and incidents are either products of the author's imagination or are used fictitiously.

ISBN-13: 978-0692854082
ISBN-10: 0692854088

Published by Arctic Night Publishing
A division of Arctic Night Productions, INC.
23901 Calabasas Rd, Ste 2018
Calabasas, CA 91302

Cover Design by Julika Kade

*In the memory of my mother, Anne H. Bakke,
who with an artist's soul and a poet's heart, gave me
the greatest gift of all – the courage to chase my dreams.*

PROLOGUE

HOLLYWOOD, CALIFORNIA – 17 YEARS AGO

The young man was born today. He would have been alive for eighteen years tomorrow at 10:26 a.m., but he was born today. The young man liked the lights. They sparkled in a great dance toward the horizon, infinite, alive, connected, like him. He was a man today. He felt it in the hardness of his body. He touched it, stroked it. He ran his hands across his body feeling his skin tingle, as if cut by a hundred shards of glass. He stood on top of the giant H of the famous Hollywood sign, the other letters disappearing into the darkness beside him. He moved to the edge of the sign and looked down at the drop. The Bender would be here soon.

The young man ran his tongue over the smoothness of his teeth. He needed his speed. He longed for its taste, its clarity. He was turned around, bent. He watched the ocean of lights moving softly below him. The City of Angels was a temptress, a bitch, a siren, as he was Ulysses. It called to him, a forbidden lover, its charms erotic, addictive, deadly.

The young man grabbed his head. The benders had turned him around. They had been hard at work, but soon he would be clear, straight. He waited for the rush, the sweet, saving rush. It didn't come. He bit down hard on his lip, feeling the taste of his blood as his mind spun. He saw his soul in front of him. He reached out and touched it. It was backwards.

The lights of the city burned into his mind. They danced and moved within, like angels in Hell. He pounded his fist into his head and spun in circles on the edge of the sign. He had always known his destiny. The wind whispered in his ear and he laughed. He could see his body dropping off into the darkness, breaking the benders away forever, as his bones shattered on the rocks below.

The wind pushed against him, as if to warn him back from the edge. How silly, he thought. He felt the edge of the sign, through the toes of his shoes. One step and he was free. The thought excited him, aroused him. He leaned into the wind, toward the touch of darkness. It would be wonderful, like entering a lover for the first time. He smiled and raised his arms. He was ready, to be free.

The young man's eyes flew open as he felt a rush and his mind lit up, the Dexedrine finally hitting him with a wave of speed. It rushed through his body. He tingled, with ecstasy, his mind racing towards clarity. The drug, unwinding and straightening him, like a thousand tiny fingers on the knots of his brain.

The roar of an engine rose above the wind, as bright lights flashed below him. He grew steady as he watched the approaching headlights. A black sedan pulled beneath him. He smiled. The Bender was here.

The young man climbed down, his body unwinding. When he reached the bottom, the Bender was waiting. He walked toward him, his clarity growing with each passing second. He had brought the Bender a gift. His skin felt cool, the shards of glass having dropped away. He stopped beside the Bender. He unrolled a long sheet of plastic, laying it on the ground. The Bender smelled of after-shave and sweet soap. The Bender looked at him, questioning.

"What the hell?"

The young man smiled. The Bender's eyes were large and wet. They glistened in the moonlight as the Bender looked down and saw the dark metal of the tire iron resting in the young man's hand.

The Bender opened his mouth to speak and the young man stepped into him, the swing full, like a batter at a fastball. The iron connected in a liquid thud. Blood blew from the Bender's back, showering the plastic sheet as he collapsed. The young man watched the Bender's eyes as he squirmed on the bloody plastic. Round, fat eyes.

Another wave of Dexedrine rushed through his brain like an orgasm. He felt it. He was in the zone now, nothing could touch him. He wiped a drop of blood off his forehead. He was on the line, clear, sharp. The Bender was trying to get away. He was crawling across the plastic, like he had somewhere to go. The young man looked out at the lights of the city.

2

It was his birthday. He was infinite, alive, connected. He smiled. The Bender screamed. No one was listening.

They were alone, in a city of millions.

ONE

LOS ANGELES, CALIFORNIA – PRESENT DAY

The pain was far away now. The blows coming down one after
another made my body tingle, took me to a place deep within, a place as
tight and as twisted as the muscle and bone I was faintly aware was
breaking in my body. The voices were muffled. The blows, soft thuds. I
was gone; so far within I may never get back. I tried to open my eyes, my
mouth, but the world was far away. Life, a thin razor cutting across my
brain. My eyes flew open, my voice ripping through the night in a scream.

I looked up at the ceiling fan spinning around in the shadows of my
bedroom. I lay still, my heart pounding, my breath shallow and quick. I
came back from the dream as I watched the blades of the fan spin around.
The dream seemed real. It once had been. I could feel my legs and arms
still tingle where they had been broken. I moved slowly, sitting up over
the edge of my bed.

A hot Santa Ana wind followed the morning light into my bedroom,
blowing across my sweat-drenched body. It was hot as hell. The Santa
Ana blew off the desert like the devil's own breath, toasting the west San
Fernando Valley and the rest of L.A. with it. I stood up and lit a cigarette,
not very smart, I know, but what the hell.

The dream was a familiar one. It had happened a few years ago while
I was working a case. As private investigators go, I'd been lucky. I was
saved by one of the guys who was beating me. He'd recognized me from
my previous profession, that of Dr. Steve Scott, the womanizing,
sensitive, corrupt, genius doctor of a prime time soap opera that ran for
six years. Apparently, his wife was a big fan, and he couldn't live with

the guilt of killing off Dr. Scott, especially, he said, after all I had been through on the show: two marriages, nine affairs, two bouts with deadly diseases, a plane crash, vasectomy, the loss of my wife and little girl in an freak amusement park accident (a giant plastic clown crushed them as it tumbled to the ground), and so much more.

The guy had driven me to the hospital himself. In my half-conscious state, I heard him talking to his wife on his cell phone, telling her that he had Dr. Scott in the car. "No shit!" He pressed the receiver in my face to say hi to her, but my mouth was swollen shut from his handiwork. He stopped the car at the hospital exit, pushed me out and took off. The hospital doctors told me I was lucky to be alive. When I got my bill from the hospital, there was a twenty percent doctor's discount on it, apparently, for being a doctor. Fame has its moments.

The role of Dr. Scott had been a blessing and a curse. I'd been a struggling actor for ten years, and the steady employment and the money that came with the role were welcome. It bought me a house and many of the things I'd wanted in life, but when it ended, so it seems, did my career. I had been so convincing in my role as Dr. Scott, that no one could see me as anything else. I was what they call in the business "overexposed." I couldn't buy a job.

On a lark I took a job tracking down a witness to a murder for a friend of mine, who is a District Attorney. My friend Blake is the closest thing I have to a brother. We grew up together. He needed this witness tracked down so he could testify. Nobody had been able to find him, so he asked me to give it a shot.

Unemployed and with plenty of time on my hands, I thought, what the hell. I took the job, found the guy, and the rest, as they say, is history. I got my license, worked for the District Attorney's office for a couple of years, and then opened up my own office, Will Spire Investigating. Spire is my real last name. My stage name had been Will Wallace, and if I ever start to get my bones broken again, I'll become Dr. Steve Scott real quick. Couldn't hurt. You never know who's a fan.

I got up off my bed and walked through the heat, naked, out the bay doors to the pool. I fell into the pool, letting the cold water wash me. I lifted my head out of the water, the dry wind licking up the moisture from my face like a parched dragon. By the time I'd reached the bay doors of the house, I was dry again. I re-lit my cigarette on the burner of the stove in the kitchen and put on a pot of coffee.

I sat down at the kitchen table and flipped open the paper, not bothering to get dressed. My house was my refuge, not large but open in the California way, with cathedral ceilings and surrounded on the outside by the bright twisting colors of bougainvillea.

I sipped my coffee as I scanned the paper. My head felt like a little man with a hammer was mining my brain. The little man had been my best friend last night, and I knew him well. He lived in a bottle with a black label, last name Daniels, first name Jack. The little man was going to town this morning, mining the brain cells he'd killed last night. I popped a couple of Excedrin into my coffee and flipped the page. Jack and I couldn't have done that much damage. I could still read.

I stepped from the shower and slipped on a cotton sport shirt and some jeans. I stared in the mirror. My face stared back, looking much older than I remembered from the day before. I was thirty-eight, thought I was twenty-eight, felt like I was fifty-eight. I didn't like what I saw. The man in the mirror seemed to stare at me as if I were a stranger on a bus. I raised my hand and waved just to make sure it was me. It was. I debated whether I should shave the few days' growth of beard on my face. If I did it would mean more mirror time with the stranger. Will Wallace, the actor, said I should. Will Spire, the PI, said forget it. I compromised and shaved my neck, leaving the rest of the stubble where it lay. I flipped off the guy in the mirror; he flipped me back.

I walked out the side door and into the garage. My black, '68 convertible Corvette Stingray still looked good. It had been the first thing I bought for myself when I got the part of Dr. Steve Scott.

I hopped over the door and into the Vette, sliding my six-foot-two frame down into the car. It fit like a glove. I turned the key and listened to the engine purr. I hit the garage door opener and pulled out past my front lawn and onto Winnetka Avenue. I took Winnetka past Ventura Boulevard and hit the 101 Freeway, taking it north toward Ventura.

Within minutes it seemed as if L.A. was behind me, the rolling hills of Calabasas appearing, not dotted with homes, but cattle, sheep, and wild oak. This was still L.A. County, but you would never know it. Los Angeles is as huge and diverse with people, places, and things as anywhere on Earth. It spreads out forever, including the wealthiest estates and the poorest slums. Its topography can go from desert, to prairie grass, to green rolling hills and babbling brooks, to mountains and the sea, all in a thirty-minute drive. Within that drive, the temperature can drop or rise from one area to another as much as thirty degrees.

Even on a day like today, with the Santa Ana condition bringing hot winds from the deserts in mid-March, making it feel like July, there is snow on the surrounding mountains. You can ski locally and be back to the beach in two hours. Six hours away in Mammoth Lakes, bowled into the Sierra Nevada's, people will be skiing until the Fourth of July. The diversity of Southern California, of Los Angeles, its ability to look like a million different places all within minutes of each other is what makes this the ideal place for the film industry.

Everything you have ever heard about L.A. is true. The good, the bad, the ugly, and everything in between; but trying to capture its essence, to label it, was like trying to grab a fistful of water. You thought you had it, then it slipped away.

I turned off the freeway and headed through Malibu Canyon toward the beach. The road was one of my favorites, cutting through rolling hills and passing mountains that looked as if they were transported from Kauai, in the Hawaiian Islands. The narrow road winds around a gorge that drops over a hundred feet to a creek that runs to the sea. I put my foot down on the gas and shot the Corvette through a tunnel carved out of rock, the scenery suddenly turning European. With the top down I could feel the heat of the Valley drop away as I approached the sea. The little man, Jack, had taken a break from pounding on my brain, the caffeine and Excedrin having caught onto his tricks. A thick marine layer hung over the coast, blocking out the sun and dropping the temperature a good twenty degrees. I wound down out of the canyon toward the coast. I passed Pepperdine University and its rolling green lawns and made a right on Pacific Coast Highway, heading toward the Colony, and my past.

The beach house loomed in the distance at the end of the private road. The house seemed larger than most strip malls, its white stucco exterior modeled after a palace of some sort. I pulled around a fountain in the center of the circular driveway, stopping in front of two large blue doors marking the front of the house. I got out of my car and looked up at the doors towering above me. The doorknocker was the size of my head. Everything about the place seemed oversized. I felt like Alice in Wonderland, or Dorothy at the gates of Oz. I avoided using the knocker. I'd probably hurt myself. I pressed my fist into a doorbell the size of a cantaloupe and waited.

My ex-wife, Stacey, opened the door of the house and smiled at me. At five-ten, the giant doors dwarfed her as they swung slowly open. She had let her hair grow since I had last seen her; it tumbled loose to her shoulders. She wore a cropped-off T-shirt and bikini bottoms, her breasts lifting the shirt off the skin of her stomach. She was tall, thin, and sensual, the kind of woman other women hated just by looking at her. Her skin was covered with small beads of perspiration that made her glow and shine.

"Hi, Stacey. You look great," I said, stepping into the house and giving her a kiss.

"You look like shit," she said, laughing. "Jesus! Did somebody beat the hell out of you? Or are those just circles under your eyes?"

"Thanks, Stacey, I was feeling pretty bad before I saw you, but now I feel all sweet and cozy inside." I took out a cigarette and lit it. Stacey took it from my mouth and threw it outside, shutting the door behind it.

"Feels like old times," I said.

I looked around the interior of the house. The house was bigger than most city blocks, with windows from the floor to the sky, showing the crashing waves of the blue Pacific on a private beach. I picked up a vase, examining it. It looked just liked one I had bought at Pier 1 Imports. It wasn't; it was Ming, the real thing.

"I was just taking a steam bath," Stacey said as she moved away from me. I watched her walk. A walk I'd seen a thousand times and had never gotten tired of, a walk that had made her big money in her younger years on runways from Milan to New York. Not enough money for this place, though. This place was Bob's. Bob Bayloff, twenty years my senior, but still a spoiled little brat.

8

Bob's specialty was playing movie producer with his daddy's millions that he'd inherited. Bob had a short man's complex—talked loud and fast, but said nothing. He'd screwed his ex-wife over just liked he'd screwed every writer and actor who ever worked for him. According to many in the business, Bob had less talent for filmmaking, or anything creative, than anybody they'd ever seen. But Bob had what Hollywood loved, something better than talent. Money.

So the name of Bob Bayloff "producer" was tattooed on celluloid in many a film, above many a star's name, even though he was known to be "missing in action" during the production of most of his films. He left the real work of filmmaking to people who really did have talent, who wanted to make a good film, who were passionate about their work. Then he took the credit, called it "his film," made millions and moved on, leaving a path of destruction in his wake. The stories were endless as were the lawsuits. He was said to have built his life on the back of other men's broken dreams. He embodied everything that was wrong with Hollywood. I hated him. Stacey had moved in with him two weeks after leaving me.

I followed Stacey across the floor. I looked up at the towering ceilings. "Nice place. Maybe the Raiders could play here. Get them back in L.A."

Stacey ignored me. Her only comment was to take her T-shirt off and pick up a towel off a large white sofa. I looked at the curve of her back running down to her G-string bikini. She turned around and patted her bare breasts with the towel. She moved the towel off her breasts, wiping the perspiration from the rest of her body. This was the Stacey I'd remembered, a little bit manipulative. She knew what she was doing, and she did it better than anyone else.

"Why don't you just take the bottoms off, too?" I said, wryly.

"Good idea," she said, as she slipped the bottoms down her legs and stepped out of them. She let me have a good look, then wrapped a white cotton robe around her naked body. She saw the look on my face.

"I didn't think it was a big deal, Will. We were married for five years."

"Yeah, well, it's been awhile. Is that what you called me over for, the morning strip show? Not that I don't appreciate it." I took a look around the house. "I take it Bob's not around. Where is he? Counting his money? Got to keep count. Wouldn't want to pay a writer or actor what they're worth."

Stacey smiled, "Have a seat, Will."

I sat down in a chair that matched the couch. I sank down three feet. The armrests were now a good foot above my shoulders. I tried to adjust myself and sank further. I figured Bob, the millionaire troll, probably had the whole place rigged like this, except wherever he sat, it probably raised up. Stacey poured a glass of orange juice from a pitcher and handed it to me.

"Bob's missing," she said. "It might be nothing, I don't know." Stacey lowered her eyes to the ground and I knew; it was something.

"He went out of town on a business trip to New York." He was supposed to be gone only three days," she said. "It's been four now and I haven't heard from him."

"Maybe he got delayed?"

"No, Will, you don't understand. I haven't heard from him at all. It's not like him. He usually calls, or texts, almost every day, when he's out of town and tells me how much he misses me."

More like to check up on her, I thought. I stared down into my glass of orange juice. "You don't have anything to put in here do you, like vodka?" If we were going to talk about Bob missing my ex-wife, I needed a drink.

"Will, I'm serious."

I was, too. I saw a wet bar across the way. I struggled to get out of my chair. I was stuck.

"I've called everybody I know. Nobody has heard from him. I don't want to be an alarmist and call the police. If I overreact and he's fine, he'll flip out! Can you imagine the publicity?"

"He's done this before, Stacey. You've told me so. Bob does what Bob wants. Right? Whether it's not calling you for a few days or flying off to Vegas, the Cayman Islands or Switzerland with his buddies, he's going to do what he wants and to hell with everybody else."

Stacey said nothing. She knew it was true.

"Did it ever occur to you that Bob isn't the noblest of men, Stacey? Maybe he doesn't want to call you. Hell, maybe he's left you."

Stacey put her glass down on the table with a bang and glared at me. "Why do you think that, Will? Because you left me?"

"I didn't leave you, Stacey. You left me! Remember?"

"You left me long before that, Will. You just didn't realize it."

"What the hell is that supposed to mean?"

I could feel the blood rise to my face as feelings too familiar arose in me. I met Stacey's glare with my own. She turned away.

"I don't want to fight, Will."

"Me, neither." I downed my orange juice.

"I found this." Stacey handed me a printed boarding pass. "It's Bob's, for his trip. I called the airline and they said he never boarded the flight. I found it in his closet. It was on top of a suitcase with his date book. I opened the suitcase and it was packed, Will. Packed! I didn't know what to do, so I called you. If you think there's something's wrong, then I will call the police."

I could see the concern on Stacey's face and I was starting to see her point. This didn't sound like Bob. He was a meticulous man, a control freak. It didn't make sense for anyone to leave a fully packed suitcase, boarding pass, and date book at home while going on a trip.

"There's this too, Will."

Stacey handed me a small cardboard box. I looked down at its contents. There were paper clippings out of a newspaper. Single, cut-out letters from advertisements and headlines filled the box. There was seemingly every letter of the alphabet represented, perfectly and painstakingly cut into little squares.

There was a small bottle of Elmer's glue and some blank sheets of paper at the bottom of the box.

"What do you make of it?" Stacey asked.

I ran my fingers through the paper letters. "What do I make of it? Trouble."

Stacey lowered her head and began to cry.

TWO

I tried to comfort Stacey, but the floodgates were open. She told me that she had had a dream that Bob was in trouble. In the dream he was white with death. He tried calling to her, but she couldn't hear him, couldn't help him. She said he was smiling.

I told Stacey that it was just a dream, that it meant nothing. I convinced her to take me through the house, room by room, to see if we could find anything that could give us a clue to Bob's whereabouts. The cut-out letters in the box were strange and raised a red flag, as I had seen such things before. People forming text from untraceable letters in order to blackmail someone, extort, write a ransom note, or commit some other crime. But on their own the letters were not a sure sign that Bob was in trouble. Bob was in the entertainment industry. The box could have come from a film he was working on, a prop, something used on set, or by the art department. It could have been left accidentally in his car or office by any number of people. I kicked myself for opening my big mouth and not realizing just how concerned Stacey was. Now, her worst fears seemed confirmed by me.

Stacey took me upstairs and showed me Bob's suitcase and his date book. I flipped through the book's pages. The last entry was the day he was scheduled to leave. He had written down all his flight information. There was no itinerary in the book or Bob's schedule once he arrived in New York, or any other clue to what business he had there.

"Anything else?" I asked. Stacey shook her head.

I opened Bob's suitcase and looked through the contents. Nothing telling, just the usual clothes, toiletries, and a couple of mystery books. I flipped through the pages of the books to see whether there was anything in between the pages; there wasn't.

"Is all this Bob's stuff? Do you recognize it?"

Stacey nodded her head, her eyes, swollen with tears.

"Does this look like what he would take for a few days away?"

Stacey nodded again. "Yes. He was reading that book." Stacey pointed to the first mystery book I had examined. *Murder At Black Lake* was written in big red letters on the jacket of the book. The letters dripped red, simulating blood, from the word "Murder," as a distorted, horror-stricken face glared up at us.

"Where did you find the box with the letters?"

"Back there." Stacey pointed to the back of a walk-in closet that was bigger than my living room. I searched the closet, turning up nothing but about fifty, stubby Armani suits.

"I've called his cell over and over but he didn't answer or respond to my texts and now it just goes right to voicemail."

Stacey sat on the corner of the bed, overwhelmed. The bed looked like it had previously belonged to Julius Caesar. Knowing Bob, it might have. It was large enough to have a rugby match on.

"Can you access his voicemail?"

"No."

"How about his secretary? He was meeting with somebody in New York. If he hadn't arrived, they surely would have tried to contact him."

"Pumpkin. He fired her three weeks ago."

"Pumpkin? That's his secretary's name?"

Stacey nodded as a smile crossed her face.

"What's her last name?" I asked.

"Pie." Stacey's smile turned to laughter as I sat on the bed next to her. "Her parents were hippies. They dropped out and turned on."

"Turned on is right. How many acid hits does it take to name your kid Pumpkin Pie?" I asked as we both started laughing.

"I swear. It's true!" Stacey said. I watched her, her face aglow, her smile bright and alive. It had been a long time since I remembered seeing her like this. It was hard for me to think of Bob making her happy, but she had chosen him; I hope he did. I took her hand and smiled.

"I'm sure Bob's fine, Stacey, don't worry." I leaned over and kissed her forehead. Stacey's eyes met mine as she put her head on my shoulder.

"I'm scared, Will." I wrapped my arms around her, holding her. It was natural, familiar, yet strange. I brushed the hair from Stacey's face as she held me.

"Let's take a look at the rest of the house," I said. Stacey didn't move. Her robe had slipped open, and I could see the curve of her shoulder and her breast beneath. She felt good against me.

She pressed closer to me and I felt the tension in her body relax. My senses were filled with her. I felt like laying her back on the bed and feeling the smoothness of her skin against my mouth, her body melting into mine as it had done a thousand times, until we were both filled with the inevitable ecstasy we physically brought to each other. Sex had never been the problem for us; it had simply been, the best.

She moved her head and I could feel her breath on my neck. I shut my eyes and I could taste her, feel me inside her as she moved against me. I ran my hand across her shoulder, moving it down toward her breast. The feeling was strong, real. The line between my mind, memory, and reality was thinning, disappearing. I felt the curve of her breast beneath my fingers, the smoothness of her thighs. Her legs slipped open as her lips brushed my neck. I stood up suddenly from the bed, bringing Stacey with me. She looked at me as our eyes met. We said nothing for a moment, our eyes locked on each other.

"We should look at the rest of the house," I said, feebly.

Stacey nodded, her eyes still on mine. She straightened out her robe and smiled softly.

"Yes, we should," she said. She took my hand in hers and led me from the room.

I could feel the blood rushing through my veins as Stacey led me down the hall, my heart pumping. My hand slipped from hers and I started to come back. I tried to clear my mind. I tried to think of other things. I thought of the DMV, global warming, Dick Cheney. I was starting to feel better. I kept my eyes away from Stacey as we started down the stairs toward the second level. That had been close, too close. I had almost forgotten the ex, in ex-wife.

We made our way through the house. The place was clean, and I mean clean. You could eat off every floor. We worked our way from room to room, and there were plenty of them. I lost count after the ninth bedroom. I followed Stacey through the kitchen, living room, billiard room, four dens and three recreation rooms, poolroom, two dining rooms, and countless bathrooms. If you had to go, this was the place to be. There were more bathrooms in this house than K-Marts in the Valley.

"That's all the rooms up here. There's a bowling alley and pub downstairs," Stacey said, as she headed toward a large wood door with a sign above it that said "BOB'S PLACE."

"Did you say bowling alley and pub?"

Stacey swung the wood door open as I followed her down the stairs, without an answer. I reached the bottom of the stairs and was confronted with a fully-rigged, four-lane bowling alley, with booths, computer scoring, even a long rack of balls and shoes to choose from, just like the commercial alleys. To the side of the alley was unbelievably, a pub. An English pub to be exact, with a long wooden bar shined to a red gleam with brass stools lining it. There were booths, carved and formed, in what looked like another century, running the length of the opposite wall along with leaded windows looking out toward the bowling alley and a fake English countryside lit by dim stage lights, early evening in merry old England. At the far end of the pub there was a small stage and dance floor. The ceiling was wood beams, rising to a pitch. I had seen a lot in my days, but this was something.

"The pub is real, right down to the last nail. It was transported piece by piece from a town in England. It was built in 1728," Stacey said. She flipped a switch and gas lights flickered on, illuminating the interior of the pub in a soft glow.

"I guess this beats my little wet bar in the corner of my closet," I said, as I made my way across the pub to the bar.

"I remember when we picked that out," Stacey said, as she moved behind the bar.

"Yeah," I sat down on a bar stool and looked around. "You must really miss it."

"Look at the bright side, Will. We've got a fully-stocked bar here and every type of beer and ale in the world, right in front of you." Stacey pulled the lever down on a tap of Bass. The dark liquid flowed to a nice head. She handed me the pint. "And the price is right."

"Good point," I said, as I raised the glass to my lips and took a healthy swig. "Did Bob seem different to you before he was going to leave? Did he act different, seem hesitant about the trip?"

Stacey shook her head.

"Bob was just Bob. He doesn't give a lot away personally, I mean. He travels. This didn't seem any different."

"There was nothing in his behavior that changed? Did he seem more stressed out, nervous?"

Stacey laughed, "Christ, Will, you've met Bob. He's always nervous and stressed out, but he acts like nothing bothers him."

"Does it? Do things bother him?"

"I don't know. Sometimes I think everything bothers him. Other times I'm convinced nothing does, that nothing gets to him, that as long as there's Bob, he needs nothing, that's it, he's fine." Stacey lowered her head slightly, running her hand across the bar.

I touched her hand and smiled. "So what else is down here?"

Stacey led me to the far wall. She opened a door to a glass room. The room was a miniature airport control tower. It looked out toward Bob's massive yard and the blinking lights of a helipad, complete with a Robinson R22 helicopter. No rush hour traffic for Bob.

"Nice," I said.

"The control tower is just for show," Stacey replied, "a place where Bob can watch his guests arrive. The only other rooms down here are the wine cellar and storeroom."

Stacey walked me through the rows and rows of bottles of wine in Bob's wine cellar. I picked up a bottle of Chateau Lafitte Rothschild 1988. I was tempted to uncork it right there. Bob was probably lying on a beach in Barbados, warm and toasty, in the company of one of the countless young actresses who felt the best place to audition for a part was not in Hollywood, but below Bob Bayloff's waist. The man was known for such auditions.

Meanwhile, Stacey, his confessed true love, was worried sick back home, leading her ex-husband through his wine cellar and nearly to his

16

bed. A more selfish man would have taken her in a moment, I thought to myself, Bob's bed or not. I felt noble for a minute, superior for my great control over my animal instincts. I watched Stacey move in front of me. That damned walk.

I held onto the bottle of Rothschild and followed Stacey around a corner. It was a sorry substitute for Stacey and sex, but it was Bob's and I wanted it. It was the least he could do for me, for making me look for him all day and for not having rolled around in his sheets with his girlfriend. I hated him for putting Stacey in this position, making her worry. Not that I hadn't done that myself a few times.

I entered the tenth row of the wine cellar. I was feeling a little grouchy, self-absorbed, and righteous. Being in "Bob's Place" seemed to have that effect on me. I grabbed another bottle of Bob's wine.

"Why did he fire his secretary?"

"I don't know."

"Have you spoken to her?"

"I called her to see if she had heard anything from Bob, but she said she hadn't. She was fired a week before he was scheduled to leave. Bob moved his office out of the studio. He was going to start working from home. She didn't mention, and I didn't ask, why she was let go."

Stacey and I moved down the last row of wine and exited the cellar. Like the rest of the house, there seemed to be no clues to Bob's whereabouts. Everything was in perfect order. I followed Stacey as we walked down a long narrow hallway built of reinforced cinderblock. She opened a large red metal door that looked like one you would see on a bank safe. It opened slowly on hydraulic hinges. I figured the thickness of the metal to be near a foot.

"This is a storage area and shelter. Bob had it specially built. It is the last room in the house," Stacey said, as we entered another narrow hallway and reached another metal door. She unlocked and pulled at the door. It opened like a vacuum.

"Bob has dry food stored, water, canned goods, a couple of freezers of meat. He figures if there is another earthquake, riot, fire, flood, nuclear bomb, whatever, he can live off this stuff down here for a good half a year."

17

The room was immense, like everything else in the house. I looked above me as ventilation fans rotated slowly overhead. I moved along the walls stacked with enough food to feed the homeless of L.A. I was growing grouchier by the minute. I could just picture Bob down here, afraid to venture outside as the screaming mass of neighbors, whose cocktail parties and children he knew well, hungry and thirsty after a disaster, huddled begging at his door as Bob screamed, "I've got mine! I've got mine, you sorry bastards! I told you!"

I moved around the room, examining the rows of stored food on shelves lit by harsh fluorescent lights. Each can, each box, was perfectly spaced and lined up, labels facing out. The walls of the room were sky blue, probably some mute attempt to make the room less claustrophobic and sterile than it was.

There was a couch, table and chairs, a bed, even a kitchen and a bathroom. But for all its comforts it felt like a death trap, built by a vision of great neurosis and ego. Bob Bayloff, the last survivor. I'd rather have the bomb, or whatever, drop right on my head than live in this place and emerge to a world of God knows what. Not that I didn't have earthquake supplies, water and such. But this was something more. This was Bob.

I glanced over at three large freezers against the wall. I looked at a can of tomato ketchup that lay on the ground. I looked around the rest of the room. Everything, as usual, was perfectly in place. I walked over to the can. It lay in a small puddle of water. Stacey reached down to pick it up.

"No!" I said, as I grabbed her arm. Stacey looked at me, startled.

"Don't pick it up." The can had fallen from a neatly stacked group of ketchup cans above it. I bent down, examining the can. "Have you been down here lately?"

"No," Stacey said. "Nobody has. What's going on, Will? It's just a can of ketchup."

The lone can seemed oddly out of place, lying in the water like a dead body in a puddle of blood, its compadres straight as soldiers on the surrounding shelves, silent, giving nothing away. I reached out and touched the puddle of water the can lay in. It was ice cold. Behind the can, at the corner of the freezer, there was a larger pool of water.

I stood up. I took my right arm and pushed Stacey gently behind me. I slipped my left hand under my shirttail hanging in front of me. I reached my hand toward the handle of the freezer that ran the length of the box. I could feel the freezer hum and vibrate beneath my fingers. I lifted up the lid of the freezer.

Bob Bayloff stared up at me, his eyes open, covered with crystals of ice. A thin ribbon of red, like a frozen necklace, wrapped around his neck. His mouth, contorted and frozen in a ghastly grin, smiled up at me as if he'd been waiting to greet me, a death mask frozen in time, capturing the last moments of Bob's life. His wrists and feet were bound, his Armani suit still buttoned. His short body fit perfectly into the freezer. Yet, he was shorter than usual, his legs had been broken and lay twisted, with the toes of his shoes pointing toward his head. His arms, also broken, lay grotesquely behind him, palms up.

"What is it?" Stacey pushed forward and let out a scream as she saw Bob. I grabbed her and pulled her back as she pressed her face into my chest and screamed hysterically. I shut the lid of the freezer and pulled Stacey from the room.

THREE

Mick liked the way he felt today. He felt clear, sharp as the blade of a knife. He rubbed his hands over the abs of his stomach, feeling them ripple beneath his fingers. He turned toward the sun, feeling its warmth upon his face. The sun lit his brain from within. He was clear, so clear. He let his hands wander over his body as he listened to the sound of the waves crash upon the shore. God, he was beautiful.

Mick felt the power of the sun upon his body. The sun was like him, bright and strong. The speed had kicked in now, his clarity was absolute. He was on the line. People tried to twist him, to bend him, to turn him around. They were jealous of his beauty and power, his intelligence. They tried to confuse him, but he refused to listen to the benders. They lied. Mick reached up and slipped another tab of Dexedrine under his tongue. He played with it, feeling its bitter taste, like that of a lover, he thought. He let it slide down his throat. He was straight now, sharp.

Mick opened his eyes. The men, the little useless men, their tin badges sparkling in the sun, were reflected in the glass of the beach house. They did nothing, they were nothing. Mick felt the surf tickle his heels. He could see her now, past the sand of the beach, standing outside with the actor. She looked beautiful, as she always did. She had found his present. She had lived with it in the house for days. Mick watched the useless men move about. They were children.

He had had fun with Bob Bayloff. Bob had cried as his legs broke. He had sobbed and begged for his life as his arm snapped and a piece of bone tore through his Armani suit. He had passed out then, but Mick had revived him. Bob had been hours of fun. Bob had tempted Mick with money. Millions of dollars for his life. But Mick's clarity had been strong. Bob was a bender, but Mick had straightened him out.

"A fool knows, only after he has suffered." Mick smiled. Hesiod wrote that in the eighth century B.C. in his *Works And Days*; it was still so true.

Mick closed his eyes again, running his tongue over the prickle of his mustache. Bob had suffered. Bob had been a fool. Mick felt the warmth of the sun. He wished she had been there to watch. She was special. He opened his eyes and stared up at the sun. They said you shouldn't, that you would go blind. He didn't believe that. The sun was clear, bright, strong. He felt aroused. He would save her for last. The universe revolved around the sun and its strength, revolved around it. Mick liked that.

FOUR

A crowd had gathered on the beach outside the house. Though this was an exclusive area, the presence of six or seven police cars was bound to draw attention. I watched Stacey, as paramedics attended to her. She was in shock. She sat in a beach chair on the brick patio at the edge of the sand, her white robe wrapped tightly around her, her arms crossed and eyes closed, as if she was trying to block out the truth of what had happened to Bob, make it go away, have it be just a bad dream. But when Stacey opened her eyes, Bob would still be dead. The image of his twisted face smiling up at her, white with death, just like her dream, would be burned into her brain for life.

I felt like shit. Bob had not been warm on a beach in Barbados, but frozen in a freezer in his own house. Though there had been no love lost between Bob and me, I was sickened to think of his death, of the horrible way he had died. It wasn't just a murder. The man had been tortured.

I saw Detective Joe Dolen walking towards me. I had called Joe's partner, Detective Dan Patrick, after we had found Bob, but Patrick had been off today, so I had gotten stuck with Dolen.

Dolen smiled as he twirled a toothpick in his mouth. Dolen looked like he belonged in Pittsburgh or Detroit rather than Malibu. He was a big man, a Slav, with a thick, black mustache and thinning straight hair that was never combed. His polyester tie was as short and as wide as any I could remember, its large stripes matching the powder blue of his wrinkled blazer. His gut hung over the waist of his pants, bending his thick belt in half with its weight. Dolen jerked at the belt of his pants trying to pull them higher, as he stopped in front of me.

"Hey, what's up, Doc?"

I smiled. "Hey Dolen, you're looking good, been working hard on that Stairmaster?"

Dolen smiled, as he looked me up and down. No matter what I said, he insisted lately on calling me Doc. Dolen insisted on doing anything that would irritate me.

Dolen moved his eyes over to Stacey then back to me.

"So, we got a little love triangle going on here, Doc? Thought you'd make it a square instead, three being a crowd and all?"

I had to smile. Dolen was a piece of work. "Yeah, that's right, Dolen, you caught me. I busted Bob up and stuck him in the freezer then gave you a call. I was bored."

"Stranger things have happened. Maybe you thought you were back on that TV show. Shit, they do stuff like this all the time."

"Yeah, I'm a delusional ex-soap actor. You sure that gold shield is yours?"

Dolen grinned. He was having fun.

"Listen, Doc, we got the lab team working things over, forensics doing their gig. What exactly is your involvement here, besides being the ex-husband of the victim's girlfriend?" Dolen took another look at Stacey. "If I was a betting man, which I am, I'd bet she doesn't have a stitch of clothing on under that robe. Something you want to tell me?"

"There is nothing I want to tell you, Dolen, but I'll say this. Stacey was concerned about Bob, and she called me to try to help find him. I found him."

Dolen twisted the toothpick in his mouth. "That's it?"

"That's it." I replied.

"What now?" Dolen asked.

"Nothing now. I found him. He's in the freezer. Why don't you go take a look? There might be some evidence there. Maybe you could catch who did it. Isn't that a novel idea?" My eyes were on Dolen. He straightened his tie.

"Hey, think you could get me on one of those soaps?"

"Stranger things have happened," I said.

"I'd love to do one of those love scenes," Dolen said, as he slicked back his unkempt hair with his hand. He smiled and winked.

23

"I bet you would."

Dolen chuckled as he turned to walk away. He stopped and turned back towards me.

"Hey, one more thing. There is a lot of blood there in the freezer. We'll be taking blood evidence, DNA from the crime scene. You haven't cut your finger on your cell phone or anything lately, have you?"

"Go have another doughnut, Dolen," I said.

Dolen laughed loudly as he shoved another toothpick into his mouth and moved away.

Stacey refused to go back into the house. I told her that I would pack some of her things for her and take her back to the Valley with me. She hadn't spoken a word since she had seen the body. Dolen and the other detectives had finished questioning both of us for now. They saw the futility of asking Stacey any more questions in her condition, and we had been told we were free to go.

I moved back around to the front of the house, trying to keep out of the way of the investigation. I had shown Dolen the box of paper letters and filled him in on all that Stacey had told me. It seemed strange to me that the murderer had left the stray ketchup can by the freezer, as if to mark the place of Bob's body. Had he wanted Bob to be found? He had obviously taken great care to make sure that everything else was spotless. No blood on the freezer or the floor, no signs of a struggle, nothing that I could see. Why had he not picked up the ketchup can? Why had he tortured and killed Bob? What was with the box of letters? My natural curiosity was sparked. These types of questions drove me crazy, but my involvement seemed over.

This was a homicide and the police investigation had begun. I was a private investigator, not a police detective. Despite the look of Dolen, he and his partner Patrick were top-notch detectives, with all the resources of their department at their disposal. There was nothing else I could do but make sure Stacey was all right. After all, she was the reason I was here.

I walked up the stairs into Bob and Stacey's room and began packing some things for her. I looked at the bed where the unthinkable had almost happened. Stacey and I making love on Bob's bed, while he lay two stories below us, frozen in a block of blood. The detectives had been

24

through Bob's stuff. I saw the mystery book Bob had been reading before his death, *Murder At Black Lake*. The distorted face on the cover, contorted from a painful death, could have been Bob's. The title could have been *Murder In Malibu*.

I looked out of the towering windows toward the ocean, sparkling with beams of light. What had Bob done? What maniac had he pissed off? Had this been over money? I saw a humpback whale less than a hundred yards offshore, his head coming out of the water as he came up for air. His head disappeared under the calm sea, his shiny back, covered with barnacles, slipping through the water in an endless arch. I had a vision of sailors throughout time recanting stories of great sea monsters, twice the size of ships, swallowing men whole. Watching the giant's back slip through the water, I could understand their fear. After what seemed an eternity, the whale's tail flipped through the air and disappeared without a trace.

I loved the ocean. I had planned to be a marine biologist in college, but my freshman year I had taken a class in drama and it had changed my plans forever. I had performed a speech by John Brown, the abolitionist, for my first assignment. It was the speech he gave on the gallows before he was hung. "The sins of this country will be purged with blood," he had said, referring to the sin of slavery. He had been right; the bloodiest war in America's history had soon followed. I looked down and saw a uniformed police officer carry a body bag into the house. Perhaps we were still purging our sins with blood. Did Bob pay for his with his life? Or was it that the real monsters to fear are not swimming deep beneath the sea, but walking among us?

FIVE

Mick watched the young girls with their school uniforms play on the blacktop. He felt good, clear. Nothing was going to bend him today. He had enjoyed his day at the beach. He bit down on a turkey sandwich, as he listened to the girls' laughter as they played tag. He liked Bob's house. He had enjoyed living there. It was very comfortable. He had slept under the beds of the different bedrooms. There were so many of them. It had been fun. Mick watched as a pretty little girl, a whalebone clip in her long blonde hair, chased a red ball across the blacktop. He smiled and took another bite of his sandwich.

His favorite place to sleep had been under Bob's bed. He had watched them living their fake lives. He would stand over Bob in the darkness, his knife silently cutting the air above Bob's throat. He had waited for Bob to wake up, tempting himself with the thought of the blade plunging through Bob's flesh and bone. Then he would pull back, grateful he had not acted on impulse. He knew he was too bright and special to act common, but it had been so tempting.

He would speed for days at a time, his clarity growing with each tab of Dexedrine. He would slither on his belly like a snake through the house as they moved all around him, disappearing into cracks and corners, a shower stall, a closet, a shadow. He was invisible. He could taste his brilliance, his power. He would watch her undress, shower, sleep. He listened as they made love. Bob was a pathetic lover, unlike him. Bob was soft and weak. Bob would grunt and groan, expecting his swollen manhood to do all the work, but his softness usually left her unsatisfied. He would then rise and move into the next room for the night. Restless, alone, she would reach for a sedative.

26

On such nights Mick would crawl from under the bed, his hands feeling the slenderness of his hips, the power of his legs. He was a man. She was so beautiful, like him. He would watch her, her breasts moving up and down with each breath, her body, unsatisfied, turning and twisting in her sleep. He would feel her breath upon his skin, as the sedative swept her away, his fingers running softly over her body, wandering lightly beneath the sheets, between her legs. She would move against his hand, wet and warm, until her body shivered. As she would awake, he would slip back under the bed, listening to her heavy breathing as she pulled the sheets tightly around her, and he smelled her, tasted her.

Mick watched as the schoolgirls played. He loved children. He finished his sandwich and took a small silver snuff container made in the sixteenth century out of his pocket. He had purchased it in a store on Newbury Street, in Boston, while getting his master's degree at Boston College. Mick opened the box and removed two tabs of Dexedrine, plopping them into his glass of Diet Coke. He took a sip of Coke and slid the snuffbox back into his pocket. He had enjoyed his lunch. The old man on the bench next to him had been quiet and silent throughout, his eyes looking off toward the playground and the schoolgirls.

Mick smiled at the old man. The old man didn't move. He couldn't. He was dead. A perfect sliver of red circled the man's neck. The collar of his shirt was soaked with blood. His head rested on the trunk of the shade tree they were sitting under. Mick had slipped the loop of the piano wire around the man's neck from behind. He had watched the wire cut back to the bone of the man's spine. The old man had jumped like he'd been stung by a bee, then relaxed.

Mick swallowed the last sip of Diet Coke. He slipped off the latex gloves that covered his hands and stuffed them into his pocket. Mick had to admit one thing. The old man made a great turkey sandwich.

Mick watched as the little blonde with the whalebone clip in her hair kicked the red ball. It was a good kick. The old man would have been proud of his granddaughter. Mick smiled and took a deep breath. Nothing would bend him today. He had had a nice lunch, a nice day.

SIX

I could see Bob Bayloff's face, white with death, the crystals of blood glistening like rubies around his neck. We were skating across a frozen pond in front of his English pub, drinking pints of Bass Ale. Bob raised his pint and took a swallow. The dark ale poured from the long slit across his throat and down the front of his designer suit. He smiled as we continued to skate across the pond. He handed me a screenplay. I looked down at the title of the script, *Murder in Malibu*. Blood dripped from the script, spotting the frozen pond like red paint on a white canvas. Bob laughed and pointed to the screenplay. "There is a great part in there for you, a starring role."

I looked down at the screenplay, blood gushing from it. Bob smiled and waved, his broken arms twisted. I watched him skate away, his shattered legs backwards and wobbly, kneecaps and skates pointing towards me. Bob laughed and spun like a figure skater from a house of horrors. Bob's head fell off as his broken, headless body continued to twirl. Bob's head spun like a top, laughing and smiling, coming towards me. I slipped and fell, hitting the blood-covered ice, sliding towards Bob's smiling face. Bob's head stopped spinning inches from my face. I stared at his ice-covered eyes as his frozen smile disappeared. His face warmed, melted, to Bob in life. "Take care, Will, they're coming!"

I woke up with a jolt, disoriented, my eyes searching the blackness, my mouth dry, my body damp with perspiration. I could feel my heart hammering in my chest. I saw Stacey standing in the doorway.

I pulled the covers from me and moved toward Stacey. "Are you all right?" Stacey didn't answer. She just stood there looking like a broken doll in the dim light of the room. I held her, her arms limp at her side. I

28

moved her hair from her face, her cheeks wet with tears. She put her arms around me and held on for life, her nails digging into my back.

"How about if I make us a drink, something to eat?"

Stacey nodded into my chest. I kept my arms around her as we moved toward the living room. I sat Stacey on the couch and opened the bay doors to the warmth of the night and the blue light of the pool. The Santa Ana was still in effect, but it had died down to a soft warm breeze. The breeze brought the sound of wind chimes softly into the house, as I moved into the kitchen to make us both a drink, Jack on the rocks for me, vodka tonic for Stacey.

The night was quiet, calm, yet there were ghosts about. Ghosts of Stacey and myself, of the life we had lived together in this house, of our past. I could feel them on another plane of existence, in this same space, moving about, loving, fighting, living, laughing. I saw them, I saw us.

I dropped two ice cubes into a crystal glass and watched the whiskey wash over them, melting them down. The glasses had been a wedding present from Stacey's sister. Stacey had left them when she moved out. She had left everything.

I remembered the first time I had brought Stacey to the house. I was so proud that I had been able to buy it, to make us a home, the beginning of a life together. I had been down for so long, unable to give her anything in the way of gifts or presents. I had placed twenty-seven cards around the house for the twenty-seven months we had been together, a type of treasure hunt, with clues on each card leading to a gift.

For years Stacey had put up with an impoverished, struggling actor. Money had never seemed to mean much to Stacey in those days. She was doing well, yet I felt helpless, frustrated, as if I wasn't holding up my end of some unspoken bargain. I had felt like a failure, but Stacey believed in my talent, in me, sometimes even more than I did myself.

"You're doing what you love to do," she would say. "You're living your dream. How many people can say that?" "Not my dream," I would say. "In my dream, I wasn't broke."

I was the one who cared about money, not Stacey. I had always felt guilty for not giving her the life I thought she should have had. She could've have been with any of the thousands of men in this town that were worth millions, like Bob Bayloff, but she wasn't; she wanted only me. And on that special day, as she moved from card to card, finding twenty-seven gifts hidden throughout the house, her face glowing like a child, her spring dress bright and colorful, I felt there was nothing in the house or the world that I could give to her that would match what she gave to me. Herself.

Five years later, nearly to the day, she'd be gone. She had opened the front door and walked out of the house one morning in May, my birthday to be exact. "Happy birthday, Will," she had said as she had swung the door open. "This is your present, enjoy it!" She had slammed the door and was gone. I waited for the door to open, for her to come back. She didn't.

Bob Bayloff had sent for Stacey's things two weeks later. The ghosts had arrived shortly thereafter. Stacey and Will, Will and Stacey; a life lived. Stacey had never set foot in the house again, ever, until today.

I finished making the drinks and started to put together a small tray full of cold shrimp and sauce, a few kinds of cheese and some crackers. I had done this a million times for us. We'd had our own little haven from the world here. We'd been happy for a long time. We had been happy just being with each other. We were each other's private paradise. The house, the yard and garden, the pool, was our island surrounded by a sea of insanity that was the city and world outside.

What had happened? What had happened to that Stacey and Will? I had liked them both. I still did. Had life changed them, or had they changed their lives? The operative word being "their." I poured some Tabasco into a small dish and set it on the tray. The ghosts of the house must be wondering who these two familiar strangers were moving among them? I know I did.

I had stayed with Stacey in the guest bedroom until she had fallen asleep. She had lain down and shut her eyes, her silence haunting. Sleep had offered her as little refuge from the nightmares of life, as life itself had. Nightmares were the order of the day.

I could still see Bob's smiling face spinning across the ice, reaching out to me from his frozen death. "Take care, Will, they're coming." I wiped a drop of Tabasco off my wrist and I shook my head. It was just a nightmare, nothing more. Yet, I had a feeling in the pit of my stomach that it was more, much more. There were ghosts about tonight, ghosts of the past and the dead, and Bob Bayloff had joined them.

I walked into the living room, placed the tray of food on the coffee table by the couch and handed Stacey her drink. I sat down next to her and smiled. She tried to smile back, but the strain and shock of the day had taken something away from her, like a piece of her soul had been stolen. The light that was Stacey seemed diminished somehow. I watched her as she sipped her drink, her slim hands shaking. She reminded me of my brother-in-law after he came back from Iraq. His eyes, like hers, seemed vacant, broken. Whatever he had lost in the desert over there, he had never gotten back. Post-traumatic stress disorder they called it.

I touched Stacey's hand and she began to cry. She buried her head in the pillows of the couch. I lay down beside her. She had still not spoken a word. I held her as she cried, soft sobs from deep within, her body limp, vacant. Whoever had done this to Bob, had done it to Stacey, too. I could feel the anger rise inside me. "Take care, Will, they're coming." I shut my eyes and listened to wind chimes mix with the sound of Stacey's tears. The ghosts were gone. They had run away, leaving only the demons of pain and suffering behind. "Take care, Will, they're coming." I could feel my blood beginning to boil. I saw the ketchup can lying in the puddle of water. Bob's eyes, crystals of ice, Stacey collapsing near the frozen, blood-filled freezer. I held Stacey's sobbing body. Let them come, the bastards. I'd be waiting and I wasn't Bob Bayloff.

31

SEVEN

Maryland was so sick of this town, but Mick loved it. He talked endlessly about it being a jewel of creative influence, of being on the edge, the real game, the big time. His voice echoed in her head. He drove her crazy sometimes. He always thought he was right. Men are like that. Put a cock on somebody and they think they know everything. She looked down at the bruise on her arm. Fuck! How many times had she told him to be careful! She was an actress, for Christ sake. She can't walk around looking like she's been dating O.J. She tried to cover the bruise with makeup. Damn! Mick was sick.

Maryland looked around the casting studio filled with a million beautiful women. Fucking L.A. She could feel the insecurities rise inside her. She stood up and checked herself in the full-length mirror on the wall. Maybe she should have a boob job. She turned to the side. Forget it. She had small breasts, but her body was tall, lean and strong. Her arms were cut, her waist slim, her legs long and sensual, fit. She looked like Linda Hamilton in *Terminator II*, when she was buffed up, but not too much. Not like those muscle-head women across the street at Gold's Gym. Shit, they were scary.

Maryland brushed her short blonde hair back, her blue eyes sparkling in the mirror. She was fine. She picked up the sides she had been studying for the audition and sat back down, waiting for the casting director to call her name. She was ready.

She put the sides down and picked up a copy of the L.A. Times crumpled on the bench next to her. Holy shit! She looked down at a story on the front page. Producer Bob Bayloff had been found dead in the freezer of his house. Bob Bayloff! She didn't even want to talk about Bob

Bayloff, the scumbag! She kept reading the story. Unbelievable! Bob had finally fucked with the wrong person. Maryland heard her name called. She laid the paper down and moved toward the casting room. Wait until she told Mick.

Maryland was happy with herself as she crossed the street. She had had a good audition. She had even mustered up some very convincing tears. The jerk-offs had probably never even seen a real actress, just the L.A. bimbos. Maryland pulled down her skintight miniskirt over the cheeks of her ass as she moved toward the curb and her car. She fumbled in her purse for her keys. She heard a whistle from one of the muscle-heads coming out of Gold's. She dug deeper into her bag. Two muscle men looked her over. She could see them standing on the curb out of the corner of her eye. One of them stepped off the curb. Shit! Where the hell were her keys?

She felt a hand brush her arm. She looked up at the smiling steroid face as her closed palm flew forward into the larynx of the man. The man went down, his head hitting a Ford Taurus behind him, putting a dent in its trunk. Maryland found her keys and opened her door, while the man rolled on the ground grabbing his throat, as his friend ran to him. Shit, that karate works! Maryland started her car. She hit the gas and pulled it away.

Maryland looked in her rearview mirror. What an asshole! She looked at her hand. Goddamnit! She'd broken another nail. That man must have been a good six-three, two-twenty-five. He's lucky Mick hadn't been there. Shit! She didn't even want to think about that.

Maryland took Sunset west, turning right at Crescent Heights. She veered right and drove under the arches that read Mount Olympus, winding up into the Hollywood Hills. She took the twisting road, pulling into a tree-shaded drive behind a pink house built into the side of the canyon.

Maryland walked into the house, hardwood floors leading to French doors that opened up onto a tiled balcony with a view of the hills and the city. The first part of the house was furnished in shabby chic, down sofas and old wood tables and chairs, comfortable, casual. Maryland moved into a second room. This was Mick's area. Mick's computer faced out

33

toward a window looking out to a small garden. The room was minimally furnished in chrome and black leather, sterile, clean, everything in place. A weight set was in the corner by the fireplace and the stereo. Hundreds of albums lined a shelf above the stereo, in alphabetical order.

Bookshelves lined the room, filled to capacity, but as neat and symmetrical as the rest of the room. Maryland ran her hand across the covers of the books as she walked by. She loved the way they felt. She had read most all of the books in the room. She loved to read, she loved to write. Besides acting, they were her two passions. Mick wasn't the only one with a brain. Maryland's hand moved from the books to her skirt, pulling it over her head as she walked.

She moved into a small sitting room next to the bathroom and a large closet. The only bedroom was off to the left. The sitting room had two chairs, a table, and Maryland's antique vanity. Maryland slid the closet door open. Mick's clothes hung perfectly in order on the left side of the closet, everything arranged by color and item, folded and hung in perfect symmetry.

The right side of the closet was Maryland's and in stark contrast to the anal order of Mick. She tossed her skirt on a growing pile of clothes on her side of the closet. She removed her earrings, placing them into her jewelry case. She looked at the large tapestry that hung directly behind her vanity, as she continued to undress. The tapestry was beautiful and very old, European, depicting a waterfall and pond in which naked young women and men, white, voluptuous, and statuesque, bathed and frolicked.

Maryland stepped out of her panties, letting them slide to the floor. She was unable to take her eyes off the tapestry. It was haunting. The figures were life size and so real. Standing there naked, it seemed as if she was one of them, as if she could take one step and join them in their lost world. She would love that, love to lose herself there, start over, and escape this town and its demons forever. She reached out and ran her hand across one of the figures. The weave of the tapestry was soft and smooth. Maryland shut her eyes and lifted the tapestry away from the wall. Mick would kill her if he knew she touched it.

She opened her eyes and pulled the tapestry higher, revealing the corner of a thick wooden door beneath it. An antique iron padlock secured the door. Maryland's hand felt the rough metal of the lock. She liked the way it felt. It felt forbidden, taboo. It was part of Mick. She held it in her hand, caressed it.

Mick had bought the padlock in London while traveling abroad in college. The lock had been used to secure chests of coins and valuables that had come from the American Colonies, as taxation to the Crown, in the early eighteenth century. Nearly three hundred years later, it looked as formidable as ever, securing not treasures of the Crown, but secret things, a secret place, Mick's place. Maryland let go of the lock and let the tapestry fall back against the wall, covering the door.

She sat at her vanity and shut her eyes, listening to the silence. She liked these times of calm and silence, of feeling whole. She was as bright and strong as Mick, she knew that, but she needed him. He added to her. He did things she never dared do. He was a man, and men are different. She knew that now.

Maryland opened her eyes and looked at herself in the mirror. Her blue eyes stared back at her, moving over her body. She thought of the audition and the room filled with beautiful women, their hair, their legs, their breasts. The way their eyes caressed her. She lifted up the top of a perfume bottle running it along the line of her square jaw. She let the smooth glass trace the curve of her breast. She felt a chill run down her spine, turning warm inside her. Her mind wandered as she ran the glass across her stomach and down between her legs. The perfume burned and Maryland shut her eyes.

She had shaved down there, she preferred it that way, but the burning wasn't from that. Her skin above her thighs was red and raw. The perfume scorched it, and Maryland bit her lip. It was from Mick. The price she paid for playing. Maryland felt the warmth of her body as she slipped the glass inside her. She gasped as she grabbed the table, the smooth glass making her tremble. She opened her eyes and stared at herself in the mirror. She laid the top of the bottle down on the vanity. She'd better not. Mick wouldn't like it. He liked to be the only thing inside her, the only one. Maryland stood up, her legs quivering.

She moved into the bedroom and lay down on the wrought iron, four-poster bed. She sank down into the softness of the down pillows. She closed her eyes, feeling a breeze from the open window blow across her naked body. She took a deep breath, trying to calm herself. Mick would be here soon.

EIGHT

The bell rang deep in my head like a dream. Like I was listening to it underwater. My eyes felt glued shut, my left arm, tingling, numb. I opened my eyes and realized the doorbell was ringing and I'd been deep asleep. I looked at Stacey lying next to me on the couch, my arm pinned under her slim body. I slid off the couch, without disturbing her. I shook my arm, trying to wake it up with the rest of my body as I headed toward the door. I looked at my watch. It was ten past nine.

Detective Dan Patrick's Irish smile greeted me as the front door swung open. Patrick was about six-one, muscular, a former pro ballplayer, a defensive back. We'd met over fourteen years ago in acting class. The Pittsburgh Stealers had just cut Dan, and he had decided to come west and try acting. He gave it a go for a while and then joined the L.A.P.D. He had moved quickly up the ranks and had been a detective for over five years now. He was considered one of their rising stars. His rugged good looks ate the cameras up, and he and the L.A.P.D. loved it, but behind it all, he was a top-notch detective. We'd been through a lot together. He was a good friend.

Dan grabbed me in a quick embrace, his blue eyes sparkling. He saw Stacey sleeping on the couch. I motioned toward the kitchen and he followed.

"How is she?" Dan asked in slight Philly accent. Dan had grown up in a tough neighborhood in South Philadelphia. He had scraped and battled for every inch life had given him. There were only a few ways out and up, away from the row houses and gangs of his youth, and all of them were tough. Dan had found one; he was a survivor, a fighter.

"She is not doing too well," I said, as I moved toward the coffee

37

maker. "She still hasn't spoken a word. I'm really worried about her."

Dan shook his head, as he pulled a chair out and took a seat at the kitchen table. He kept his head lowered, running his hand across the wood of the table. Dan had known Stacey as long as I had, longer even. He had met her right after she had moved out from New York. He had introduced us. It seemed a lifetime ago, yet like yesterday. I switched the coffee maker on.

"They performed the autopsy on Bob last night."

I looked over at Dan. "What? So soon?"

"My superiors want to move quick. The press is all over this, Will. The story was in the papers and on the news before we had even removed the body. Bob Bayloff, dead in his freezer. The man made a lot of big films with big people. His murder is big news."

I listened to the coffee starting to brew. Dan was right. This thing was big and Stacey was going to be right in the middle of it. I'd have a part, too. The thought made me sick.

"To say there has been a leak to the press is an understatement," Dan said, "More like a flood. They have the names of all the players, you and Stacey included."

"Shit." I turned the sink on and splashed cold water onto my face. I toweled off and took a deep breath. I was hoping I would wake up any minute in my bed and this whole thing would be a dream.

"There is another thing." Dan got up and moved toward me. He took a moment. "Bob was raped, sodomized. We found no trace of semen or sperm, but he was definitely violated. He didn't leave much physical evidence behind. No fabric or hair, prints, nothing. It was like he was never there. Incredibly clean."

My eyes found Dan's. "Jesus Christ!" I moved to the table and sat down. Dan grabbed a couple of mugs out of the cabinet and poured us some coffee. He handed me one of the mugs and sat down across from me.

"Whoever did this, Will, was one sick son-of-a-bitch. Bob was tortured. The killer took his time, enjoying his work. When he was done playing, he used the piano wire from behind."

"Any suspects?" I asked. A slight smile came to Dan's lips. "Dolen

38

thinks it was you, but nobody else is buying it."

"What a guy, he just loves me."

"Dolen knows you didn't do it. He just wants to yank you around a bit."

"Tell him not to yank too hard. I'll yank back."

Dan's blue eyes lit up. He knew me. He knew I wasn't kidding. He smiled, "I'll tell him."

He took a swig of his coffee, taking a moment. "There is one more thing. An old man was murdered in Santa Monica yesterday. He was found on a park bench across from an elementary school. Apparently, he went there every Tuesday to have lunch and watch his granddaughter play, same bench, same time. He was killed with a loop of piano wire, cut straight back to the spine, just like Bob Bayloff. Otherwise, he was untouched. His name was Alfred Green. He was a film agent. You ever heard of him?"

"Alfred Green! Hell, yes!" Alfred Green was not just some agent. He had gotten his start back in the day. At that time he was a wonder kid, tall and handsome with a silver tongue. He wooed some of the biggest stars in Hollywood away from more established agents. He was a legend who had built a personal empire. Today, in an era of mega agencies with hundreds of agents wielding more power and clout than some studios, Alfred Green preferred to remain independent. Over the years, he had put together some huge deals. He was well liked, well respected. He was Bob Bayloff's agent.

Dan looked at me, reading my mind. "We know he was Bob Bayloff's agent. We are working on that connection. Can you think of any? Common enemies, people they may have pissed off?"

"Only about a million. Both Bob and Alfred Green were in the business. They made and screwed over hundreds of people over the years. Hell, I bet every day a deal was going bad and somebody was getting hurt. Who the hell knows? Professional jealousy? People who felt they didn't get a big enough piece of the pie or the credit they deserved? They made careers and broke careers, it's an insidious business, Dan, you know that. The possibilities are countless. These guys were major players."

Dan leaned back in his chair and slipped a toothpick into his mouth.

"Well, playtime's over."

I took a sip of my coffee as I watched Dan gnaw on his toothpick. It was over all right for Alfred and Bob. No more lunches, meetings, deals, or tomorrows. But for playtime, I had the terrible feeling, that in some horrible way, it was just beginning.

NINE

Mick liked the boys on Santa Monica Boulevard. He liked to watch them move, the way they leaned and stood on the corners, the way they walked, like they were sliding on ice, so casual and cool. He watched as a young blond boy talked to a man in a black BMW, his face lit by the headlights of a passing car. The boy leaned against the car, caressing the windshield like a lover. The door to the car flipped open and the boy slid in. The car pulled away as the boy's head disappeared beneath the dash. Sex for sale, twenty-four hours a day. Mick smiled; this was his kind of town.

Mick sat in his brown '73 Chevy van. He was parked on Santa Monica Boulevard, in Hollywood, across the street from The Miracle Works Playhouse. He leaned down and did a line of cocaine off the dash of the van. He washed it down with a Diet Cola and a tab of Dexedrine.

Mick pressed his fists into the side of his head. It was buzzing. He could hear every voice, every thought on the entire planet in his mind. The white noise of life surrounded him, threatened to drown out his existence, his spirit. The molecules of the universe felt like sledgehammers zipping across his brain. He put his hands over his ears, trying to drown out the voices, the noise. He could feel the pressure of the molecules against his skin, burning him, passing through him, re-energizing, protons into electrons, potential to kinetic, kinetic to potential, energy, pure energy. He laughed and smiled and twirled his head. It was beautiful!

He was brilliant. He was special. The voices and noises told him so. He was a lightning rod, absorbing the energy of the universe. It was the price he paid for being chosen. He was illuminated, unique.

"He is great, who is what he is from nature and who never reminds us of others." Emerson wrote that in his "Uses Of Great Men."

Mick laughed. He was a great man. Nature had made him who he was. There was no one like him, no others. Maryland understood that. She knew, deep down. She understood everything. She couldn't do what Mick did. She was a woman, not a man. To be great, truly great, you needed to be a man. The world was ruled by men. The rules were different for women. Emerson knew that. Maryland knew that now, too. Mick had taught her.

Mick watched a tall, black transvestite walk toward the van. Her large breasts pushed hard against the material of her skimpy halter. Red hot pants revealed that she was as much man as woman. Mick laughed as he took another sip of his drink and sniffed the hit of coke further up his nostril. Why settle for half the package when you could have the whole thing in one shot, breasts and a cock? There was a type of poetry to it, an indefinable beauty. He loved it.

The transvestite leaned up against the passenger door of the van and smiled. Mick looked at the large, dark cleavage rolling over the open window and into the van. He smiled back. She looked at the trail of coke dust that lined Mick's dashboard and winked, "Party time, playboy? I'm just your kind of girl."

Mick leaned over and opened the door, and the pro slid in laying a large hand on Mick's crotch. "Ohh...looks like my baby's ready to roll! Large and hard, sweet words to a girl's ears." The hand moved up, unbuttoning Mick's pants and sliding them down.

The transvestite stopped, looking down at Mick's crotch. "Oh my."

She moved her eyes toward Mick. He grinned, "Just do it." The transvestite smiled large as her head went down. Mick fondled her breast with one hand as his other hand slid across the seat, finding the man in her, hard and ready. He leaned back and closed his eyes. He thought of Emerson's "Uses Of Great Men." Here was one use, the whole package in one shot. He laughed and spun his head. He loved this town.

42

TEN

Mary Higgins watched the young girl on the stage. The girl had talent. Though she was new to the class, she held great promise. The words flowed from her smoothly. Her monologue was strong and real. Mary looked around at some of the other faces in the Miracle Works Playhouse. She had been a professional casting director for over twenty years.

She saw the dreams of young people from every corner of the country shattered on a daily basis. Few would make a living in this business. Fewer still would realize their burning dreams of stardom. She knew the statistics. Ninety percent of the members of the Screen Actors Guild made less than five thousand dollars a year and those numbers didn't even include actors who were non-union and trying to break in.

She looked back at the young girl on the stage. She was good, very good, but there were no guarantees in this business. Mary had seen the most talented people fail, the least talented succeed. Fate, timing, luck, talent, who you knew, they all seemed lost as one, mixed together into a huge dream called Hollywood.

Luck, timing, talent, it became hard to separate one from the other these days. There was either success or failure, and the reason for one or the other seemed irrelevant. As Humphry Bogart had said, "If you come to Hollywood and a certain number of accidents happen to you, at the right time, in the right place, you'll be a star."

Yet, there was something pure in the student's faces as she glanced around the room. A light that comes from those who chase their dreams, who feel they must "act." A light that comes from the pure joy the chase gives them no matter how impoverished or exhausting or against the odds

43

it may be. The freedom that comes from never looking back on one's life and saying, "What if..." Mary knew that in this place, for at least one night a week, they had achieved part of their dream. They were all "actors."

Mary loved the faces. It was the reason that after an exhausting day of casting, she liked to teach the scene study class. She was nearing fifty now, and had never married. Her work had been her life, these students, and all the others before them, her children. She could feel their energy, their desire and drive. It made her feel needed, a part of something bigger.

Over two decades ago it was Mary who had been the bright pure face on the stage. But Mary had soon realized that her talent lay in spotting talent, not being the talent, so she had given casting a try. She had been very successful. She had made a name for herself in a tough business. She knew stars. She had discovered some herself in this very room. But it was in a class like this, that she felt the most alive, the most rewarded. She understood in the deepest part of her soul, the dreams, the pain, the pure love of acting.

Mary watched as the young girl on the stage finished her monologue. The girl took a moment and then looked up at Mary for the critique of her work. "Very nice, Amanda. I didn't feel you were acting at all."

The young girl smiled. She knew that this was the highest praise. Mary turned to the other faces in the class, hanging on her words, eager to learn their craft, pick up something they could use, something that could spring them to another level in their work, make the difference between just having an audition and getting the part.

"You see what Amanda did was real, she didn't pretend to have emotions, she was really feeling them. She found a way to get in touch with her emotions, her life, her past, her pain and joy, and bring them to the character. They were real, so her performance was real. Remember, there is nothing worse for an actor than for people to see you as "acting." You must feel your performance and make it your own. It was very nice, Amanda."

The young girl moved off the stage to the applause of her classmates. Mary smiled and shut her notebook, signaling the end of the class. Her students filed by, chattering, laughing, saying their good-byes. She watched them disappear through the front door. Mary took a deep breath and removed her glasses, enjoying the first silence of her day. She could still sense the energy and the presence of the students in the room, like a fog across the floor of the stage. Mary smiled, enjoying the moment, taking it all in. After all these years, the feeling of warmth that teaching brought her seemed as new as the day. She stood, collecting her things. She switched off the stage lights and moved toward the front of the theatre and her office.

Mary entered her dark and cluttered office. There was still some work to be done before her long day was over. She switched the light on over her desk, and a faint glow lit the room. She looked down at her desk, puzzled. Her desk was covered with a white drop cloth, like one a painter would use. She looked down at her feet. She was standing on the cloth. It spread out across the floor. Mary turned as the door behind her shut.

A tall, slim man was standing in the darkness. Mary fumbled for her glasses. "Who's that? Who's there?"

A soft voice came from the shadows. "I've come to audition for the part."

"Part?" Mary's mind was racing. Had she scheduled an audition this late? "What part?"

The man stepped into the light. He wore painter's coveralls, a stocking cap, and glasses. Green plastic trash bags were wrapped around his feet, rubber gloves over his hands. He smiled, his perfect white teeth glowing in the dim light. "Why, the part of the killer, of course."

The man's right hand jabbed out and there was a flash of blue light in the darkness. Mary felt herself leave the ground, the jolt of electricity, from the stun gun, lifting her off her feet and spinning her around. Mary landed face down on her desk. She tried to move, but her body wouldn't respond. Her face twitched on the drop cloth covering the desk. Saliva dripped from her mouth onto the cloth. Her body felt as if it was on fire. She moved her legs, trying to stand.

"That was very good, Mary, but now try it with more feeling." Mary managed to stand, when she was hit with another jolt, and she flew back onto the desk. "Oh, that was much better, there was no acting going on there." The soft voice laughed. "Don't you remember me, Mary?"

The man stepped toward Mary, staring down at her face. He removed his glasses. His eyes looked black as coal.

Mary tried to speak, but her jaw was locked, her body shaking. She could smell the scent of electricity and burnt skin in the air. She could feel the warm wetness of her own urine running down her leg. She was going to die. She shook her head at the black-eyed monster.

He smiled and rolled her over. Mary felt her hose rip off. She was filled with incredible pain. The pain shot through her. She screamed as he thrust. She clawed at the cloth and kicked her legs. She raised her arms to fight, and there was a flash of shiny silver in the darkness and a prick against the skin of her throat. The soft voice spoke to her as she watched her blood run across the white cloth as he continued his business.

"Now you remember? Don't you? Don't you, Mary? Now you know." Mary's blood flowed from her throat. She watched it, as if it wasn't happening, the soft voice fading through the pain, the world becoming distant. Know what, she thought to herself. Know what? For the only thing that Mary Higgins knew, was that she was dying. She saw the faces of her class in front of her, so much youth and promise. Her last thought was a prayer to Jesus to protect them. Protect them all, from the black-eyed monster.

ELEVEN

Daisy moved her hips slowly, grinding to the music. The stage lights glistened off her black body like the sun off coal. She was the sexiest thing I had ever seen. No matter that she was nearing seventy and near two hundred pounds. The woman could flat out sing the blues. She ripped your soul out with her voice, then played sweet music with it. She sang from her heart, down low and up high, with a lifetime of pain and experience, until you felt that life was the most horrible and beautiful thing in God's universe, a tragedy, not to be missed. Blues, when Daisy sang it, was life.

I sat at the Jewel, in Hollywood, waiting for Blake, letting the music wash over me. Inhaling it, like a fine tobacco. Stacey was still at my house in the Valley. Her doctor had come by to see her earlier in the day, and Stacey had been unresponsive, still not speaking, not eating much, not sleeping, just staring blankly as her body shook, her lips quivering uncontrollably. It broke my heart to look at her.

The doctor had given her a sedative. He said it would let her sleep through the night, and that he would be back to see her again in the morning. Dan had come by after his shift had ended at work to see how she was doing and had volunteered to sit with me. Shortly thereafter, Blake had called. His voice was calm, but I could tell something was up. Dan had offered to stay with Stacey while I drove over the hill to meet Blake, commenting that it would be good for me to get out of the house for a while. The Jewel, as usual, had been our choice as a meeting place, our home away from home.

It calmed me to be here surrounded by the music, the people. I watched the stage lights flicker off the hundreds of old forty-fives and

47

black-and-white pictures of blues men that lined the walls. The placed smelled of good Southern cooking, whiskey, wood and sweat, and the memories here for me were good. The waitress brought me a beer and a shot of Jack. The beer I had ordered, the Jack seemed to have found its way over by itself, like a bad running buddy who always gets you in trouble, whom you're both happy to see and not happy to see at the same time.

I looked up at the waitress, questioning the arrival of my friend. She motioned to the far wall and a crowded booth. Lawrence, one of the two brothers that owned the place, lifted his glass to me, the candlelight from the table in front of him reflecting off the thick lenses of his horn-rimmed glasses. He was sandwiched in the booth between a tiny brunette, her head barely visible over the top of the table, and an Amazon blonde, a good head higher than him. I smiled, the image comical, like a scene from a Groucho Marx film.

In the old days, long before Stacey, the house, or the show, I had put some money into the Jewel. Not much, but it was all I had at the time. Lawrence and his brother Jake, a blues guitarist, had scraped together their savings to buy the Jewel dirt-cheap but they had come up a little short, and that's where I came in. I closed my meager savings account, wrote them a check, and jumped on board.

The Jewel had originally opened in 1932 and had been a mecca for the blues, attracting all the top names of the day. Urban decay had gotten the best of it, though, before Jake and Lawrence arrived. They hadn't changed it much, keeping it dark and simple as in its heyday. To Jake, the "Blues Man," the music was all that mattered. There had been only beer and wine served during our reign and liquor had to be sneaked in like during prohibition. This, apparently, had been my job. Thinking back, I realized you had to be so young to be so stupid. We had almost gotten caught and gone under more than once. It was a time when ignorance was truly bliss.

The Jewel had eventually taken root and flourished, the music of Daisy and others like her leading the way. This was the place people came for the real thing. No glitz, no Hollywood glamour, just the blues.

I never did make a dime off my investment and I couldn't have cared less. I eventually got my money back and put it toward trying to start a life with Stacey. Lawrence and Jake found big investors from Texas and finally got a license to sell liquor. They had prospered, but had never forgotten the old days when we were full of youth and foolishness. I raised the shot glass of Jack toward Lawrence for old times' sake, and we put him down together.

At first glance to an outsider, I must have looked like another normal, happy, customer, smiling and toasting from across the room, but inside I was anything but. The smile was an attempt to be human, but down deep, I felt like a train had run through my bowels. My gut was twisted into knots and nervous energy flowed over my body like electricity. I was shaking. Not from shock like Stacey, but from anger, and there was something else, a taste, like bile on the back of my soul, disgusting and repulsive. I recognized it. It would listen to no logic or reasoning. It was primeval, as old as the beginning of time, and I hated it. It was fear.

Stacey was broken, and that scared me, and the sick thing that had done it was out there, reveling over the twisted legs and arms of Bob Bayloff, of grandfather Alfred Green's faded life, of Stacey's smashed psyche. I looked around the room at all the people in the club, into the cracks and crevices of the darkness, off the reflections of the flickering light. The boogeyman was out there. He was somewhere close and he wanted to play. I felt it, like an approaching storm. It was just a feeling, nothing more, and that scared me most of all.

Put a man or two in front of me where I can see them, look them in the eyes, and the fear evaporates like a pool in the desert leaving only the dry hard surface of action. But in the shadows of the mind, fear plays games, teetering and tottering around, popping up like a jack-in-the-box and running off to the dark edges of your imagination where goblins and visions of childhood nightmares live. Where your mind photographs the horrors of life and plays them over and over on the screen of your subconscious, where common sense and reasoning are two playmates not allowed. This was where fear thrived, the boogeyman's playground.

Fear though, had its purpose. To make us aware. I had to use it, channel its energy into construction and action, and not let it blur me with its numbness. Fear was even worse when it was not fear for yourself but

49

for another, someone you cared for, like Stacey.

It was the loss of control, the helplessness that fear preyed on. Keep the edge, I thought, don't go numb. I looked down into my beer and wondered whether I was losing my mind. I rubbed the temples of my head. I needed some distance. Because of Stacey, I was too close. I had seen murders, bodies, people shattered, but this was different somehow. I was too close. The shot of Jack settled in my stomach like a warm storm, unwinding the knots in my gut for just a moment. I closed my eyes, listening to Daisy's velvet voice wrap itself around me, and told myself to calm down, that it wasn't my affair.

Stacey was my ex-wife. The last thing I needed was to get involved with the murder investigation of her lover. I told myself to remember to take a look at Stacey's and my divorce papers when I got home, to remember where I stood in the equation. Yes, I was a friend, but outside of Stacey's well-being, I had no role; that was it. Distance is what I needed.

Except that feeling, a bump in the night, someone watching, a chill on the spine, footsteps behind, the boogeyman. I opened my eyes and saw Dan standing in front of me, and the bile of fear reached up and grabbed me by the throat.

"What going on! Where's Stacey? Is she all right?" I said as I stood up.

"She's fine, Will. She's fine."

Dan put his hand on my shoulder. I took a breath and felt my spine relax.

"I got a call and had to leave. Your neighbor, Mrs. Trimble, is sitting with her. Where's Blake?"

"He hasn't shown up...."

"I'm right here."

I looked over Dan's shoulder as Blake walked up. It was good to see him. He wore a leather jacket, black T-shirt, jeans, and boots. The same thing I was wearing. We looked like brothers normally, even though he was more than a few inches shorter than I, but tonight we looked like thirty-eight-year-old twins whose mother had dressed them alike. I looked him up and down. This had been happening all the way back to high school. He looked at me and shook his head

"Nice outfit," I said.

"Fuck you," was his only reply. It was our normal phrase of endearment to each other, a throwback to our adolescence. Dan looked from Blake to me.

"What's going on, Dan?" I asked.

Dan hesitated a moment then said, "You remember Mary Higgins?"

"Our acting coach, yes, of course."

"Well," Dan said, as his eyes flicked away, "We're going to go see her."

TWELVE

Mary Higgins was on stage, her favorite place to be. In the dim light of the Miracle Works Playhouse, the stage spotlight cut through darkness like a laser, illuminating Mary. She sat in her favorite chair, her legs crossed, her notebook folded on her lap. Her eyes were open, her head straight, staring out into the darkness to where her students would be seated. Her right arm was raised, her finger pointing out toward the empty seats. Her left hand held a pen and was curled over the top of her notebook. It was a familiar pose for Mary, one I had seen a thousand times over my years of studying with her, and for a brief moment, I expected to see a smile break across her face as she broke out in laughter, striking her pen loudly against the arm of the chair. But she didn't move. She never would again.

As I got closer, I could see that her pantyhose had been put on neatly, but were backwards, the creases running up the front, not the back of her legs. Her face was pale as snow. Her blouse, which I first thought was red, I realized, was originally white, turned dark, with the color of her blood. A thin gash traced across her neck as straight and smooth as a surgeon's cut. Yet there was no blood on the stage or anywhere around her. Dolen was leaning over the body. He looked up and saw me and shook his head, the normal playfulness gone from his eyes as they met mine. He stepped off stage and approached Dan, Blake, and me.

"He tied her hand, finger and head up with stage wire. It's attached to the ceiling. Quite the production," Dolen said, as he pulled a chocolate bar out of his blazer and took a bite. "It's clean, like Bob's scene. Been dead about four hours. According to her students, class ended at seven, which would make the time of death right around then. Her car is in her parking space, engine's cold as ice. We believe she was killed here or nearby, then placed on the stage. A student who had come by to pick up a script found the body. The front door was left open as if it was an invitation." Dolen took another bite of the chocolate bar.

"If he killed her here, where's all the blood?" Blake asked, hands in his pockets, eyes toward the stage.

Dolen shrugged, "He's Mr. Clean, a regular white tornado."

Dolen shoved the rest of the candy bar in his mouth and smiled, his teeth blacked out by the chocolate, making him look like he was the third cousin of an Ozark family, like his brother was his papa.

I felt like decking him and wiping that smile off his face. That was my friend on stage with her throat slit. My friend. I took a seat and looked up at Blake as his eyes caught mine. He knew my feelings for Mary. She had been a mentor of mine.

It was on this very stage, in which her lifeless body now sat, that I performed my first scene in L.A. It was an audition to get into Mary's scene study class. Fresh out of college and the American Academy of Dramatic Arts, I wanted a critique from someone known in the business, someone who dealt with the reality of acting and making it.

After I was done, she had pulled me aside and took my hand. She had smiled and nodded her head, not saying a word, but I knew what it meant. She squeezed my hand then turned and walked away. That moment had meant more to me than all the years of school and critiques put together, for she was the real thing. Her world was the real world of acting, and she'd just let me in.

From that day on, if there was anything she could do for me she would. There was camaraderie among the actors who studied here. Most of us were broke, spending what money we had on studying and headshots, working odd jobs to get by. I cleaned carpets, drove limos, waited tables...anything I could. But that wasn't my life; my life was here within these four walls and the dreams and people they held. It was in this very room, during a showcase for casting directors and agents, that I was first brought in to read for the show. I had been here and on other small stages around the city for nearly seven years. Within three days after the reading, I was in New York screen testing. Another week and I was on the set back in L.A., a three-year contract in hand, and the years of struggle before washed away into memory. I made more money my first month than I made the whole year before and my life would never be the same. And it had all started here, with Mary.

Dan came over and laid a hand on my shoulder. "You all right?"

"Yeah, thanks," I said as Dan removed his hand. I looked at Dolen staring at me. "What? What are you looking at?" Dolen said nothing, smirking, his eyes locked on me.

"You better not be thinking what I think you are! That I had something to do with this!" I stood up and Dan got between Dolen and me.

"Take it easy, Will, you know we don't think that," Dan said as Dolen ran his tongue over the chocolate on his teeth, his eyes still on me. "I have to show you something, though."

Dan put his arm around me and led me away, as Blake and Dolen followed. Dan led me toward the last row of seats in the dimly lit playhouse. Out of the shadows a body formed, with a white shiny face peering toward the stage. As I got closer, I could see that it wasn't a body at all, but a stage dummy, a prop. It was seated in the last seat of the last row, posed in a relaxed position, a notebook folded in its lap. Where its face would normally be there was an eight-by-ten glossy headshot stapled to the dummy, giving it the appearance of having a live, smiling face.

The eyes of the picture looked directly toward the pointing finger of Mary on stage. I stared at the picture. It was like I was looking in the mirror. It was my face, my headshot. The dummy was me, smiling grotesquely upon the dead body of my teacher.

"Jesus Christ," Blake said as he stepped forward. The eyes of my headshot sparkled at me in the changing light as Dolen stepped up. He hoisted his belt up over his gut and smiled.

"What's up, Doc? Why's she pointing at you, huh? Looks like a private party, just the two of you. Maybe she was more than just your acting teacher. Maybe she taught you a few other things on the casting couch, you know, you and her getting it on."

I exploded at Dolen, my right fist connecting to the soft side of his head. Dolen's feet left the ground as I put him down on his back. I was on top of him, my left fist taking in most of his right eye. Dolen squealed to stop, as I felt the barrel of his revolver under my chin, while my Smith and Wesson found its way to Dolen's jaw.

"Hold it! HOLD IT!" Dan screamed, "Goddamnit! Put them away! NOW!" Dan took a step forward. "JOE! NOW!" Dolen slowly removed his gun and I followed. I stood up as Dolen sat, staring at me.

"You're fucking under arrest, Spire! You-son-of-a-bitch!" Dolen said as he clumsily tried to stand, his eye already swelling up. He pulled a pair of handcuffs out and stepped toward me. Dan stepped in his way.

"Back off, Dolen. Nobody's arresting anybody. You were out of line."

"Fuck that!" Dolen screamed, pointing a finger at me." That little actor boy attacked me!"

"Watch it, Detective," Dan said, "I used to be a little actor boy myself."

"As on officer of the court, it would be my recollection that you attacked Mr. Spire and he was just acting in self-defense. Isn't that right, Will?" Blake said as he lit a cigarette. He lifted the pack towards me and I took one, lightning it on Blake's open lighter. I took the smoke in, then let it out in a gray stream toward Dolen.

"Absolutely, counselor. He had his gun to my head."

"This is bullshit, Dan! You going to let them get away with this?"

Dan took a deep breath. "Listen, Joe, Will's my friend, as are you. You're my partner, but I told you what Will's relationship was with Mary. I knew her, too," Dan said pointing to the stage. "She was my friend. She's dead, Joe, and you were out of line, and this goes no further. That's it."

Dolen looked at Dan for a long moment, and then lowered his eyes. When he raised them again, they were on me. He pointed his finger at me. "This isn't over, Spire." He slipped his handcuffs back inside his jacket, turned, and stormed away.

Dan looked at me and shook his head. "You feel better?"

"No." I turned toward the stage and looked at Mary.

"Your partner's out of control!" Blake said. "How are you going to handle this?"

"I'll handle it." Dan stepped toward me. "Will?"

"Yeah," I answered, my eyes still on Mary.

"Whoever did this is someone you know or knows you, someone who studied here."

"You studied here."

"Yeah, well, after tonight, I might be next on Dolen's list of suspects."

Blake sat on the arm of one of the seats and crossed his arms. "Excluding you and Will, that would leave a lot of people that passed through these doors over the years. Doesn't narrow it down very much. I'm sure the killer knew that, not wanting to give too much away."

"Well, there's more," Dan said.

I turned toward Dan. "More?"

"Yeah." Dan looked down at the notebook in the dummy's lap. He pulled a pair of latex gloves from his pocket and slipped them on as Blake and I moved closer. Dan reached down and flipped open the notebook. There was a picture inside. It was of Stacey and me. We were sitting on Bob Bayloff's bed, our arms around each other, Stacey's robe half open, her head on my shoulder.

"Son-of-a-bitch," I said staring at the picture. "He was there, he was in the house. That was the day we found Bob's body." Dan's eyes were on me. "It's not what it looks like, Dan."

"Okay, Will, if you say so."

"It's the truth."

"I believe you, Will. Maybe you can help me with this next part." Dan lifted up the photo. Underneath was an old script.

Pasted over it where the dialogue would be there were little clippings out of a newspaper. Single, cut-out letters, strung together, just like the ones Stacey had found in Bob's closet. I looked down at the words they formed. "It's Latin," I said, my eyes skimming over the words.

"I know," said Dan, "can you read it?"

"Yeah." I looked down at the first words and translated. "'He that dies pays all debts.'"

I looked up and took a deep breath. "It's Shakespeare," I said, "from *The Tempest*."

"What's the next line?" Dan asked. I glanced down again at the script.

"'Death surprises us in the midst of our hopes.'"

"Shit! What a sick bastard," Blake said as he stood up.

"Is that it?" Dan asked.

"No, there's one more, from Shaw."

"Who?"

"George Bernard Shaw." I slipped my hands into the pockets of my jacket, trying to control my emotions.

"'He who can, does. He who cannot, teaches.'"

I looked at Mary, her pale skin glistening in the harsh glare of the spotlight. I felt the anger rise inside me like a tidal wave as my eyes filled with tears. So much for getting some distance. This guy was mine. And God help him, when I found him.

THIRTEEN

I took deep breaths, pulling in the night air like it was life itself. My head was spinning, my stomach in upheaval. I stood out in front of the Miracle Works Playhouse bent over, my hands on my knees. The air was cool as I breathed it in, the heat of the day having washed away with the night. I straightened up and looked across the street at the blinking neon sign of the Jewel. Close, the bastard had been close all right. He had been just across the street. The medical examiner and forensics team had arrived on the scene and were beginning their work.

Dan had sent two black-and-white units out to my house, even before he had seen me at the Jewel, to check on Stacey. Dan said they had radioed back that everything was fine and that one unit would stay the night. He had suggested that we move Stacey soon, to somewhere safe, perhaps out of town. I could not have agreed more.

I took in another deep breath and shut my eyes, feeling my senses coming back to me. This animal had gotten to me, overwhelmed me with his little show. What was my connection to him? Was it Stacey? He could have had her at any time. She could be in the freezer dead with Bob Bayloff. The guy had been in the house! He could have killed both of us. Abducted Stacey, done away with me. The horrifying options could go on forever, but he didn't do anything but take a picture.

It was the game this guy liked, the control, and to this point he was in control. We were pawns, and he was moving us around his little game board at will. What was this guy up to? He was an animal, an animal that rapes, tortures, sodomizes, and kills, while quoting Shakespeare and Shaw and writing in Latin. He was brutal, that had been obvious, but what was worse was that he was intelligent. We had stepped into something

58

dark and twisted and all of us were players. We didn't know the game, only he did. But one thing was for sure. It was a game of life and death.

Blake walked up to me, laying his hand on my back. "You all right?"

I nodded my head. Blake handed me a bottle of water. My mouth felt like it was stuffed with a hundred cotton balls. I took the water and drank it down.

"Remind me not to meet you anywhere again," Blake said. "I could do without this kind of social life."

I smiled at Blake. In all the horror of the evening, I had forgotten to ask Blake why he had wanted to meet me. Dan walked up joining us.

"I forgot to ask you, Blake. On the phone, it sounded important. Why did you want to meet? What's up?"

"Well," Blake said, as he looked at Dan and then to me again. "Not wanting to be outdone by tonight..." Blake stopped and took a deep breath.

"Yeah?" I said. Blake's eyes met mine.

"Blue is out."

I felt my heart move into my throat. "What?"

"He's out," Blake repeated.

"Since when?" I said, my voice trailing away.

"Three weeks," Blake answered. "It was a mistake, a computer glitch. He was released, furlough. They gave him his walking papers, and he just strolled out the front door with twenty other prisoners."

I sat there not believing my ears. Blue, or Bud Williams, his real name, one of the most brutal sex offenders I'd seen, had just been released into society on a computer glitch.

"How could this have happened?"

"It was a major screw-up, Will. He was transferred and came in under a different name. Buck Williams, a drug offender. He was furloughed by mistake. We found out when the real Buck Williams' attorney started asking questions about his client's release. That's when they realized they had furloughed the wrong Williams."

"Oh, my God! Where is he?"

"We don't know. So far the manhunt for him has turned up nothing."

I looked at Blake and could tell that he knew what I was thinking even before I asked it. "You think this is him?"

Blake glanced at Dan. Dan crossed his arms, looking down at the ground.

"It could be," Dan said, as he ran his shoe over the cement of the sidewalk. His eyes came up and met mine. "Blue knew you and Stacey. He didn't study here, but he hung out here. He knew a lot of people you did, the same circle of friends. There's a connection there."

"You're the one who found him, when no one else could," Blake said. "He wasn't very happy. As you remember, Will, he swore if he ever got out he'd pay you back the favor. That's another connection."

"But Blue never killed before, he was a sexual deviant," I said.

"Never killed before that we could prove," Dan answered. "We only got him on the Wilkins' case, but we suspected him of dozens more, including some where the victims were murdered. We just couldn't get those to stick. Not enough physical evidence. The crime scenes were too clean. Sound familiar?"

I thought of Blue. I had put him in the recesses of my mind, locked him away, where I had hoped I never had to see him again, but there he was, like a nightmare come to life. Tall, dark, he moved like a cat. I could see his smile as they led him from the courtroom, his eyes on me. He had brushed by me and whispered, "You're mine." They were the only words he had spoken through the whole trial.

It had taken me nearly a year of hard work to find Blue. In doing so, I had also found the Wilkins' girl. She had been tied to a tree, naked, showered, clean, blindfolded, her body covered with bruises and cuts. All her hair had been shaved from her head and body. She had been raped repeatedly, but she was alive. Blue played rough, but she had been a good girl, not resisting and pleasing him, so when he had tired of her, he had let her go. He tied her to the tree so the world could see "What a little whore she was."

The only physical evidence was some gold paint under one of her fingernails. She had been abducted after her shift, as a waitress, at a local pizza joint. She was eighteen at the time. But unlike the other girls Blue had been suspected of taking, who never saw their abductor and were always kept blindfolded, she had seen something.

A mole on the side of her abductor's neck, two numbers on a house, two letters on a belt buckle. It was the belt buckle that was the break. It was an antique, from the dress uniforms of a U.S. military officer during the Spanish American War. It was rare, and I traced it down to the store it was purchased from in Vermont. From there, I worked my way through various dealers and previous owners.

With some luck, I found myself at an address in Chula Vista, California, south of San Diego, about ten minutes from the Mexican border. The first two street numbers on the small wood house were the same as the Wilkins' girl had described. When the police arrested Blue, he was wearing the belt buckle.

Blue acted nonchalant, unfazed by the arrest, claiming his innocence. He claimed he had never seen the girl in his life. He thought himself too bright to be caught and that we had nothing on him. Unfortunately for Blue, lab tests proved that the paint under the Wilkins' girl's nail, which was a rare mix of paint and real gold, matched perfectly with a paint sample taken from Blue's belt buckle, and there was a mole on Blue's neck, just like the girl had described. The clincher, though, had been one strand of bloody hair, found under Blue's bed. DNA tests matched it perfectly with the Wilkins' girl. Blue was sentenced to twenty-five years.

"Why would he have targeted Bob Bayloff?" I asked.

"Blue wanted desperately to be something in the business," Blake said. "We know he had some type of a breakdown before he moved down south. He told everybody for years he was a big film producer. He could have known Bob."

I thought back to when Stacey and I met Blue at a friend's party. He said his name was Bud Williams. He had told us he was a film producer and went on to describe all the projects he had in development with big name stars. He dropped names and lines on every girl he met, including Stacey. He was handsome, very handsome, intelligent, and charismatic. In this town, in the film business, where busboys become stars overnight, it is hard to decipher the truth. You have to take people at their word, or not at all. He seemed to be everywhere, knew everybody, just another producer trying to make a name for himself in Hollywood, trying to close the deal.

Had Blue known Bob Bayloff? Had he bullshitted Bob like everybody else? Had Bob found out he was a phony and pissed Blue off, exposed him for what he was to the real players in the business? It was possible.

I had seen Blue at the Miracle Works Playhouse on more than a few occasions for talent showcases and had spoken with him. He had called Stacey a few times, even met her for lunch once, saying he had a film project she would be perfect for. Then he disappeared. I didn't see him again until Chula Vista, and the arrest.

When the police walked Blue out of his house, he looked tattered and thin, but his eyes were the same and I recognized him for the first time. Blue, the serial rapist, the man I had been hunting for over a year, was Bud Williams, the wannabe Hollywood producer. In truth, Bud Williams was Blue, and the only thing he had ever produced in his life was pain.

Dan took a deep breath and rubbed his hands over his face. It had been a long day, and a longer night.

"Listen, Blue is a good place to start," Dan said. "Maybe it's him, maybe not, but right now it's all we have. Hopefully, the forensics guys can come up with more physical evidence from the crime scene, give us something more to go on."

"Either way, whether Blue is this guy or not, he's out of prison, free as a bird," Blake said. "You know what that means, Will."

I nodded at Blake. His meaning was clear. Be ready, be on guard, Blue could be around the next corner.

"The lone good news of the day, Will," said Blake, "is that I've convinced the D.A. to hire you. Who better to go after Blue than the guy who found him before? What do you say?"

"I say yes! Hell, yes!"

"I brought your name up as soon as we found out Blue was loose."

"What about this case?" I asked.

"Your job is to find Blue. If you think the two cases are connected then follow any lead."

I smiled. I don't know how Blake had pulled it off, but he had just put me right where I wanted to be. No longer was I just a victim, a person tied up personally with the case, I was part of the official investigation. I held my hand out and Blake slapped his hand down into it.

"Thanks, buddy," I said.

"No problem."

I looked over Blake's shoulder as the coroner wheeled Mary's body out. She was zipped up in a blue body bag. Blake, Dan, and I watched as they loaded her into the back of the coroner's car. Dolen stood supervising. He gave a glance over toward our direction, his eyes freezing for a moment on me. He then turned and moved away.

"He's not going to be too happy about me working this," I said, as Dan turned to me.

"You just see what you can find out to help us, Will. Take care of yourself and Stacey, and I'll take care of my partner. He's a good cop, just keep clear of him for a while."

"Fine by me," I said.

"There's one more thing, Will," Blake said. "The last psychological evaluation we have on Blue is not good. He was on medication in prison, but now that he is out, it's unlikely he's taking it. He was in prison for five years, and his mental condition deteriorated considerably. He is apt to be even more unstable than before."

I thought of the Wilkins' girl tied to the tree, the vacant look in her eyes. More unstable? It was not a good thought. I watched as the coroner's car pulled away with Mary. I felt the weight of this night on me like a wet blanket and I wished in the deepest part of my soul that it were just a dream. I watched as the car turned the corner and Mary was gone.

I would never see Mary again. Only in my mind would she appear. There she would live forever in my memories alive and happy, a friend who had helped me discover myself. There was only one thing left that I could do for Mary. Find her killer. If it was Blue, and I found him again, his days of trials, furlough, and computer glitches were over. All that lay ahead for the killer of Mary and the destroyer of Stacey, was me.

FOURTEEN

Maryland bit her lip, her body shuddering as Mick moved between her legs. She moved with him, feeling she could take no more of him inside her. She gasped for air as he thrust harder and faster, her body enveloping him. She reached down between her legs feeling his hardness move within her, her eyes shut, her thoughts racing. She screamed as she came, her voice piercing the room, her mind and body separating from reality. She grabbed at the sheets of the bed as Mick thrust deeper, faster, harder, her pain mixing with the gasps of another orgasm as she arched her back, her legs quivering as wave after wave of orgasms shook her.

Maryland lay still in a warm fog as Mick withdrew. Small beads of perspiration felt like chips of ice upon her breast, as a breeze blew through the open window. She ran her hands over her body as her mind swam away, floating in a timeless void of peace. Slowly she came back.

Maryland laughed as she got up off the bed and moved into the bathroom. She turned the shower on hot and hard. She stepped in letting the water wash over her, her mind still floating on the wings of her orgasms. Her knees were weak, and there was a pleasurable throbbing between her legs. She smiled and was happy.

She thought of the time Mick wasn't in her life. When he had been away from her. How they had taken him away. She had been incomplete, lonely. She had felt vulnerable. Mick made her feel safe. She needed no one else. The years they had taken him from her had been horrible. On the outside she had appeared normal, content, but inside she had felt as if she were dying. Mick was like a dream.

He asked nothing of her that she too did not want, even if at the time she did not know it. He knew what was right for her, even more than she did herself. Other girls complained how their lovers or boyfriends were not there when they needed them, but Mick was. He always would be. Nothing or no one would harm her with Mick around. She knew he could be violent. She knew he had secrets that they would never share. But he was there always for her, and she knew deep within herself that no matter what, he was hers.

Maryland let the hot water run over her until the shower was filled with steam, the skin of her chest turning red with the heat. She could have stayed in the warm cocoon of the shower forever, but she had to get ready to go. She did not want to be late. It was not something one was late to. She washed and rinsed her hair quickly, then stepped from the shower. She grabbed a towel and wiped off the steam from the mirror. Her blue eyes stared back at her from the reflection. She stared at her naked body in the mirror. Perhaps she should go like this, naked. That's the way he had preferred her. Actually, on her knees from behind was the way he had preferred her.

She brushed the thought aside as she picked up her blow dryer and started to blow-dry her hair. You must not speak ill of the dead, she thought. She looked down at the newspaper lying on the sink. The service started at noon, the paper said. Everyone would be there, she thought. After all, Bob Bayloff had been a big man. Maryland smiled and laughed to herself. She couldn't help it. She thought of Mick, a big man. She found that term when used to describe Bob extremely amusing.

FIFTEEN

Stacey had insisted on going to Bob's funeral. Her insistence, whispered earlier in the day, had been the first words she had spoken since the day we had found Bob's body. Her older sister by five years, Brenda, had arrived from Big Bear, a town about two hours east of L.A., in the San Bernardino Mountains. She stood next to Stacey and me at Forest Lawn Memorial Park, her hand clasped tightly around her sister's. White clouds moved slowly across a pale blue sky, casting shadows down upon the gleaming black of Bob's casket. The preacher's words bounced numbly off me as my eyes scanned the crowd. Dan was nearby and a police presence was evident past the line of more than two hundred mourners that had come to pay their last respects to Bob.

Many in the crowd were recognizable celebrities, and it seemed to be a who's-who of Hollywood. The tabloid shows and papers were out in full force, as were the L.A. Times and the more legitimate rags. The police had had their jobs cut out for them earlier as we ran a gauntlet of cameras and press, pushing and shouting like a pack of wild dogs to the kill.

The press had also been camped outside my house for two days, and I had been tempted to practice my marksmanship with the new Beretta handgun Dan had given me. It held fifteen rounds, including one in the chamber. Its weight and shape fit my hand nicely, and its action had been smooth and crisp at the firing range. It was large and not as easily concealed as my snub nose Smith and Wesson, but it nearly tripled the number of rounds ready to fire, and the extra firepower that the Italian 9 mm gave me let me feel a little more prepared for Blue, or whatever else this town decided to throw at me. Unfortunately, there was no law against

66

the press being camped outside my house, so my target practice would have to be limited to the gun range and a good grouping of shots on the paper target. I had only pulled my gun twice during my job as a PI, and I had never shot anyone. I had no doubt that I could though, if it came down to protecting someone from the monster that had slit Mary's throat and broken Bob up like a wooden doll.

Part of me, a dark part that I didn't want to acknowledge, was hoping for it. Hoping for the opportunity not to group the shots at a paper target, but at the monster's head. But the monster, in reality, was just a man, one of God's children, and I hated him for making me think such thoughts. I knew it was not my job to play God, judge, and jury. But here I was, the weight of the Beretta on my hip and my eyes scanning the crowd, praying for a glimpse of his face and the opportunity to take him down.

In this world there were no Godzillas or monsters from the Black Lagoon. The monsters wore faces like ours and were our neighbors. They had names like Bundy, Manson, Berkowitz, and Dahmer. They were no one and they were everybody. They were violent, dark, sick, twisted, and evil. Yet, they were not born from a lagoon or an erupting volcano; they were born in small towns and big cities across the country. They had brothers and sisters and families. They passed us on the road at night, sat next to us in church and school. They had played Little League, believed in Santa Claus and loved their mothers.

We struggled to understand them, to see what went wrong, what could be done, so that we could learn from our mistakes and make no more monsters, just happy, well-adjusted children who would grow up to become better human beings than those of us who came before. But in the end, they were here, walking and living among us, and forcing an ex-actor to think about blowing another man's head off. I preferred Santa Claus and Little League and I loved my mother, but against her wishes, I had grown up. The innocence in me seemed gone. Pain and anger does that to a person. That is how the monsters in all of us are born.

I looked around and the world I saw in the reflection of Bob's casket and Stacey's tears, I didn't like at all. But we take what life gives us and we do our best. So with that in mind, I felt the weight of the gun on my hip and looked for the monster. He had trapped us in his world of violence and fear, and like an animal that will chew his own leg off to be free from a trap, I would gladly put him down to free us all. And if in that moment, I become him, a killer, then let it be, for perhaps he will see in that last moment of life, how precious it is, and what a thief he has been.

I looked at Stacey and thought of Mary and hated myself for such thoughts of what amounted to revenge. I knew I was too emotionally involved with the case. But I could find Blue, and if Blue wasn't the killer, then I would find out who was.

The preacher finished speaking and my eyes came to rest on Bob's casket. In life, he had not been one of my favorite people. Yet strangely, I was connected to him in death in a way that was eerily close and disturbing. I felt sadness, remorse, and a touch of guilt that comes from being the lone survivor of a two-way rivalry for Stacey's heart. Stacey had stopped crying. She seemed numbed, her eyes staring over the casket toward the white clouds tracking across the sky.

After the service, Brenda would be taking her back to Big Bear with her. She had a nice house on the lake there with her husband. It was made of logs, yet modern throughout with long windows looking out onto the lake. It was another world up there at nearly seven thousand feet above sea level. The town was small, with three ski resorts nearby that were flooded with people fleeing Los Angeles to the sanity of the mountains during the weekends. It was beautiful, and Stacey and I had enjoyed many wonderful times there over the years.

I looked at Brenda. She was slim like Stacey, her brown hair was cut short in a no-nonsense look that suited her and her lifestyle, her jaw line was clean and sharp. Her brown eyes showed intelligence and caring and could sparkle with laughter in a split second. Indian sliver and turquoise adorned her hands. She was dressed in a simple black dress. Yet her beauty, glowing from the inside like a mystic flame, seemed to outshine the most glitzy and glamorous of the Hollywood celebrities that surrounded her.

I had always liked Brenda. We had remained friends even after the divorce. She was easy to talk to, grounded, and stable, unaffected by her beauty, secure with who she was. Like Stacey, she had grown up in Pasadena, near Los Angeles, yet she had never been attracted to the trappings of L.A. or the film business. In a way I saw the reflection of two opposites in Stacey and Brenda, yet their similarities were undeniable, their laugh and smile, their mannerism of speech and sense of humor. Though at times the difference in their lifestyles had strained their relationship, the two sisters were close and Brenda had always been there for her little sister, as she was there for her now.

Brenda turned her head toward me, her eyes catching mine. She smiled a sad smile. I loved them both. To me they were family, and no court or divorce papers could ever change that. It was a matter of the heart. Brenda owned a small café in town, while her husband Bill worked as the local sheriff. He was a twenty-year veteran of law enforcement and a good man. He had grown up in the mountains and was fifteen years Brenda's senior. He loved Brenda and she loved him. At times I envied them and their life together, their happiness in the clouds above the City of Angels. I could not think of a better place for Stacey to stay than among the quiet and serenity of the mountains with Brenda and Bill.

I reached out and took Stacey's hand. I shut my eyes and gave a silent prayer of thanks that Stacey was here among us. I thought of how the killer had been in Bob's house watching. It made my blood run cold. I pushed the feeling down and thought of the mountains and their beauty, of Stacey slipping and sliding across the ice of the lake, her eyes alive and sparkling as we laughed together. What happened to those days, to us? I had let her leave, walk right out the door to Bob. I held Stacey's hand tighter. It was true. I had pushed her away with my distance. I knew that, but deep in my heart she had never left, and I had never let her go, and in an odd way that only love understands, I never would.

SIXTEEN

Stacey watched the clouds move across the sky. They were the type of clouds that puffed and billowed, white as the purest snow. They reminded her of clouds she had seen on a large oil painting at the Louvre in Paris, of angels playing in heaven. The angels were lit with a golden light that pierced the clouds in beams and shone down upon the sinners of earth, the mortals, such as herself.

She tried to imagine Bob as an angel among the clouds, lit with golden light. But as hard as she tried, it seemed impossible. All she could see was his twisted body, his face frozen in a ghastly grin, his ice-covered eyes seeming to laugh at her is if it was all a sick joke. She concentrated on the clouds and tried not to think. Her throat was dry and she felt as if she was crying, yet the tears would no longer flow. She tried to pretend that she was floating on the clouds to a place far away in a fairy tale she had once read about, where things such as death and fear did not exist. But all she could see was blood and Bob and his grin of death.

She had told Bob that she felt that they were being watched, that she had heard noises in the night. Bob, having taken his sleeping pills each night, had heard nothing at all. She could feel it though, someone watching, the weight of their eyes upon her, and there was a smell in air like plastic, sterile and clean. At times she thought she was going mad, that her life with Bob, with its great insulation of wealth, so safe and secure, was driving her to these illusions, these fears of someone being in the house. Her life, once so creative and full, had been reduced to the role of pleasing Bob, of entertaining his guests and business partners. She was the perfect hostess, and in turn, she had no needs or wants for material things. Yet, she felt as a bird in a gilded cage. Part of her, the part she

70

loved the most, had been lost within the confines of Bob's world, of Bob's life. Her independence, her drive and sense of self, the essence that was her, seemed gone forever. She had created her own prison out of the white sands and glass of Malibu. She had everything, and she had nothing. She was a prisoner of her own conscience. Yet, with all this said, she still felt the eyes upon her and smelled the sterile stench of plastic.

Unable to sleep, she would take Bob's pills, falling into a heavily drugged slumber. Then the dreams would come, erotic and frightening, that would awake her with the shudder of her own orgasms. She could feel the touch of someone lingering on her body like a ghost in the darkness. Yet, there was no one there, the silence of the night freezing her until she could barely breathe. She would lie there paralyzed, wishing Bob would be there, would hold her, as she knew a man could, with both body and soul.

She loved Bob, that was true, but it was different, calculated and safe. She felt in control. Passion was limited to comfort and security. Stacey knew there was more to love, that true love had no control. That being in love meant giving up calculation and safety to run with the wolves of one's heart and go where they may lead you, be it to pleasure, or to pain. It was that fear, the fear of being out of control, of being hurt, that had led her to Bob and away from the wild and reckless passion of the wolves, and of Will. Stacey felt Will touching her hand, and she knew that the deepness in which his love had touched her would never be equaled by another man. She felt it even now, at the funeral of the man she had left him for. The strength and rawness of it frightened her still, and she felt like embracing it and running from it at the same time.

She had picked safety over love and passion because it was safer to her heart. Yet, in the safety lay a lie. A lie to herself about the true nature of love and happiness, of giving up fear for hope and taking the good with the bad. Love's nature, Stacey knew, was not one of control but one of emotion, trust, and the fear of putting part of your dreams and happiness into the hands of another, as they have put theirs in yours. Control is an illusion, Will had told her, and as she brought her eyes down from the clouds and watched Bob's casket being lowered into the ground, she realized that once again, he had been right.

71

SEVENTEEN

Mick liked Bob's casket. It had a nice gleam to it, very tasteful. He watched as it disappeared into the grave and felt that the ceremony, overall, had been quite nice. The preacher, he felt, rambled on a bit as they always do, but at least it was a nice day for the service. Mick reached up and adjusted his Versace sunglasses, then flattened his tie down over his silk shirt and Armani suit. Mick wondered if they had been able to straighten Bob out. If not, they could have saved some money by using a smaller casket. The last time he'd seen Bob, they could have fit him into a shoebox.

Mick smiled and tried to keep from laughing. It was hard though; he was so witty. Mick had caught Maryland on the way out of the house planning to go to the service. He knew about her relationship with Bob, but he would have none of that. He had forbidden her to go. This was his party. Without him, none of these lovely people would be here. He had such a way of bringing people together. A good host always does. He scanned the faces of the celebrities in the crowd, their expressions so solemn and sad. Mick smiled; he truly had touched the stars.

Mick took a deep breath of satisfaction as his eyes found her. It was almost time. Her hand was clutched tightly to the Actor's as they moved toward the parking lot. She looked beautiful, somehow more than ever. Grief suited her. Mick shut his eyes. He could taste her even now. His being was filled with her senses. The softness of her skin, the whiff of her fragrance, her hushed noises of excitement, like the purring of a kitten. Mick opened his eyes as she turned with the Actor and walked toward him, escorted by two uniformed policemen. Mick adjusted his glasses, his head up, his eyes on her. He watched as she drew closer, the Actor by her side, joined by the blue-eyed detective and the short-haired brunette.

Mick slipped the stiletto knife down from his sleeve and into the palm of his right hand. It had been specially made in South America, its blade long and razor sharp, with a strong spring that slid the blade out with the power of a punch and then back in, in the blink of an eye. In his other hand Mick held the small, plastic remote and the wet handkerchief lightly in his palm. Mick's eyes never moved from her as the group came toward him.

The press now gathered around in frenzy, the two uniformed officers trying to clear a way, the blue-eyed detective helping out. He could see her now clearly, her skin glowing in the sunshine. She was almost there. He smelled the scent of her perfume as she brushed by. The blue-eyed detective stepped beside Mick as the crowd pushed in, and Mick pressed the lever on the remote.

Three explosions, like gunshots, rang out from a tree twenty yards behind them. On the third BANG, Mick thrust the stiletto deep into the detective's back. Mick felt the thin blade skip over the bone of a rib and into the detective's lung, then retract quickly, back into the handle of the knife. The detective made a hushed, breathless sound, like the whisper of the wind, as air escaped his lungs, and he grabbed his back. People ran and dove for cover as a fourth explosion rang out, and Mick moved away.

EIGHTEEN

I was on my knees, my Beretta pointed toward the tree and the sound of the shots. People screamed and pushed as the grip of complete chaos and panic broke out. Police, private security guards, and the bodyguards of the stars had their clients on the ground, guns pulled. I scanned the tree line as people ran by me and through my sights, my heart pounding, Stacey, under my knee, lying on the pavement of the parking lot, her hands over her head. Then I saw him. Dan was standing ten feet behind and to the left of me. His face was pale, his eyes glazed over, his gun held limply in his hand. His eyes caught mine with a look of puzzlement as he took a step forward and collapsed, the back of his blazer covered in blood. Brenda, lying on the ground near him, moved to his side.

"Officer down! Officer down!" I screamed as I leapt up and ran toward Dan, my gun raised. The two uniformed officers moved with me. I crouched at Dan's side as one of the officers called on his radio for an ambulance and backup. I lifted Dan's jacket up. His shirt was soaked with blood. Dan looked up at me, his eyes moving back and forth, his breathing, heavy, liquid, and labored. He tried to speak. "Hold on, buddy! Hold on! Help is on the way!"

I took my tie off and pressed it into the bubbling wound in his back, applying pressure. Dan's blue eyes looked up at me as Brenda took his hand in hers. I took my jacket off and put it behind Dan's head. Blood covered his lips as he tried to speak. His lips moved, but all that came out was a crimson mist. He focused his eyes for a second on mine, and I lowered my ear close to his mouth, yet all I could here was the pain of his breathing. Dan shut his eyes, focusing all of his strength for a moment, then whispered "Stacey?"

74

I felt like I was hit with a hammer as panic gripped my soul. Stacey! Stacey! I turned and looked to where a moment ago Stacey had been safe beneath me and knew before my eyes reached the empty spot that she was gone.

NINETEEN

I sat in the hospital waiting room, my head in my hands. Dan had made it to the hospital with his life, and now he was in the hands of God and the surgeons. A search of the park, for Stacey, had turned up nothing. She was gone, vanished right in front of me. I kept my eyes shut tight, my mind spinning. The monster had her. He had been there. He had staged the whole thing. Planned chaos.

I had a panicked feeling in my body, making me sick to my stomach. My head pounded and I felt as if life was swirling around me at a different speed. The noises and voices of the waiting room blurred into an endless, irritating buzz in my ears. I stared down at the black and white tiles on the hospital floor and they seemed to be floating. Blake had shown up soon after our arrival at the hospital and was with Brenda. A doctor was checking her out. She somehow had remained calm and clear through the whole thing. Every reaction perfect, focusing on the moment and what needed to be done to save Dan and find her sister.

How did this happen? How did I let this happen? The monster had baited me and I had bit. I was the perfect pawn. I could still feel Stacey beneath my leg. Feel where her body was pressed against mine safe and warm. I smelled her perfume on my clothes. Saw her face. I would rather be dead than to have let this happen. I would have gladly taken the monster's knife right into my heart to keep her safe, to keep her from him. But I failed. I tried to focus, but my mind ran in circles. He had her. The monster had her. I tried to move and couldn't. I felt out of body, intoxicated. Life seemed surreal. I needed to act, not just sit here, but do something to find Stacey. But what?

I felt a hand on my shoulder and looked up to find the fleshy face of

Dolen, his expression solemn and sad, a novelty for him. Two men that looked like Siamese twins stood next to him in conservative suits and short haircuts, and I knew even before Dolen introduced me that they were FBI.

The men pulled out their badges and identified themselves as Agents Black and White. I stared at them and felt as if I was in some type of morbid comedy. Were they joking? I started laughing.

"You sure you're not Frick and Frack?" I asked.

The FBI boys didn't smile, but Dolen chuckled as he slipped a toothpick in his mouth.

"We would like to ask you some questions, Mr. Spire."

I looked from White to Black, then from Black to White. They looked like they were made of plastic.

"Do you guys melt if you're left in the sun?"

White's lips flinched in what could be conservatively called a smile, and I was fascinated that his face didn't crack.

"We know you've suffered a shock, Mr. Spire. We can talk later. We believe you could be very useful in the investigation."

"Oh, gee, do you think?"

White held onto his smirk as I glared at him. Then he turned and moved away. I watched him go and wondered how he could walk without bending his knees. Black remained where he was, staring at me. I looked over toward Dolen and pointed at Black.

"Do these guys come with a warranty? Because I think this one's broken."

Dolen chuckled and twisted his toothpick into his mouth. I looked down at Black's shiny shoes and saw the reflection of my face in them. I thought to myself that if I was going to throw up, this would be a good time. Black turned and moved away, taking the vision of my blurry face with him. I immediately missed myself. I shook my head and ran my hands through my hair.

"So the Feds are involved. I'm so excited."

"It's kidnapping now, Spire, it's their ballgame. They'll be running the show."

"They're assholes. They'll cut you guys out and pressure me to stay

out of it. They strictly operate by themselves like the egotists they are."
My dealings with the FBI, to say the least, had not been very positive. But
I couldn't help but be glad deep inside that they were on the job of
finding Stacey. That is if they could. With all their resources and high
technology they hadn't been able to find Blue. An actor turned PI had,
and it had pissed them off.

The whole time I was looking for Blue, they had been on my back
like I was the criminal. They tried to shut me down and block me at every
turn. I couldn't understand it. I thought we were on the same team, had
the same goal. But it was all about them. They threatened me, bugged my
phone, and had me followed. I had shared all my information with them,
and they had shared nothing with me.

Finally, tired of the one-way information relationship and of being
used, I got smart and lifted their file on Blue from the back of the lead
agent's car. In typical FBI arrogance, they felt no need to lock their car. I
looked at Frick and Frack as they huddled together across the room. If
they, or anyone else, thought they were going to keep me off this case,
they were terribly wrong. They would have to kill me to do it.

"Don't worry about them," Dolen said, as he saw the target of my
glare. "You and me, Spire, we've got some unfinished business to take
care of."

I looked up into Dolen's pink pudge and found his small, black eyes
pinned on mine. I thought for a second he was going to take a swing at
me. I could have cared less. I hoped he knocked me out.

"We've got to find this asshole, find Stacey, fuck the FBI," Dolen
said, his middle finger raised in the air to further his point.

"You and me?" I asked.

"Yeah, you and me, Spire, no matter what."

I looked into Dolen's eyes and knew we were on the same track. I
nodded my head.

"And when we do find that cocksucker, there's something I want to
give him."

"What's that?" I asked.

Dolen twirled his neck around and there was an audible crack as it
loosened up. "You're the fuckin' actor, Spire, use your imagination."

Dolen stood up and pulled his belt up over his gut as he waddled across the hospital floor. The guy was a piece of work. Like Dan had said, though, he was a good cop and had been a good friend, and as I shut my eyes and prayed for Stacey and Dan, I thought that right about now, I could use both.

TWENTY

The music was soft and muffled and there was a low humming sound, constant and close. Stacey opened her eyes but was met with only darkness. Her head was pounding. Her throat and mouth were dry and her body ached all over. She tried to raise her hand to touch her face but she couldn't. She tried to focus her eyes and remember. Something horrible had happened.

She felt enclosed, as if she was in a coffin. Her mind was clouded and hazy. She took a breath and her lungs burned and she realized that her hands and arms were bound, her mouth gagged. She smelled the scent of new carpet and gasoline. A slim ribbon of dim light traced a line across the blackness above her and she realized that it was the light of day trying to press in. The humming continued, low and smooth. Tires, she thought. The sound was the spinning of tires beneath her. She was not in a coffin, but the trunk of a car.

She tried to think through the fog of her mind. Back to what had happened to her. The explosions, Will holding her down, the panic of the crowd, the acid stench of a cloth pressed to her mouth, the face of a man. She was trapped. She had been taken. Abducted. She listened to the tires spin as she reached her feet up feeling the top of the trunk with her toes. Her shoes were gone and she thought foolishly for a moment that that was too bad, they had been her favorite. She closed her eyes and felt as if she was going to be sick. Perhaps this was just a dream, a nightmare that she would awake from at any moment. But she knew it wasn't. She struggled against her bindings and a sharp pain shot through her head. This was no dream. The nightmare was real. It was as real as Bob's death. He had her. Whoever had tortured and killed Bob had taken her.

She listened to the music flow in muffled waves from the front of the car. She recognized the song that was playing, a slow melody, sentimental and melancholy. The title of the song was "Love Is Blue." She felt a chill, like ice on her spine. Blue, she thought, "Love Is Blue."

The song finished playing and there was a moment of silence interrupted only by the hum of the tires beneath her. Then it started over again, the same song, "Love Is Blue." The notes echoed through the trunk in haunting waves. He was going to kill her. But first he would torture her like Bob. Stacey began to cry softly. Her lips moving beneath her gag in a silent prayer. She asked God, begged him, to let her die now. Not to let her live long enough to see the trunk open, revealing the face of her killer and the unimaginable pain he had planned for her.

She concentrated on her heart, its sound pounding in her ears. She concentrated with all her strength and prayed with all her faith for it to stop beating, for God to take her. She prayed for the light of the angels to appear and bring her to heaven where there was no pain. But her heart kept pounding, its beats, morosely keeping time with the soft notes of the melancholy tune.

Stacey listened as the sound of the tires spinning changed suddenly to a coarse rumbling that jarred her with vibrations as the road turned rough. Gravel and rock, she thought. They had gone off a paved road. Where was he taking her? Where were they? Was he taking her far away to a remote place to torture her, to kill her? To bury her where she would never be found? She thought of Will. He would be looking for her. That is, if he was alive. She prayed he was.

The sliver of light above her was dimming, fading. Darkness was approaching. Stacey kicked her feet against the top of the trunk, trying in vain to get it open. She would throw herself from the car, she thought. If she could just get it open. She would throw herself onto the road. Anything would be better than to be at the mercy of the killer. She continued to kick frantically, her feet stinging from the metal of the trunk. Please, she begged, please God, let it open, let it open! She clenched her teeth into her gag as she continued to kick until she felt as if she would pass out from the pain in her legs and feet. Yet, the trunk did not budge. She was imprisoned. Helpless.

Stacey kicked once again and the car suddenly stopped, throwing her forward and jarring her body against the back of the compartment. She listened to her breathing and the engine idling. What was happening? She heard a door open. Then footsteps, the crunching sound of dirt and rock. Her breath stopped. He was coming. He was coming for her. She lay perfectly still as if she was hiding. Trying not to move or to make a sound. But he knew where she was.

The footsteps stopped behind the car. Stacey shut her eyes. She was going to die a horrible death. She saw Bob's face in her mind, the pain frozen on it, the blood and his broken bones. She began to shake uncontrollably. She waited for the trunk to open, but nothing happened. The music played and in the darkness of the trunk Stacey waited. Waited for the killer. She pretended she was invisible. That nothing could hurt her. She held on to the last seconds of solitude with herself before his hands would be on her. Violating her, touching her. Forcing her to do the unimaginable. But the trunk remained closed.

Stacey listened as a slow scratching sound echoed through the trunk. Then again, above her. It was like fingernails on a chalkboard. Then again. But this time more muffled and soft. It was his hands, she thought. Again, but even softer, slow and deliberate, like a caress. The sound moved over Stacey like a thousand needles. She squirmed, twisting and turning trying to push the noise away. Then the scratching stopped and there was a tapping sound above her. Fingers, she thought, fingers rolling one after another as if from boredom. Stacey buried her face in the carpet of the trunk feeling her breath on her cheeks. The sound thundered in her head like a cannon. Slow, playful, teasing. TAT..TAT TTAT TAT...TAT.

Tears flowed from Stacey as she began to sob. She recited the Lord's Prayer in her mind. Quickly. Over and over. He was torturing her, without even touching her. He had begun. There was a jingling sound. Then metal on metal. The sound of a key fitting into the lock of the trunk. Stacey screamed in her mind.

Please God! Don't let this be happening! Please! Please!

Her breathing was short and quick and she realized that she was moaning. The music stopped playing and the sound of Stacey's moans echoed through the trunk. Seconds felt like minutes. The key jiggled in the lock. Stacey gasped for breath. Time was up. It was over. She was his. She waited for the trunk to open, For him to take her. Yet, there was only silence.

Suddenly, there was a rumbling sound above her as the car sank down onto its shocks, and Stacey realized that the killer was on top of the trunk. She heard a soft voice whispering through the metal above her. She turned her head away as the voice continued. Close, he was so close.

The voice was repeating something over and over again. Stacey held her breath. She heard the words, understood them. They reverberated through the metal of the trunk, inches from her face. The voice, muffled and metallic. "I love you. I love you. I love you." The car began to rock softly on the springs of its shocks "I love you. I love you. I love you." Stacey shook her head violently, trying to block out the voice. But it continued, "I love you. I love you. I love you." Stacey gasped for breath, her head spinning, her lungs on fire. The rocking stopped and she heard the sound of metal on metal as the key slipped out of the lock. Then the soft voice, sweet and caressing, promising, "We'll be together soon, my love."

Stacey felt herself break. She lashed out with a kick toward the voice, her feet slamming into the metal above her as a scream came from deep within, pushing through her gag as it filled the trunk with the sound of horror, as her mind fell away. She didn't hear the footsteps moving away, or the sound of the car door opening and shutting, or the melancholy notes of "Love Is Blue" as it began once again, or the tires spinning beneath her. All she heard was the chilling scream of a horrified woman and a small voice in the back of her mind telling her that God had forsaken her. For she was still alive. Alive in hell. In the hands of a madman.

TWENTY-ONE

Slim had the needle stuck deep in his arm. The plastic syringe hung limply against his wrist, the form of the needle visible under his translucent skin. He sat in a tattered La-Z-Boy recliner in a broken-down, one room dump near Dodger Stadium. A clattering, old, metal fan spun in the open window, bringing in the fumes and smog from the roaring freeway below. I was back on the job, on the street where I belonged, trying to find Blue and any clue to Stacey's whereabouts. I had come to see Slim, one of my best sources on the street. But it seems I was a little late. Slim had been on his favorite ride, the black horse of tar heroin. This last ride had taken him to the limit and beyond, over the edge. Slim was dead, overdosed. The last step in a junkie's decline from what was once a promising man to what now lay in front of me, a frightening vision of total addiction.

I had been on a trail of dead-ends for two days straight, trying to track down Blue and find Stacey. I had had high hopes for Slim, having heard through the grapevine of the street that he had seen Blue. Apparently, Blue had been subsidizing his premature parole by dealing a little cocaine and heroin, and Slim had been one of his customers.

I took a deep breath and sat down across from Slim on a pile of old newspapers. I looked at his hollow face. His eyes were still open. They showed no pain as they had in life. He looked calm, comfortable. His struggles with the demons of his addiction were finally over. He'd lost.

Slim was fifty-three. He had once been a pro baseball player. A shortstop. He had played in the minor leagues for years and made it to the "Show" one season with the Atlanta Braves, his year, culminating with a pinch-hit RBI in the World Series. That had been before the horse had run him down and taken everything he was and ever would be. That pinch-hit had been the high point of his life. Death with the needle, in this lonely room, the obvious low.

Slim had tried rehab seven separate times. Eventually, he had given up and given in and like so many other addicts before him had embraced the drug completely. Embraced it, until there was nothing much of the human being left in Slim, just the constant cycle of the needle and the high, the endless craving and the fix. I reached over to the cluttered TV tray by Slim's side, picking up an old picture of him taken during his playing days. The young man in the picture, athletic and smiling, bore little resemblance to the pile of skin and bones in front of me.

The only recognizable trait were his eyes. Eyes that had seen and experienced what every little boy dreamed of, a packed stadium, the ball cracking off the bat to the screams of millions of fans around the world. I looked out the window, catching a glimpse of Dodger Stadium past the freeway. It seemed a very long way from there to here, from the playing fields of the Major Leagues, to this dirty room and the tattered La-Z-Boy. I guess it was closer than one would have imagined. I laid the picture back on Slim's TV tray and made my way into the hall littered with trash, roaches, and the sound of junkies arguing over the quantity of their stash. I moved to a window by the stairs and pulled my cell phone from my pocket and called the police.

I emerged from Slim's dark hole of despair and squinted at the sun, its light casting long shadows across the white asphalt of the street. The sun was an equal opportunity planet, which shone as brightly here in the dilapidated areas near downtown, as it did on the glittering sands of Malibu. The same could be said for the heroin Slim loved. It was an equal opportunity addiction. From here in the bowels of the city, to the estates of Malibu, it had spun its web, the comeback drug of the decade.

I took a deep breath, trying to clear my head from the vision of Slim and the needle. It was a tragic waste. I slipped on my sunglasses as I came to my Vette. Two boys who had told me they would look after my car while I went into the flophouse stood nearby, their large eyes showing much more than the few years of life they had seen on this earth, which I figured between the two of them didn't total twenty. I slipped a five-spot into each outstretched hand and they ran off to their next adventure, which in this neighborhood amounted to living another day.

I started my car and pulled away, heading toward the freeway ramp. I took the Hollywood Freeway North toward Hollywood. I had planned on visiting Dan at the hospital. But that now would have to wait. Dan was in stable condition and the doctors felt good about his chances. The blade of the knife had missed severing his spine by less than an inch. If that had occurred he would have been paralyzed for life. In the dark scheme of things he had been lucky. Brenda had gone back to the mountains to be with her husband. After her calm and poise the day of the attack, she had broken down like the rest of us, the stress of her sister being abducted too much for her to handle. She would try to do what she could, which she knew wasn't much, from her home in the mountains. This city was nothing but pain for her.

With Slim dead, my only shot now was to head down to Hollywood and into the underbelly of sleaze to try to find Timmy Bates. A little midget of a man with a temper four times his size. He had served time for putting a man twice his height through a plate glass window and then cutting off the man's middle finger. The man had apparently flipped Timmy off and "Tiny Tim," as he was known on the street, hadn't liked it. Timmy had served time with Blue and, from what some people said, might be supplying Blue with his dope. I didn't know exactly where Timmy hung out, but I knew in what direction his tastes ran.

Dolen had been in contact with me on regular basis. Keeping me abreast of the situation with the police and the FEDs. The explosions that were set off in the park were the type used on film sets for the special effects of gunfire. They had been placed on the trees sometime before the service and activated by a remote triggering system. Dolen, with help from agents Frick and Frack from the FBI, were trying to track down where exactly the explosive special effects had originated. The theory was that they were stolen. The FBI had also confiscated every piece of video that was shot during Stacey's abduction and were trying to isolate an image of her abductor.

I didn't need to see an image. I had one burned into my brain. More than ever, I was convinced that we were after Blue. This all seemed too personal. Targeted at Stacey and me, Blue making good on his courtroom threat. He knew that hurting the ones I loved was the best way to hurt me. Bob's death hurt Stacey, which in turn hurt me, and drew me into the equation. Then there was Mary, my headshot smiling at her dead body, then Dan, and now Stacey. In my mind Blue was the man. He was slowly dismantling my life. Though there were some pieces that didn't fit. Alfred Green for one. Where did he fit into the puzzle, something to throw us off, a trick? Maybe. The monster had waited for a public place to show his control. He could have taken Stacey any time he wanted from Bob's house. But where's the challenge in that? The sport? The game?

The profile of a controlling game player, bright and calculated, fit Blue well. It was the brutality of the killings that puzzled me. It had not been Blue's method of operation in the past to kill. Not that we could prove. Yet with his deteriorated mental state and the time he had served behind bars, it was not a great leap to imagine that he had become more violent and demented than before. Blue to me was the key. Find him and I would find Stacey.

Time was now an enemy. It frightened me. Every minute, every second that ticked by was agonizing to me. I had to push down the thought of what she might be going through. What he might be doing to her. It didn't do Stacey or me any good to think about it. I had to focus on my job with a singularity of purpose. Find Blue. Find Stacey. Focus.

I felt like I was running on the fumes of adrenalin. I had not slept in days and was seeping further down into the sludge of the mud-people of L.A. Somehow though, I felt good, useful. Stacey was on my mind every second. But I had to keep moving, keep working, and not let the horror of the monster having her slip into my thoughts.

I watched the sun beginning to set in a bright orange and yellow haze over the hills of Hollywood. The day was disappearing. Tiny Tim and others like him that feed on the night and slime of the city would be out soon and I would be joining them in the twilight world of L.A., where reality is but a theory, ready to be bent to suit personal taste. The monster lived in his own reality, his own world. He had Stacey down in the shadows and the darkness. To find him I needed to be there, to join him. Enter his world. I looked forward to it. I felt comfortable with it. I felt like embracing the darkness. Pulling it up over me like a black blanket and hiding from the world. Creating my own reality. I watched as the sun disappeared over the hills bringing on the night. Comfortable was the word. I felt comfortable with the darkness. As comfortable as Slim, his needle, and his tattered La-Z-Boy chair.

TWENTY-TWO

She looked like Kansas. Fresh, clean. I saw golden fields of wheat, blue skies and fresh air in her eyes. She had the winning smile of Homecoming Queen and a body to drive the farm boys wild. She belonged to Middle America, to the best of us, but I could still smell the scent of the Greyhound bus she had rode in on hanging over her like a fog. She was dressed in a black leather teddy; a whip, a cat-o'-nine-tails, hung from her hip. She touched my arm lightly and asked me what my pleasure was. I knew the question had a double meaning. I smiled, slipped her a twenty, and ordered a Jack on the rocks. She turned and moved away the black leather of her dominatrix G-string cutting her ass in half like the night sky across a full moon. I knew the story. She had come to Hollywood with a dream. To be a star, an actress. She was acting now. But in a few months Kansas would be gone from her eyes, and she would wake up to realize that her dream had been turned upside down. That make-believe was reality, and reality was make-believe.

I was standing in a crowded room at a place with no name. A fetish club that moved from week to week to a different location, word of mouth and paper fliers the only roadmap. I looked around at the crowd looking for Tiny Tim. This was his kind of party. He followed the circuit of S&M like a gambler follows the horses. Leather, chains, whips. Women with women seemed to be the theme tonight.

Kansas walked back towards me with my old friend Jack in her hand. She was beautiful. Like air and water she flowed toward me. I felt like grabbing her and taking her away with me before the wind and wheat of the plains were gone from her eyes forever. This town was going to eat her alive. It was a crime waiting to happen. A crime in progress. Kansas leaned over and whispered in my ear as she handed me my drink. She told me softly to come with her as she took my hand and led me through the crowd.

I followed Kansas toward a back room. I watched her move. I was hypnotized by her, the rhythm of her walk, the smoothness of her skin. We stopped at a red leather door guarded by one of the largest men I had ever seen. I took a sip of my drink as I stared at the man's right arm. It was as big as my whole body. Jack traced a path to my empty stomach and without passing go raced straight to my head. The man leaned over toward Kansas, bending his massive body in half as she whispered in his ear. He looked like a giant tree that could move and talk, like the ones in the Wizard of Oz that threw apples at Dorothy.

Jack hit my brain like a hurricane as I watched Kansas talk to the tree. I could swear her leather teddy and stiletto heels had disappeared being replaced by a blue-checkered dress, pigtails, and red ruby shoes. I looked down at my feet, checking for any sign of Toto and the yellow brick road. The tree stood erect and opened the door behind him and waved me in with a hand the size of Russia. Kansas took my arm and led me past the threshold of reality and over the rainbow.

The room was small, hot, and smoky. There was a crowd of people standing and sitting around a small stage. On the stage, strapped to an iron bar and blindfolded, was a tall blonde girl. Her back was to the crowd, her arms above her head, her legs spread apart. She was naked except for high heels, black hose, and a leather garter. The place was silent but for the sound of leather whipping through the air and connecting with the flesh of the blonde girl's ass. She moaned in what seemed part pleasure and pain as the crowd politely sipped their drinks.

A tall brunette, her hair cut short and straight above her shoulders, was doing the whipping. She wore a black metal studded outfit that exposed all the erotic parts of her body while covering the rest. Against the black backdrop of the stage it seemed as if the white skin of her breasts were floating in the air, independent of the rest of her. She moved around the stage like a cat, slow, deliberate. Teasing the blonde with soft touches, kisses, and the whip, before striking her with another lash. Kansas squeezed my hand with each crack of the whip, her eyes peeled to the blonde on stage, opened wide, like a kid at Christmas. If only the boys back home could see her now. Kansas wasn't in Kansas anymore.

I looked around the room, into the faces distorted by the light and shadows. I was down in the trenches of Hollywood. I was swimming through a sea of alternative tastes. The faces were no different than any others I had ever seen. The room wasn't full to the capacity with the Blues of the world, just people, for the most part as harmless as the next person, with just a different twist on an old theme. Sex.

My head grew light and foggy as Jack took up residence. He took a bit of the edge away. Softening things. An edge that, since Stacey's abduction, had been so sharp it had been cutting my brain in half. I had stepped into a different world down here and was happy about it. The one I had been living in had not been too good lately. The show in the real world made the one on stage look like a production by Barney, or Ronald McDonald, what was a little naked whipping compared to murder.

I felt the muscles of my mind relax for a moment. I had been running on empty. I was as tight and as wound up as I could remember. Ready to explode or collapse at any given moment. Stress after a time breaks you down from yourself. Makes you think and act without clarity, just emotion. I closed my eyes, feeling Kansas' touch upon my skin. It felt good, human and real. I needed to be out of my head. I had been living in there too long. In the what-ifs and could-ofs of my life. I needed to be out, to feel alive. And with her simple touch, I was, and did.

Kansas ran her fingers softly over mine with the rhythm of the whip. I took another sip of Jack and felt the stress slide off me like a discarded suit of armor. And then I saw him. Tiny Tim stood by the side of the stage, his chin propped up on it. He had a grin on his face like he had just killed his wife and enjoyed it. He was staring straight up into the crotch of the brunette as she paced back and forth on stage. There were times in my life that I had considered myself lucky. But luck scares me. It's too easy. And this had been way too easy. To find Tiny Tim on my first try made me very uncomfortable. Finding him should have been a little easier than finding a needle in a haystack. But here he was, right in front of me.

In the land of OZ, Tiny Tim fit right in. He looked like a demented Lollipop Kid. His head was shaved smooth, his skull bumpy and gnarled.

His bare arms were stubby, but muscular, showing his time inside. They were tattooed, showing more ink than skin. He had a nose ring with a chain running to a pierced ear and dangling down near his cheek. I looked for his partner in crime, Luke. A massive idiot of a psychotic whose one love of life was smashing anything with a higher IQ than his, which made everybody a target. I kept my eyes on Tiny Tim but saw no sign of Luke. When I did talk to Tim, I didn't want Luke around. Job safety was a priority to me.

Tiny Tim watched in fascination as the brunette slowly removed the blonde's garter belt and hose, leaving on nothing but her blindfold and heels. She spun the blonde around so that her naked body was facing the crowd and flicked the flame of a lit lighter quickly over the blonde's breasts, and then cooled the heat with the wetness of her mouth. This brought on purrs of delight from the crowd and her capture.

The brunette then removed the blonde's blindfold, revealing to her the many eyes and faces of the audience in front of her. The blonde's blue eyes moved quickly across the faces of the crowd as her breathing became heavy, her body shaking. The brunette then stepped behind her and the lash of the whip began once again.

Kansas stepped back into me, her eyes frozen on the stage. She wrapped my arm around her chest and I could feel the leather of her G-string and softness of her skin press into me.

The whipping continued, faster, harder. The blonde becoming more aroused and excited with each stroke, her eyes open wide to the crowd. Kansas' chest moved up and down quickly with each crack of the whip. My mind floated on the intoxication of her scent. She smelled like innocence, sex, and desire. Her body melted into mine as if she'd been made for me. She took my hand, placing my fingers in her mouth as the blonde's excitement grew. The brunette continued the whip, as she moved her body slowly against the blonde. She reached her hand down between the blonde's legs, touching her, as she whipped harder, faster. The blonde screamed as she climaxed in pained ecstasy, and Kansas bit down hard on my fingers. A sharp pain ran up my arm colliding with the Jack in my mind and becoming not too un-pleasurable. I could feel the skin of Kansas' thighs as I spun her around. She released her grip on my fingers and slowly pulled them from her mouth, her eyes on mine.

She took my fingers, still burning from her bite, and placed them between her legs, sliding them under the thin leather of her teddy. Her mouth came slowly open as I felt her warmth on the tips of my fingers. "I know who you are...," she gasped as her lips brushed my neck "...I watched you for years." Her breath smelled like honey and she felt good. We were two adults, standing in the middle of a fetish club, turned on beyond the limit.

I wanted her. She wasn't just a fan; she was a dream, a fantasy. But not now. Not with the monster out there in the darkness somewhere with Stacey. I slipped my hand from Kansas as her lips found mine, sweet and soft. I pulled away, her taste lingering on me. "Another time," I said softly in her ear, "another time."

Kansas looked up at me with eyes like shattered glass. I kissed her once again, then turned and moved away. I walked toward the stage, leaving the golden fields and sunshine of Kansas, for the stormy black land of a demented munchkin and his psychopathic giant. Another job, another time, I would have thought myself crazy. But this wasn't just a job. It was everything. It was all there was.

I tried not to think. Not let my mind run away, but to focus on finding Blue. I reached behind my back feeling the hard comfort of my Beretta tucked into the waist of my pants. Tim moved away from the stage and through a side door. I took a deep breath, the taste and warmth of Kansas still running through my mind. I tried to focus as I followed Tim through the side door, and into the unknown darkness of his twisted world.

TWENTY-THREE

Tiny Tim stood under the glare of a bare light bulb hanging from the ceiling and lit a cigarette. We were both standing in a dark hall that ran behind the stage of the fetish club. I pressed myself into a bend in the wall melting into the darkness, keeping out of Tim's sight. In the harsh glare of the light bulb I could see a bump where the tail of Tim's shirt met his pants. He was packing a gun. That was a new twist. He had been strictly a blade man before. His time in prison must have brought him a new sense of self.

I scanned the darkness looking for the massive vision of Luke, but there was still no sign of him. Tim brought a small vile up to his nose and took a long hit from it. It was a "glass bullet," probably filled with crystal meth or coke. Gun and dope, Tiny Tim was the picture of rehabilitation, the perfect parolee.

Tim stepped forward and knocked on a door in front of him with his elbow, his head barely reaching above the doorknob, his arm as thick as he was tall. The door opened and Tim's face melted into a smile that almost made him look sweet, like Spanky, from *The Little Rascals*, with a nose ring and tattoos. The brunette from the show stepped out into the light of the hall. She bent over and kissed Tim. Not friend kiss, but a real one, deep and passionate. Tim slid his hands up her legs as she grabbed the chain that ran from his ear to his nose. She pulled on it hard and Tim let out muffled cry of pain as their passion grew. It was like watching a bad episode of Fantasy Island, Tattoo and the Dominatrix. They continued going at it and I wondered how much more of this I could take without another drink. Then the blonde from the show appeared from the door and to my nauseating surprise started in on Tim herself. Tim was

94

lost for a moment in a frenzy of female flesh. He then reappeared, grabbing both the woman as best he could with his stubby arms and pulling them into the room, slamming the door behind him.

I stood in the darkness. Now I was sure of it. The world was upside down. Tiny Tim, the munchkin felon, was having sex with two women while I stood alone in the hall, having left Kansas, to find a serial killer who had abducted my ex-wife, who had left me for another under-sized human male named Bob. I rubbed my temples trying not to think so much. My mind was getting loopy from no sleep and either not enough or too much alcohol. I bet it was the former, and I raised the last sip of Jack to my lips.

I never saw it. The punch came hard and quick to the back of my head. My body flew forward against the wall, shattering the glass of Jack in my hand. I tried to turn as another blow hammered my right side pounding into my kidney and bringing me to my knees. I gasped for breath as a massive hand grabbed me by the neck and slammed my face against the wall. I heard the crack of my nose and felt the warm wetness of blood fill my nostrils.

The hand grabbed me again, ready to send me on a return trip into the wall. I turned quickly, violently, spinning my body, the point of my right elbow catching the side of a knee the size of a redwood and buckling it. Luke's face fell from the shadows and into the light as he went down to a knee. I continued my turn, slamming my left fist up into Luke's groin and bending him over at the waist. Luke let out a deep groan of pain as he grabbed his crotch. I stood up, bringing my right knee with me and into Luke's head like a missile, dropping the giant straight to the ground in an avalanche of muscle and bone. I tried to catch my breath, sucking air through the blood and broken cartilage that was my nose. I reached behind my back for my Beretta, but before I could pull it free, I felt the unmistakable hardness of a gun barrel pressed into my ribs.

"You looking for me, pretty boy?" I looked down to find the round face of Tiny Tim. A Colt .45, that looked comically big in his small hands, pressed into my side. The brunette from the show stood by Tim. Tim motioned to her. She reached over and pulled my gun from under my coat and proceeded to hold it on me.

Tim smiled. "You don't look so good, Spire. You bump into something in the dark?" Tim glanced down at Luke. "Hey, get up!" Luke lay by my feet, not moving. The brunette bent down, slapping Luke's face. Luke slowly came to and shakily stood up, towering over all of us. He rubbed his crotch, his eyes glassy with pain.

Tim motioned with his gun toward a bathroom across the hall. "In there, Spire." The brunette opened the door as Luke grabbed me and pushed me inside. The three of them followed me in. I caught a glimpse of myself in the bathroom mirror. I looked like I felt, bloody. My head and face were on fire. I turned my back on Tim as I ran some water into the sink.

"This isn't one of your brighter moves, Tim." I splashed cold water onto my face, watching my blood swirl down the drain.

"This isn't just me you're fucking with. The FEDs are involved. Everybody's involved. This is big-time. You're better off dealing with me than them. I may be wrong, but if they see you with that big gun in your hand, you might be going away for a long time."

"Why the fuck you following me?"

"I like you, Tim. You're sort of my idol."

I grabbed some paper towels and looked at my nose. It had been broken before, a defensive end. I reached up with my fingers and snapped it back as best I could. I thought I was going to pass out from the pain. I went black for a second and held onto the sides of the sink. I turned toward Tim, who seemed impressed with my nose trick. I leaned my head back against the bathroom wall, trying to stop the bleeding.

"If I found you, Tim, don't you think they will? You pull this shit on the FEDs, they'll kill you."

Tim looked at me, his mind working. "What do the FEDs want with me? What the fuck's this about?"

"It's about murder, kidnapping." I brought my eyes down on Tim. "It's about Blue." Tim suddenly looked nervous.

"Hey, I don't know nothing about any murder or kidnapping, and I don't know any fucking Blue."

"Cut the shit, Tim, I know you served time with him, so do the FEDs. Word is you've been supplying him with dope. And unlike the cops, I could care less what you do with your free time. Guns, drugs, S&M, circus acts, I don't give a shit. All I want to know is where he is. Where's Blue? Tell me and I've never seen you."

Tim kept his eyes on mine. "That motherfucker's crazy. Sick crazy." Tim lowered his gun, slipping it into the waist of his pants. He took out a cigarette and lit it, inhaling half of it in one hit. He exhaled. I tried to see his eyes through the cloud of smoke that surrounded him. He looked like a stump that was on fire.

"Yeah, I knew him inside," Tim said, "So what? Everybody did. They knew to stay the fuck away from him."

Tim pointed a thick stub he called a finger at me and shook it. "And you should know, Spire, to stay the fuck away from me." In one sweeping motion the giant pulled a metal blackjack from his pocket and slapped it against my head and I went down toward the white tile floor, the light spinning away into blackness.

TWENTY-FOUR

Mick was happy with his new place in the desert. It was very unique. A cavern, deep within the shaft of an abandoned silver mine. The silver mine had not been worked in over a hundred years. All that was left were a few crumbling buildings, the mineshafts themselves, and the desert heat. But to Mick, it was the most beautiful place he had ever seen. It had taken Mick only two weeks to make the place uniquely his. He had shored up the walls of the # 8 shaft and made the cavern below it beautiful. He'd hired some illegal aliens, day workers, from Mexico to do it. He'd met them in the parking lot of the Home Depot out in Hemet and they'd done some fine work.

He'd decorated the cavern with some Persian rugs, along with a couple couches, a French armoire, a coffee table, some leather chairs, and, of course, two beds for his guests. A Honda generator powered the whole place, which Mick thought, was amazingly quiet. He had also built some special compartments in the back that he would utilize a little later in his production.

He sat in his new place, staring down at the beauty of his face through the lines of cocaine that ran across a gold-rimmed mirror. Small lights, powered by the generator, and hanging from the old wooden support beams above, lighted his face. He leaned down and sniffed up a line, feeling it burn, in a pleasurable sort of way. The cavern had a damp, musky smell of earth and rock and Mick liked it. He leaned back and let out a scream that echoed through the cavern. He felt renewed, alive. Better than he had felt in months. As a child, he'd once had a place like this, a secret place. Some teenage boys had dug it out of the woods behind his house years before. It had been his refuge, a place of his own, where he could hide and be safe. It too had smelled damp and earthy. That is until the Bender found it and it was no more.

Mick reached into the pocket of his blazer and took out an ornate, gold pocket watch, flipping it open. He had a small errand to run in a little while, nothing big, just part of his production. He had been told the watch had belonged to Louis XIV. He wasn't sure if that was true. But it was beautiful. Beauty was important to Mick, as it should be to all cultured and civilized men. Mick shut the watch and closed his eyes, letting the sound of Mozart's Fifth Symphony move across his soul in waves of pure pleasure.

Time was an interesting concept, Mick thought. Time was who he was. Endless, forever. Slipping across people's lives and then vanishing, leaving them grasping for a destiny unfulfilled. Time was relevant only to one's own situation. A minute of ecstasy seemed fleeting, a minute of pain, eternal. Both sixty seconds. Yet, in the clock of one's mind, they were hours apart. "Time is the longest distance between two places," said Tennessee Williams in *The Glass Menagerie*. How true Mick thought, how very true.

Mick raised his hands in the air, conducting the symphony in his mind. Mozart was brilliant. Mick tried to remember if he had ever met him. He couldn't recall. Maybe. Mick had lived so many lives. But surely he would have remembered Mozart. He laughed, of course. How silly of him. Mick thought that Maryland would be proud of him for creating this place. Of course, he could not tell her certain things. But he knew she sensed the contentment and happiness in him. His goal was her happiness. Yet, it was better that she knew only what he chose to reveal to her. She was not like Mick. She was fragile, delicate. Women are that way. He would shoulder all the burdens of their happiness. He would take care of and protect her. That is what men did for the woman they loved.

That Mick should have a distraction every now and again, a tryst of seduction, was no concern of hers. Men always had, through the ages, been distracted by the beauty and pleasure of others. Mick was no different. It was a right that came with being a man. Men took what they wanted, some by power, money, seduction, or by force. It had always been so. It did not eliminate his need or love for Maryland. No one could ever replace her. She was part of him and he was part of her. Life without her was simply impossible.

Mick leaned down and did another line of cocaine off the mirror. He looked at his watch again. It was time to run his errand, a little social visit. He turned the pocket watch over, admiring it. His fingers ran across the beautiful engraving on the back. He smiled. Alfred Green had had good taste in watches.

Mick raised his eyes toward one of the two beds in the cavern. The curtains that enclosed the area were open. She was finally here. She lay tied to one of the beds. Her eyes covered with a red velvet blindfold. Her black dress from the funeral was folded neatly over a chair by the armoire. Mick's eyes moved over her body and the black lace of her underwear. She was beautiful. He would have to take it slow with her. They needed time to be reacquainted. Seduction was the art of men, the skin of their lovers, their canvas. Mick placed a tab of Dexedrine in his mouth, rolling its bitterness around with his tongue as his eyes caressed her. Yes, Mick thought, beauty did have its place.

TWENTY-FIVE

My eyes came slowly open. I saw the stained porcelain of a toilet bowl under the door of a stall, and blood pooled in red puddles on the white tiles of the bathroom floor. My head was pain. My face throbbed. I heard a numb rumbling in my ears, like an echo of people talking far away. My eyes focused and I saw the smooth skin of a girl's leg and the black leather of her shoes near my face. I lifted my eyes and saw Kansas. She was kneeling beside me, holding my hand. The giant tree, who had guarded the red leather door to hell, was standing next to her. He was talking to Kansas as she shook her head. There were tears in her eyes and I wondered what she was crying about.

I tried to speak. But no words came out. I tried to move but only my eyes flickered. I watched as men in latex gloves and white uniforms moved into the room. Paramedics. Not for me? I just needed to catch my breath. The men in white kneeled beside me and a bright light was shone into my eyes. They took Kansas from my side and she stood up, her hands over her face. I wish she wouldn't cry. I tried to reach out and touch her, to tell her so, but one of the men in white was holding my wrist.

I watched the flurry of activity around me. I tried to move my legs to stand up, but I remained where I was. The echoes in my ears grew louder, faster, more frantic. The men in white placed a long wooden board next to me and I was turned over. My eyes stared up at the rusted pipes of the ceiling. I watched a cockroach scurry across the wall. Kansas' face came into view looking down at me, her eyes, red and swollen. She looked beautiful. I tried to smile at her. But she kept crying as something soft was slipped around my neck.

I watched four latex hands move above me. They were wet and red

101

with blood. Somebody must really be hurt. I felt my body raised up toward Kansas and then lowered back down again. If they'd just help me up, I could go. I could help. I just needed to catch my breath. I wondered where my car keys were. I would need them. Did I drive here? Where exactly was here? I watched the men in white move around me as Kansas continued to cry. One of the men leaned down toward me. He was talking to me with an underwater voice. I wondered how he did that. The lights began to dim and the echoes grew distant. This was silly, all this fuss. I was fine.

TWENTY-SIX

Dolen looked at the young woman. She was dead, naked. Her mouth was gagged. Her head shaved, her throat slit. A lamp, from across the room, was tilted to shine directly upon her. The spine of her back lay against one of the four wooden posters, of her four-poster bed. A red wig had been placed on top her shaved head, her hair laying in clumps by her feet. Her face and lips were smeared with make-up, making her look like a clown of horror. Dolen took a deep breath and hoisted his belt up over his gut. Son of a bitch!

Dolen slipped on a pair of latex gloves and moved toward the body. Were the hell was Spire? This was definitely the work of their boy. He had been trying to reach Spire for over a day now. But no one had heard from him. Dolen looked closer at the young woman. Their boy had done a real job on her. Dolen examined the back of the post by the woman's neck and ran his glove lightly over it. He looked at the tiny black shreds of leather on the fingertips of his gloves. The killer had tied the woman to the post with a black leather strap, or belt, while he had been busy with his work. Another belt was still in place, wrapped around the woman's waist and the post of the bed.

Dolen stepped back and called over one of the lab boys to take a sample from behind the post. The killer had had time. He had tortured her, like Bob.

There was no sign of forced entry. No sign of a break-in. Dolen looked into the woman's open eyes. They were sky blue. He could tell even in this state that she had been a looker. Dolen thought that she looked better dead than most of the woman he had dated alive. Their boy had been busy all right. Ten to one she had been raped, they'd find signs of a forced entry there. Dolen leaned over and spit a stream of Skoal into a plastic cup. Yep, the son of a bitch had been busy.

Dolen looked down at a small table next to the body. A script lay neatly on the table. The FBI twins had told him not to touch anything until they arrived. But he was an L.A.P.D. homicide detective, for Christ sake, and he was going to do his job in his city. He'd take it in the ass before he'd listen to a couple FEDs who needed permission to breathe. Spire was right. Fuck them.

Dolen picked up the script and knew before he opened it what he would find. Perfectly cut-out letters, from a magazine, pasted over where the dialog would be. The letters formed two sentences.

The first one read, "Our last garment is made without pockets." That's about death, Dolen thought.

The next sentence was, "How much better a thing it is to be envied than pitied."

Dolen looked at the girl's body. The killer had either envied or been envied by the victim. In either case, it was the victim that was pitied now. The killer had made sure of that. Dolen reached into his pocket and pulled out a pad of paper with the quotes from Mary Higgins' crime scene that Spire and he had gone over.

The first, "He that dies, pays all debts," referred to the first killing, to Bob Bayloff. The killer felt that Bob had owed him something.

The second, "Death surprises us in the midst of our hopes," referred to Alfred Green, in his twilight years, watching his hope for the future, his granddaughter, as death surprised him.

Then of course there was Mary Higgins, the teacher, and the third quote: "He who can, does. He who cannot teaches."

An obvious dig at Mary's teaching and her failed acting carrier. Dolen looked again at the new script. It was written in English not Latin. Why? He bet if Dan were here he'd know. He had that whole artist thing going on. Spire would probably know, too. He was another one. Dolen looked down at the quotes again, the fucking psycho.

Dolen lay the script back down as he examined the crime scene. He would bet his balls that when the boys were done dusting the place there wouldn't be any prints from the killer. The place would be clean. They knew that the killer had used commercial cleaners to cleanse Mary Higgins' crime scene, and Dolen was sure the killer had done the same here.

A uniformed officer came up and laid a folder in Dolen's hand. The victim was Shari Canes. She was thirty-four, single. No record. Her present employer was Tell Tone Films where she worked in the wardrobe department. She also did hair and makeup as freelance work. Dolen brought his eyes up to Shari. Their boy had done some freelance work on her. What the hell did she do to piss him off? Or was this random? Doubtful, their man picked each victim for a reason. They had all been in the entertainment business. And all but Alfred Green had a connection to Spire. Did Shari? If that actor-fuck Spire was here he could ask him. Where the hell was he?

Dolen's eyes moved over Shari. She was so young. For what, why had she died this fucked-up death? This girl was about as far down on the totem pole from Bob Bayloff and Alfred Green as they come. What the fuck did she do? Dolen didn't like this. He didn't like this shit at all. It wasn't normal, even in the world of homicide. This wasn't a gang shooting, a jealous lover, or a good old-fashioned murder for hire. This was something different. Evil and sick.

The psycho was smart. That was true. So fucking what. Dolen was smart, too. He might not read Shakespeare or Shaw. He might be fat, wear cheap suits, and never get laid without paying for it. But he was smart. He had twenty-five years in homicide. He had solved more cases than most other detectives put together. He had been decorated for bravery three times. Shot twice. And his life was his job.

He'd been married once but it didn't last and he didn't have any family. His family was his partner and his fellow cops. He spent most of his time not in his lonely one-room apartment, but at the station house. He had saved every penny he had ever made. So what? What was that, a new suit, a new car? His suit was just fine, and his car was a classic. All that material shit meant nothing. This was all that mattered. His job—solving murders. And he did it well.

So why the fuck did this guy bother him so much? It wasn't the bodies, the games, the torture. He had seen just about everything in his quarter century on the job. More broken bodies and lost lives than he cared to remember. Few had gotten to him, though. Really gotten to him. There was something in this case, something more than torture, murder, and rape. More than the attempted murder of the only friend he had in the world, his partner, Dan. It was a bad feeling that he couldn't shake, a feeling that this was the one, the guy from his dreams, the guy who would end Dolen's life.

Dolen had had the dream ever since he'd joined the force. The dream was a nightmare. One that always ended the same way, with Dolen gasping for breath in a dark, lonely place, his hands over his throat, the warmth of his blood slipping through his fingers, the killer stepping from the shadows and Dolen's realization, the killer's true identity finally becoming clear. Yes, of course, he thinks, of course. But it's too late, too late to warn anyone, too late for Dolen, for he's become the killer's next victim.

Dolen knows that it is just a dream. Or is it? Perhaps it's a premonition. He feels deep down that it is. He's certain that this is how he will die. Alone, killed by a case he couldn't solve until it was too late. Dying, with the useless knowledge of a dead man. When he awakes from the dream, he always struggles to remember his killer's identity. But he never can.

He looked up at Shari. He wondered if she had known, if she had felt that way in her last moments of life. He pitied her if she did. Pity. It is better to be envied than pitied. The killer had made sure of that. The son of a bitch! Dolen let out a stream of Skoal into his plastic cup and sighed. Where the hell was Spire?

TWENTY-SEVEN

I had dreams, dreams that were fractured and torn, dreams that were filled with pain and the feeling that they may not be dreams at all, but my reality. I dreamed of a hospital, nurses, and doctors, of the beauty of Kansas and a burning pain in my head. Of a bright, small apartment filled with sunshine, plants, and flowers. I dreamed of sounds and tastes, the whistle of a kettle, water running, classical music, vegetable soup, the warmth and softness of a fragrant body next to mine. I dreamed that time was slipping away. I dreamed of a monster in the darkness, and of Stacey.

I opened my eyes slowly. My head was sharp with pain. It was hard to breathe. My eyes focused and I saw Kansas. She had her back toward me. She was standing near a window, its sheer yellow drapes blowing in a light breeze beside her. A white towel was wrapped around her body, and beads of moisture sparkled on her skin like diamonds.

She looked beautiful. My eyes moved to the small apartment I was in. I had seen it before in my dreams. Like a flood, it all started to come back to me. Tiny Tim, Luke and his blackjack against my head, the hospital, Kansas, the ride to her place, and the softness of the bed in which I lay. I watched Kansas as she let the towel drop, unaware of my eyes upon her bare body. She sat down at an antique vanity and began to brush her hair. I saw her face reflected in the mirror of the vanity as her eyes caught mine. She smiled and turned toward me.

"Hi," she said. Her eyes danced and shined. She turned, unabashed by her nakedness. "How are you feeling?"

"Great." I tried to smile, but it was a weak attempt. Kansas stood and moved toward me. She took a blue silk robe from the back of her chair and slowly wrapped it around her body. She was a vision. She saw my

107

eyes upon her. She smiled and sat on the edge of the bed.

"How long have I been here?"

"Two days."

"Did you find me?"

"Yes. I went looking for you after you left. I wanted to talk."

"Sorry that I left like that, so suddenly. I needed to find someone. I still do. It's very important."

Kansas dropped her eyes. She ran her hand slowly across the sheets of the bed and the form of my leg. "They came and took you to the hospital. They treated you. We didn't know who to call, what to do, so I brought you back here." Kansas brought her eyes up to mine. The wind and wheat of the plains was still there. She had a warmth to her, a light from within.

"Thank you," I said, as I reached out and touched her hand. Kansas wrapped her fingers around mine as she smiled.

"I was so worried. There was so much blood. I thought... Well... the Doctor said that you were lucky. You've had a concussion, ten stitches in your forehead, cracked one rib and bruised the others, and your nose is broken."

Kansas leaned toward me and brushed the hair away from my forehead, like a mother would do with her child. She reached over to the bedside table and poured a glass of ice water from a pitcher and handed it to me. I drank it down. The coolness of it on my throat was heavenly. She placed her hand in mine and I held it.

"Is it a woman you're looking for?"

"Indirectly."

Kansas caressed my hand. She smelled like flowers and fragrant oils.

"Do you love her?"

"Always."

My eyes stayed on Kansas. She reached up to my face, gently running her fingers across the line of my jaw to my lips, touching them lightly, her eyes never leaving mine. "Then I hope you find her."

Kansas smiled as she stood up. "Are you hungry?" she asked. I nodded my head. She turned and moved away toward a small kitchen off to the right. She pulled out some pots and pans and some food from the refrigerator and went to work.

I watched her. I had been here two days. Two more days that the monster had been loose, that Stacey had been gone, that she had been in an unimaginable place. Was she alive? I knew that she was. He had her because of me, because I had played his game. What was his ultimate plan? I didn't know. But he wouldn't kill her, not yet. He didn't stage the whole abduction at the cemetery to take her away and kill her. He was a showman. It was the game he liked. If it was Blue, I knew that he was ultimately after me. He would use Stacey to infuriate or control me. For now at least I felt her life was safe. But then again, there were worse things than death. I thought of the Wilkins' girl tied to the tree, the look in her eyes, as if her soul had been stolen. I stepped back from the memory.

In trying to find the monster I had underestimated the danger of Tim, and those like him. I had been as alone as I had ever been on the white tile of that bathroom floor. The doctor had been right. I'd been lucky. My life could have seeped away as I bled to death by the toilet of a dingy fetish club. Sometimes I wondered how I had come to this place in my life. The truth was, I loved my work. The pure reality of it was more rewarding than any role I had ever played as an actor. This was real. It didn't get any more real, and perhaps a blackjack against the head every now and again to remind me of that was a good thing.

I looked at Kansas. With little fanfare she may had saved my life, and perhaps in doing so, saved Stacey's, too. I would find Stacey. If I had to go through twenty-five Tiny Tims and Lukes and the beatings they gave me to do so. I would find her. And I would find her alive.

Kansas broke some eggs into a bowl as I moved my legs. They were stiff. My whole body was stiff. I felt like a plane crash. I felt as shattered as the eggshells that were cracking in the kitchen. It was a good rule in the game of private investigating not to get hit with anything hard, and not to fall on anything hard. I had done both.

Tiny Tim had done a real job on me. More than I would have suspected. But that told me two things: he had seen Blue, and he was scared, real scared. I had seen it in his eyes. He thought he could beat the fear away by giving it to me. But he hadn't. All he had done was buy some time and piss me off. He was on the top of my list of favorite people to visit. I knew where we stood now, and I was looking forward to our next little chat. Kansas turned toward me.

"Do you like spinach omelets?" she asked.

"I love them." Kansas smiled as she moved about the kitchen, pleased that I was pleased. I sat up in bed. I raised my head to place a pillow behind it and a sharp pain ran up my side. They had worked my ribs. Worked them good, a few kicks when I was down, I suppose. I bet even the brunette from the show got in a couple of good shots. I must have been the life of the party. Too bad I had missed it and had been out cold. I reached up and felt the metal splint and bandages that ran down the ridge of my nose. Another bandage covered the gash on my forehead. It was on the left side of my head, up high, near the hairline. I could feel the coarse thread of the stitches running beneath the bandage as I ran my fingers across it.

"Do you know a guy from the club circuit named Timmy Bates? Everybody calls him Tiny Tim. He's very short, stocky, covered with tattoos..."

"Yes, I know who you're talking about." Kansas looked at me. "Did he and that thing, that giant, do this to you?"

I smiled. "Yeah, that thing and him did this. Do you know where I could find him?" Kansas didn't answer. She acted as if I had never asked the question.

"Are you still acting?"

"No," I answered. "Dr. Steve Scott ended my career. Well, that's not completely true, I made a life change, I'm a private investigator."

"You're a private investigator? You're kidding? You should of kept acting, you're wonderful." Kansas kept her eyes from mine as she continued her work. "Really, you are."

"Thanks." I tried to adjust myself again, to get in a position so that my eyes could see hers. "Listen, Tiny Tim, it's very important that I find him. Do you have any idea where I could look for him?"

Kansas just kept working. The sound of traffic floated in through the open window, filling up the empty space in our conversation.

"Maybe," she finally answered. She stared down into a large mixing bowl she was holding. "Maybe not." She raised her eyes to me. "Maybe I don't want you to find him"

Her eyes stayed on mine. We seemed locked together. She put the bowl down and moved toward me. I could feel her energy flow across the room. She reached me and bent down and kissed me, deep and passionate. The pain in my head seemed to disappear and all I knew was her. She pulled away and without a word went back to her bowl and her mixing.

"I know a place he may be. I'll take you there."

I watched her. I had lost two days, dreams, pieces of dreams, is all I had to show for the loss. Dreams, and the sweet taste upon my lips from a young woman, cooking me an omelet, in a blue silk robe, who was no dream, but perhaps more reality than I could take.

TWENTY-EIGHT

Stacey's eyes were open. Yet, there was only darkness. Her mind was foggy and dreamy from whatever the killer had given her. Her body was covered with silk sheets, her arms were tied to the bed she was lying on, her eyes, blindfolded. God had died. He did not exist. Stacey knew this was true. She seemed to have a sense of clarity deep within her soul. She was alone. There was only her. There would be no help. There would be only pain and the destruction of herself. The killer would twist and torture her from within. He would start deep within her soul and work his way out toward the mortal parts of her, to the ends of her nerves, where pain was born.

Stacey listened to her breathing in the darkness of her mind and felt helpless. How long had she been here? She had no sense of time, hours, days, weeks? The killer had been drugging her, feeding her, talking to her in a slow, soft voice. She had heard music and laughter floating into her sedated dreams. He had touched her, letting his fingers run the length of her body. He had caressed the softness of her skin beneath her bra and panties.

Stacey had struggled through the drugs trying to move, but it was as if her body was weighted down. Eventually, he had pulled away. For now. Soon she knew he would want more. Much more. She dreamed of escape. But how? She was not strong enough, physically or mentally. So her dreams turned to a wish, a wish that she would never wake up again to his voice, or his touch. She was too weak to take it. She knew he was going to kill her eventually. So she wished for death.

She fantasized about it. Fantasized that he gave her too many drugs and that she never awoke. In her fantasy she could see the frustration and anger of the killer as he found her limp, lifeless body. How enraged he would be that all his twisted plans of seduction and torture had been spoiled. That he was no longer in control. That he no longer held any power over her. Stacey held onto this vision. She found joy in it. It calmed her.

Stacey listened to the silence surrounding her. She sensed that the killer was not near. The room was so quiet. She felt the velvet bands that bound her to the bed with the tips of her fingers. They were wrapped around her wrists and ankles. She took a deep breath. The air was cool and crisp and reminded Stacey of mornings in the mountains when she and Will used to wake up early, and walk down to the lake from her sister's house to watch the sunrise. She thought of those times, of Will's touch and the colors of light rising from the darkness, shimmering on the surface of the water as a new day was born.

It seemed a dream now, a fantasy. Had there been anything so beautiful in this life, so peaceful, so calm? With her eyes closed and the coolness of the air filling her lungs, she could taste those times as if they were today. She could smell the scent of the tall pines that lined the shore of the lake, see the glistening patches of snow up high on the peaks of the surrounding mountains. She could see Will's smile, his eyes on her, his cheeks colored red with the brisk morning air. Stacey breathed deep again and tried to hold on to the feeling that this was her reality, the lake and Will, but the feeling of the binds that held her down, brought her back to the reality of the killer's bed.

Stacey felt her eyes fill with tears under the softness of her blindfold. She didn't really want to die. She wanted to be free. She wanted more than anything to live, to breathe, to see the sunrise again, to feel as she had those mornings in the mountains. We don't know how wonderful life is, she thought, what a gift we live every day, until it is all taken away. We always want more and more, when we already have so much. We are blinded by greed and ego, always in a hurry to race to something better, living our lives somewhere in a theoretical future, where life is somehow better.

In reality, she thought, the moment that we are living, that we are so eager to race by, could be the best moment of our lives. Stacey was guilty. She had raced toward and lived in the future, always seeing something bigger and better around the next corner. Not seeing the full wonder of the moment. Now, in the darkness, tied to the killer's bed, she struggled to remember what it was she'd been racing towards. What could have been more miraculous, more precious, than the simple beauty of a new day dawning, shared with the one you love? And what was the cost for such a priceless moment? Not Bob Bayloff's millions, or a starring role, but simply life.

Stacey tried to stop the tears but she couldn't. She had no control over it. She had no control over anything. She had never felt so helpless.

From the sting of her tears and the depth of her helplessness, Stacey began to feel the anger rise. She wanted to see the sunrise again, to be grateful for every moment, every day. She struggled against her bindings. She pulled hard on them in anger and frustration. She wanted to live!

She jerked her arms and pulled with her legs as her tears continued to flow. How dare he! How dare he do this to her! He wasn't God! He was just a man. He had no right! No right! Stacey pulled violently on her bindings and to her surprise felt the band on her left hand move. She pulled again, the band tightening over her hand. But it had moved. Yes, it had slipped!

Stacey arched her back and pulled with all her strength, putting all the pressure she could bear on her left arm. She felt as if her wrist would break as she turned and twisted, when suddenly her hand slid free.

Stacey lay frozen for a moment, listening to the silence of the room. Her breath echoed in her head like a storm. She tried to calm herself. Was he watching her? Was he there? Was this a trap?

Her left wrist throbbed and her fingers tingled. She grasped the blindfold on her face and pulled it away. The room was lit with bright stars floating in the air, and as her eyes adjusted, she realized that the stars were candles covering the room. In the soft, flickering light, she looked for the face of the killer, but found only the dark shadows of a room of rock, furnished with antiques. Stacey's heart raced as she reached over and untied her other hand and then her legs. Could this be happening? Had God listened to her? Had He heard her prayers?

She stood up and felt as if she was going to pass out. She reached over to a chair next to her, steadying herself. The candles flickered and danced, and to Stacey the floor looked like a lake of mercury, shimmering and moving. She saw curtains, cutting the room in half. She tried to move toward the curtains but her head spun in pain and she went tumbling to the ground.

She pulled herself up. Her legs were weak and feeble. She could barely breathe. Her body ached all over. The drugs the killer had given her were still with her. She moved slowly. It was if she was walking on water. The light of the candles danced around her like playful fairies, the room spinning. She must hurry! He would be here soon! She knew he would! She said a silent prayer as she stumbled toward the curtains. Stacey felt a rush of freedom as she pulled the curtains open. She moved passed them, out into the darkness, and stopped.

She was standing in a cavern of rock and dirt, lit with the dull glow of black lights. The lights eerily illuminated her pale skin into a fluorescent glow. She looked down by her feet as the ground fell away into a deep shaft. The shaft was narrow, but wide enough to make a leap to the other side impossible.

She looked into the shaft, no bottom visible, only darkness. Stacey put her hands to her head, gasping for breath. Where was she? Where had he taken her? What was this place?

Then she heard it. The soft notes of the melancholy tune "Love Is Blue" playing behind her. The song found her spine like the blade of a knife. He was here. He had been watching her. She felt the chill of his eyes upon her as she stood, frozen. She heard the sound of ice cubes dropping into a glass and smelled the heavy scent of a cigar as it drifted towards her. She began to sob, softly. She stared into the darkness below. It seemed calm and limitless and she knew she would never see the sunrise again. There would be no pain she thought, just an end to the nightmare.

Stacey closed her eyes and asked God to forgive her. Forgive her for what she was about to do. She would never go back to his bed, to his touch. Never. She felt a wave of calm wash across her. It was over. She closed her eyes and thought of the beauty of the lake and of Will. She smiled as she saw the light dance across the water in her mind and she took a step toward the ravine. A soft voice rose behind her. "I kill him if you do." Stacey stopped.

"The actor. I kill him."

Stacey didn't move. The waves of the song moved through her. She felt the essence of herself drift away on the notes of the tortuous song. She stared down into the abyss and could see herself falling into the blackness. She put her fists to her eyes, overwhelmed. He would kill Will! He would kill him! But Will would be hunting the killer, Stacey thought. He would be looking for him. It was the killer that was in danger now. Will would find him. That is, if he was alive.

"He's alive and he's looking for you," the voice answered her, as if reading her thoughts. "He'll never find us, though. But I'll spare his life if you come back inside."

The soft voice got closer. "Come, let's have a drink together." She could feel the killer now; feel the presence of his body in the space behind her. He was humming along with the tune. She could smell him. It was familiar and horrifying. She thought of Bob and the freezer.

"I have prepared your favorite, a tray full of cheese and crackers, some shrimp with Tabasco sauce, and of course, your vodka tonic." He inched closer. She felt his breath on her neck, his heat.

"I know who you are." The words came out of Stacey's mouth more steady than she could believe. They hung in the air. She listened to the killer's breathing, inches behind her.

"Well, of course. We have always known each other."

"Your name is Blue. You're Bud Williams."

"I have had many names, many lives, just labels for a transitory passage. It's my soul you recognize. Souls are eternal, they require no such labels."

Stacey listened to the killer's voice. It was soft, like a whisper, not deep in pitch. She tried to remember Bud Williams' voice. She couldn't.

"I recognized you from a former life. I was drawn to you as I have always been and always will be. I had come to you for an entirely different purpose at first. Then I realized that it was you. I saw you. Truly saw you. You're me, backwards."

Stacey continued to stare down into the darkness. He was insane.

Beyond insane. More than she could have imagined anyone to be. But if she could keep him talking...

"What was your purpose...the first reason you came to me?" Her voice trailed off into the cavern. She heard the killer take a deep breath.

"To kill you of course."

Stacey wrapped her arms around herself as the blood rushed from her head. She tried to breathe, to speak, but the word came out as a whisper, "Why?"

"I believed you were a bender. Then I saw it was you. My love."

Stacey's body was shaking. Her eyes burned and the killer's voice echoed in her head.

"I knew that in time, time with me, you would cast off the confusions of this life and remember the clarity that was us. There are few of us that are straight and clear. I can see it in you. Though there have been people, certain forces in this life that have tried to bend your clarity. Your soul is sharp, on the line, like a razor. I can see it clearly, even as we speak. For that reason I have always known that... I love you...I love you..."

The killer's voice vibrated through Stacey. She could feel his breath, his words, one by one, on the back of her neck. "...I love you... I love you... I love you..." He pressed his body into hers. She felt his excitement, his hardness, against her as he continued. "...I love you ...I love you ...I love you..." Stacey thought of Will as the killer's lips found the skin of her shoulder, her neck, her ear, and she stepped off into the emptiness of the black ravine.

TWENTY-NINE

Stacey felt herself falling. She didn't brace herself. She was ready to die. She landed with an explosive thud that knocked the air from her lungs. She rolled over and gazed up at the black lights above, her mind spinning. She gasped for breath and felt the softness beneath her and realized her fall had been broken. Laughter floated down to her from above. The killer's voice reached her.

"I trust you're all right, my love. Your performance was wonderful." Stacey felt the softness beneath her once again and realized she had landed on an air bag. Stacey looked up toward the voice in confusion. The killer had staged the whole thing, like a scene from a film. She half moaned and cried, her voice trailing off into the darkness.

"I am disappointed that after expressing my feelings that you preferred death, over trust. You've been away from the clarity that is us for too long." Stacey tried to move, but she couldn't. She tried to scream, but she had no voice. The only sound in her head was the killer's voice.

"Think back to your dreams at the beach house, to the pleasure that would come to you in the night. Think, my love. There is no need for another take! You were marvelous!"

The black lights above Stacey went out and Stacey was left alone in the pitch black of the shaft. She heard "Love Is Blue" echoing down toward her from above like a broken record in her mind. She gasped for breath as her insides wretched and her stomach gave way and she vomited violently, her body shaking in waves of dry-heaves. God was dead. She was sure of it. She reached out, feebly, finding the stonewalls of the shaft as she fell within herself, slipping away into the depths of her mind, and the mercy of unconsciousness.

THIRTY

The club was called Frog's. There was no marquee, no sign. From the outside it looked like a house, but inside, it was a world of its own. Kansas and I sat in my Vette across the street from the club. Kansas gazed out the driver's side window, her right hand fidgeting with the steering wheel. She had driven me here after we had found my car unharmed, and un-towed, right where I had last left it in the parking lot of the fetish club. I had been amazed that it was still there and had taken that as a sign that my luck was changing. I had then pressured Kansas to drive me to where she thought Tiny Tim would be, and Frog's had ended up being our destination.

Kansas looked over toward me as the light of a passing car caught her eyes. She looked like a cat in the night. She had a talent for making me feel uncomfortable, in a pleasurable sort of way. She blinked slowly and I thought for a moment that she might curl up on my lap. I ran my hand down my side and felt the medical tape that covered my broken rib through the thin fabric of my shirt. My ribs hurt with each breath I took and my head wasn't much better, feeling like an early morning wake-up, after a long night out with Jack.

I didn't have time to be in pain, I had work to do, and with each ache I became a little angrier. I didn't want to be here. I felt like staying in bed for a decade or so, having Kansas stroke my head and cook me spinach omelets. But I needed information, and I needed it fast. And then there was that voice screaming in the back of mind. Screaming for help. A voice that was desperate and pained. A voice that had been raised at me more times than I cared to remember, until answering it was no longer my responsibility and my head was filled with only the silence of my

119

thoughts, and an emptiness in my life that had yet to be filled. The voice was that of my ex-wife, and my friend, somewhere out there with the monster. So Kansas, the omelets, and the decade of sleep would have to wait. I had a job to do, and I needed to start doing it. I reached into my coat pocket and pulled out the pain pills the doctor had prescribed for me, Vicodin, the Cadillac of painkillers. I took one out and popped it into my mouth, swallowing it down. Kansas just stared at me.

"That's your second one," Kansas said with more than a hint of condemnation.

"Thanks, Mom, I'll keep that in mind before I go out and play," I replied.

Kansas smirked at my sarcasm and shook her head. Kansas' real name was Laura Boyd. She was from a small town, a farm to be exact, right outside of Wichita. Kansas was from Kansas.

She kept her eyes on mine. "You sure you want to go in there?" she asked. "You're not in much shape to be confronting anyone."

"Who said anything about confronting anyone? I just want to talk," I said as I opened up the glove box and pulled out my old Colt revolver. I smiled at Kansas as I slipped the revolver into the waistband of my jeans. "You think he's in there?"

Kansas nodded at me. "He comes here with Renee from the club, the girl from the show."

"Yeah, we've met," I said. "What time do they usually show?"

"When it opens, after two," Kansas said as she pushed the hair off her forehead. She was wearing black leather boots that hugged her legs to her knees, and a black miniskirt with a midriff shirt with spaghetti straps and a black leather coat. She looked good, real good. I tried not to notice.

I looked at my watch, it was ten after two in the morning, and I was again in the shadows of the City of Angels, outside a place that didn't exist. "You stay here," I said to Kansas as I took her hand in mine.

She smiled at me and opened the driver's side door. "What, so I can find you in the bathroom again? No way. I'm coming with you. Try and stop me and I'll punch you in the ribs, take you home, and put you back in bed." Kansas' hand slipped from mine as she got out of the car and slammed the door. I sat in the car watching her cross the street toward the club. Son of a bitch! I opened the door and stepped out of the car, wincing over in muffled pain as I closed the door and followed her.

I reached Kansas, who was standing in front of the house, her arms crossed. "Look at you, you can't even stand up straight!"

"Yeah, I can," I said defiantly. I tried to straighten up, but it didn't really work.

"Will, what are we doing here? Let's just call the police!"

"I already have," I said, as I grabbed Kansas by the arm and led her toward the front door of the house.

"Will? The entrance is around back."

"Oh," I said as Kansas slipped her arm around mine and led me away. I held my ribs as I moved along after her, bent over like the hunchback of Notre Dame.

I had never been to Frog's, but I knew people who had. The place was only open one night a month, and the night always changed. It wasn't a club really, but a private residence with no legitimate paper trail to the real owners. Its clientele, Hollywood stars to select lowlifes like Tiny Tim. It was buried beneath a sea of distortions, legal mazes, and good old cover-ups. Kansas led me along an overgrown brick path toward a black door and under the roof of an old wooden porch.

"Can you get us in?" I asked. Kansas turned toward me and kissed me as her hand found my jeans and she slid her fingers down into them. She grabbed hold of my gun and pulled it from my pants. "Yes," she said. She smiled and slipped the .38 under her skirt and into her panties. I watched her as she turned and knocked on the door, her face fresh and innocent. She looked like a Girl Scout selling cookies door to door, not like a dominatrix waitress, packing a .38 in her panties. I smiled. I was beginning to really like this girl.

A hatch on the door slid open, and two baseball size eyes looked out at us. The hatch slid closed and the door swung open. I had a bad sense of déjà vu as the giant tree of a bouncer, from the fetish club, stepped out onto the porch. He looked me over slowly as I tried to stand up straight, the metal splint on my nose reflecting the porch light into my eyes. I squinted and the tree smiled at me with teeth the size of piano keys and laughed the laugh of a god. He slapped me on the shoulder, almost knocking me off the porch. I smiled through the pain as he motioned for me to raise my arms in the air. I did so, slowly.

"Be careful. He's still hurt," Kansas said, as the tree began to pat me down for weapons. The tree moved his paws over and across me. He pulled from my pocket a police blackjack like the one Luke had slapped against my head. He looked at it for a moment than handed it back to me and signaled that it was all right for me to enter. He winked one of his baseballs at Kansas, and we moved by him and into the club.

Inside, the house was huge, craftsman in style. To the left there was a living room that had been gutted, and booths and tables occupied most of the floor space along with a couple of couches and comfortable-looking chairs. The wall was lined with various framed pictures of celebrities and stars, most of them signed. To the right was a den that had also been stripped down. It had a jukebox, its neon lights keeping beat with a sultry jazz tune that floated intoxicatingly through the air. A few couples danced on the shiny wood floor, oblivious to the world around them. I followed Kansas as she led me past the booths of the living room, toward what would have, in a more traditional setting, been the kitchen of the residence.

Wooden stools lined a long breakfast nook. I had a feeling though that milk and cornflakes weren't being served this morning. One hint. The doors of the kitchen cabinets had been taken off and were filled to capacity with different types of liquor. A woman was working the bar, adorned with a lip ring, and pierced nipple, which could be seen quite clearly through the lace of her top. Kansas walked up to the bar, and the pierced woman moved toward her.

"I'll take a glass of merlot, and an ice water, and whatever you've got for fifty," Kansas said. The pierced woman nodded. She returned in a moment with the drinks, and Kansas reached her hand across the bar slipping the money into the palm of the pierced woman's hand, in a half handshake. Kansas turned to me and handed me the glass of water. I stared at the benign liquid. It wasn't Jack.

"You shouldn't mix alcohol with prescription drugs," Kansas said. I looked down and saw the folded corners of a small paper packet the pierced woman had slid into Kansas' hand. I figured it to be about a half of a gram, fifty bucks worth of cocaine. I brought my eyes up to Kansas.

"I find that comment very humorous, ironic really, considering." I glanced down again into Kansas palm. "Is it the prescription part of the phrase, drugs, that's confusing me?"

"Yes," Kansas said as she took my hand and led me away from the bar.

We walked down a hallway and into a room painted with the color of flashing lights across fluorescent walls, as two girls in skimpy outfits danced in gold-painted disco cages hung from the ceiling. Patrons moved to the beat of the music on the dance floor beneath them, as we made our way through the room and into another hallway. There were five doors in the hallway. One was open. It was a bedroom, complete with a bed, a mirrored table, a couch, and two chairs.

A couple lay on the velvet-covered bed, staring up at a spinning strobe light above them that spun out different colors across the room. Kansas shut the door of the room, sat down on the couch, and opened up the paper packet, sliding some of the white powder out and onto the table. She cut out four lines and pulled a silver straw from the pocket of her coat, taking one of the lines up her nose in one quick stroke. She looked up at me and smiled and extended the straw out for my taking. I shook my head as I looked down at the lines.

"That shit will kill you," I said.

Kansas smiled at me and laughed. "Oh, you're one to talk. You and your buddy Jack?"

She had a point, but I tried not to think too much about it as my fingers fidgeted with another tab of Vicodin. It's not that in my day I hadn't been a bad boy, but I had hoped time had taught me something of survival, survival in the city, and survival with myself. I nodded at Kansas, acknowledging her point, and tried not to judge, but couldn't help but wonder where she would be in ten years. Wonder whether she could take it, or it would take her. Only time would tell.

The couple on the bed broke off their gaze at the strobe light, seeing that the party favors had arrived in their absence. Kansas passed the straw around and they both did a line and introduced themselves, Kansas knew the girl, and they immediately struck up a conversation. I laid my hand on

Kansas' head and she closed her eyes, and I could swear I heard her purr like the slinky feline she was.

"I'll be back in a minute," I said. Kansas took my hand as I began to slide away. She looked up at me with a deep look of concern.

"I'm coming with you," she said as she stood up.

"No, you stay here. I'll be right back." Kansas didn't like it. She stood there for a moment, the height of her black boots bringing her up almost to eye level with me. She saw in my face that there was no negotiating this point. She took my hand and slid it under her skirt and I felt the hardness of the Colt between her legs. I slipped it from her panties and into the waistband of my jeans. I smiled and squeezed her hand and she sat back down, her eyes never leaving me. I opened the door.

"If you're not back..." she said, but I never heard the rest of her sentence as I shut the door and moved down the hallway, leaving Kansas with her new friends in the decadence of the endless L.A. night. I moved down the hall. I slipped another Vicodin into my mouth as ribbons of pain entwined my body, the pain reminding me of how badly I wanted to see my old pal Tiny Tim.

THIRTY-ONE

I looked around at the light flickering through the fog of a large room at the back of Frog's. There were couches, tables, and chairs peppered with various patrons enjoying themselves, a type of communal lounge. Old, silent movies cast their images on the walls along with psychedelic colors dissolving and reforming. Dancers, naked but for the bright paint that covered their bodies, danced eerily through the crowd like troubled spirits from Timothy Leary's mind. My eyes scanned the faces hidden in the shadows. I was looking for a little man. A little man in big trouble. Tiny Tim was here. I knew it. I could feel his presence on the nerves of my psyche. I slipped my hands into the pocket of my jacket and felt the hard, leather-covered metal of my blackjack. If Luke was around, I had a present for him.

The Vicodin had kicked in. My head was light and soft, the pain muffled, and for the first time I was able to stand up straight. Music vibrated off the walls, mixing in a kaleidoscope of images and sounds. My eyes caught the form of a painted girl swinging slowly overhead from a trapeze as I made my way through the crowd. She moved in and out of the lights, changing colors, like a chameleon. The crowd was growing. It was prime party time for the after-hours gang, and the place was like a carnival.

I wondered how Kansas was doing. This was part of her world and she could probably take care of herself, or at least she thought she could. Every girl that Blue had grabbed had probably thought the same thing, and I couldn't help but worry. It seemed to be all I did lately, was worry. It was the loss of control that did that, the loss of control over my life, over a situation that thrived on control. For control is what the Blues of the world were all about. It is what they thrived on, taking it, and keeping it.

I scratched at the bandage that covered the wound on my head as I concentrated on the faces moving around me, and there she was. Renee, the girl from my private party in the bathroom, the one with a taste for Italian handguns, S&M, and tattooed trolls, stood sipping a glass of red wine, her armed wrapped around the thick neck of Tiny Tim.

Their backs were to me. They were involved in a conversation with a group of people lounging in front of them. One of the crowd was Luke. He was seated on a large couch that with his size, he made look like an armchair. They were all laughing and having a good ole time, while I stood there trying to breathe through a metal splint and popping pain pills like they were M&Ms.

I watched Renee kiss Tim, and I thought how far away Stacey seemed to be. How far away I seemed to be from finding her. I watched Tim laugh and felt the anger rise inside me. He knew. He knew where Blue was. That's why I had gotten the beating. He thought the beating would keep me away. He didn't know about Stacey, or where she was; if he had, I'd probably be dead. He would have had to have killed me. He would have known that as sure as he loved a good S&M whipping, I'd be back for him, again and again.

I slipped down into a soft chair and into the shadows. I'd wait and watch. I reached into my pocket and pulled out a pack of cigarettes and slipped one into my mouth. I'd been trying to quit, but like a lot of other things in my life lately, I wasn't having much luck. The light of the flame flickered off the metal of my splint as I lit the cigarette and watched Tiny Tim move. He walked away from the crowd as Renee took a seat near Luke. He walked away, alone.

I stood up and kept my eyes on Tim as he pushed his way through the crowd. He made his way to a small bar at the front of the room. He got a beer and turned and took a seat by himself at a table for two. He leaned his chair back against the wall and took a swig of beer as he watched one of the painted dancers move by. I slid slowly towards him, using the cover of the crowd to approach at an angle. Tim's eyes were pinned on the dancer as I slipped into the chair across from him. Tim looked over at

126

me, and the look on his face was one of shock. He soon recovered, though, and smiled a shit-eating grin as he looked at my broken nose and blackened eyes.

"Hey, Spire, you have an accident?"

"Yeah," I replied, as I slipped my Colt free and slid it under the table and into Tim's crotch. Tim's eyes went wide. "Accidents will happen," I said, as I pulled the hammer back on the gun. Tim tried to speak, but no words came out.

"Now maybe I'm mistaken, Tim, but you don't have much going for you, and if I pull this trigger, you'll have even less. So unless you want to put a whole 'other spin on that name, Tiny Tim, I'd come with me."

I reached across the table and grabbed Tim by the collar and pulled him up. I slipped the gun into my coat pocket, pressing the barrel into the back of Tiny's neck, as I pushed him through the crowd.

Tim looked back over his shoulder as my free hand went to the small of his back and I felt the metal of a handgun tucked into the waist of his pants. I could tell by its form, even before I pulled it free, that it was my Beretta.

"Finders keepers, Tim," I said, as I slipped the Beretta into my coat pocket. Tim's eyes scanned the room as I continued to pat him down.

"Luke's not coming, Tim, he's busy with your girl. She was tired of that knee-high loving you give her, like a dachshund in heat. She's going for the grande package."

I saw a door open on my right. A bathroom. I pushed Tim inside and locked the door behind me. The bathroom was large, and better yet, it was empty. Tim turned around and glared at me. He started to speak and I brought the metal of the Colt down on the bridge of his nose. The crunch was audible, like the cracking of a walnut. The power of the blow sent Tim through the door of the bathroom stall, splattering its walls with a freckling of his blood. Tim grabbed his nose, his pain coming out in guttural groans of rage.

"What's the matter, Tim, have an accident?"

Tim's eyes were on fire as he brought them up to mine. He charged me as I brought my blackjack out and slapped it against his head, up high, near his vacant hairline. Tim's scalp opened up, and he tumbled over and hit the floor hard. I reached down and grabbed him by the collar, pulling him over to the urinal and slamming his head into it, his face toward me. Tim's eyes rolled up into his head as I flushed the urinal over his face and put the barrel of the .38 down his throat.

"Let's pick up where we left off, huh, Tim? Where's Blue?"

Tim looked up at me, his eyes, bloodshot and glassy. He made a gurgling sound and I slipped the gun from his mouth.

"What's that, Tim? You'll have to speak up!"

"You're dead, Spire. You better fucking kill me, or you're dead!"

I slapped the gun against the side of Tim's head.

"Wrong answer, Tim!" I put the barrel of the .38 back into his mouth. I took a deep breath. "I'm tired, Tim, my nose hurts, I've got to piss but your fat head's in the urinal, and to top things off, your buddy Blue, he took Stacey. He's got her. So don't think for a fucking second that I won't pull this trigger and flush your brains down this toilet!"

Tim's eyes changed, like a light of reality had gone on inside. He believed me. He was going to talk. I took the gun from his mouth. He started to speak and the bathroom door exploded off its hinges as Luke's massive body came flying in.

Luke grabbed me, lifting me into the air and body-slamming me into the wall. My breath flew from my lungs as pain ripped down my spine. I brought my gun down hard on Luke's head and it bounced off a scull that was thick as a grizzly's. He squeezed me and I felt another rib crack. I screamed and heard Tiny Tim yell, "Kill him, kill him, Luke!"

I fumbled for my pocket and slipped my blackjack out with my left hand and smacked it against Luke's temple as I continued bringing the Colt down onto his head. Luke's grip softened as I played "Little Drummer Boy" on his skull. He went down to his knees and I slipped free. I wound up like a batter and took a full swing, bringing both pieces of metal in my hands to the side of Luke's head, sending him down for the count. Luke's falling body revealed Tiny Tim, holding a small, .22 caliber handgun, his right pant leg pulled up above his black boot. His boot, I'd forgot to check his boots. Tim pointed the gun at my head.

"You're dead, Spire."

In a flash I raised the .38 toward Tim and we fired together. Tim's bullet whizzed by my ear, taking a piece out of the wall near my head as Tim's feet left the ground and he went down onto his back, his gun slipping from his hand. I stood there looking down at Tim, a ribbon of gun smoke twisting over his body. The scent of gunpowder, burnt and sweet, filled the air. I raised my eyes to the shattered doorway and found Dolen's large body framing it, two uniformed officers standing behind him.

"What the hell took you so long?" I gasped.

Dolen took in the scene, gnawing on a toothpick. Tim moaned, his legs moving through the air. The round from the .38 had caught him right below his left collarbone. One of the uniformed officers spoke into his walkie-talkie, calling for an ambulance.

Dolen casually kicked Tim's gun away, then bent down, examining Tim's wound. He looked up at me and nodded his head in approval.

"You all right?"

My legs were shaking, my heart pounding. The .38 felt like it weighed a ton in my hand. I could still hear a buzzing in my ear from Tim's bullet passing by. I put my back against the wall and slid to the ground. "Yeah, I'm fine," I said.

Then I leaned over and threw up.

THIRTY-TWO

Mick watched the fat cop and the actor as they walked out of Frog's. They walked next to a gurney being wheeled to an ambulance. A man, bloody and shirtless, was handcuffed to the gurney. Mick recognized the man as Tiny Tim. Mick sat in Maryland's black BMW, across the street from Frog's. He caught a glimpse of himself in the rearview mirror. He looked good. The wig he wore was spiked and white, his glasses and mustache, dark. Mick thought that he looked a bit like Billy Idol back in the '80s. He smiled as he took a sip of diet cola, laced with Dexedrine, and watched the actor pace back and forth on the sidewalk.

Mick had enjoyed his night. His characters had performed beautifully. He had sat in the shadows of Frog's and waited, waited for the inevitable. He had seen the actor walk in with the waitress. She was pretty, but not Mick's type. He had watched as the actor led Tiny Tim to the bathroom for a little payback. He had seen the fat cop enter, clearing out Frog's with the shine of his badge quicker than a fire could have. Mick had seen everything. He had heard from his friends on the street about the beating the actor had taken at the fetish club, and it hadn't taken a genius to figure out when the actor would be looking for Tiny Tim, and where. Of course, Tiny Tim had not been bright enough to figure it out.

Mick laughed. Sometimes his players were so predictable. For example, the actor, he was purely emotional, but Mick liked that about him. Mick took a sip of diet cola as he watched the fat cop spit on the sidewalk. Mick had enjoyed the show. The scene had gone well. A good director should be proud of his own work, Mick thought. After all, it's his legacy.

"Are we ready to go?" a young voice asked from the passenger's seat of the BMW. Mick turned his eyes to the smooth face in the seat beside him.

"Yes, Richard, almost," Mick answered. Mick had met Richard in the club, at Frog's. Richard's eyes shone through the darkness toward Mick. He smiled as Mick stroked his hand gently across the boy's face. "How old are you, Richard?" Mick asked. The boy shut his eyes, enjoying Mick's touch.

"I'm eighteen," he answered.

"Eighteen? Well then, you're a man now, aren't you, Richard? " Mick leaned over and gave the young man a kiss. The young man wrapped his arms around Mick, enjoying it. Mick pulled away, the young man's breathing, heavy. "You're lucky, Richard, very lucky." Mick slid his hand up Richard's leg, feeling the firmness of the young man's excitement.

"Remember, Richard, to be born a man is the greatest gift of all. Yet, in this life, you can be anything, or anyone, anytime you want."

Mick caught the form of the actor crossing the street to his Vette. Mick watched as the actor climbed into his car and pulled away. The actor followed the bright lights of the ambulance down the road. Mick smiled, pleased with himself, and as his head went down to taste the youth of the young man, he felt that his own brilliance was unsurpassed. His plan was going perfectly. Perfection, Mick thought, was what he was all about, as young Richard would soon find out.

THIRTY-THREE

Maryland had to keep telling herself that she was doing this for Mick. She sat in the sunshine of the patio of the small café and waited. Waited for part of her past to arrive. She sipped her glass of chardonnay. She was nervous. The feelings she had about the man she was waiting for were strange and confused. It had all been so long ago. But Mick knew what he was doing; he always did. He had a reason for everything, including her coming here, and she trusted him completely. Maryland looked around the café, at the bright faces of L.A. Fuck! She felt like getting up and leaving. She didn't like the past, not hers. Mick knew that. He would never have asked her to do this if it wasn't important. Very important.

Maryland glanced at her watch. She had so much to do. She had to drop by her agent, then meet with a photographer for new headshots, then go to a callback for a commercial. She never seemed to have as much time as she used to. She had so many things she had to do, including finishing a script she'd been writing. Yet, it seemed lately, that time just slipped away and then the following week she had the same things to do as she had the week before. Maryland took another sip of wine. Goddamnit! She didn't want to be here.

She looked down at the sheer black blouse she was wearing. It was sleeveless. She had worn a black wonder bra beneath it, in an attempt to give herself some cleavage. She had also worn black silk pants and three-inch heels. She loved the heels; they made her height about six-foot three. He was that tall, the man she was waiting for, if not taller. Maryland looked into the mirror of her compact and checked her makeup. She wondered if she had used too much mascara. She didn't think so; it made her blue eyes stand out. Perhaps the blouse she had worn was too provocative. She let her fingers run over the skin of her bare arms, feeling the tightness and cut of her muscles. Fuck it, she thought, who cares. Maryland stared down into her glass of wine, running her fingers in a circle around its rim until it hummed. She was a wreck inside. She couldn't wait to get to the gym. After a good workout, she'd relax.

She looked up at a man across the room sitting alone at a table for two. He had been staring at her ever since she had walked in. He smiled and raised his glass toward Maryland. Christ! She felt like getting up and pouring his drink in his round little lap then breaking the glass over his bald head. Instead, she smiled politely. You never knew, he probably owned a studio or something. She'd probably run into him in a casting session, and he'd remember her as the girl that smashed a glass over his head. That was the problem with this town; you had to be nice to everybody. One day a busboy, the next day the hottest new director. He kept staring at her and Maryland lowered her eyes. He was starting to piss her off. She was not in the mood. This whole situation made her agitated. It brought up memories and issues that made her uncomfortable. But then again, Mick knew best. He always did.

Maryland took a deep breath. Perhaps he didn't get the message. Maybe he wouldn't show. She knew he had to be careful. She had never really believed all the things they had said about him. All the things she had read. But you never knew for sure. Maryland tapped her foot against the leg of the table as she continued to run her fingers across the rim of her glass. Shit! She didn't want to be here.

Then Maryland felt it, a presence in the room, as if the air around her had become weighted, heavy, and she knew he was there. She looked up from her glass and saw him standing in front of the table. He smiled a perfect smile, his eyes sparkling. He was as handsome as he had ever been. Maryland smiled as her gaze caught the man's eyes. A man she had known a long time ago, in a place she had tried to forget, a man who had been a friend and more, a man she had known as Bud, but everyone else called Blue.

THIRTY-FOUR

Maryland watched Blue sit down. He was thin, wiry. He wore a steel blue blazer with black slacks and a white satin shirt that matched the gleam of his smile. He looked good, every bit of him Hollywood. His eyes moved quickly around the room, then over Maryland. He took out a pair of designer sunglasses and slipped them on, his eyes still visible through the blue lenses. He laid a newspaper on the table in front of him and touched Maryland's hand.

"Hi, Maryland. It's been too long. You look great." Maryland felt the coolness of his touch on her hand in the warm sunshine of the patio. It brought back more than she cared to feel.

"So do you," Maryland said, as she gently slipped her hand away from his and picked up her wine glass. "I wasn't sure you would show, whether you got the message from Anna."

"Well, I did. I was happy to hear from you. How did you know Anna could get in touch with me?"

"Didn't, not for sure. But I knew that if anyone could, she could. You two had always been so close."

"Do you stay in touch with anyone else from Group?" he asked. Maryland lowered her eyes.

"No, I have only heard from Anna twice in ten years. But I knew where she was, where she has always been."

Blue leaned back in his chair. "Anna is misunderstood. I knew that ever since I met her in Group. She is better off where she is, in the institution. This world is not for her."

Maryland looked at the form of Blue's face. It was the face of a man she once would have done anything for. It was a time in her life when she'd been forbidden to see Mick. When he was gone from her life altogether, a time when she'd found a friend, a lover, in the face now before her.

"How about you, Maryland? I heard you finished graduate school and have been acting. Things going well?"

"Yes," Maryland answered. She smiled. His voice was somehow soothing. Fuck! He was so good-looking! She watched him as he leaned toward her, his mannerisms smooth and polished. He touched her hand again, and she wished Mick was there. She saw his eyes through the lenses of his glasses.

"Is it true, what I read, what they say you did to those girls?" Like an out of body experience, Maryland heard herself ask the question, but didn't believe she had.

"No." Blue slipped off his glasses, his eyes pinned on Maryland. "No, it is not true. You know me better than that."

Maryland lowered her eyes. Yes, she did know him.

"Look at me, Maryland. Look at me." He squeezed her hand. "You know what it's like, Maryland. You know what it's like to be accused of something you didn't do. That you, as a person, didn't really do. Don't you? You of all people know what that's like."

Maryland raised her eyes to his. His eyes were blue, dark blue and piercing. She nodded lightly. She didn't want to think about it. She didn't want to hear about it. She was here for a reason.

"Mick, he wants to meet you."

"Mick?" Blue slowly removed his hand from Maryland's and leaned back in his chair. "Mick's back in your life?"

"Yes."

Blue smiled a bright shining smile that made Maryland uncomfortable, almost angry. "I need him," she said, trying not to sound defensive.

Blue's eyes moved over Maryland. He nodded. "You always did."

Maryland fidgeted with her napkin. "You were the only one...who ever understood...who ever believed that," she said. She stared at the form of his lips, his mouth. It had been so many years, yet it felt like yesterday.

"I'd love to meet Mick," Blue said, as he kept his eyes on hers. "I've heard so much about him from our days in Group that I feel I know him. It would be my pleasure."

"Great," Maryland said. She felt a wave of relief wash over her as she watched Blue get the waiter's attention. He ordered a scotch and another wine for her.

"I can't stay for long, though I'd like to. But we can have a drink together." His smile and face were so disarming. Maryland watched as he reached down and flipped open the newspaper on the table. "Any idea why Mick wants to meet me?" Blue kept his eyes on the paper.

"He didn't say, but I am sure it's very important. Or he wouldn't have asked."

"Oh, I'm sure it is." Blue turned the paper towards Maryland. "Have you heard about these killings? They found another one, a girl killed in her bedroom."

Maryland kept watching him. She had put so much away over the years. They had told her not to. They had told her to confront her feelings. But it helped her to separate things, to put things away.

"It's the fourth killing," Blue said. "They think that they are all connected, along with an abduction. People in the entertainment business are getting jumpy. What do you make of it? Being in the business and all? What does Mick think?"

"I don't know."

Maryland didn't look down at the paper. Her eyes were on him. She remembered him now, things she had tried to forget.

"You hurt me. You know that?" Maryland was surprised by her words. Their meaning and the feeling behind them had been buried for so long. Blue said nothing. He just looked at her.

"I trusted you. You made that place bearable," Maryland said, her hands shaking. "You didn't have to be there. You committed yourself because you were troubled. But I had to be there. And you made me feel whole, special. Until..." Maryland lowered her eyes, fighting back tears.

"I didn't mean to hurt you, Maryland. You know that?"

Maryland shook her head. Blue leaned toward her, his voice soft and gentle.

"You and Anna, I would never hurt either of you. There is a kinship

136

between us, something others don't understand, don't have. We are different, special in a way. I understand that now. I understand that I wasn't sick. That it wasn't you, or me, or Anna that had problems. It was the world around us. Anna, she can't take it. She's too fragile. You, you have Mick. Me, I live within myself. My world. But I would never hurt you. Never, not on purpose."

"You did," Maryland said softly, her head still down. She felt the coolness of his hand again upon hers, his fingers touching her lightly.

"I'm sorry," he said gently, Maryland lifted her eyes to his. He bent down and gently kissed her hand. "I truly am." She looked into his eyes. Perhaps she was blind. But she could only see what she could see.

Blue reached over and touched Maryland's face gently. "I have to get going. Tell Mick that I'll meet him any time. Get a hold of me through Anna. She knows how to reach me."

Blue finished his scotch. He picked up the newspaper off the table and tucked it under his arm. "I have a feeling that your Mick and I are going to get along well. We may have much in common."

Blue laid some money on the table as his eyes caught the form of a young blonde girl moving past, her breasts swaying under her bra-less blouse. Blue smiled at Maryland, as he leaned over and gave her a kiss on the cheek. "It was great to see you, Maryland. We'll talk soon," he said, as he slipped on his glasses. He turned and moved away.

Maryland watched as the young blonde girl moved outside the café and across the street. She watched as the girl disappeared around the corner followed closely by a man in a steel blue blazer and black pants. A man she had known a long time ago. A man she had known as Bud, but everyone else called Blue. And as Maryland watched the man turn the corner, she wondered if he would hurt the young blonde girl, as he had once hurt her.

THIRTY-FIVE

I watched Tiny Tim through the one-way glass of the police interrogation room. Just like on TV, I could see him, but he couldn't see me. The room was sparsely furnished—four chairs, a table, and a holding cell. Blake and Dolen had been going at Tiny Tim for over an hour now. Yet, Tiny Tim didn't have much to say, even though he was looking at twenty-five years to life for his third felony strike. Tim was staring straight at me. He knew I was back there, behind the glass. He sat in a wheelchair that was handcuffed to the table, his shoulder bandaged and taped, his arm in a sling. Dolen had pulled him out of the hospital as soon as he could, seeing that questioning him down there was leading nowhere, and thinking that perhaps a trip to the police station and the bars of the holding cell would loosen his tongue. It hadn't.

Tim was scared, but not by the police station, Dolen, or Blake. He was looking at more time down the road than he could do, hard time, but he still wouldn't give up any information on Blue. He knew Blue was on the outside and if Tim talked, his life would be over. In prison, or on the street, Blue had friends. A thought, that with my past with Blue, had not escaped me. The FBI boys were on their way and the word was that they would offer Tim a place in the witness protection program, if he gave them the information they wanted. But my guess was that Tim would have none of that. Maybe time would change that, but for now, when time was of the essence, he wasn't going to talk.

I watched Dolen as he worked himself into a frenzy trying to get Tim to talk. Then Dolen lost it, slapping Tim in the head and kicking his wheelchair just as Tim's lawyer walked into the room. Tim's lawyer pointed a finger at Dolen, threatening to bring Dolen up on charges of assault. This set Dolen off even further as he got up into the counselor's face. Blake stepped in and pulled Dolen away and Dolen stormed out of the room. Tiny Tim was nonplussed by the show going on around him. His silence was only less intense than his eyes focused on the one-way glass and me. Dolen was replaced in the interrogation room by two other police detectives and Frick and Frack from the FBI, who had just shown up. Dolen entered the back room where I was, out of breath, his face red as a boiled beet.

"Son of a bitch! That fucking asshole knows where Blue is and now he's lawyered-up!" Dolen took a white handkerchief from his pocket and wiped the perspiration from his face. "Shit! The FEDs aren't going to get anywhere with him and he's all we fucking have."

"You're right, they won't get anywhere with him, but he's not quite all we have."

"What the hell you talking about?" Dolen asked.

I reached into my coat pocket and pulled out a worn, leather business card holder. I reached down into it and slid out a yellow piece of paper with a phone number written on it. I handed the piece of paper to Dolen.

Dolen looked at the piece of paper and the tattered cardholder and raised his eyes to mine. "Don't tell me you removed evidence from a crime scene, Spire?"

"All right, I won't, I won't tell you that this holder belongs to Tiny Tim, that I picked it up off the bathroom floor on the way out, and that I called that number in your hand and found out something very interesting. But I did."

Dolen took a quick look around as another detective entered the room. "And?"

"And I think we should take a ride. You up for it?" Dolen smiled and nodded his head. He closed his hand over the yellow piece of paper and swung the door open, slamming it against the wall. He strode out of the room, with me following close behind.

THIRTY-SIX

Anna watched the spider climb up the wall of her room. She tried to listen closely to what it was telling her, but the sound of the rain against her window was drowning out the spider's words. Anna moved her head, sliding it against the dull, white wall, toward the spider, her eyeglasses scratching the peeling paint. She held her breath, listening. The spider's voice was tiny, like a scream. She shut her eyes, concentrating. The spider was warning her. Warning her that bad things were coming. Bad things from the outside, from that world where the other people lived. The world that made no sense. The world of blame and judgment and riddles. The world of the crazy people.

Anna was scared. Her friend Bud, who everyone called Blue, was out there among the crazy people. They wouldn't understand him. They would judge and blame him, like they did with her. Like they always did. Like they had done with her friend Maryland. The spider moved closer. Anna could see his little mouth moving. It was His voice. He spoke to her in many ways, in the air, in the rain, in her mind, through animals and silent people, alive and dead. But it was always Him. He guided her and loved her. He never judged. Anna listened as the spider spoke and she understood. They were coming. They wanted her to become a Judas, to tell them things, to betray. The crazy people were coming to try to turn her into one of them. But she wouldn't let them.

Bud had told her that the greatest power she held was being normal. For the crazy people feared her, because they couldn't make her be like them. They couldn't make her live by their rules in their world of riddles and lies. She and Bud and the other normal people were special, for they were the only ones truly free. That scared the crazy people, so they locked them up and tried to change them.

Anna whispered to the spider, thanking him, and he turned and went back toward his web and a fly he had caught. Anna watched as the spider began to eat the fly. The fly was paralyzed, but still alive. It wasn't cruel, thought Anna. It was beautiful. It was God's way, His plan. Everything in nature killed. All of God's creatures lived off the death and pain of another. It was His will.

Anna pushed her glasses up onto the brim of her nose and thought about this. God had had his choice of how he wanted the world to be, being God. God could have chosen to let the fly live forever, thought Anna. He could have created this planet with little green creatures that never got sick, have pain, disease or death. That was the point of being God. He could have done anything He wanted. Yet, He had created a world of pain, violence, and death.

Anna knew from the Bible that man had brought pain and suffering upon himself. But take man away, thought Anna, and God's creatures, all of them, from the time of Creation, suffered, died, killed. Was God a masochist? Did He enjoy watching suffering? Did He revel in pain? Did He like watching the fly being eaten alive, held captive? He must. It was His idea. The crazy people would lock God up for this behavior in their world. They would kill God. They would call Him immoral, twisted, sick, to cause such suffering. They would judge God! They were so arrogant, so self-righteous! It was God's will. He had set up the whole system. Violence, pain, killing, dying. It was God's plan. It was normal.

Another fly flew into the spider's web and the spider moved slowly towards it. The spider was normal, normal, like Anna and Bud. The spider understood God's truth. Lived by God's law. The crazy people pretended that they were different. Better. They wrapped up their death, their murder, in little plastic packages and called it hamburger, veal, sushi, and sold it in bright stores with music and housewives and tried to forget that they were killers. Why did they fight so against God's plan? They were such hypocrites. They picked beautiful flowers at the height of their life and placed them into bowls of water, feeling they were being kind to them, as they watched them slowly die. Ha! That is so them, Anna thought. They were crazy!

141

Anna watched the spider bite the new fly with its venomous fangs, paralyzing it. Anna smiled. What imagination! Think of it! Watching, helpless, as you are eaten alive! Only God could have thought of that. He was Brilliant! If the crazy people had it their way, there would be no spiders, no Annas, Buds. There would be no God. There would just be lies and them.

Anna rolled over onto her back and watched the rain sliding down the pane of her window in long, clear streaks. She liked the rain. It made her feel close to herself. It was like a cocoon, she thought, a cocoon of emotion and time. A blanket of gray shadows wrapped around her, insulating her from the frantic brightness and chaos of the world outside. The world where the other people lived. She thought of Bud. She was worried about him.

Anna wrapped her arms around herself and turned over into the softness of her pillow. The wind whipped the raindrops against her window and she could hear His voice in the softness of its sound. He was whispering to her that they were here. Anna turned her head toward the dull, yellow paint of the door and a moment later she heard the lock click open.

There were three of them. Anna's eyes flicked across their faces. Crazy as loons, all of them. She could see the arrogance in their eyes. They had come, just like the spider had told her. Just like He had told her. The doctor, a fat man with a badge on his chest, and the TV actor who had caught Bud.

Anna looked at them all and wished she was a big spider. She would wrap all three of them up into her web and eat them one at a time while they were still alive. She would talk to them with every bite she took. She would ask them about God, about why they lied. She would ask them how it felt to be eaten. How it felt to be trapped, imprisoned, helpless. How it felt to be living in a land of riddles and rules. How it felt to be scared of the normal people. She would ask them how it felt... to be crazy.

THIRTY-SEVEN

Her eyes were on fire as they flicked back and forth from Dr. Jackson, to Dolen, to me. Her name was Anna Burnside and she had been behind the walls of this institution for nearly twenty years. She had returned home one Christmas break, during her sophomore year away at a prestigious Ivy League college, and had proceeded to kill her whole family, her mother, father, eighteen-year-old brother, and her fifteen-year-old sister. She had shot them as they slept, with her father's 12-gauge Remington shotgun, his favorite, that he used regularly to duck hunt with, on the small lake that lay on their hundred-acre Connecticut estate. She then proceeded to open up all the presents that lay under the thirty-foot Oregon pine that was their family Christmas tree, before she lit the whole house on fire.

When the firemen arrived and finally put out the fire of the twenty room mansion, they found Anna's father, a small, slightly built man, who had made his fortune in plastics, stuffed up the chimney, still dressed in his red Santa Claus costume that he had worn for their annual Christmas party just hours before. When the police asked Anna why she had killed her family and stuffed her father's body up the chimney, she had told them that He had told her to do so. That it had been God's will. She had then smiled and wrapped the pink silk robe her father had bought her at Tiffany's around her slim sorority girl shoulders.

I could still see the blue blood of her upbringing in her all these years later. She was attractive, thin, her blonde hair pulled neatly back off her face. Her posture was erect, her legs politely crossed and at an angle. Just, I'm sure, as the French finishing school she had attended in Europe, during the summer of her sixteenth birthday, had taught her. I looked around the stark, small room. At the pale green hospital robe that clothed Anna, this was not the place one would expect to find a former millionaire and Ivy League debutante.

I listened as the wind slammed the rain against the window of the room as Anna smiled at me and I wondered what she was thinking. I didn't like being here. The whole place had a feeling of suffocation to it, energy of darkness and despair. I felt like turning and running out the door and into the rare Los Angles rain, letting the rain wash me, cleanse me. It was a place of forgotten people. Of dirty lies and family secrets locked away and too horrible to mention, secrets that scare all of us. Secrets that deal with the dark, twisted side of the human mind and the places of violence, loneliness, and disassociation it can take us to. Of the larger human family and the struggle we all have to learn why. To try to understand insanity, and to try to understand the fear we feel when we come face to face with it, as I was now.

Perhaps it comes from the fear deep within us all, that in the blink of an eye, in the chemical misfiring of the mind, in a momentary, traumatic detour from reality in which we cannot return, that it could be us behind the barred windows and pale green hospital gowns of the asylum. That we could be the faceless, nameless souls society locks away and labels crazy. I looked into Anna's eyes and thought that she appeared no more insane than I. And perhaps, until the moment her brother and sister awoke, to see Anna standing over them, their father's shotgun raised in her hands, their parents' blood splattered across her white prep school nightgown, neither did she, to them.

I took a seat on a stiff wooden chair by the door, the yellow piece of paper that I had found in Tiny Tim's cardholder clutched tightly in my hand. I had called the phone number on the piece of paper and gotten the institution and immediately put the connection together. I had been to this place once before during my first pursuit of Blue. I knew he had committed himself into the institution years before under his real name, Bud Williams. He had been here for over six months and had been in what they termed "Group," or group therapy. Anna had been one of the members of Blue's Group, along with some fifty other people who came and went throughout Blue's stay. Anna was the only one of three who still remained in the institution.

There had been seven members of Blue's Group still in the institution, the last time I was here. After painstaking research, they had led me to nothing. But now there was Tiny Tim's cardholder and the number on the yellow piece of paper.

Dr. Jackson, a stout man in his sixties, was head of the institution and knew, as well as I, that the phone number belonged to the public phone in the patient's recreation room. Because it was a pay phone, he had no records of out-going calls, but he did know that Anna had received several calls since the time of Blue's mistaken parole. The other two former members of Blue's Group, according to the nurses, had received none.

I looked at Anna. She was the perfect front for Blue, the perfect contact. Nothing she said could be considered reliable. Nothing she said could be used in court or against Blue. Her eyes found mine as she scooted back on her bed and against the wall. She pulled her knees to her chest, suddenly looking very child-like. She smiled at me and giggled, and I could swear that she knew exactly what I was thinking. And I couldn't help but wonder just how sane one really was, if one was insane.

THIRTY-EIGHT

Stacey's eyes were open. They had been for a long time now, yet she felt there was nothing else in life worth seeing with them. She felt them as useless as the rest of her, skin, bones, blood and breath, held together just for the sheer amusement of the killer. There was nothing of her left, just a shadow of flesh, void of all things that had once been her. Yet, her eyes, she could not take them from the form of the glass pitcher. It was filled with ice water, high above her, on the edge of the black ravine, lit brightly with the glow of a white light.

Stacey couldn't remember how long she had been down in the shaft. She remembered falling, welcoming death. She remembered how she had been tricked and had landed on the softness of the air bag. How the killer's voice had floated down from above, how it had nauseated her, and how unconsciousness had been welcome. But how long ago had that been? She had no idea.

All she knew was that she couldn't take her eyes off the pitcher of water. Her throat burned with a thirst like she had never felt. As if a hot iron from a fire was being pressed down her throat. Had it been days since she had last drank or eaten? She didn't know. All she knew was that she would never leave the shaft. She would never climb the rope ladder the killer had lowered down the side. She would never climb it, because that is what he wanted. For he was up there, waiting. She would die down in this shaft before she gave him the satisfaction.

But the water, above, she could see its clear, cool wetness. She believed the ice, floating and reflecting the light, to be the most beautiful thing she had ever seen. She didn't know there could be such thirst in life, such a burning. She had been hungry, painfully hungry, but that had passed, and now there was only the thirst. She tried to take her eyes from the water, but she couldn't. She could feel the coolness of it flowing down her throat, the burning being quenched by the heavenly liquid. Stacey had lost any sense of time. Her mind, in the endless darkness, was removed. She dreamed, wide-awake. She saw things, visions, like movies played out on the walls of the shaft. She had smelled the warm, soft fragrance of food above. Had seen it sitting on the edge, like the pitcher. But the water was different. It was from another world, from a land of light and liquid and life.

Stacey bent her head back, looking up. The pitcher seemed to be getting closer and closer to her. She could see it more clearly now. It seemed to be floating down to her from above. She smiled and laughed. It was, it was getting closer! She didn't know it, but she had begun to climb the ladder. Putting one hand over the other, she climbed. She felt as if she was flying, dreaming. She was delirious. There was nothing of her or the world, just the water, getting closer and closer, until she could see the beads of moisture on the smooth glass of the pitcher. They shined like jewels of light. She could feel it now, the coolness of the glass in the palm of her hands. Then it was there, like a miracle, cold and wet, running over the fire in her throat, cooling and quenching it. Stacey was crying with happiness. Never had she felt anything so wonderful. Never. All she knew was the ecstasy of the liquid, the feeling of the ice and moisture in her mouth just as she had dreamed. Then in a flash, the pitcher was grabbed away and Stacey's eyes flew up, meeting with the dark blue eyes of a tall man, and his bright smile.

"Take it slow," the man said gently. "Or you won't hold it down." The man handed the pitcher back to Stacey and she continued to drink, slower this time, her eyes on the man. Was he the killer? Stacey tried to think, but she couldn't. He turned and walked away and sat down inside the killer's lair, in a large leather chair. He put his feet up on a matching ottoman and lit a cigarette. He smiled at Stacey, then opened the leather-bound book resting on his lap and began to read it, silently.

Stacey brought the pitcher down from her mouth as she continued to stare at the man. Stacey felt herself start to come back as the water ran its course through her dehydrated system. She realized now that she had climbed the ladder, though she had sworn to herself that she never would. But at this moment, with the burning beginning to fade, she didn't care. For at this moment, as she raised the pitcher once again to her lips, she couldn't help but be happy. Happy for the cool wetness that had become all she knew, all she cared about, all she felt. All she felt that is, for now.

THIRTY-NINE

Mick was clear, sharp as the blade of a knife. He slid on his belly, his mind racing with his own brilliance, his genius. His lives were as countless as the stars and the seasons. Yet, in all the infinity that was his time, she had been by his side, his lover. In many different forms, with many different names, but it had always been her. She was safe now, for the time being, with Blue, back at Mick's secret place. He had had to leave her while he ran his errand. But he knew she was safe. Blue and Mick had a deal. A deal sealed in blood.

Mick watched the fire from the fireplace throw shadows against the walls of the house. He had entered the house easily. He was invisible. Hiding in cracks, corners. He was a shadow, a burst of air. The softness of his coveralls slid silently across the floor, every inch of his body black, covered, and muffled a trail of smoke drifting toward his victim. He heard the young woman's breathing. He smelled her scent.

She was not the one, not his lover, but she was part of her and equally as special. Like mercury, Mick flowed toward the large brass bed. The wind brushed the branches of an overhanging tree against the window of the bedroom, softly, like spirits of the night begging entrance.

He had watched the young woman from outside, through the bright glass of the windows. He had watched her undress, her body white and sweet, her curves and skin perfect. She had run a bath, pouring fragrant oils into it. She had slipped into her bath as Mick slipped inside the house and under her bed.

He had watched her from there as she let the warm water of the bath flow over her, losing herself in the sensation, her hands moving lightly over her glistening skin. He had waited until the fire had grown dim, then he had moved, hiding in a closet, behind a couch, in the corners, listening, watching. Mick was like chill in the night. She sensed him, but she would not let herself believe that he existed as she slipped into bed. She was too grown up for that. There were no monsters in the night, no boogeymen, or were there?

Mick moved from the shadows, reaching the edge of her bed. He felt the white lace of its covers. It smelled of her. She turned in her sleep, brushing the covers gently away from her body, then settled again. Her bare legs, glowing silky white in the flickering light of the fireplace, seemed erotic creatures of their own. Mick licked the white lace of the covers, tasting the fragrant oils of her skin as he listened to her slow, sensual breathing. He rose, hovering over her. The shadows and light played across her naked form, disclosing all of her immense beauty to him. Oh, how she smelled like his lover.

Mick inched closer and felt the cold hard metal of his knife as he slid it from its sheath. A glint of light reflected off its silver blade, catching his eye. It was long and razor sharp. Mick slashed the air above the woman's throat, quickly, then moved the knife lower, slowly tracing the space between her legs. Flesh and bone, Mick thought, was not much to hold such beauty together. A quick cut, a slice, and it fell apart so easily.

He closed his eyes. The moment of ultimate clarity was at hand. It excited him. It filled him with a feeling of power and peace. The voice of the benders were far away, nothing but a distant tickle in his mind. They could not touch him in this world. Here, he was God.

Mick's eyes flicked open, coming to rest upon the form lying next to her in the bed. It was the form of a large man, her man. The hair on the man's chest was thick and dark. The shadow of his muscles, large, the lines on his face cut deep with time. A gun, its holster draped over the post of the bed, lay near the man's head, a silver badge clipped next to it. The man was on his back, and by the sound of his breathing, Mick knew that sleep had taken him far away.

Mick held the blade of the knife up into the light of the fire, admiring the rainbow of colors that danced across its steel blade. In a flash, Mick brought the blade down hard and smooth across the man's throat. The man's eyes flew open as his hands raised off the bed for an instant, then settled back into the softness of the covers as a breathless sound escaped him. His eyes were frozen and void, the light of life vanishing from them, being replaced by the dim flickering of the dying fire and death.

Mick felt calm and warm inside. He listened to her deep breathing, undisturbed by the man's silence. He wiped the blood of the knife off onto the sheets and slipped it back into its sheath. Suddenly, her eyes flew open wide as Mick's hand came down over her mouth and she began to scream. Mick clamped down as his free hand flew to his pocket. She kicked and clawed, struggling against Mick's weight, as Mick pulled the cloth from his pocket and pushed it into her mouth, a whiff of its chloroform filling the air. He watched as her eyes rolled back into her head as her struggling stopped and her body grew limp.

Mick pulled away, his heart pounding. He pulled off the black mask covering his face, his skin flushed with excitement. He looked out the window and to the lake beyond, the moonlight shining off the thin layer of ice that covered it.

Mick's heart began to slow as he looked at the snow-capped mountains in the distance. Spring was coming, Mick thought, even to the mountains.

Mick's body felt as light as air, his head a rush. He took a tab of Dexedrine from his pocket as he listened to the spirits of the night still scratching to be let in. "Come in," Mick whispered, "the door is open." Mick smiled as he slipped the tab of Dexedrine into his mouth, the roughness of his rubber gloves brushing against his tongue. Why do people in the country never lock their doors, Mick wondered? Perhaps it would scare them more to believe that they needed to, than to live in the denial that they don't. That he didn't exist. That he wasn't out there, waiting.

Mick swallowed the tab of Dexedrine, enjoying its taste. Around these parts, after tonight, he bet all the doors would be locked tight for a long time. For a very long time.

Mick noticed suddenly that he was very hungry, famished actually. He couldn't remember when he had eaten last. He glanced at the young woman in the bed. She looked so peaceful. Mick slowly moved out of the bedroom and into the kitchen, opening the door to the refrigerator. He pulled out some cold cuts and bread and began to make a sandwich for himself.

A gold-colored cat hopped up onto the table near Mick, watching him, his eyes opening and shutting slowly in the dim light. Mick smiled and reached out, petting the cat. Mick liked animals. They were certainly better than people. He couldn't ever recall being hurt by an animal, insulted, taken advantage of, fucked over. An animal had never broken a promise to him, lied to him, used him, called him names. An animal had never locked him away, told him he was nothing, beat him, raped him. An animal had never hurt the ones he loved, like Maryland, made her life unbearable, unless he existed in it. In the animal kingdom there were no benders to do such things. There was only truth, life, death, love, survival. An animal loved, as Mick did, forever.

Mick finished eating his sandwich, pondering the animal kingdom. Then he cleaned up, wiping the crumbs from the counter and placing his plate into the dishwasher, before turning it on. He then opened a can of cat food and fed the gold cat, making sure its water bowl was full.

Suddenly, Mick's eyes lit up as his mind went sparkly and cool, like chips of ice pressing against his brain. Mick stood still, letting the rush of Dexedrine flow over him. He breathed deeply, hearing his blood pulse, listening to the muffled chatter of the planet. Mick laughed loudly and the gold cat scurried away. God, he thought, as he placed his hands over his ears, listening to the voices of enlightenment streak across the synapse of his brain, he was so lucky to be him!

Mick moved back to the bedroom, his laughter still echoing in his head. He stood over the young woman, slipping his mask back on. He reached into the pocket of his coveralls, pulling a small plastic bag from it, giggling at his genius.

He opened the bag and removed a single, black, plastic button, holding it carefully by its sides. The owner of the button had not yet realized it was missing from his coat. But it was, and of course, like everyone else, the man had buttoned his coat up with his fingers, leaving his print.

Mick smeared some of the dead man's blood onto the button. He then lifted the woman's right forefinger finger, pressing it against the back of the button and letting the button drop to the floor. Mick watched as the button rolled beneath the bed. He smiled. The seed had been sown. The scene had gone very well.

Mick brushed the woman's dark hair gently from her face. She was not for him. She was a present, a gift, part of a bargain. Yet, Mick still leaned down to steal a kiss. How could he not? After all, he was him. And as he did, he could not help but marvel how, in so many ways, she was like his lover. After all, in this life, the two women were very connected. Sisters, Mick thought, always were.

FORTY

Blue watched the young woman. She was dressed only in black lace underwear. He let his eyes wander over her breasts, her nipples raised by the coolness of the cavern. She reminded him of that girl in Mississippi. The one he'd kept tied and gagged in the closet of his room at the Motel Eight. He'd met the young lady at Spanky's Bar down by the Gulf around Christmas waiting tables. She'd thought he looked like a movie star. They all did. She'd never seen him as she walked to her car after Spanky's closed and he'd taken her from behind. She never saw him, ever. He'd played with her for a couple days and then made her bathe and shower, twice, before he tied her to a flagpole near the Nativity scene of the town hall. In the holiday spirit he'd tied branches to her head like antlers and put a red sock over her nose and another one up her sweet little bare ass, like a tail. Rudolf the red-nosed slut.

Blue smiled. Yeah, that's who this girl reminded him of. But he knew this one. Stacey was her name. He remembered her. She had been married to the man that had put him in prison. The man he was going to kill.

Blue had met Mick like Maryland had asked. Mick had brought him here to this crazy place. Blue had to laugh. It was some sick shit Mick was doing. But hey, to each their own. Everybody's taste bends in different directions. The guy certainly had a sense of style, you had to give him that. Blue liked Mick. He knew he would after all he had heard about him back when Maryland was in Group. Yet, he had to admit one thing. He was amused, and a little shocked when he first saw the guy. He was a piece of work. Incredible. Just like Maryland had described. It's amazing what the human mind can do. Especially a twisted human mind.

Blue exhaled a stream of smoke from his cigarette and thought of the bargain he and Mick had struck, a bargain that would be beneficial to both of them. Blue would help Mick baby-sit Stacey and form a plan for him to get away with her. In return, Mick would deliver what Blue wanted most—Will Spire—deliver him right here to this crazy place, where Blue could take his time making him uncomfortable. Make Spire feel all the pain Blue had dreamed of making him feel for years.

It was fucking perfect. And when Blue was done and Spire was dead, Mick would help Blue throw Spire down one of the old mineshafts and bury him there, maybe even bury him alive. It was a sort of fishing expedition between two buddies, and the bait was sitting right in front of him dressed in black lace panties. And just to put a cherry on top of the whole thing, as a reward for helping Mick, Blue would get a plaything of his own. One that he could take with him across the border, one that Mick said was every bit as sweet as the prime pussy sitting in front of him right now. In fact, Mick said, they were sisters. Blue smiled as his eyes moved over Stacey. Yeah, he liked Mick's style. He understood now why Maryland needed him. He was one sick son-of-a-bitch.

FORTY-ONE

Stacey recognized him now. The water and food he had given her having brought her back to her situation. She was in some sort of cave. She had been taken, abducted, held captive. Fuck that, she thought. That was Bud Williams sitting across from her, relaxed in a large leather chair. He sat there calmly, like he was watching a big screen TV as his eyes moved over her. God was dead? Is that what she had thought? Well maybe, but obviously, Blue wasn't. And neither was she. She wasn't going to ask God for any more favors. She was alone, with only herself to rely on, her fear having seemed to wash away with the coolness of the water.

She had been taken, stuck in a trunk, molested, and all the time she had been scared to death. Of what, she thought? A man? One man? Of Bud Williams? She knew what he had done to those girls. She had watched him in court, his blue eyes and good looks hiding the sickness that lay within. He had frightened her then with just a glance or a smile. But it was different now. She was different.

She held his gaze for a long moment. "I know who you are," she finally said. She took another sip of water. "How you doing, Bud?" She could see the annoyance in his eyes for calling him Bud.

Blue smiled, acting amused. "I'm fine Stacey, how are you?"

"A little tired," Stacey said, "I haven't been sleeping too well."

Blue let out a loud laugh. "I'm sure you haven't."

Stacey kept her eyes on Blue, feeling the anger rise insider her. Don't be a victim. Isn't that what Will had always said about life? Don't be a victim, Stacey.

Blue motioned to the shrimp, cheese, and crackers lying on a silver

156

tray in front of him. "Come, have some more, and join me?"

Stacey's eyes met his. Somehow when he spoke, his voice, its tone and resonance, his speech, was different than the memories of her abductor. Then there was the calm about him. As if the air was thick with him. It seemed somehow not to fit in her mind. The whole energy around her, the sensation of the room, was not as it had been since she was taken. Yet, there he was.

She thought of the Wilkins' girl naked and tied to a tree. Yes, she remembered him, remembered his deeds of violence that she had read about in the paper. Remembered his cold threat to Will as they had pulled him from the courtroom. She remembered his arrogance, his swagger. Well, fuck that.

Stacey thought of her life with Bob Bayloff and wondered where Will was, if he was safe, if he was looking for her. Her anger cooled for just a moment as she lowered her eyes. Bob. The lies to yourself start small, don't they? Lies of happiness and contentment. But soon they grow to a point that they are all you have. Stacey had run toward her lies and the white sands of Malibu as a safe haven from the real problems of her relationship with Will. It was easier, she had thought, than dealing with the hard choices and pain that came with reality. But in the end, the lies had buried her. Because no matter how much she lived them, she still knew down deep that they were just that—lies. Soon, they had suffocated her with their weight. Lost in self-delusion and denial, she had struggled to find a way out, but the search led her only deeper into the twisted maze that had become her life and Bob's. Then Bob disappeared and Will had shown up.

Stacey raised her eyes and found Blue staring at her. His eyes, like stars, held her gaze. "Feeling better?" he asked as he smiled softly.

Stacey felt her anger rise inside her again, raw and hot. She stood up and dropped the empty pitcher to the ground. She moved toward Blue, his gaze taking in the full length of her body. She watched as Blue picked up a silver knife off the tray of food that lay in front of him and sliced a piece cheese with it, laying it upon a cracker and sliding it into his mouth. Stacey felt the anger twist inside her body, her eyes burning, her muscles hard and tight.

Stacey adjusted her bra, seductively, the piercing of Blue's eyes taking it all in. She kept her gaze on him as she ran her fingers lightly down the flatness of her belly toward her lace panties. "Aren't you going to offer me a seat?" she asked.

Blue smiled softly. "Of course." He stood up, and as he reached back to pull up a chair beside his, Stacey lunged.

Like lightning Stacey grabbed the silver knife off the tray, and as Blue turned back toward her, plunged it into his body. Blue went tight as Stacey felt the knife hit bone. His fist caught the side of Stacey's head as he stumbled back and she went tumbling to the ground.

Blue stood, the knife protruding from him, its blade having disappeared into the muscle beneath his shoulder. He grasped the knife's handle, his eyes open in shock, as he lost his balance and collapsed onto the table in front of him, shattering it. Stacey stood quickly, bringing the full force of a bare kick into Blue's face, the blow, snapping his head back.

"Don't be a fucking victim!" Stacey screamed as she kicked again. Blue blocked the blow, grasping her leg as she pulled away and leapt over him and ran, reaching the edge of the dark shaft.

She could hear the sounds of Blue stumbling to his feet as she saw a ladder lying in the shadows to her right. Stacey grabbed it, lifting it into the air and dropping it, its far end falling across the ravine and reaching the other side.

Blue yelled her name as she scrambled across the ladder. Suddenly the ladder was pulled from beneath her as she leapt the last foot to the other side. Not looking back, she ran, following a set of metal tracks, up, up, toward a glimmer of light, realizing that she was in a mineshaft of some kind. Stacey reached the top of the shaft out of breath and exhausted and was bathed in a blinding glow of sunshine and suffocating heat.

She stumbled, covering her eyes, trying desperately to see, to focus. Blinded, she fell, the skin of her knees opening on the hard pack of the ground. She pulled herself up as her eyes began to clear, revealing the nightmare of what lay in front of her. Nothing but endless miles of parched land, cactus, and scrub. Stacey froze for a moment, turning in circles, looking out at the vast desert landscape, the only sign of life, barbed wire, a bunch of broken-down shacks, and an old pickup truck. Stacey ran toward the truck yanking its door open, and searching desperately for the keys. Then she heard it, her name rolling across the desert. Stacey glanced out of the back window of the truck and saw Blue standing by the entrance to the shaft, an automatic handgun raised in his hand, his shirt covered in blood. Stacey stepped slowly out of the truck, facing him. She looked at the blue metal of the gun, the sun shining off its barrel, and she could think of only one thing—run.

Stacey turned and ran as a shot rang out, shattering the rear window of the pickup as she fled toward a dusty stretch of worn desert and tire tracks. She ran as fast as she could as two more shots rang out, kicking up dust to the side and in front of her. Yet, she kept running, her bare feet falling hard, being cut by rock and countless patches of cactus. Her lungs and legs burned as she ran toward the vacant horizon. Her thoughts focused on one thing. She was free, free!

Her mind was numb, but it flew with images of her life as a child, of people and places she'd known. She was running toward all of them, toward herself, toward life. She could see herself as a child, standing in the waves of heat billowing off the desert floor, urging herself on. It was a vision of her as she had once been, honest, true. She ran towards it and away from the lies and the guilt that had become her life. The heat was overpowering and her muscles ached. She thought she was running fast, flying, but as she looked down, she saw she was barely moving as the sound of an engine rose behind her. Suddenly, Stacey was overcome by a gust of dust as the pickup spun around her. She fell, her elbows slashing open upon the jagged ground.

Blue spun the wheel of the truck. He drove around her in circles, fast, faster, enveloping her in a blinding cloud of dust. Stacey coughed and choked, staggering to her feet, the trucks tires crunching on the hard-packed desert. No! Stacey thought. No! He would not have her! She was free! The roar of the pickup was deafening. Stacey stumbled, her lungs filling with the desert as she caught the form of something dark moving towards her through the dust. Stacey screamed as Blue slammed on the brakes and her world went black.

FORTY-TWO

Mick liked the mountains. The fresh air, he felt, had done him good. The benders were far away now, nothing but a tickle on the back of Mick's mind. He felt clear, sharp. The scene in the cabin had gone perfectly. The seed had been sown. Mick smiled as he took a sip of Diet Coke, laced with Dexedrine, and drove his Chevy van down the twisting mountain road. He reached the bottom of the mountain and turned onto the highway, heading out toward the desert with Blue's plaything. His gift for Blue was tied down tight to the floor of the van, gagged, blindfolded, and covered with Mick's painter's tarp. Though Mick smelled a hint of urine coming from the back, he was sure she was fine. Anyway, Blue wouldn't mind if she was a little wet. Not when he saw her.

Mick felt the thin air of the mountains disappear, the weight of sea level focusing him, the noises of life, of the universe, touting his brilliance. "War is politics by other means," Mick thought. How true. He tried to remember who had said that. It didn't matter. Mick was political, Mick was at war, a war of retribution, of justice, of right over wrong.

"There is no right, no wrong; there just is." The thought shot into Mick's head like a bullet blinding him with pain. He could hear the Bender laugh as he'd said it, see his eyes. Mick tried to shake the thought off, the tickle on the back of his brain now like needles pressing into his skull. It hadn't happened! It hadn't happened to him!

Yet, Mick remembered the rough touch of wool, the darkness of the closet, the stench of mothballs, and his slender body. Mick's eyes suddenly cracked with emotion. It had not happened to him, it had not! Tears began to flow as Mick shook his head violently. He fumbled for more Dexedrine, slipping it under his tongue, tasting it before swallowing. Yet, the Bender's voice echoed in his mind, deep, hard, calling to him. Mick could feel his young body tremble with the resonance of the Bender's voice. He knew what would happen if he found him.

If only he was a man, a man grown tall and strong, he could stop the Bender. Stop his voice and deeds forever. A man protects who he loves, protects them! But his youth and build were no match for him. No match. Mick saw, as if yesterday, replayed on the screen of his mind, the light filling the closet as the door opened. He screamed through the memories as the Bender's hands found him.

Mick pulled the van off the road, shaking his head violently, the pain cutting his brain in half. It didn't happen! Not to him! Not to him!

Mick pounded the steering wheel, grabbing his head, the tears flowing. He could see the Bender as he climbed off him, feel the warm trickle of blood running between his legs, and hear his own weak sobs that it wasn't right.

"There is no right, no wrong; there just is," said the Bender buckling his belt as he walked away.

Suddenly Mick's mind lit up, the rush of speed hitting him hard. Mick's eyes flew open as his brain went sparkly and cool. The tears stopped. Mick stared out into the brush by the side of the road. He saw a cricket there, clear and sharp. He could hear it talking to him in high clicks. He began to calm with the rush.

There were many benders in life, Mick thought, those trying to bend him to their will. But he was straight now, on the line, sharp. Mick sat, listening to the cricket, the brown, dead brush around it, waving in quick, jerky motions.

Mick heard soft moans coming from the back of the van. They soon grew loud drowning out the chirp of the cricket.

Mick unfastened his seat belt and climbed into the back of the van, screaming and shaking the tarp violently until the moaning stopped. He then climbed back into the driver's seat, sitting perfectly still. He listened for the cricket, but it was gone.

Mick's mind returned to the mountains and the seed he had sewn. He had left the house clean, untouched. Except, of course, for the button under the bed. Mick looked to the jerky grass, jumping in the sunshine. Yes, there were many benders in life, in many forms. But he was a man of men. He knew that now. He believed it. The seed had been sown.

FORTY-THREE

I stared down into my palm at the shadowy white form of the pill. It was the last of my Vicodin, yet my ribs still ached as if the girl from the show had just finishing stomping on them in the S&M bathroom with Tiny Tim. Fuck. I popped the pill into my mouth and swallowed it down. I was back. Back to the bright apartment filled with plants, sunshine, flowers, and girl called Kansas. She was in the kitchen making lunch, the smile on her face revealing the pleasure taking care of me gave her. That is what she was doing, wasn't it? Taking care of me? I had come over to her apartment after seeing Anna in the institution, not wanting to go back to the isolation and memories of my house. A house that was now alive with ghosts. Ghosts of Stacey and Will, of Will and Stacey, a life lived. Instead, I had come back to the warmth and sunshine of Kansas, her energy alone making me feel strangely at peace, at peace in the middle of a storm. Making me feel as if I belonged. Belonged to what exactly I didn't know, and for the moment, didn't care.

I looked down at a piece of paper marked with sixty-two names. It had taken some doing to get them and the accompanying patient synopses. A federal warrant had been necessary to be exact. Frick and Frack from the FBI had helped with that and Dolen had passed it along to me before we left the institution. They were the names of all the people that had been in Group or group therapy during Blue's time there. The list was alphabetical and Anna Burnside's name was the first. Dolen had been struck by the woman as I had, the perfect front, the perfect contact for Blue.

We would work on the theory that she and the institution were the key. That a string ran through her and that place, perhaps tying all things together. At least we knew the string ran from Anna to Blue. The FBI boys had helped there too, another federal warrant to tap the phone in the patients' recreation room. If Blue called her again, we'd be ready with a trace.

But something in Anna's eyes, something beyond the insanity, beyond the Remington shotgun and her father's Santa Claus draped body stuffed up the chimney, told me that she was on to us, that we might have to dig deeper to find the strings that led to Blue.

I slipped the papers into a manila folder, the file I had been keeping on the case, as I listened to the soft sound of wind chimes from Kansas' patio mix with the notes of Mozart. Uncharacteristically, the dominatrix waitress, with a flair for cooking and cocaine, was also a classical music freak. Like her, the wind chimes and music seemed part of the calm in the storm, the eye of a hurricane.

With all the madness going on around me, being here, I was able to focus and not let my mind run away with the thought of the Monster and Stacey and what she must be going through, while I sat having a nice lunch. That did me, or her, no good.

I looked up as Kansas laid a bowl of salad, topped with pine nuts lightly sautéed, accompanied by a lemon and herb chicken, with fresh string beans. I stared down at the food as Kansas started to serve the two of us. It certainly beat my normal lunch fare of a tuna sandwich accompanied by a fading hangover and stale bread. I raised my gaze to the freshness of the young woman's eyes. The golden fields of wheat and blue skies were still there.

She had her hair pulled back, with no makeup on, her skin, flawless. I would hate to be the one to take the wheat and skies from her eyes, to be the one to cause her any pain, to steal that smile from her face. I had seen enough pain in the eyes of women, of Stacey, to last me a lifetime. Part of me told me to go now, to leave Kansas and the herb chicken and walk out the door forever. To leave her to others better suited. Leave her to someone else to take the sky from her eyes, someone else to drive her to the Bob Bayloffs of the world. But I didn't move, I couldn't.

My eyes slid over her translucent skin, down the form of her sensual body, settling on the plate of food in front of me, and I stayed. I took a bite of chicken and felt it melt away in my mouth. Kansas smiled seeing my reaction, pleased that I was pleased.

I stayed but should have gone. Was I selfish? Or, I thought, as my eyes fell upon Kansas once again, was it something more? Was something melting in me, something deep inside, something hard and painful and held way too long.

FORTY-FOUR

It was their boy all right. No doubt. Dolen stood in the bedroom of the cabin looking out across the frozen lake to the mountains. He took a deep breath and lowered his eyes to the bed and the large form of a man lying there. The man was heavily muscled with wisps of gray hair on his chest, a gun belt and holster with an old .38 hung from the bedpost, a sheriff's star clipped to it, like a scene out of an old Western. A lot of good it did him, that gun, Dolen thought, as he gnawed on his toothpick. The man's face was calm, his eyes open, staring blankly to the ceiling. His neck was cut open. Blood pooled in circles around his chest and onto the sheets. Sheriff Bill Benson couldn't have raised his hand for his gun even if he'd wanted to. The only thing the sheriff could do was die.

Dolen kept his eyes on the scene. He wondered if he'd seen him? If the sheriff had gotten a glimpse of the killer, had recognized him in his last seconds of life as in Dolen's reoccurring dreams. Dying with the useless knowledge of a dead man. It made Dolen shiver to think of it. Fuck, he didn't like this. The whole fucking case gave him a bad feeling, one he couldn't shake.

Dolen brought his eyes to the imprint of the ruffled sheets next to the man. Their boy had taken her, just like her sister, Stacey, wisped her away in the night like a fucking magician. Dolen remembered Brenda from Bob's funeral, her looks, her calm and poise when Dan was stabbed. How she helped save Dan's life. She'd kept her head better than most rookie cops and some veterans would have, and this was her reward, her reward for helping save his partner's life. Fuck his bad feelings and his dreams, this guy was going down. This guy was his, he and Spire's. Besides, what's the worst that can happen, Dolen thought, as he put a

166

pinch of Skoal between his cheek and gum and looked at the dead sheriff. It didn't look so bad, kind of peaceful really.

Dolen spit a stream of Skoal into a plastic cup and watched the forensics boys do their work. The two FBI assholes were there, too. What'd Spire call them? Frick and Frack. Dolen had to laugh at that. They did look like they were made of plastic. Spire was all right, not bad for one of those little actor boys. Dan had been right about that.

The FBI twins were looking over a piece of paper that Bill's deputy had found, when he came over, after Bill didn't show up to work. Dolen had already had a good look at it. The same as the others, perfect cut-out letters from a magazine spelling out a quote. This time the quote said, "It's better to give than to receive." It was spelled out in English not Latin, otherwise it had all the markings of their boy.

Shit, fucking Spire! He was going to be in even more pain when he found out their guy had taken Stacey. This shit didn't make sense to Dolen. In all his years in homicide, this was fucking weird. Was Spire himself the key? Three of the murder victims had big personal connections to Spire—Bob Bayloff, Mary Higgins, and now Bill, his ex-brother-in-law, not to mention Stacey and Brenda. Then there was Blue, the prime suspect, the one with the best motive to fuck up and torment Will's life. Was he their guy?

But where did Alfred Green, the agent, and poor, beautiful Shari Canes fit into this? These killings were for revenge, payback. Dolen seemed sure of that. The quotes seemed to support that, but payback for what, for who? And if it was payback for Will and Blue's situation, then why were Alfred Green and Shari Cane involved?

And another thing, Dolen wasn't sure Blue was their guy. Though a lot of the shit fit. He wasn't sure. And what about that Anna character in the institution? What the hell's up with her? Dolen liked her looks, tall and sophisticated, crazy, like a debutante on crack. It turned Dolen on.

Plus, Dolen kind of admired her flare—that whole Santa Claus thing with her father and the chimney showed imagination. Hell, Dolen had come close to doing something like that with his own dad back in Detroit. His dad, feeling the best holiday cheer, was tying one on and then beating the shit out of his mom, all the while wearing a Santa hat with "Father"

167

written in magic marker on the front of it. It had seemed to be a holiday tradition.

Father my ass, Dolen thought. Just because he'd fucked his mom and got her pregnant didn't make him a father. Being a father took a hell of a lot more work than that and that ass-wipe hadn't put a minute into it, ever, not in Dolen's life. Dolen never called him father or dad, just Pop. Because that's what Dolen wanted to do to him, pop him right in his fat, sweaty mug, and that's exactly what he finally did one Christmas in high school. Popped the man right through a pane glass window after he'd started in on his mom, laid him outside on the cement stoop for the whole neighborhood to see. By the time the police came to pull Dolen off, the white of the fat man's Santa hat, where it said "Father," was red with blood, and it wasn't Dolen's. The ass-wipe never laid a hand on his mother again. Ever.

Dolen watched as one of the forensic boys approached him. He handed Dolen a small evidence bag with a single black button in it. A large button, like from a coat. Dolen examined it. "Found it under the bed," said the forensic boy, "seems to have some blood on it."

Dolen examined the button. He thought to himself that the sheriff wasn't sleeping with a coat on and he doubted Stacey was, either. Could it be their guy? Could it be his button? Had they finally caught a break? Most people, even criminals, button their coats with their bare hands, not gloves. Could they get a print of the killer from it? The button might have been torn off the killer's coat if Brenda had struggled, which Dolen bet she had done, and the blood on it could link it to the crime.

"Any blood found under the bed?"

"Nothing," replied the forensic guy.

Dolen nodded his head. It could have rolled under there, he thought.

"Send it to the lab, see if they can get any prints off it."

A button, Dolen thought, as he watched the forensic guy move away. It had always been his belief that no matter how good a killer was the odds of something going wrong were just too great. There were just too many variables. They'd always fuck up and give the police something. Could this be it? Could this be part of the puzzle, something to tell them they were on the right track? Tell them who their boy was. Could they lift a print, find some DNA? Even Mr. Clean here, the sick son-of-a-bitch, would have his day, Dolen believed that. Even he would fuck up. Was today the day?

A button, Dolen thought, as he spit a stream of Skoal into the plastic cup. Please, God, let it be. Let them nail this motherfucker before he killed again and again. They needed a break, God, you hear! Help them out, for Christ sake!

Dolen wasn't a religious man, but as he looked out at the beauty of the snow-capped mountains across the ice of the lake, he thought that if God could do that, create the mountains the sky, and the lakes, he could certainly help them catch one douche bag-motherfucker serial killer. Couldn't he? Dolen spit out another stream of Skoal, keeping his eyes on the mountain. Fuck, yeah. You're damn right he could.

FORTY-FIVE

Mick couldn't believe his eyes. He stood in the darkness of his cavern in the desert looking at the form of his lover. She was tied to the bed, her body illuminated by a black light. Her skin was covered with bruises and dried blood, shining purple in the light. She lay unconscious, her breathing slow and steady. Mick reached down and touched her hair softly, pushing it off her forehead, its strands caked with blood. Mick took a seat near Stacey. He looked around the room, at the broken coffee table. Where the fuck was Blue? What had happened here? Mick felt the buzz in his head grow louder as if the volume of life had been turned up to intolerable. He let out a scream as he put his hands to his ears and he felt the anger rise inside him. He thought of Maryland. His lover so reminded him of her. Why is it that others can't see the light of their souls? Why is it that others hurt and abuse them, bend them as if they were common creatures?

He had left Blue here to keep her safe, to watch over her. Blue, of course, did not know of Mick's grand plan, the beginning of the third and final act of Mick's production, the plot point that would change the entire direction of his masterpiece. But Blue had known that Mick was bringing him a gift from the mountains. A woman he could enjoy and more bait for the actor, Will Spire, to fly to their trap and give Blue what he really wanted, revenge.

Mick had hatched the plan, the gift to Blue, to keep Blue close. A good director should always give his actors motivation. Mary Higgins at the playhouse, had said that. It's what Mick was doing. He was giving Blue motivation to play his part well, to have his pivotal scene go perfectly, but now this. He needed Blue here for his production to be a success. He needed his star, but where was he?

Mick untied the binds that bound his lover, laying her arms gently across her belly. She was still dressed in her lace underwear, and as Mick dipped a soft washcloth into the cool water of a silver basin, he couldn't help but marvel at her beauty. Mick began to wash her with the cloth, moving it gently and with care across her body. Had Blue done this to her on purpose? Why? Why would he do this? But Mick knew deep down why. It was Blue's nature to hurt. Well, Mick thought, he had a nature of his own.

Blue, Mick knew, had hurt Maryland once, too. She had told him so. It was during the time Mick was forbidden to be in Maryland's life, a time in the institution when Mick had gone far away from her. Maryland had forgiven Blue for hurting her. Mick had not. Mick never forgave anyone or anything. How could he? He was him. He was born of non-forgiveness.

Mick felt the white noise of life soften as he cleaned his lover. He remembered Blue's gift, Stacey's sister, still tied to the floor of Mick's van. He'd better go get her. Soon the van would bake her like an oven in the desert heat. That wouldn't make a very good gift, now would it, Mick thought? Mick had counted on Blue being there to help him bring his gift into the cavern, but he guessed he would just have to do it himself. He still needed Blue to play the villain in an upcoming scene. It was very important. Mick looked down as the dried blood of Stacey turned red with the wetness of the cloth, and Mick knew that he had cast the part of the villain perfectly and that soon, as all good directors do with their leading men, Mick would make Blue a star, a star that would not soon be forgotten. But where had he gone? Anna would know.

FORTY-SIX

Maryland didn't understand why she was here. Mick did some weird shit, she knew that, but what was with this place? She'd been here for almost an hour, waiting for Blue to come back and she still didn't like it. It was a cave, an old mine shaft actually, a furnished mineshaft in the middle of the desert, with a generator for electricity and a moat kind of thing, that you had to go over to enter. Mick had summoned Maryland here because he needed her help. He wanted her to wait for Blue and if he didn't show, to find him and bring him back here. Maryland looked around at the setup. Jesus!

She didn't even want to know what Blue and Mick were up to here. No fucking way. All she knew was that she was supposed to be at a casting call for a national Head and Shoulders commercial at three-thirty, one that would pay the big bucks if she booked it. But instead, she was eighty miles away in a cave in the middle of the desert. Fuck! And her hair looked good today, it really did!

Maryland had wanted to call Anna at the institution on her cell phone right away, thinking that would be the easiest way to contact Blue. But Mick had said no. No calls to the institution at all. If Blue didn't show, she was to go to the institution, contact Anna, find Blue, and bring him back to this hole in the ground.

Maryland looked at the heavy, red velvet curtains cutting the room in half. Mick had forbidden Maryland from looking behind them, just like he forbade her from opening the door that lay behind the tapestry in their apartment, because it was his secret place. Maryland stared at the curtains. Here was another one, another secret place, within a secret place. Mick was gone, though. He had left her with his instructions and taken off. He wasn't here to stop her from looking behind the curtains now, was he? Maryland thought about this. No, he wasn't.

Maryland took a step toward the curtains, the only sound, the hum of the portable generator somewhere in the recesses of the cavern. What would it hurt if she did? Big deal if she did open them. There was no lock on them, nothing to keep her from seeing what Mick's big secret was. Men always have secrets, she thought, isn't that why they're men?

Maryland reached her hand out taking the fabric between her fingers. She felt her heart racing as she felt the slickness of the velvet. It felt taboo, like the antique lock on the door behind the tapestry in their apartment. Maryland stood not moving for a long time. She then let her hand fall to her side. No, she thought. She stepped back. Mick had told her not to. He trusted her and she would not betray that trust. We all have secrets, thought Maryland. We all have curtains hiding parts of ourselves, parts we don't want anyone else to see. Maryland knew she did. Mick was no different. Perhaps his secrets were larger, darker, more eccentric, but they were his nonetheless.

Maryland suddenly felt guilty for even thinking about doing it. Mick had been nothing but good to her. She couldn't live without him. There had been a time once, after the institution, that she had been happy without Mick. Even after Blue had hurt her, she'd stayed away from him. The doctors in the institution told her she needed to. That she needed to stand on her own two feet. They said she used Mick, transferring her problems onto him and expecting him to deal with them, instead of handling them herself. They said that she didn't need Mick at all, that she was strong enough to handle anything in life herself. That's what she'd learned in Group.

For many years after the institution she had been happy on her own. She had gotten her master's degree, dated, worked as an actress. She'd worked hard at her craft, until she had met a producer who had promised her everything, a part in his film, a permanent part in his life. He was wealthy and powerful. He treated her to many things, introduced her to many people. For the first time in her life Maryland felt special. She felt she belonged to that exclusive club at the top of the pyramid that was Hollywood. She felt a breath away from happiness, from all that she desired, from a life in film and fame.

Then he'd kicked Maryland out of his house by the sea and moved "her" in. He moved her into his life, exchanged the two of them like they were parts of an engine, his engine, an engine of greed and selfishness. The delicate strings that he had attached to Maryland's career were cut. The pyramid collapsed. The people she had met through him would not take her calls. It was as if they had never known her, laughed, ate and drank with her. It was as if she had never existed.

She struggled like an actress starting out. The film he promised her, one that would have launched her career, went to someone else. Maryland went to see the film, watched what should have been her up on the screen. By then, Mick was back, watching the flickering shadows of celluloid with her. He told her not to worry, that she would still be a star, his star.

After, with Maryland in tears, they sat alone in the dark theater and Mick made Maryland promise that she would never mention the little man's name again, that the name Bob Bayloff, would never cross her lips.

Maryland stared at the velvet curtains in front of her, thinking for a moment that they looked like the ones covering the movie screens in old theaters. Maryland lowered her eyes. Mick had been good to her. He had never hurt her, ridiculed her talent or dreams, or betrayed her. He was the only man she had ever known who hadn't. He had protected and taken care of her. Suddenly, Maryland didn't want to know what was behind the curtain. She realized she never had. She didn't want to know what Mick did, or what was in his secret places. She just wanted him to be there for her.

Mick knew the dark side of life, the painful side. He knew how to handle it; Maryland didn't. She never had. She didn't want to. She just wanted to be happy and loved. She didn't ever want to know what was behind the curtains. Whatever it was, she could see it was dark and forbidden. She'd rather stand on this side of life, this side, where shampoo commercials were her greatest concern. She'd leave the dark places of the world to Mick. She knew those places, she'd been there, in the institution, but she wouldn't go back again. Ever.

Maryland turned away, clutching her keys, and as she moved toward the exit she realized that Mick had been right, what was behind the curtains was not for her, not part of her life, but part of his. And as she climbed toward the heat of the desert she thought about finding Blue. Anna would know where he was. If Mick wanted to see him, there was good reason, for the one thing that Maryland was sure of, was that Mick knew best. He always did.

FORTY-SEVEN

Dolen's head hurt. He stared into his glass of bourbon and wondered when, if ever, he was going to get laid again. Bobby, behind the bar, had a few middle-aged hookers who would fuck the tailpipe off an old Chevy if you paid them. But that's not what Dolen meant. It would be nice, for once, to have the woman who was sucking his cock, really want to suck his cock. His! Not every motherfucker with a Hamilton.

Dolen rubbed his temples and wondered where the hell Spire was. That little actor boy was probably taking it up the ass somewhere, auditioning for his comeback. Dolen took a swig of his drink and knew that wasn't true. He was just jealous. He bet Spire had had a better piece of ass with his first one than Dolen had had in his whole fucking life. But where the hell was he? Dolen hated to admit it, but he was worried.

Dolen looked around the bar, Hanks. It was his home away from home and he'd come here the minute he'd gotten back from the mountains. Bobby even had a shower and cot in the back in case Dolen didn't feel like stumbling across the street to the emptiness of his own apartment, which most nights, he didn't. Dolen tapped the rim of his empty glass and Bobby poured him another as the jukebox moaned Frank Sinatra's "Strangers in the Night." Dolen felt like going over and kicking the shit out of that jukebox, beating it to a pile of junk with his blackjack.

Strangers in the night my ass. Same old fucking people who'd been here the last thirty years. If a stranger walked in here they'd think they were in the Twilight Zone. The place hadn't changed since 1978. There was still a re-elect Nixon poster hanging in the men's room. But hell, that's what Dolen liked about it. He hadn't changed. Why the fuck should anything else?

176

Dolen pressed his palms into his temples. He was in a bad mood. This whole case seemed to be closing in on him. He couldn't sleep at all now no matter how many drinks Bobby poured him. And when he did, he dreamed the dream. Dying, with his throat slit, on a case he couldn't solve until it was too late. Dying, with the useless knowledge of a dead man.

Dolen raised his eyes to the Budweiser Clydesdales circling over the bar encased in glass. How the fuck was that thing still working after all these years? It wasn't like they had a guy, a Budweiser, miniature Clydesdale guy, to come and fix the thing, did they? Hey, maybe Dolen could get that job after he retired. He liked Clydesdales. He liked bars. Dolen didn't know how that thing kept going round and round, year after year, but it made him feel good that it did. That it hadn't broken down like the rest of the fucking world.

Dolen looked across the bar at a woman with a red scarf. She was in her sixties and her face looked like his. Maybe she would suck his cock? He should probably just go over there and ask her. Hell, he'd be happy to do whatever she wanted. To tell the truth, he'd be happy just for the company. Just as long as it didn't require cash up front.

Dolen looked down into his drink and thought how there had been a time, when he was young, that women had been attracted to him. He wasn't good looking; he never had been. But that didn't matter. It was the way he'd carried himself, the confidence he'd had. He'd been a hotshot, the youngest detective in the department, a young bull, ready to take on all comers.

But life hadn't turned out the way Dolen had planned. The job and the street had broken him down, robbed him of everything. As a cop, you live in a world rubbed dark with ugliness. The only people you can talk to, who understand, are on the job. The rest of the world lives in a fucking fairytale.

It's hard even to talk to the others, to hear their petty complaints, about traffic, work, their marriage, blah, blah, blah. You want to just grab them and tell them how lucky they are that nobody ripped their heart out today. That nobody raped their kids and sawed off their legs. That nobody skinned their husband or burned their mother's house down with her in it. To go home and hug their wives and kiss their kids because it might be

177

the last time they see them. That there are people out there waiting to do all those things to them and more. How did you know? Because you've seen it. You've lived it.

That's what you want to tell them, but you don't. Because the fairytale people don't want to see how the world really is. They see only what they want. Believe only what they want. They believe that if they work hard, love their family, are nice to others, pray and believe in Jesus that some maniac won't stick an ice pick in the back of their head just to see what it feels like.

So, with that in mind, you just smile and nod as they talk about American Idol and the power of positive thinking and you realize how far away you've moved from all of them, from the world, because you'll never again believe in fairytales. How could you?

Dolen raised his eyes to the woman in the red scarf. The ugliness had robbed him of everything—his marriage, his friends, his youth. But what the fuck was he supposed to do? He wouldn't trade a day of it for the most beautiful woman in the world. He loved his job. Whether he ever got laid again or not, he loved it. And late at night, when he was staring up at the ceiling, the one comfort he had was that he'd made a difference.

There were people alive because of him. Murders in the making that had never happened because he'd stopped them, put the motherfuckers who would commit them in cages like the animals they were. He would have liked to see more of them burn, or get the needle, but he'd seen what prison was like. Let the rapist get raped and the killers die in their cages. That was just fine with him. The fairytale people would never know. Never know how close they were to being the next "victim." But Dolen knew and that made all that he'd lost over the years worthwhile. And he knew one more thing, more than he'd known anything else in his life. Their boy was next. He was going down, whether Dolen's dream was true or not. That douche bag-motherfucker was going down.

Dolen finished his drink as a man pulled a stool up next to him. Dolen looked over, finding the sparkling blue eyes of his partner Dan Patrick. Dolen smiled.

"How did you know where to find me?"

Bobby slid a beer across the bar to Dan. "I'm a detective." Dan gave

Dolen his Irish shit-eating-grin and took a sip of his beer.

Dolen laughed loud, his first laugh of the night, maybe the year. It was great to see Dan. He was recovering and back on the job. They had put him on light duty, at his desk. But he was back. Dan paused for a moment, folding his hands and staring down at them.

"You know that button you found under the bed at the Benson crime scene?" Dan asked.

"Yeah?"

Dan reached up and pulled a folded piece of paper from his coat. He laid it on the bar in front of Dolen. He tapped on it with his knuckles and took another sip of his of beer.

Dolen looked at Dan, who revealed nothing. Dolen picked up the paper and unfolded it. He froze.

Dan smiled. "The print they got off the button was clear and complete. It's Blue's. We have his print, along with Brenda's."

Dolen raised his gaze to Dan.

"We can place him at the scene." Dan said. "The blood on the button is the victim's. Just as you thought, it was probably torn off the killer's coat as Brenda struggled for her life. Blue's coat."

Dolen took a moment. He then slowly folded the paper laying it back on the bar. "Son of a bitch. It's him. It's fucking him."

"It fits," said Dan. "We don't know yet why he killed Alfred Green or Shari Canes, but it all ties together. His time inside must have twisted him even tighter. He's on some kind revenge kick, that's for sure. And you know who's on top on his list? "

"Spire."

Dan nodded. "Have you heard from him?" Dolen asked.

"He's waiting for us at the institution. Said he's found something."

"Fucking A!" Dolen said, clapping his hands together. Dolen stood up, suddenly feeling like he was twenty years old again. He threw some bills onto the bar for Bobby as he winked at the woman with the red scarf. The woman smiled and Detective Joe Dolen smiled back as he and his partner Dan Patrick headed for the door.

FORTY-EIGHT

Maryland didn't move. She stood at the reception area of the institution, her head down, her pen frozen on the line of the sign-in sheet where she had just scribbled her name. Her eyes were focused on the name directly above hers, Will Spire. She knew that name. It's the name of the man who'd caught Blue, the actor, from the Miracle Works Playhouse, the one who'd become a private investigator. What the fuck was he doing… But before she could finish her thought, she knew. He was looking for Blue, too.

Maryland slowly raised her eyes and put down the pen. The woman at the desk handed her a guest pin that she slowly clipped on her blouse as her eyes scanned the institution. This wasn't good. Mick had sent her here to talk to Anna so she could find Blue and bring him back to the desert. But now that guy was here, that PI guy.

Maryland smoothed out her skirt over the firmness of her legs. Fuck! Why did Mick do this shit to her? She already blew her shampoo commercial; never made it to the audition because Mick had her drive out to that hole in the desert to pick up a message for Anna! And now this!

Oh, my God! Shit! There he was! Walking right towards her!

Maryland turned away. She fumbled quickly through her purse as the PI approached the reception desk.

Maryland found her sunglasses and slipped them on and everything went dark. She straightened out the glasses as her eyes slowly adjusted to the light. Did they look suspicious, sunglasses at night? What was she talking about? This was L.A. for Christ sake; everyone wore sunglasses at night.

Maryland grabbed her cell phone from her purse and pretended to dial it as she heard the PI talking to the receptionist.

"Two detectives with the L.A.P.D. are on their way. Joe Dolen and Dan Patrick. I'd appreciate it if you could show them back to room eight. Dr. Jackson and I will be waiting there."

"Of course, Mr. Spire."

Room eight, Maryland thought. That was Anna's room. Fucking great. They were all coming to see Anna. Could it get any worse?

Maryland heard the PI begin to move away when the receptionist spoke.

"Oh, Mr. Spire? I didn't get a chance to tell you before, but I loved you on "Legends." My sister and I never missed an episode. Just great, really great"

"Why, thank you. Thank you very much."

Maryland thought she was going to throw up. The guy was a private investigator! He hadn't acted in years! He was never any good when he did, anyway. Well, he wasn't bad. But Jesus! Don't people ever forget?

Maryland lowered her phone as she listened to the PI's footsteps move away and she knew they didn't. They never forgot. Marilyn Monroe would be famous long after everyone alive today was dust. That's one reason Maryland had wanted to be an actress from the time she was a child. It's a type of immortality. Frozen in the most attractive years of your life. Your talent, charm, and wit, played over and over again to countless new fans throughout the years. Your performance, seen a hundred years later, as fresh as the day it was filmed.

And as for you, the actor, long dead and gone, you haven't aged a day and a new generation is falling in love with you. Of course they never forget. When they do, thought Maryland, that's when you're really dead.

Maryland turned slowly. The PI was gone. She slipped off her glasses and gave the receptionist a quick smile.

"Excuse me? But aren't you here to see Anna Burnside?" the receptionist asked.

"Yes, I am," Maryland replied.

"Well, she is with a doctor right now. You are welcome to wait here or in the cafeteria down the hall."

"Do you know how long she'll be?"

"No." The receptionist gave Maryland a long, sweet smile, before returning to her paperwork. Too long and too sweet, thought Maryland.

Maryland saw the PI in the distance. He was down the hall, past the cafeteria, talking to a doctor. She wondered if he would even remember her, recognize her. It had been a long time since they had both attended class at the Miracle Works Playhouse. Either way, she didn't want to take the chance. She didn't want to be linked to this place or Blue. No way.

Suddenly, the door behind Maryland swung open and two men walked in. One was good looking with blue eyes, the other, round and balding. They flashed their badges at the receptionist. Just like the PI had said, detectives. Fuck, she didn't want to be here. This was bullshit.

The round one gave Maryland a good looking over, his eyes running the length of her, before he and his partner followed the receptionist down the hall. Fucking pervert! She felt like putting her palm to his nose, flattening him out like the muscle head from Gold's.

Detectives. How the hell was she supposed to see Anna? Let Mick come out here and find Blue. Maryland didn't want to be here and she definitely didn't want to see Blue. The time in the café had been enough. More than enough. She felt nauseous. She hated it here. Hated it! She wanted to be back in their apartment in the hills, reading or trying to finish her script, not in some mental institution filled with detectives. Not trying to find a man who had once hurt her so deeply it was like her soul had been ripped out.

Maryland saw the receptionist staring at her and she took a seat on a nearby chair.

She could see them talking down the hall—the detectives, the doctor, and the PI What the hell was Mick doing with Blue anyway, and what the hell was that hole in the desert? Maryland fidgeted. Well, she knew, but she didn't really know. Didn't want to know. That was Mick's business. She stayed out of his stuff. He told her just what she needed to know. That's how she liked it. That's how it worked. If he asked her to do something, then she did it, then it must be important. Especially this. Maryland took a deep breath. She was getting agitated.

Mick knew how she hated this place. How she had spent two years of her life trying to get her shit together here, trying to get away from him.

Maryland looked around at the dull green walls. It seemed like yesterday that she had arrived. The place looked just the same. They had brought her here after her father died. After her breakdown. She was just a teenager. Her mother had been gone for years. The only person she had in her life was Mick. Nobody liked that; nobody thought that was a good idea, nobody, but Maryland and Mick.

Looking around now it was as if Maryland had stepped back in time. Like the bell was about to ring, signaling lights out, and Maryland could stand up and walk right down the hall, make a left and a right and enter room 212. Her room. At least she'd had a room to herself, she thought. Her father had left her some money… well, more than some, so she could afford it. The room where Group 22 met was right across the hall. That's where she'd had group therapy. That's where she'd met Anna and Blue.

Maryland couldn't believe Anna was still here after all these years. Anna's family had enough money to keep her locked up for the rest of her life, and that's just what they were going to do. Fuck, thought Maryland, she'd rather be dead than still be here. Not that this place hadn't helped her. She guessed it had. She'd gotten out, gone to college, and started a new life. But she'd hated it here. Hated it. First, they'd forbade her to see Mick; then, they'd introduced her to Blue.

How ironic, Maryland thought. Mick had never hurt her. Blue, on the other hand, had nearly destroyed her. For a long while he had been her lover and friend. Blue and Anna had made this place tolerable, had made her feel normal.

Then, one night, Blue decided to wake her by stuffing a rag into her mouth. He then tied her hands behind her back and had his way with her. Every which way he could think of. And Blue could think of a lot of ways. He was very imaginative. Maryland would have given him anything he wanted. Done anything he wanted. But where was the fun in that?

By the time Blue slipped out into the darkness of the hall, Maryland could barely move. The pain was everywhere, but it was worse inside, deep down, where she held love and trust. Where she held herself. The next day she pretended she was sick with the flu in order to get out of Group. Blue popped in to see her and acted as if nothing had happened, as if they were still friends, as if it had all been fun and games. He discharged himself a day later.

Maryland had not seen him again until their meeting at the café. She had read about him in the papers. Followed his trial. And no matter what he'd tried to tell her at the café, she knew the things she'd read were true. What he'd done to the Wilkins' girl and the others.

Maryland lowered her eyes. She had never told anyone what had happened down the hall in room 212, including Mick. But Mick said Maryland had told him everything one night up at the Chateau Marmont when they were fucking and doing blow. But she knew he was full of it. She knew it. Because if Mick had known what Blue had done, she wouldn't be looking for Blue, Blue would be… Well, she didn't even want to think about that.

Maryland lifted up, straightening her skirt. She was sick of sitting here with this dingbat receptionist staring at her, and she was hungry. The receptionist was rumpled and frumpy and couldn't take her eyes off Maryland. Maryland wondered if the woman had ever been fucked in her life. Didn't look like it. Maybe she just masturbated to re-runs of "Legends." Or maybe she was a lesbian and wanted to fuck Maryland. No doubt. Well, that wasn't going to happen. Not that Maryland hadn't been with a woman or two in her life. She had, but not one like this, no way. Maryland stood up, her six-foot frame towering over the receptionist. The receptionist looked down quickly at her desk. Maryland stood, glaring at the frumpy lesbian woman for a moment, before she slipped on her sunglasses and headed toward the cafeteria. God, she hated this place.

FORTY-NINE

He had told Anna they were coming. But she had been ready. The crazy people, with their lies, had not touched her. They had stood with their mouths open, sounds coming out, like bird talk. They talked a lot, but she would have nothing of the bird people's betrayal. She sat on her bed, with her knees pulled to her chest and watched them. She wished she had been back at her home in Connecticut. She would take her father's key that he hid in the china box on his desk, and open his gun cabinet. Then she would shoot the birds, just like her father had done each year down by the lake.

After, she would pluck the liars and cut them open. She would baste them with apple butter and roast them on a spit, like her grandmother had done with a pig each Thanksgiving. She would leave their heads on and watch the bird people's eyes bubble and pop in the fire. Maybe then they would speak the truth. No matter that they were dead; the dead spoke too, all the time.

Anna turned her head away from the yapping birds. They were talking about her friend Bud. They called him Blue. She didn't mind that. Everybody called him Blue. What's in a name? A rose is a rose… she thought. No matter what they called him, he was her friend.

Bud had called her on the phone in the recreation room. That's what they were worried about. Bud and she hadn't said a word. But they'd talked. They'd done some business. Anna felt a giggle inside, deep down where nobody could see it.

Blue had needed Anna's help and she had given it to him. That's what friends were for. The giggle grew larger. It came up from inside until her lips slid across her teeth in a large smile. They all thought she didn't know things, her family and the crazy people. But she knew things. They thought because she was in this place that she wasn't smart anymore. That's why they were so crazy. They forgot that she'd been a Rhodes Scholar, that she'd had all A's since before prep school. They forgot how she listened and learned and remembered. If she heard it once, if she read it once, there it was, like a picture in her brain.

Anna looked out the window. Since she didn't have the key to her father's china box, she wished the bird people would fly away, high up to the trees outside. Then across the city to never come back. Though He had told her they were coming, whispered it to her while she was in the shower, she still didn't like it.

Anna brought her gaze back to the cackling crows. They were looking at her paintings taped up on the wall, finger paintings. They wouldn't let her have a paintbrush here. They said it was too dangerous. Anna started to giggle again inside. They had no idea what dangerous was. It wasn't a paintbrush.

The giggle came up again, all the way this time, and Anna started laughing out loud. She couldn't help it. How stupid could they all be?

The bird people were angry now. They were flashing their badges and wanted to know why all her pictures on her wall were blue. Nothing but blue and blue. Blue, blue, blue, blue, blue!

Anna's laughing grew louder, stronger. She jumped up and began ripping the paintings off the wall. She scared the bird people, as her laughter became hysterical. It was all too funny! Blue, blue, blue, blue, blue! Anna ripped and clawed at the paintings.

Suddenly the door flew open and two men in white grabbed Anna, forcing her down onto her bed. She felt the restraints of the straightjacket being slipped around her and the prick of the needle. The world slowed down, the bird people's voices became faint, the lights streaked, then dimmed. But Anna's laughter only grew in her head, a paintbrush, dangerous? Not as dangerous as what was outside, she thought, a normal person, like her, among the crazy people.

FIFTY

Maryland looked down at the piece of crap in her hand. It was supposed to be a sandwich, but it looked like a piece of crap. She sat in the cafeteria of the institution, pissed. The cafeteria was closed, so she'd been forced to get the piece of crap out of a vending machine that distributed pieces of crap, for money, to starving idiots like her. She was pretty sure it'd been sitting in that machine since she'd been locked up in this hellhole years ago. It had been sitting there all that time, just waiting for Maryland to get it out. And now she had. Maryland lifted up the corner of the sandwich. The mayonnaise on it would probably kill her in less than an hour, so it didn't really matter that Mick had sent her here to talk to Anna and find Blue, because she'd be dead soon from fucking mayonnaise botulism!

Maryland threw the sandwich in the trash and took a sip of her Diet Coke and wished to God that it had some rum in it. She hated this place. She swallowed the Coke, trying to wash the crap from her throat as she raised her eyes to the four men talking down the hall. Christ! She was pissed! Pissed at Mick! Oh, right, she was sure he had a great reason to send her here to try and find Blue. But let him come to this place and eat a piece of crap out of a rusted vending machine while sitting near a doctor, two L.A.P.D detectives, and a private investigator, all of them having just talked to Anna. Maryland ran her lipstick across her lips as she looked at the men down the hall and her anger grew. This was bullshit!

Maryland watched as the men turned and began walking toward the cafeteria. Maryland froze, unable to think or move as the four men entered the cafeteria. Shit! She slipped her sunglasses back on and lowered her head as the men, deep in conversation, moved toward the coffee machine. Maryland pulled her phone from her purse, pretending to be busy. She hadn't done anything; she was here to see a friend. But she didn't want the actor-turned-PI, Will was his name, to recognize her, to talk to her. She didn't want to be linked to Blue, or this place, or any of the shit Mick was up to.

The PI got his coffee and moved away from the group toward Maryland. Oh, fuck, Maryland thought. She felt like she was going to be sick as he took a seat at the table next to her. He glanced over at Maryland and smiled a soft smile, nodding his head, acknowledging her.

Maryland managed a half smile, but thought she was going to throw up the half-eaten piece of crap all over him. Would he recognize her from her days at the Playhouse? Would he? Maryland closed her eyes behind the lenses of her glasses, trying to calm herself, as the other men took a seat with the PI

The PI looked away and Maryland felt herself breathe. He hadn't recognized her, or if he had, he hadn't said anything. The PI raised his hand toward the other men, his voice suddenly becoming agitated.

"All we know is someone tried to contact her three times. A man. But according to the FBI, when Ms. Burnside got on the phone, a few keys were pressed from the other end, then more tones from her end and then the guy hung up. That's all we know."

Maryland kept her eyes down. They were talking about Anna. The round detective spoke up, his voice loud and rough.

"Yeah, a few tones, a fucking signal. It happened in three separate phone calls. You don't think it was our boy, Spire? You think somebody else was calling playing row, row, row, your boat to her?"

The blue-eyed detective spoke calmly.

"The FBI are running the tones through their computers to see what possible sequences of words, sentences, or signs they could be."

"And they're going to come up with nothing, I'll tell you that," said the PI "If it's anything, it's their own signal. It's just between the two of them. The guy's smart, that's why he didn't stay on the line long enough for us to get a trace, I think she knows everything that's going on. Everything. You guys saw the paintings. What do you think that was all about? She's fucking with us. I'm not sure she's half as crazy as they say she is."

The men fell silent. The round detective looked over at Maryland. His eyes stayed on her. Maryland felt like her heart was going to pop out of her chest. She had to do something. She had to move, or eventually they were going to talk to her.

Maryland looked up and saw the receptionist walking toward the cafeteria. Shit! The frumpy lesbian was coming for her. Coming to tell her it was all right to see Anna now. Maryland could feel the men's eyes on her. She was fucked! They would know she knew Anna and it wouldn't take them long to know she knew Blue too, that she once had been his lover. That she had once been locked up here. That she had been one of them.

The round detective looked like he was going to speak when Maryland suddenly stood up, grabbing her purse, and moving quickly toward the receptionist. She could feel their eyes on her back as she intercepted the receptionist outside the door of the cafeteria.

Maryland shut the cafeteria door just as the receptionist told her that she was free to see Ms. Burnside. Maryland thought of leaving, of fleeing, but that would make her look even more suspicious. They may question the receptionist about her. Who knows what they'd fucking do? Mick would be angry, too. He would not be happy if she left without seeing Anna. And as pissed as she was at him for sending her here, she didn't like to see Mick upset and angry. So Maryland smiled hard at the frumpy lesbian, who smiled back as if Maryland had just made her come. Maryland turned her back on the receptionist and moved away. She took a deep breath, trying to calm herself as she moved quickly around the corner, feeling the men's gaze vanish with the welcome wall of the hall.

FIFTY-ONE

The best place to hide was in plain sight. Blue's father had taught him that. Blue had been tempted to go inside the waiting room of the institution and hang out. Wait for Maryland and get a good view of his buddy Will Spire, the man he was going to kill.

Instead, Blue sat across the street in his new set of wheels, waiting. Blue had fucked up out in the desert. He knew that. He'd gotten carried away with Spire's ex-wife. He hadn't raped her or anything, but he'd hit her a little too hard with that truck. Mick wouldn't like that.

Blue needed to make things right with Mick. Maryland could help him do that. Maryland had gotten a contact number for Blue, from Anna, and called it from her cell phone. Blue had gotten Maryland's message. She was waiting for him at the institution. Blue knew why. Mick wanted him back in the cave to complete their plan. That was just fine with Blue. He hadn't left for good. He had just needed to take care of some business. Now that he had, he was looking forward to getting on with things, especially taking care of Will Spire, and Mick's cave was the perfect place. Blue should have just played it straight until Mick had gotten back from the mountains. But that bitch had put a knife in him and pissed him off.

He'd had the wound patched up in a little shit-hole hospital out in the desert, but it still burned like hell. He'd told the nurse there that he'd fallen off a ladder trying to fix his roof and had landed on something sharp. She knew he was full of shit, it was a clean knife wound, any idiot could see that. But Blue had smiled and flirted with the young nurse, who probably hadn't seen a man, other than the methed-out locals, or the leather-skinned regulars down at the Oasis Bar, in years, so she didn't ask any questions. When she was done, she played with her hair and laughed as Blue finished his story of what a clumsy handyman he was. He used one of his fake IDs at the counter and paid cash for the service, no questions asked. He winked at the nurse as he left and could feel her eyes follow him into the night. Fucking women, they were all the same.

Blue flicked the butt of his cigarette out of the open window of the car and thought about Spire. He'd thought about Spire a lot these last years. Spire was in the institution right now with those two detectives. Blue could follow Spire, when he left, and kill him tonight. But where was the fun it that? Blue wanted Spire to be in real pain. Like the pain Blue'd been in the last five years in the four-by-six cell Spire had put him in. The kind of pain Blue had felt when he'd been raped and beaten senseless in the showers of Folsom his first day in.

Blue hadn't known that each ethnic group claimed a different showerhead, or that using the wrong one could mean death. He'd just stepped into the shower and turned it on. He'd been spared being butchered with a shank only because he was new, fresh meat.

During his time inside, he'd seen it happen to others, though. Men cut to pieces in a flurry of violence, left naked and bleeding on the shower floor, their lives spinning away down a rusty drain. That place was filled with animals, thought Blue. It wasn't this world, it was hell, and Spire had put him there.

Blue wanted Spire to see those he loved fucked, like Blue'd been, Will's ex-wife by Mick and her pretty little sister by Blue. Maybe they'd switch off. Maybe Blue would pull a Folsom shower scene on Will. Give him a little taste of that. The girls could watch. Wouldn't that be a fucking kick?

In fact, he might take Spire with him down to Mexico, put him in his trunk so the fun and games could continue south of the border. When he was done with Spire, he'd just stick him under one of those half-finished houses they've got everywhere. Christ, don't they know they haven't got enough money to finish those things when they start them? Those two hot shot detectives would have their hands full trying to find Spire's body in that country. Yeah, thought Blue, as he lit another cigarette, admiring himself in the rearview mirror. Good luck with that.

Mick could make Spire's pain complete. So Blue needed to make things complete with Mick. Make things right with their deal. All Mick wanted was a little help getting away clean with Spire's ex. That was fine with Blue, like a cherry on top of Spire's chocolate sundae of pain.

Blue looked out at the lights of L.A. He took a deep breath and could smell the scent of the city, taste the sweetness of being on the outside. Out here, he was everyone and no one. He could turn on the charm, flash his million-dollar smile, and make anyone believe he was anything they wanted him to be. That was his real gift. His father had recognized that early on. He had taught Blue the power of the con. The power of giving people what they need while you take what you want. He'd taught Blue that the world was one, big insecurity, waiting for you to compliment and cuddle it, while you steal it blind. And if along the way, you chose to abide in your own pleasures, then so be it. Use the world; don't let it use you, his father had said.

Blue didn't see the connection between what had happened to him in the showers of Folsom and what he'd done to the Wilkins' girl, though some people tried to make it. What had happened in prison was about men exerting power over men. What he did with certain women was just fun and games, sex, with a little twist.

Besides, after taking one look at him, his car, the cut of his body, and the wad of bills in his pocket, they were the ones, the women, that wanted to play him. How many women had he met that thought they could play him? Play him with their tits and ass that they thought were so special he should give up all future pussy, for the honor of fucking theirs for the rest of his life. So special, he should hand them the keys to his Kingdom just to get a little taste, hand them the big house and big lifestyle they all thought they deserved for being born without a cock between their legs.

Yeah, thought Blue, that pussy was like a credit card on crack. That's what we get for bringing up our daughters in a world of Ken and Barbie and frogs turning to princes just because the little darlings kiss them. More likely, Ken was going to take some naked shots of Barb and post them on the Internet. And as for the frog, well, he really was a fucking frog; she just couldn't see it through all the princess magic she was brought up to believe.

Or worse yet, he wasn't a frog at all… he was Blue.

Oh well, like his dad had said, "There's the way you think the world should be and then there's my fucking way." And Blue's way was to take, fuck, and taste anything he wanted, anytime he wanted. As for his so-called "victims," well, fuck' em if they can't take a joke. He'd showed them a good time.

Blue adjusted the side mirror on the Aston Martin, keeping an eye on the front doors of the institution. He'd rented the car down on the corner of La Cienega and Beverly, in Hollywood. Hollywood suited him, he thought. Prison didn't. Up in Folsom, his good looks had been a curse. But here in Hollywood, they were gold.

In Folsom he'd had a target on his ass, literally. He'd had to join the Aryan Brotherhood just to get some protection. He hated those crazy motherfuckers with all their racist bullshit. Hell, Blue's first love had been an African princess. He loved the dark side. Loved it. His second love had been a nice little Jewish girl he'd run away with to New York. But he'd towed the line on all their Hitler-worship-redneck-crap in order to survive. He'd had no choice.

It was the Brotherhood for Blue. Or becoming somebody's bitch, and no way that was going to happen. Sex was a weapon on the inside, the ultimate power grab. In that world, Blue was going to be the pitcher, not the catcher, the giver of pain, not the receiver. You've got to be an animal to survive among animals, thought Blue, as he adjusted his crotch through the silk of his pants; otherwise, you're nothing but a meal.

Blue and his new friends had taken care of some business though, doled out some payback for Blue's beating in the shower. Blue had worked in the kitchen, filling the inmates' trays with food as they passed by. And the Brotherhood had been nice enough to smuggle him in some arsenic. Over a three-month period Blue poisoned the two main culprits of his shower scene. The guys had been cellmates and they were always sick. Soon, even their friends wouldn't go near them for fear of catching something, and the doctors couldn't figure out what was happening.

Care comes slow in prison. The "I give a fuck" factor is pretty low there. When the men finally got transferred to the prison infirmary, it was too late. One of them died the first night he was there when his organs shut down. The other got transferred to a private hospital and died on the outside. In the end, thought Blue, that first day in the showers, who really got fucked?

Blue smiled. Don't mess with him. Just don't do it. Spire should have remembered that.

Blue took another hit of his cigarette as he looked around at the interior of the handmade auto. It was beautiful. He'd rented the car with the last bit of money he'd made from the heroin he'd scored from Tiny Tim. Making any more cash on that gig, though, was up. Tim had got himself busted, by Spire, no less, and was headed upstate. Blue was sure Tim would keep his mouth shut when it came to his dealings with him. If not, Tim's time inside would be shorter than he was. One word from Blue and the Brotherhood would plant Tiny Tim in the ground for good.

Selling smack on the street was too risky anyway, thought Blue. It was fine for some walking around money. But it couldn't score Blue the type of cash he needed to vanish, because after he'd dealt with Spire, that's just what he was going to do. Poof! Gone! So Blue had had to think hard of another way to get liquid. That's where Anna had come in. She'd taken care of him. He'd always known she could. That's why it's so important to keep up with old friends.

Blue moved his gaze to the leather satchel sitting on the seat next to him, his hand resting comfortably on it, near his .38 revolver. Some action from inside that satchel should square things with Mick, Blue thought, because he was liquid now, motherfucker, liquid as a fucking lake.

FIFTY-TWO

The clock was ticking. I stared down into my coffee. I could feel my guts tying themselves into knots as I thought of how Stacey was still with the monster. Bill Benson, my former brother-in-law, was dead and Brenda, Stacey's sweet, angelic sister, had been abducted. And guess what? It was all because of me. Blue was cutting a trail to me through the people I loved, but it was me he really wanted. Everyone else just seemed to have to pay the price.

I took a deep breath and closed my eyes. This was not good. The way I felt was not good. Dolen and Dan had left the institution, off to answer a call. But I couldn't seem to move. I was tired, more tired than I had ever been. In reality, I would have liked nothing more than to be in the cocoon of a bright yellow apartment filled with classical music and the touch of a young woman from Kansas. Was that such a crime, wanting to be happy? I saw the dead faces from the case flash across my brain. Yeah, I guess it was. There could be no happiness until it was over. Until life had a path toward something other than dead bodies, cops, madmen, and mental institutions. Until life led to a world filled with possibilities, not pain and the exceptional finality of failure.

I had to do something, go somewhere, but what, where? I thought I'd found something here with Anna. That's why I'd called Dolen and Dan. But I had nothing. Anna Burnside was crazy all right, crazy like a fox. We had her insanity, a few dial tones, and a button with Blue's print on it. Blue, on the other hand, had Stacey, Brenda, and our balls in a vice.

I looked across the room and suddenly realized I was starving. I saw a vending machine across the way and got up and moved toward it. I leaned over, looking through the window of the machine at little cut

195

sandwiches, stuffed into oversized triangular boxes. I stared through the window for a long time, examining them. They looked like crap.

I stood up and felt dizzy for a moment. The Jewel wasn't far away. I could get a real meal there. I wouldn't mind a drink either, or the sound of Daisy's velvet voice if she were onstage tonight. Maybe after, I could think a little clearer, a little better. There must be something, something I was missing that could end this thing. And still the question remained, if it was Blue and he was after me, what was with Alfred Green and Shari Canes? Why had he killed them? They had no connection to me. I rubbed my hands over my face and could taste the steak and collard greens already, feel the fingers of Jack and Daisy's voice unwinding the knots in my brain. Yeah, that was the call. The Jewel was the ticket.

FIFTY-THREE

Blue's finger twitched on the trigger of his .38 as he watched Will Spire walk out the front door of the institution. His eyes burned and his blood pressure rose to the point of uncharted violence. His mouth dried with adrenaline and his muscles grew taught. Yet, he kept his feet anchored firmly to the floor of the Aston Martin. He watched as Will moved toward a black Corvette parked in the shadows across the street. He could see Will clearly, the stubble lining his jaw, the stress under his eyes, the shine of his watch, and it took every ounce of Blue's energy not to leap from the car and kill him. Blue let his mind run, seeing Spire's face turn toward the click of his footsteps, hearing the crack of the gun as Spire's eyes flew open in shock and his brains scattered across the perfectly waxed hood of his car.

But Blue didn't move. He just kept breathing slow and steady, his gaze flicking to the form of a tall blonde girl leaving the institution behind Spire. Blue watched as Maryland paused, seeing Will. She lowered her head, looking through her purse as if trying to find something, waiting for Spire to start his car and pull away, which he did. Maryland raised her eyes as Will's car passed her and she continued across the street toward her black BMW parked in front of Blue. She gave a quick glance after Will as the lights of his car disappeared around the corner.

Blue watched Maryland as she walked toward the BMW. He flipped open his gold lighter, compliments of Anna, and sparked the wheel, bringing its flame toward the unlit cigarette in his mouth. His face glowed in the light of the lighter as Maryland's eyes found his through the open window of the car. Blue was impressed that she gave nothing away as she opened the door to her Beemer and climbed inside.

Blue slipped his .38 into the waistband of his pants and fired the ignition on the Aston Martin. He listened to the deep purr of the engine as he watched Maryland pull her car into the darkness. He waited for a moment, enjoying his smoke, his blood slowly cooling. He then put the car in gear and fell in behind Maryland. He drove, the taste of Spire, of what could have been, still with him. Patience, he thought, be patient, you've waited five years, don't be rash. Do it right. He took another hit of his cigarette, keeping his eyes on the glow of Maryland's taillights up ahead, doing what his father taught him, using the world. Following close, but not too close.

FIFTY-FOUR

I sat in my car, the engine running, pulled over to the side of the road around the corner from the institution. Stunned. I felt like I had been hit over the head by a brick. What the fuck? I slammed the car into gear and punched the gas. The Vette's tires screeched as I whipped the car around into a tight U-turn and blew through a stop sign. The roar of the engine vibrated through my body as I flew by the institution's front doors and screamed, "I know her! I fucking know her!"

I picked up the taillights of two cars in the distance as I flew down the dark, vacant road. The cars turned right, their lights now moving perpendicular to me. I thought the tall blonde had looked familiar when I saw her in the cafeteria of the institution, but I couldn't figure out from where I knew her, or if at all. But I did know her, from the Miracle Works Playhouse! I downshifted and the Vette hunkered down like a caged animal as I made the hard right. I moved the gears quickly through their sequence, gas and clutch, the 400 horses pushing me back into my seat.

She had studied at the Playhouse when I had been around. She had studied there when Blue had been around! When Blue had been Bud Williams, the wannabe producer! I was gaining and close enough now, that even in the darkness, I could see the two cars clearly. One was a black Beemer; the other, a late model Aston Martin.

FIFTY-FIVE

Blue watched the lights of the approaching car in his rearview mirror. The car was moving, coming fast. The car flashed under a streetlight and Blue saw that it was a black Corvette and he knew immediately that it was Spire. Blue's hand found his .38. Maybe that whole "...put Spire in the trunk and go to Mexico..." thing was now out of the question. If Spire had seen him, he'd take Spire's head off tonight.

But how could he have seen him? Blue had been sitting in the dark and Spire had not even glanced across the street as he walked to his car, not for a second. Blue paused and it hit him. It was Maryland. Spire had recognized Maryland as he drove past, remembered her from back in the day. Blue watched as Will's car fell in behind him. He'd never said Spire wasn't smart. After all, he'd been the only one to find Blue. The only one who'd had a fucking clue. But it was Maryland that Spire was following now. Blue would bet his life on it. He was.

Blue brought his hand slowly from his gun back to the steering wheel of the car and thought about his options. The darkness and the tint of the windows would keep him hidden from Spire. For now, Blue was a nobody, just another flashy car moving through the L.A. night. There was no reason to escalate things, not with unfinished business at hand, not with a liquid satchel on the seat next to him. There was no reason to draw attention to himself, to alert Maryland with a flick of his headlights. No reason to leave any dots that could be connected to him by Spire or the police. Maryland could handle herself and if things got too tough for her, she could always call on Mick. Blue smiled a wry smile. Mick and Spire, Blue would pay to see that.

Blue looked up ahead at an exit forking off to one of the multitude of freeways that connected the city to itself. He put on his blinker and slid slowly over into the exit lane. He veered away from the main road toward the freeway as Spire's Vette passed him, just like he thought it would, following Maryland's BMW into the night.

His meeting with Mick would have to wait. Blue's hand found the leather of the satchel feeling its contents pressing against his hand. It was good to be free. Free to do what he wanted, when he wanted, bound by nothing but him. Maybe he'd hit a couple of strip clubs down in Hollywood, see what he could find of interest. There were a lot of motel rooms there too, and after, a lot of canyons through the hills, deep, dark canyons, where a boy like Blue could howl at the moon and fun could be had by all.

FIFTY-SIX

Stacey had almost worked the tie loose. She listened to the steady hum of the cave's generator, her eyes closed, concentrating. Her right hand was nearly free. She had worked the velvet strap that circled her wrist, down toward the bottom of her thumb. Stacy paused, trying to gain some strength. She took a deep breath, the cool air of the cave filling her lungs. How long had she been tied to this bed? It had been hours since she had been conscious. Her body ached all over and the cuts on her elbows and knees burned like hell. Yet, someone had bandaged them, had washed her. Who? Bud Williams? No way.

That Blue hadn't finished the job he'd started, after he hit her with the truck, hadn't raped her and tied her to a cactus to die, was shocking to her. Why hadn't he raped her, Stacey wondered. That's what he did, that's who he was. Why would he take the time to bandage and clean her after she had put a knife in him? From what Stacy had heard at his trial, bandaging and cleaning were not part of his MO. Was there more to all of this than just him and her? Stacey thought she'd heard someone else in the cave, a voice, someone moving about, but that was long ago. There seemed to be only one explanation for any of this, for this crazy cave, for the difference in Blue's voice from that of her abductor's, for her not being raped and left to bake in the desert. Blue had a partner.

Then, Stacey heard it, a voice, like a pained whisper. Stacey lifted her head up, trying to locate the sound through the darkness of her blindfold. There it was again, soft, inaudible, but definitely a voice, a woman's voice. Stacey swallowed. Her words came out, hoarse and hollow. "Who's there?" Stacey listened for a response, but heard nothing but the hum of the caves generator. Then, a gasp, "Please…help me…"

Stacey held her breath; there was someone else here, another girl. The voice came again, clearer, stronger. "I'm tied down…I can't move…please help me…please…"

Stacey froze. She felt sick and panicked. Oh, my God! Her voice broke with emotion. "Brenda? Brenda is that you?"

"Stacey?"

"Brenda? Brenda!"

Stacey listened as Brenda tried to respond, but all that came out were deep sobs and breathless gasps. Stacey's tears pressed against her blindfold, the voice of her sister ripping her open. Emotions held deep and tight came up in a violent surge that burned her eyes. Her voice came out like the screech of a wounded animal.

"Brenda…I can't move…I can't…"

Stacey pulled violently against her bindings, screaming, twisting, turning. Yet, her bindings held tight. Finally, she stopped struggling, her arms shaking in spasms, the pain in her head and body overwhelming her. She lay gasping for breath, listening to her sobs mix with that of her sister's, unable to help either of them.

FIFTY-SEVEN

Dolen stood on the back patio of the Holmby Hills mansion. He looked out at the acres of manicured lawn lit by a variety of colored lights. This area of L.A. is not where the 99 percent lived, or even the 1 percent, but where the .01 percent resided. Where tens of millions of dollars could buy you a cozy nine bedroom Tudor manor like the one Dolen was visiting. He and Dan had been at the institution with Spire trying to figure out their next move, when officers responding to a break-in had called them to this location. Dolen spit a stream of Skoal into a plastic cup. Well, not really a break-in, he thought, more like I have the security code to your front gate and door, so I'll just let myself in "kind of deal and while I'm there, I'll open your safe and help myself to everything in it because I also have the combination to that."

Dolen shook his head and let his eyes wander over the expanse of the estate. He couldn't help but admire the large fountains, three of them, stretching out in even spaces toward the horizon, each one, he'd been told, exact reproductions of the fountains of Versailles. Fuck that, these people were idiots, thought Dolen. He felt like walking across the perfect lawn and pissing in one of the fountains. Taking a nice, long, taxpayer-paid civil servant piss into the first one he came to. If he pressed real hard, he might even reach the tits of the pretty marble lady in the middle, whose toga seemed to be falling off.

Why the fuck not, he thought. The owners weren't here to complain. They were in the Cayman Islands, escaping the horrible, brutal, sunny L.A. winter that only middle-class mopes like Dolen stayed around for. Oh, my gosh, honey, it's dropped below 70 degrees, we better head to the Islands! It's the same thing, like clockwork, that the owners had done for the past thirty years. A detail that had not been lost on the combination burglar who had gotten away with a little over $425,000 in cash. Just some walking around money, thought Dolen, kept in the house for a rainy day, when the owners, tired of watching reality TV, might want to buy a yacht, or a racehorse, or part of a fucking racehorse or whatever!

Dolen threw his plastic cup down, watching his tobacco-stained spittle splash across the Italian tile of the patio. Fuck it! Their boy had walked right in and gotten enough cash to disappear and never be found. That kind of money can buy a lot of protection and time. You could be king of a Third World country with that type of cash, buy a new face, IDs, passport, whatever the fuck you wanted. Dolen looked up at the light in the window above him. He saw Frick and Frack from the FBI standing next to Dan. The feds had done their analysis on the phone calls Anna had received in the institution, like they'd all thought, the random dial tones turned out not to be so random after all. The tones, translated to numbers, in sequence of the phone calls she received, had been the gate code, door code, and combination to the safe in the house.

It seemed that the patio that Dolen had just decorated with his spittle was the property of John and Betty Burnside. The couple had never had any children of their own and had taken an early liking to the very bright and beautiful daughter of John's brother, Ralph Burnside. In fact, the couple had doted on the young girl, Anna, paying for her schooling, traveling the world with her, and insisting that she spend her summers with them, in L.A., at their Holmby Hills home. That all ended when the girl killed her father, John's brother, Ralph, and stuffed his body up the chimney of his Connecticut mansion, one Christmas day. Having killed the rest of her immediate family too, John and Betty Burnside had taken over reluctant guardianship of the girl and had paid for her extensive therapy and institutionalization. Since Anna's committal to the institution, they had never thought to change anything about their lives, including their security codes or combination to their safe. Why would they?

Dolen let out a sigh and reached down to pick up his plastic cup. One reason they should have, he thought, was that their niece had a photographic memory, a friend named Blue, and was crazy, as Spire had said, like a fox.

Dolen looked over as the patio door slid open and Dan stepped outside. "Too much for you to handle in there?" Dan asked as he closed the door behind him.

"Not a big fan of Frick and Frack." Dolen answered.

"You mean Agent White and Black?"

"Whatever," Dolen replied, sliding another pinch of Skoal between his cheek and gums. "They give me the fucking creeps."

Dan slipped his hands into his pockets. "Not having a good night, are we?"

Dolen looked over at Dan, his eyes burning.

"Are you? That's Blue on the security tapes. I know the guy's got a mask on and we can't see his face. But it's fucking him. He drives up in that high-end car, so as not to raise suspicion of the neighbors, and makes off with nearly a half a million dollars. That these knuckleheads keep in a safe, hidden under a pull-out painting in their bedroom, just like in some cheesy movie. And on top of that, he grabs an AR-15 assault rifle and a couple of boxes ammo from these morons' gun cabinet, so now he's better armed than we are! When he's had his fill of fun, Dan, he's going to kill Stacey and Brenda and be gone. That's what this little raid was all about. Going-away money. So, no, I'm not having a good night!"

Dan lowered his eyes.

"Besides that…" Dolen said, his voice growing soft, "he's not going to be done until he kills Spire."

Dan's gaze met Dolen's. They looked at each other for a long moment. They both knew he was right.

"We'll make sure that doesn't happen," Dan said.

"Yeah. Like we made sure the rest of the killings didn't happen." Dolen brought his gaze to the darkness past the fountains.

"What's going on, Joe?" Dan asked, marking Dolen's long silence. Dolen hesitated.

"I think this case is going to kill me."

"Kill you? You mean you're tired…"

"I mean a blade across my throat. I mean dead. Dying with the useless knowledge of a dead man."

Dan took a step toward Dolen. "That's just a dream, Joe. That's all that is. You've had that dream for years."

Dolen spit another stream of Skoal into his cup. " It's not a dream, partner. It's a premonition."

"You can't believe that?"

When Dolen finally answered, his voice was soft, almost a whisper. "More than I believe anything in my life."

"You're not going to die, Joe, at least not from this case. You'll probably live to be a hundred and be twice as ugly and five times the pain in the ass you are now. It's just a dream. It means nothing."

Dolen kept his eyes toward the darkness.

"Who keeps over four hundred thousand dollars in their house?" Dolen asked. "What kind of people do that?"

"Rich people," Dan replied. "Now let's get out of here and get a drink."

Dolen didn't move. "What do you say, Joe?

"I've got to piss," Dolen said, as he stepped off the patio and onto the perfect lawn. He walked straight toward the first fountain. Dan watched as Dolen unzipped his pants and a perfect stream of pee arched through the colored lights landing smack on the breasts of the sculpted lady in the middle of the fountain.

FIFTY-EIGHT

Maryland had her car pulled over on Melrose Boulevard, down the street from Paramount Studios, in Hollywood. She had been sitting there for a while watching the black Vette that had been following her and getting her more and more pissed off. The Vette was parked four spaces behind her, the PI who had caught Blue sitting coolly in it smoking a cigarette. It's not like the guy had tried to keep Maryland from knowing he was tailing her. He'd been doing it for over an hour, all over the city, and making himself very visible. When she pulled over, he pulled over, when she took off, he took off. Christ! What did he think? That she was going to let him follow her home? Let him know where she lived? Invite him in for tea and a blow job and tell him where to find Blue? Fuck that! She wasn't about to go home and she wasn't going to lead him back to that hole in the desert where Mick was, where she was supposed to be, the place Blue was supposed to follow her to, before he took off and left her alone with this PI piece of shit!

Maryland glared in the rearview mirror. She was fucked! And why the hell was he just sitting there doing nothing? Why didn't he get out of that car and do something? Anything! Maryland was at the end of her rope. She slammed her hand down on the horn of her BMW. It blared, loud and sharp. "Do something, you fuck!" Maryland screamed, her words being drowned out by the loud screech of the horn. She looked in the rearview mirror, keeping her hand on the horn, and saw the PI calmly smoking his cigarette.

"Fuck this!" Maryland wailed, as she yanked the car door open and stepped out into the street. She slammed the car door shut, strutting, with purpose, toward the black Vette, her high heels clicking on the pavement.

208

The PI didn't move as she reached the car. She stared at him through the driver's side window, before rapping her knuckles against the glass.

"Hey!" she screamed. "Roll the window down!"

The PI smiled a soft smile and slowly rolled the window down, his cigarette dangling from his lip.

"Can I help you?" he said softly.

Maryland, flustered for a minute by his mellow attitude, thought for a moment she had the wrong guy. But no, it was him!

"Yeah, you can help me," she said. "You can stop fucking following me!"

"I'm sorry," said the PI, in barely a whisper, "but I can't do that. It's my job."

"Fuck your job!" screamed Maryland. "You think I'm just going to let you follow me all over the city? Follow me home so you know where I live... so you can..."

"You live at 2244 Liverpool Lane," said the PI. Maryland's mouth dropped open. "I had the police run your plates," said the PI as he opened his car door and got out.

Maryland took a step back. "Don't touch me!"

The PI raised his hands. "Not to worry. I'm a private investigator. My name is Will Spire."

"I know who you are," Maryland snapped. "But that doesn't give you the right to harass me."

"I'm afraid it does, Miss Sharp. You are Maryland Sharp, aren't you?" Maryland didn't answer. "I'm working a case and I believe you could be of some use. Maybe there is somewhere we could talk for a moment?"

Maryland looked the PI up and down. "You studied at the Miracle Works Playhouse, didn't you?"

"As did you," said the PI. "That's one of the things I'd like to speak to you about. Maybe I could buy you a drink and we could just talk for a few moments?"

"I want you to know I have a boyfriend."

The PI smiled. "I understand."

"And he's the jealous type."

The PI pointed across the street to a coffeehouse. "Just a coffee?" He kept smiling. He had a nice smile. Maryland had always thought that when she used to watch him on TV.

She stood for a long moment with her arms crossed, staring at him, before she nodded her head.

FIFTY-NINE

Maryland was asleep now. Mick stared out of the window of their Hollywood home, looking at the sparkling lights of the city below. Maryland had told Mick about the conversation she had had with the PI and how he'd asked her why she was visiting the institution. Maryland had told the PI that she had known Anna Burnside from the summers Anna spent in L.A. That Maryland's father and Anna's uncle had both been members of the Brentwood Country Club, and though Anna was a couple of years older than Maryland, they had been friends. The lie, like all good lies, held some truth. It was true, Mick thought, that Maryland had been friends with Anna and that both women had spent their summers at the Brentwood Country Club. But they didn't meet there. They'd met in group therapy at the institution, years later, at a time when Maryland was forbidden to see Mick. That was when and where their friendship began.

Mick felt the hair on his arms stand up as he felt Maryland's energy move through him as if she was there, listening to his thoughts. Mick smiled; it had always been so. Mick reached out to steady himself, feeling the wave of Maryland wash across him. His smile grew, his mind and body having been a lightning rod for such things. He didn't like that the actor had questioned Maryland. The actor was a player in Mick's production, but Maryland was not. She worked behind the scenes, like a good Art Director or First Assistant Director would. Helping Mick make his vision come true.

Mick remained perfectly still as he stared at the city lights dancing like fireflies toward the horizon. Besides his annoyance with the PI, he felt good. He felt enclosed in his own membrane, straight, on the line. His

211

thoughts came to him, fired into his brain, clear, hard, sharp. It was Blue's fault that Maryland had been questioned. That she had been made so uncomfortable and frightened that she needed to reach out to Mick. Mick had plans for the PI, as he knew Blue did. But what Blue didn't know was that Mick had plans for him, too. Mick laughed as he thought about the bloody button under the bed. The seed had been sown.

Mick knew about the money Blue had scored from Anna's uncle. Anna had told Maryland. Blue was smart, real smart. But Blue hurt his friends and used everyone around him, including Anna and Maryland. He had no loyalty, but to himself. He didn't love like Mick did. He had no one in his life like Mick had Maryland and Maryland had Mick. He would never feel pain so deep for someone, that he knew he was alive. See him or her so unhappy that he would do anything to save them even if it meant his own destruction.

For Blue, there was no one worth dying for, living for, or killing for, but him. Blue was the center of his world, the only one that mattered. What a hollow existence, thought Mick, feeling Maryland's energy vanish as quickly as it had appeared. He remembered what Maryland had once said. "Not to love, or be loved, would be to live, but not be alive."

Mick closed his eyes. There would be time for everything. Maryland would understand when she saw Mick's lover for the first time. Maryland would see that her soul was like theirs. She would know that the three of them were the same. That Maryland and Mick had known her in many lives, in many forms. That their connection, the three of them, surpassed this time and place. Maryland would look upon his lover, and within her eyes, see herself. She could lay with her and love her as Mick did, for the three of them were made for each other.

Mick opened his eyes and took a deep breath, elated. The day was near, the plan almost complete. Justice is rare in the universe. The benders seldom allow it. The actor would play his part as would Blue. And now that Maryland was on stage, she too would have a role. In the end when the curtain fell, there would be a happily ever after and three destinies fulfilled.

Yes, Blue was smart, but not as brilliant as Mick. Mick was glad that Anna had told Blue about the money. In this life, money comes in handy and one can never have enough. Though Mick had money of his own, family money, the three of them, Maryland, Mick, and his lover, could always use more. Besides, where Mick was sending Blue, he wouldn't need any.

SIXTY

I sat in a white Chevy Malibu up in the Hollywood Hills. I'd rented the car just down the street from where I'd had coffee with Maryland Sharp. Having left my Vette parked safely in an underground parking garage, I had proceeded, unnoticed, up to Mt. Olympus and the pink bungalow marked 2244 Liverpool Lane. I'd parked down the street on Orange, around a corner and behind a tree, but with a line of sight that gave me a clear view of the house and Maryland's black BMW parked in its driveway.

I watched as the sun began to rise, cracking the darkness with streaks of orange and yellow. I had dozed off a few times only to awaken with a start, the large coffee I bought at the bottom of the hill, hours ago, still clenched in my right hand. I brought the coffee up to my mouth and took a cold swig, as I watched the colors of the sunrise spread across the city. I didn't think I'd missed anything. The BMW was still in the driveway and the lights that had been on in the house were now off. Maryland Sharp was most likely curled up and sleeping in a nice warm bed, unlike me.

It was all just probably a wild goose chase. I had no real reason to suspect her of anything, besides visiting an old friend in the institution, but something didn't feel right about her. It wasn't just the fact that the friend she was visiting had murdered her entire family, but something was off with her, with Maryland. She was lying, or at the least, omitting things. Why? Was she scared of me following her? Wouldn't anyone be on guard, holding back, when being tailed throughout the city and then interrogated? I rubbed my eyes. Of course they would. It was probably all a wild goose chase.

I was tired of all of it, though. My thoughts were jumbled, unclear. I could think of nothing but trying to find Blue, of saving Stacey. But I felt,

214

as my mother used to say, "discombobulated." Time was running out. I could feel it ticking away with each beat of my heart. Helpless? Was I helpless to stop this thing? I refused to believe that. I would press on, until the ticking of time or my heart itself stopped. That was what I would do. That was what I had to do.

I had been thinking about Stacey a lot, well, more about Stacey and Will. Was there a Stacey and Will, I wondered? There were the ghosts, the marks made by us on time as it had passed. But was there an "us"? Not in the way I thought, perhaps. I knew I would always love Stacey. But that love was built on stones of what could have been, on what had been, and a fleeting hope of what could be. If only... I took another sip of coffee. If only what, if she'd left Bob and had come back home?

I had waited. Waited for the door to open, for Stacey to walk back through it. For her to shoo the ghosts away as we picked up our lives and lived happily ever after. But that had never happened. She never left Bob. Ever. Bob had left Stacey, when a maniac broke him into pieces and stuffed him into his freezer. That was the only time Stacey had come back. After all the years, months, days, hours, and minutes that she could have, she never did, until Bob was dead.

Eventually, I had gotten tired of staring at the door, waiting for her to return. I dated. There had been no shortage of women. My running buddy, Jack, and I tore up the town. But it felt like nothing. I still held on, down deep, in a place no woman could touch, a place I didn't even seem to have access to, I held on. That is until a young, dominatrix waitress from Kansas came into my life and my grip on that place began to slip away. I awoke in her apartment in the real world, not a fictionalized one made of memories and hopes, but the moment. The moment is what life is; all we can touch, hear, and feel is now. What we were is our past, what we dream to be, our future, but life is now. The moment is where I needed to be, less ghosts, more life, more now.

Like the classical music that had seeped into my half-conscious mind, soothing and buffering me from the nightmares of my other reality, Kansas had given me, with her touch and kindness, a sense of peace. Strange that at a time high with stress, death, and disaster that I could say that. But it was true.

I thought of Kansas, of her music, of the soft breeze blowing through her yellow curtains, of the comfort of her bed. I didn't know what the future held for us, if anything. But I liked to think of her. And as I did, I was unaware that my eyes had slipped closed and that I was drifting away, away to somewhere safe and warm and over the rainbow.

SIXTY-ONE

Blue watched the sunrise over the desert. He was standing on the edge of a cliff. He was smiling, looking out at the miles and miles of nothing but miles and miles. Streaks of light rose above the mountains in the distance, surrounding them in a halo of colors. Blue took a deep breath and felt free. Free to do what he wanted, to be whom he wanted. He thought of the men in Folsom waking up to the bars of their cells and another day of trying to survive. Survive the dead wait of time slipping slowly by, survive the other animals they were caged with. He would never go back. He'd rather die out here in the desert, surrounded by the endless spaces than to be put back in a cage for even an hour.

Before his night out in Hollywood, Blue had returned the Aston Martin, its task, making him unnoticed in Holmby Hills, done. There was no chance of anyone tracing the car to him. He'd rented it with a fake ID, compliments of Tiny Tim, who'd set him up with four such "ID Packages," including stolen credit cards, driver's licenses, and Social Security numbers. Identity theft was big inside Folsom. The gang members on the inside used the members on the outside and ran it like business, hitting mailboxes, trash bins, and setting up scams on the Internet to get the numbers they needed. Before the owners of the real IDs knew it, the boys could take them for thousands. When the cards were shut down, the boys dumped them and moved on to the next victim. Each package had a shelf life and Blue was always aware that the clock was ticking. He'd settled his bill on the Aston Martin with cash and dumped the ID Package he'd used for the deposit into the hands of a homeless man on the corner of Hollywood and Vine, who in gratitude, gave him a lapel pin of Marilyn Monroe.

217

Blue walked back from the bluff he was standing on and leaned against his new car, a late model, black Shelby Mustang. Being liquid is a beautiful thing, he thought. Cash is definitely king, especially at a used car lot. Blue lit up a small cigar and wondered what the boys in Folsom would think if they could see him now, with the whole world spread out before him, people and places to see. All there, like his father used to say, "ready to be taken." And take was what Blue planned to do. Once he'd made it back to Mick's hole and collected his gift, he planned on putting some things into action.

In a moment of clarity, the night before, while stuffing a hundred-dollar bill into the G-sting of a redheaded stripper, with a dragon tattoo on her ass, Blue realized he didn't need Mick or anybody's help at all. That he didn't have to give money to Mick to square things. Or help Mick get away with Spire's ex. Blue didn't owe anybody anything. It pissed Blue off that he'd ever considered helping Mick. Especially with all the shit Mick was involved with. Blue could only rack up his actions to some fucked-up sentimentality he had toward Maryland from back in the day, that, and extreme curiosity at seeing her boy Mick, whom he had heard so much about in Group.

Blue didn't need anybody. Not one fucking person. But Maryland and Mick's sickness could help him. Blue's goal when he got out of Folsom was to get liquid and square things with Spire. He'd accomplished one of those goals, and with the help of Mick and Maryland he would accomplish the other one and lay the blame right at their feet.

Spire's ex was the perfect thing to bait Spire with and Mick's crazy hole the perfect place to set the trap. When the cops found Spire's body down Mick's rabbit hole, Blue would be in the clear, case closed. There would be nothing between Blue and the border but a little bit of desert and some good times. Blue was angry that he'd ever considered paying Mick some of his hard-earned cash, just for tapping that little twat with a pickup truck. Mick was lucky Blue didn't have his way with her, all his ways. But that could still happen. The whole situation could be very useful to Blue. After a night of fun and relaxation, he saw it all clearly now. Blue took a deep hit from his cigar, feeling the cold of the desert night vanishing with the sunrise. Mick had dug himself a hole all right,

218

thought Blue, one he'd never get out of.

Blue moved his eyes from the sunrise as he heard a noise coming from the back of the Mustang. He walked to the back of the car. The noise was coming from the trunk, soft and muffled. Blue stared at the trunk as he pulled a pair of latex gloves from his pocket and put them on with a tight snap. He took the car keys from his pocket and popped the trunk, which opened slowly, revealing a naked, redhead girl, with a dragon tattoo on her ass.

The girl was lying on a sheet of plastic, gagged and blindfolded with her hands bound behind her back. Blue reached into the trunk grabbing the girl's arms and lifting her effortlessly out. The girl, crying through her blindfold, put her feet shakily into the dirt of the bluff, standing, with the help of Blue.

Blue brought his mouth toward the girl's ear, whispering. "I'm going to let you go now, but you have to trust me. Do you trust me?" The girl nodded her head as her sobbing grew. "I'm going to let you walk away. But it's important that you listen to me and do exactly what I say, understand?" The girl nodded again, choking on her fear.

Blue grabbed the girl by her shoulders and turned her until she was facing the cliff. He then stepped back, his gaze taking in her form from head to toe.

"Walk," he said.

The girl, naked and shivering, took a trembling, blind step, toward the cliff, then another. "Keep going," said Blue. The girl stumbled forward toward the rising sun and the hundred-foot drop.

Blue leaned against the car enjoying his cigar, watching as the ground beneath the girl's feet began to quickly run out. His gaze fell onto the girl's ass and her dragon tattoo.

"You know what I always liked about dragons, besides that they breathe fire?" Blue watched, mesmerized, as the girl approached the edge. "They can fly," he said.

Blue counted in his head. The girl had about three steps left. One…two…her next step would be nothing but air. "Stop." Blue said softly. The girl stopped, inches from the drop.

Blue smiled, pleased. "Very good. Now, turn slowly toward my

219

voice. But make sure it's toward my voice and don't go any further forward."

The girl, gasping for breath, standing bound and naked on the edge of the cliff, did exactly as she was told. Her bare feet, twisting in the soft dirt of the bluff, without moving forward, until she was facing Blue.

"Very good," Blue said. "Now walk toward me and don't stop until I tell you to." The girl did as she was told walking back toward the car and Blue. "Keep going, you're doing fine." The girl stumbled, stepping gingerly, the ground growing rockier beneath her bare feet as she moved ever so slowly past Blue.

"I want you to know," Blue said as the girl passed by, "I had a wonderful time last night." The girl gasped for breath between her sobs as she kept putting one foot in front of the other.

"Don't stop, now, keep going. You'll be just fine," Blue said as he pulled his latex gloves off and shut the trunk of the car. Blue watched as the girl headed slowly out into the desert. "Keep going," Blue said as he opened the door to the car and climbed inside. He took one last look at the beautiful girl, lit by the rays of the rising sun, heading out into the miles and miles of nothing but miles and miles, before he put the car into gear and drove away.

SIXTY-TWO

I woke up to find a gun pointed at me. The gun, large and silver, was held in the steady hand of a six-year-old boy dressed in a cowboy outfit. The boy had the gun pointed at me through the driver side window of my rent-a-car. "Bang! Bang!" the boy screamed, before turning and running across the street toward the shelter of a treehouse, next door to Maryland Sharp's. I rubbed the sleep from my eyes and tried to sit up as I watched the boy climb the ladder of the treehouse, before turning and firing off a couple more shots at me for good measure. My body was cramped and my left leg was asleep. I put the cold cup of coffee, still clenched in my hand, down on the dash as I noticed how high the sun was in the sky and that Maryland's black BMW was gone. I looked at my watch. It was nearly noon.

I opened the door to the car and stepped outside into the sunshine trying to stretch my cramped body back into shape. I'd been deep asleep. I'd missed Maryland leaving, and whatever else, if anything, had happened. Apparently, the coffee had not been enough to override my body's exhaustion. Time, eventually catches up and shuts you down. I'd learned that over the years. One, or a hundred-one coffees, it didn't matter, when it was time, it was time.

I pulled my cell phone from my pocket. I'd missed five calls, three from Dolen, one from Dan, and one from Kansas. I'd had the ringer off on my phone and apparently the vibration had not been enough to wake me. I hit the voicemail button and raised the phone to my ear as I stared at Maryland Sharp's empty driveway. I lit a cigarette, though I knew I shouldn't, and lowered the phone from my ear. Dolen and Dan wanted to meet me for a late lunch at two. Kansas wanted to be, well, Kansas. She

221

was there for me. I had to admit, that felt good.

I took a long hit from my cigarette as I looked around. Maybe I should have tried a pint of Jack to stay awake and not a coffee. Probably not. I smirked at my cigarette with sudden disgust, before throwing it on the ground and stepping on it. Breakfast was over. I ran my hands through my hair, slipped on my sunglasses, and headed across the street.

From the look of things, Maryland's house was empty. But it was hard to tell in the daylight. I stepped up onto the sidewalk and smiled at the boy in the treehouse next door. I waved at him. It was good cover for any of the neighbors, or someone in the house, checking me out. Just a friendly friend of the neighbors, that's all I was. There was a fence around the neighbor's house, but not Maryland's. Her house had a few trees and a garden with a small path marked with flat stones running along the neighbor's fence toward the rear. I stepped up onto the path of stones as my young cowboy friend eyed me from above. I raised my hands, as if giving up, as I walked slowly backwards along the path.

The path led to a bench overlooking a canyon with a beautiful view of Hollywood below. The city looked soft from up here, with the blue, cloudless sky above it. It looked angelic. The load-bearing wall of the "City of Angles." Soft, it was not, glittering and hard as a diamond and just as impenetrable. It was littered with the souls of the "what ifs and could haves," the dreamers, who if they had made it would have been called Stars. Hollywoodland is what the housing developers first named it. That's what it was, a land. A land far away from the rest of the country, the rest of the world, inhabited by different creatures, living different lives. If it all broke down they had the city, the sunshine, the beach, and the mountains. Not a bad place to live a broken dream. You'd be hard-pressed to find one person who came from somewhere else, which was just about everyone, to say they regretted doing it. There was no losing in this city, just adjusting of expectations. Soft, it was not. But where else in the world could you be more of who you could be, just by trying?

I took in my surroundings while thoughts of Hollywoodland flittered through my mind. The windows on Maryland's house, though covered with closed plantation shutters on the front, were uncovered in the back, in order to take in the view. I slid behind the branches and the cover of an orange tree, making my way toward the back of the house. I saw no cameras, wires, or any other signs of surveillance on the property.

Now out of sight from the neighbors and their cowboy kid, I concentrated on spotting any movement from inside Maryland's house. Though it was probably all for nothing, I wanted to have a look see, to see what I could see. The garden on the side of the house wrapped around to the rear and a large bay window. One of the panes of the window was open, letting in a soft breeze that rattled a wind chime hanging over the back door. With the shade of the roofs overhanging, taking away the glare on the rear windows, I had a clear view inside. Shelves of albums and books, black leather and chrome furniture, a rack of free weights and a weight bench were all in view along with a desk and computer by the bay window. This wasn't a girl's room. Maryland had a roommate. Question was, was he her husband, boyfriend, or just a guy helping with the rent?

I thought for a moment how easy it would be the reach my hand through the open window, grab the handle, and roll it further open, maybe even enough to squeeze my body through. I paused for a moment. Why was I so fixated on this girl? Because she had visited Anna in the institution, and studied acting like a hundred other people at the Miracle Works Playhouse? I mean, what did I really have on her that I would consider breaking into her house, breaking the law? Nothing, that's what, nothing, but that pesky thing down deep. Like indigestion on my soul, that thing that made me twitchy and wanting of action not thought, nagging and uncomfortable. My gut said roll the window open and go inside, Will. That there was something there, something I had to see. Do it, it told me. I took a deep breath. I knew the feeling all too well, and I knew it could mean trouble.

I stayed for a moment in the shade of the house, listening. There was nothing but the soft sound of the wind chimes. I looked out again at Hollywood and the blue sky above. I watched a lone, white cloud over the city, drifting. It looked soft and billowing, like the ones Stacey used to love. I watched it for a moment, alone, surrounded by the vast emptiness of the sky, before I turned back toward the house and reached my hand through the open window.

The crank on the window turned more smoothly than I had expected.

It slid the vertical windowpane open about nine inches. That was all I needed. Pulling my hip up onto the windowsill, I scrunched down and turned sideways. I put my head through the opening first and then pulled the rest of my body through, ending up inside, just under the desk. I glanced quickly around, no sound or sight of a dog or anyone. Convinced no one was home, at least no one who was not sleeping, I crawled from under the desk and stood up.

I took in my surroundings. I could feel my heart pounding. Breaking and entering seemed to have that effect on me. The room I stood in, sterile and black, led to another room decorated in marked contrast, white and shabby chic. That was Maryland. I looked down at the desk I had just climbed out from under. I picked up a neat stack of bills off the desk. They were addressed to a Mick Carter. I put them back just as I found them and took a step into the other room and stopped. Wait? What the hell was I looking for, exactly? I had to admit, I didn't have a clue. Not a very good plan, but now that I was here, what the hell. In and out, in and out, just a quick look.

I moved into the adjoining room. The room was bright and lit by a large window that took in the view of Hollywood, its walls, lined with shelves of books. To the left of the window was a back door leading outside to a brick patio covered with wrought iron lawn furniture, with yellow cushions. To the left of the door was the dining room and an open kitchen decorated with Mexican tile. The house was clean, decorated nicely, but odd in the contrasts from one room to the next, as if two very different people shared it.

I moved toward the front door and down a hallway to the left. I stopped at the end of the hall, admiring a large tapestry hanging on the wall near an antique vanity and a small dressing room. A large bedroom was off to the left. The tapestry was beautiful, as was the rest of the house. I moved quickly into the bedroom, comfortable casual and neat, with a large king-sized bed covered with a white down comforter. The artwork on the walls looked original, like the tapestry. Bookshelves, like the ones in the living room, lined the wall, their titles speaking to education and intelligence, more than light reading. One bed, one bedroom, Maryland's roommate was more than just that. The bathroom was also nice and clean, showing both male and female products.

I moved out of the bedroom and toward the white vanity. It too looked like the real thing. Someone had some taste, if not some money. I poked my head into the dressing room. Like the two rooms out front, it showed two very different people lived here, one very neat, one, from the look of it Maryland, not so much. My eyes once again found the tapestry. It was haunting in its beauty and obviously very old. I found myself drawn to touch its soft weave. After a moment, I lowered my head. What was I doing here, invading these people's lives? There was nothing to see here, but someone else's life. I thought of Stacey, of the life we had had, of our house, our things. The things that say this is "our" life. The operative word being "our." Suddenly I felt as if I was trespassing, which of course I was, but it was more than that, as if I was violating a life.

I must have been crazy to think that some random girl could have anything to do with abducting and murdering people. What the hell was I doing in this girl's house? I must be out of my mind, desperate and out of my mind. Just because she knew someone in the institution didn't make her involved. Hell, half of L.A. knew someone in an institution. Or they belonged in an institution. Same fucking thing… I rubbed my hands over my face and was overwhelmed with the feeling that I had to get out of the house now. Right now.

I began to move and suddenly stopped, as I spotted a stack of old scripts on the floor of the closet, on Maryland's side. The red cover of one of the script caught my attention, showing the gold letters A.F.G., The Alfred Green Agency. I leaned down and picked up the script titled "All Gone."

I flipped through the pages seeing highlighted sections for the female character, Marla. The pages of the script were the traditional different colors of a "shooting script," one that had been made, or was being made. Near the back of the script I came to the "call sheet." A sheet given out to the actors with their call time, or time that day they needed to be on the set. Included in the sheet were the names of the producers, director, writers, and production people for that day's shoot.

My eyes went right to the name on top of the sheet, to the Executive Producer, Bob Bayloff. Actress, Maryland Sharp, had an 8:00 a.m. call.

She was playing the part of Marla. It was dated four years ago and was for the first day of Principal Photography. I scanned the production departments and names listed on the sheet and suddenly froze. I stood, feeling my heart move into my throat as I stared at the names listed under Wardrobe Department. The first name on the list was Shari Canes. I felt like I was suddenly in a vacuum; the world had gone silent. Shari Canes. Shari Canes? Alfred Green, Bob Bayloff, and Shari Canes all listed on a call sheet with Maryland Sharp. Was it the case of a small world, small town, and even a smaller business, or was it something more?

I tried to process it. Three of the victims involved in the same film as Maryland Sharp? I needed some more time in the house. I began to go through the other scripts in the closet when suddenly, I heard the lock on the front door click open.

I dropped the scripts and glanced down the hall as the front door swung open and a man's paint-stained work boot stepped inside. I turned quickly, moving into the bedroom and pressing my back against the wall, as I heard the front door shut and footsteps clunk down the hall, towards me. The footsteps suddenly stopped. I looked over at the window, on the far side of the bedroom. It was closed. But if I could make it there... The footsteps started again, moving closer. I dove for the bed, sliding underneath it and concealing myself behind the hang of the comforter.

I looked out from under the bed, as the black boots entered the room and stopped just inches away from my face. I held my breath, as the boots pivoted away from me and the mattress sank down, as the man sat on top of the bed. One by one, the boots left my view. The man pulled them off and then dropped them back down onto the floor with a thump. The bed then rattled and sank further as he lay down on it. I couldn't believe it. I was hiding under the bed like a kid. Like I was in a Three Stooges movie, but there was only one stooge, me. Great going, Spire, real topnotch PI work. Break into a house with no plan and get caught there. A white sweatshirt, marked with paint, dropped to the floor near my eyes. The bed rustled again as the man got comfortable. I listened to the soft breathing coming from above me as I closed my eyes and cursed my stupidity.

SIXTY-THREE

Stacey lay in the warm wetness of her own urine. Her burning thirst had returned, yet she could do nothing. Her arms and legs were numb from being tied to the bed for so long. Her eyes, open under the black of her blindfold, danced with images of her and her sister throughout their lives together. She saw the two of them splashing in a plastic pool filled with a garden hose, riding bikes, driving in John Smiley's convertible; Brenda, beaming with happiness, at her wedding to Bill. The images shone upon Stacey's blindfold like movies upon a screen. She and Brenda had talked, through the pain of their imprisonment, for what seemed liked hours. Their words, comforting each other, until the burning thirst and dry cracking of their throats took their voices away.

Yet, the images of their lives together, of happier times, still flickered across the darkness of Stacey's mind. Though she was horrified that Brenda had been taken, that what lay ahead for them was nothing but pain and probably death, in a selfish place held deep within us all, she couldn't help but be relieved that, for the moment, she was no longer alone.

Were they going to die here, sisters to the end, die of thirst and starvation? Maybe, thought Stacey. But maybe she had injured Blue more than she had known? Maybe, even killed him? The thought excited her. If she had nicked an artery, he might have bled to death before he could reach help. She thought of Blue's pickup sliding off the road and into the desert, as he collapsed against the steering wheel. Her cracked lips parted in a smile at the thought. The smile faded quickly though, as she realized that Blue's death might guarantee theirs. That is, unless one of them could break free of their bindings. And what of Blue's partner, and she was convinced, that he had a partner. Who else would have washed and

227

bandaged her? If Blue was dead, what would he do? Would he come back for revenge and kill them, or flee and let the desert do the deed for him? It's not like anyone would find them in this hellhole, thought Stacey. Not ever.

Stacey closed her eyes. She had no more tears. She wished she could just shut down. Hit a switch and turn life off. But she couldn't. She had to lie there in her own urine and feel everything that was pain and helplessness and take it. She listened to her own rhythmic breathing and tried to sleep, tried to separate herself from reality and fall into a state of dreams. Nightmares were not to be feared, she thought. She was living one.

What if she could escape, she thought, letting her mind run away with the fantasy, if suddenly her bindings unraveled and she was free? What would she do? Would she and her sister lie in wait for Blue to come back, ambush, kill him, and then flee with his truck? It was the only thing they could do. Stacey had seen the miles of desert, felt its heat and pain. It was not made for life, just death. Without a vehicle, they would never make it through the desert to the road, or to somewhere or someone who could help them. But could they kill Blue in cold blood? Could she? Yes, she could. The voice that told her so, that rang in her brain, seemed foreign to her. But it was nonetheless, her voice. Not the "her" that entertained Bob and all his guests or pampered herself in the glass house by the sea, or even the one that built a life with Will. This voice belonged to a new Stacey. One that was forged from abduction, rape, imprisonment, and being pushed passed the edge to the dark side where she had come face to face with evil.

They would wait, she and her sister, hidden in the darkness of the cave; there was everything they needed here to survive but freedom. That would come when either Blue or his partner returned. Then they would drive to the nearest town and call the police. But was killing that easy? Was lying in wait and then striking a deadly blow so simple? Taking a man's life? Stacey's eyes flickered beneath her blindfold. She could only pray that she would have the chance to find out.

It was at that moment that there was a burning light, tremendously bright. Stacey blinked, and shook her head violently, as she realized that

228

her blindfold had been ripped off.

Her eyes focused, finding the handsome and horrifying face of Blue smiling down at her.

"Did you miss me?" he quipped.

Blue flicked open the blade of a buck knife and cut the ties to Stacey's hands. He fiddled with a cell phone in his other hand, flipping it over and over.

"I took the liberty of recharging your cell phone. This is your cell phone, isn't it?" Stacy's gaze flicked to the phone, but she said nothing.

"Well, when I tell you to, you're going to call your ex, the wonderful Mr. Will Spire. You're going to call him for help. Tell him, where I tell you to tell him you are, and he can then come save you like the hero he is." Stacey kept her eyes on Blue, but remained silent.

"No? Won't do it? Not ever? No matter what I do to you? I actually believe that, you're very strong," said Blue.

Blue brought the point knife to Stacy's chest.

"But here's the deal," Blue said casually. "If you don't call and tell him exactly where to meet you, no cops of course, just the hero, if you don't do that, then I'm going to put this knife through your sister's heart and cut it out of her chest right in front of you. Then you can hold it, keep it as a souvenir, to remind you of what a wonderful decision you made."

Stacy's eyes filled with tears as Blue folded his knife back up and put it in his pocket.

"Now get cleaned up. We're expecting company."

SIXTY-FOUR

Where the hell was Spire? Dolen and Dan had called him more times than Dolen had gotten laid and they hadn't heard a word. They'd even put an APB out on his car, which had been found in an underground parking garage in the Valley. A look at the security camera's footage showed a casual Spire walking out of the garage thirty-six hours ago and vanishing into a crowd. Dolen was worried. He would flat out admit it. He was fucking worried. Their boy was on the loose with nearly a half a million in cash and killing Spire on the top of his psycho-to-do-list.

Dolen closed his eyes and sighed. He was in the middle of relieving himself. He had to go way too often these days. His prostate was probably the size of his head. He knew he should have it checked out. But to be honest, he didn't like having a man's finger up his ass. Call him old-fashioned, but that was just something that he didn't like. Maybe Spire or Dan did, they'd been actors. They'd probably tried all kinds of stuff. Maybe they'd even had a class in it at that Miracle Works Playhouse. Scene study, cold reading, and a finger up your ass class. If you planned on working in Hollywood, Dolen thought, that class probably came in pretty handy.

Dolen shook himself and zipped up his pants. He hated worrying about Spire. It pissed him off. He'd thought his pissed-off level had reached its maximum about two weeks ago, but it just kept going up. His prostate was the least of his worries. Fuck it. If he was right, and this case was going to kill him, what did it matter?

Dolen stared down at the cactus he'd just pissed on. It was a gnarled, twisted, ugly looking thing. It reminded him of the face of a cop he used to know. If Satan himself had made a plant, that's what it would look like.

230

Everything out here looked like that.

Dolen hated the desert. Not the money desert, with the pools and the palms, but the real desert, like the one he was standing in. Nothing good ever happened out here. Even the plants were fucked up. They knew it was a shit place so they covered themselves with needles and thorns so they could pass on their pain to anything that got near them. Meth labs, dead bodies, and white trash, that's all Dolen had ever found in the desert.

Dolen raised his eyes to the edge of the cliff and the forensic boys taking moldings of the tire tracks there. Oh yeah, and a naked stripper with a dragon tattoo on her ass, half dead, burnt to a bright bubbling red, her feet and body filled with cactus needles. He'd found that, too.

Dolen wiped the sweat from his face with a white handkerchief. Well, he hadn't found her himself, exactly. A trucker had, thirty yards from the black assault of Highway 72, lying motionless. Lucky for the girl, Carrie Pressley was her name, that the trucker had known exactly what to do. Another hour in the desert, the doctor had said, and she'd have been dead.

Carrie Pressley was twenty-four years old, from a small town in Montana. Her Hollywood dream had not included stripping at the Studio Gentlemen's Club, or meeting a man like Blue. But dreams run both ways, good and bad. As bad ones go, they didn't come much worse than a night in a dark canyon with Blue and a naked trek, bound and blindfolded, across a needle-filled desert.

Blue had taken her, like he'd taken many of his other victims, alone, in a dark parking lot, after she'd finished work. He had easily overpowered the 105-pound girl and shoved her into the open trunk of his car. But not before Carrie had seen Blue's face and the type of car he was driving, thought Dolen. Not before she'd seen three letters on the scumbag's license plate.

Dolen walked up toward Dan and the forensic boys. He pulled out his cell phone and tried Spire once again. Spire's phone didn't even ring and went right to voicemail. Dolen slipped the phone back into his pocket as he reached the edge of the cliff. Dan turned toward him.

"Blue bought the car in Hollywood. It's on tape. He paid cash."

"Of course he did," Dolen said. "Compliments of the idiots in Holmby Hills."

"We also have the abduction on tape," Dan replied.

"Great. Few more feet of footage and we can make a home movie," Dolen said as he slid a pinch of Skoal into his mouth. Dan said nothing and Dolen took a deep breath and looked around. "Why out here?"

Dan eyed Dolen, puzzled.

"Why did he drive two hours from the canyon in Hollywood and drop his plaything off here?" Dolen asked.

"I don't know," Dan replied. "Why?"

"Maybe he had something going on out here?"

"Like what? There's nothing out here."

Dolen looked up at the burning sun and at the miles of parched land. "How do we know what's out here? She was out here."

"What are you saying, Joe?"

"I'm saying, it makes no sense that he drove out here to just dump the girl. He could have left her in the canyon tied to a tree. That's his MO. Why take the ride? "

"To throw us off."

"Maybe, but he knows we'd know it was him either way. I don't think he gives a shit that we know. I think he gets off on it. Maybe he had some business out here, somebody to meet."

"Or he could have been passing through?" Dan raised his eyes toward the bluffs in the distance. "Arizona is right past those mountains to the east. All he has to do is make a right turn for a hundred miles and adios, Mexico."

Dolen said nothing. Dan stared at his partner. He had seen this a thousand times. Dolen was in one of his moods.

"Fine, Joe. What are you thinking?"

"I don't think he's going to Mexico. Not yet." Dolen pointed toward the desert. "We head out there."

"What's out there?"

"He is."

"How do you know that?"

Dolen ignored the question and spit another stream of spittle onto a cactus. He watched the spiny, thorny piece of crap glisten in the sun. This one looked like a girl he used to date. It seemed his whole social scene

232

was represented in this fucking wasteland.

"I don't know, Dan," Dolen finally answered. "How does anybody know fucking anything?"

Dolen hoisted his belt up over his gut and stomped up the hill toward their car. Dan lowered his head and sighed, before following his partner.

SIXTY-FIVE

I was in physical pain. My bladder could only take a little more of being stuck under this bed. The guy above me had not been sleeping. I didn't know what the hell he'd been doing all this time. Reading, I think. But he had not slept at all, not gotten up, not left for one minute so I could slip out from under the bed and out of the house. I closed my eyes and tried to think about something else besides the agonizing feeling to relieve myself. I tried to concentrate on the script I had found with the names Bob Bayloff, Alfred Green, and Shari Canes, all connected to it and in a way, to Maryland. I knew it was thin, not proof of abduction or murder, but it was something. Suddenly, the springs of the bed above me creaked and two sock-covered feet swung onto the floor near my face. The man stood up, the mattress rising above me with the release of his weight. Thank, God. Movement.

The man reached down and picked up his paint-stained sweatshirt off the floor. I strained to get a look at him from under the bed, but my view was cut in half. All I could see was the man's torso moving into the bathroom where he stuffed the sweatshirt into an open hamper. His socked feet then returned, moving past me and out of the bedroom to the dressing room beyond.

I slid closer to the end of the bed trying to get a better view and got a glimpse. He was tall, slender with dark hair and dark eyes that sat behind a pair of gold-framed glasses. He stood facing the tapestry on the wall. He reached out, pulling up one corner of the tapestry and revealing a dark wooden door beneath it. He hung the corner of the tapestry from a hook above the door. Reaching into his pocket, he pulled out a set of keys, bringing them toward a large padlock that secured the door. What the hell

234

was this, a painter, with a hidden door? The man found the key he was looking for and rattled it in the lock, until it finally opened. He hung the padlock on another hook on the wall and pulled open the door. He then vanished, stepping into the room, or whatever was beyond the door and out of my sight.

In a flash I was out from under the bed and into the bathroom, the urge to urinate, overwhelming. I fumbled with my zipper. Fuck! I couldn't go in the toilet, too loud and I'd have to flush or he would see it. My only choice, the sink! I leaned over the sink and let go. I thought I would pass out from the pure pleasure of it all and for a brief moment, I didn't care if the man walked in and caught me; the feeling was so incredible. Done, I zipped up and ran some water into the sink when I heard the sound of a door closing. I went quickly to my knees, scrambling back under the bed just in time to watch the socked feet move by me and into the bathroom.

The man paused by the sink. Shit! I hadn't had time to dry the water in the basin. How the hell had I let myself get in this situation? What kind of private investigator had I become? The man stood by the sink for a long moment as I tried to calm my breathing. He then brought his hands slowly down to the faucets, tightening them, as if they'd been leaking and then closed the bathroom door. I shut my eyes in relief as I heard the sound of the shower being turned on and the shower door closing.

I pulled myself from under the bed and moved out of the bedroom and into the dressing room. I stopped by the tapestry listening to the flow of the shower coming from the bathroom. I lifted up the corner of the tapestry, revealing the hidden door and large lock beneath it. I took the lock in my hand. It was heavy, old and formidable. What the hell was going on here? I put my ear to the door and for one brief moment wondered if Stacy was behind it. Only silence met me from the other side. I pulled away from the door, hearing the flow of the shower once again.

This was fucking weird. I guess people were allowed to have hidden doors and secret rooms in their house. But something was off here. The same feeling that made me think something was off with Maryland Sharp. Fuck. I felt like getting a crowbar and stripping the lock right off the door. That was the way to do it. Don't mess with that big metal thing, go right around it and rip it out where it's screwed into the wood of the door. Shit, I wanted to see what was behind there. But I would need a warrant for that and I did not have enough evidence for a judge to serve a search warrant. Then there was the whole problem of how I came up with any evidence I found, by breaking into the house. Not good. I put my ear against the door again. I felt like slamming my fist against it or knocking, to see if anything came back from the other side, but I couldn't take the chance. If I was caught here, that was it, game over. Unfortunately, the answers to what lay beyond the door would have to wait. I turned and moved away quickly, making my way back towards the man's office and climbing out the open window in which I came.

Crouching down, outside the house, I rolled the bay window shut to how I had found it before I entered. Keeping low, and hopefully out of sight of the neighbors and their cowboy kid, I moved behind the cover of the orange tree until I made it to the flat stones of the path. Once there, I stood upright and tried to look casual as I walked down the path toward the sidewalk. I looked over into Maryland's driveway, spotting an old, tan Chevy van, license number 4JUL178. I made a mental note of it as I crossed the street to my car. A secret door and a script with three of our murder victims' names attached to it. Hell, maybe this wasn't such a wild goose chase after all.

SIXTY-SIX

Mick felt odd. The world seemed far away. He had airplane noise in his head. That soft, buzzing sound you can't escape when you're flying. It surrounds you, drowns out the clarity of the world. Mick shook his head as he climbed into his van. He couldn't get rid of it. It made everything slow, dull. Even the leaves on the trees looked less bright. He stared at the pink paint of his and Maryland's house and it looked tan and faded. Mick shut his eyes and shook his head again, but when he opened them everything still looked dull, fading even more to the shades of an old photograph.

Mick put the van in gear and pulled out of the driveway. The shades of the world irritated him. He reached for his snuff container, but knew even before he picked it up that it was empty and he was out of Dexedrine. He lifted the van's ashtray out of its place, on the dash, looking beneath it, to his secret stash. There were two empty pill bottles and no coke. He was out of everything. The airplane noise was getting louder, the gray colors of the world around him bleeding into each other in an annoying celebration of bland.

Mick blasted the air conditioning as he felt the sweat building on his forehead. He wiped the sweat off in a manic motion as he drove down the winding road toward Hollywood below. "Fuck!" he screamed aloud as he tried to focus on the moving lines of the road. He had to see the Beaver. He could hook Mick up, but that old fucker was not answering his phone. A car came up the hill toward Mick, screaming its horn, as Mick crossed over the line and into its lane. The car passed him in a streak of gray, which seemed to float in time, before finally vanishing. The horn, long past, followed Mick, like a slow recording, echoing in his head, as he reached the stop sign at the bottom of the hill.

Mick sat, listening to the rumbling of the old Chevy engine, his breathing shallow and quick. The perspiration running down his neck felt like it was alive and crawling across his skin, just to annoy him. He closed his eyes, trying to calm himself as he thought back to the phone call. Blue had called from the desert. He was there now with Mick's lover and her sister, waiting for him.

Suddenly, there was a distant tickle on the back of Mick's brain. It rose to a voice. The Bender was whispering to him, telling him he wasn't a man, that he was nothing, worse than nothing. That he was as bland and gray and slow as the world around him. That Blue was the real genius; Mick, just a pawn. Mick sat at the vacant stop sign and wondered how he had ever thought he could pull this off. His production was going to fall apart, collapse! He began to shake uncontrollably. But the seed had been sown! Hadn't it? It was perfect. Right? The police knew only of Blue. Mick was just a whisper, a shadow in the night. He was invisible to the men with the tin badges. He was enlightened, brilliant, chosen. Or was he? What was he chosen for? Mick struggled to remember. The pieces of his mind seemed to be slipping away. It was all a black hole now, bottomless and pointless. What had he been thinking? Blue would kill him. Kill him! Or the police would catch him! Mick didn't want to die, he didn't! Maryland would die too and so would his lover, their souls separated forever.

The Bender's voice grew louder, abusing and teasing Mick. Mick felt the sting of tears fill his eyes, as he lowered his forehead to the steering wheel. What had he been thinking? What? Horns blew from three cars back and still Mick didn't move as the Bender's voice became all he heard. Cars pulled around him, their drivers screaming and blowing their horns, but all Mick heard was the deep voice of the Bender calling to him, all he felt was the rough scratching of wool against his skin, all he saw was the darkness of the closet in which he hid. Mick could see his young body trembling, see the thin sliver of light penetrating beneath the closet door. He knew what would happen if the Bender found him. He saw the sliver of light break as the Bender's shoes blocked it out. Mick screamed as the door to the closet flew open and the Bender's hands grabbed him.

Mick's scream turned into the quick wail of a siren. Mick's eyes flew open as he came back to the faded colors of the day and the siren gave another quick burst. Mick looked in the rearview mirror of the van and saw the flashing lights of a police car behind him.

The driver's side of the police car opened and the lone police officer stepped out. Mick listened to the sudden, deafening silence in his head as the officer approached the van. The officer rapped his knuckles against Mick's window. Mick reached down to the window handle of the old van and rolled the window down.

"What seems to be the problem, sir?" asked the officer.

Mick said nothing. The Bender had found him.

"You do realize you're blocking traffic, don't you? Can I see your license and registration, please?"

Mick just stared at the Bender. He knew he was still alive. That he could change forms. That he had been looking for Mick for years. And now, here he was.

The officer gave Mick a moment to respond. He then began to speak, but before he could, Mick pulled a .357 handgun from his back waistband and pulled the trigger. The shot hit the officer in the forehead taking the back of his head off, in a burst of red, as he fell straight back to the pavement.

Mick stared down at the dead officer, blood seeping slowly from the man's open skull, toward a storm drain. It was frustrating having to kill the Bender again, he thought. Mick slid the gun back into his waistband and put his blinker on, checking carefully for traffic both ways, before turning left and continuing down the hill toward Hollywood.

SIXTY-SEVEN

Mick felt a sense of calm wash over him as he crossed over Sunset Boulevard. His breathing was slow and steady again. He was on his way now. He would get clear, sharp. The Beaver lived only a short drive from where Mick had killed the Bender. A few more blocks and he'd be there.

Mick made a left turn down an alley by an old strip mall. He drove past the plastic trash containers and blue recycle bins, looking for the red bandana. He spotted it tied to a chain-link fence and turned the van into the back drive of the house. He parked the van next to an old blue Volkswagen Bug, covered in rust, and a gold '72 Oldsmobile Cutlass Supreme that had seen better days, but still looked pretty sweet. The large driveway looked like a hoarder's paradise, with everything from old machinery, to furniture and children's toys stacked about. A junkyard. Mick shut the large sliding gate to the driveway and locked it. He knocked his knuckles on the back door of the house. Getting no response, he opened the door and went inside.

The interior of the Beaver's house was like a maze. Piles of old boxes and newspapers, stacked taller than Mick, lined the rooms. Mick could hear a TV on in the back and eventually came to what was the junk of the Beaver's living room.

The Beaver sat on his couch, remote in hand. His long gray hair, tied in a ponytail, hung down to the only colorful thing in the room, his tie-dyed T-shirt. His eyes, wide open, stared up at the ceiling through his round spectacles. Mick had seen plenty of dead people and the Beaver was dead.

Mick didn't move for a moment, taking it all in. He went to the Beaver's side and slipped a gold key chain from around the dead man's neck, before moving back toward the front door and out into the junkyard.

In the yard, Mick found the back half of an old car, junk metal, pinned between a broken outboard motor, a massive tractor tire, and a door-less refrigerator. He slipped one of the keys from the Beaver's key chain into the lock of the car's trunk and opened it. He then pulled out the panel, which was covering the bottom of the trunk, revealing an old iron safe, fitted into the compartment where the spare tire used to go. Mick opened the safe with another key from the Beaver's key chain and pulled out an old Army duffle bag, covered with peace signs. He unzipped the bag. It contained every type of drug, bottled or bagged, that Mick could ever want.

Mick quickly rifled through the contents of the bag, finding the familiar, tiny tabs, of Dexedrine. He swallowed three of them and then laid out a line of coke, the size of a rope, on the bumper of the car. He sniffed it up, in three consecutive hits, and immediately felt his mind go sparkly. Mick leaned back against the tractor tire, as the colors of the world came flooding back.

The Bender had twisted him. Turned him inside out. The Bender was good at that. Always had been. But he was dead. Mick had seen the Bender's brains scattered across the road. The Bender thought he could trick Mick. But Mick had seen his round, fat eyes, smelled his sick scent of aftershave and sweet soap.

Mick sniffed the hit of coke up his nose and the world became brighter. How many times would he have to kill the Bender, he wondered? No matter, as many times as it took, he thought.

Mick looked around. He felt good; he was coming back to himself. His brain was unwinding. He was becoming clearer by the second. He laid another line out on the bumper and hit it up, his head snapping back as he finished it. He stood up and listened as suddenly the buzz of the world got turned up ten notches and the Dexedrine hit him with a rush of brilliance.

Mick grabbed the giant tractor tire, steadying himself. He looked down at his palms and they flowed with color and deep lines of knowledge. He tried to swallow, but his throat was too dry. A beer would be good right about now, he thought. He reached down and slung the bag of drugs over his shoulder and headed back inside to see the Beaver.

Mick sat across from the Beaver, on a stack of old boxes, drinking a can of PBR. He was clear, sharp as the blade of a knife. There wasn't a mark on the Beaver. Looks like the "summer of love" had finally caught up with the old hippy, thought Mick. He downed his beer and threw the can onto the floor, with the rest of the Beaver's junk.

Mick had been thinking now, with a mind connected. Connected to all about, to all that was here and all that would ever be here, to time and space itself. He had been careless, killing the Bender out in the open. His mind had been twisted by the voice of the Bender in his head, by his lack of clarity. He had backslid to a time when he wasn't the man he was today. A frightened time, in which he was not in control, he was not the director of his own destiny, his own production. He had been weak, weak and careless. But no longer.

Mick opened the duffle bag, transferring the majority of drugs inside, to the plastic bag by his feet. He zipped up what drugs were left into the duffle bag, and stuffed the bag under the couch next to the Beaver. He then took the gold key chain and slipped it back around the Beaver's neck, while grabbing a set of car keys off the coffee table.

It was not like him to kill without a plan. To possibly be seen, to be careless. But sometimes you have to take the shot, he thought. Sometimes your back is against the wall. Sometimes there is no other choice. Mick made a promise to himself, long ago, that he would kill the Bender on sight, in any life, in any time, on any plane of existence. And he had.

Mick walked over to the TV that was still on, and turned up the volume. A man was on the screen, trying to convince people how good his adult diapers were. Well, at least the Beaver didn't ever have to worry about that now. He'd made it as far as he was going to go in this life and would never have to feel the humiliation of an adult diaper being slipped over his wrinkled, skinny ass. A victory for any man, Mick thought.

Mick moved next to the Beaver. He took the remote from his hand and placed it on the table. He then slipped from his back waistband the .357 handgun he'd killed the Bender with, and lifted the Beaver's right hand, putting the Beaver's index finger on the trigger of the gun. Mick then placed the barrel of the gun against the Beaver's temple and pressed down hard on his finger.

The shot blew a hole in the Beaver's head the size of an orange. Blood, brain matter, and pieces of skull splattered the wall and the couch. The blast pushed the Beaver onto his side, the gun resting in his lap, his finger still on the trigger.

Mick picked up the plastic bag full of drugs and walked out of the house and into the junkyard. He then soaked the interior of his van with paint thinner, before lighting it on fire. He slid the door to the driveway open, and with the bag of drugs in hand, climbed into the Beaver's '72 Cutlass Supreme. He started it with a rumble as he watched the van slowly burn. He spun the Cutlass around, past the piles of junk, moving through the gate. Escaping, before the heat and flames of the fire reached the gas tank of the van, leaving a dead Beaver to take the rap for killing a cop, who was really nothing more than the Bender in disguise.

SIXTY-EIGHT

Anna had seen a leprechaun once. It lived in the woods behind her house in Connecticut. She had been eight years old and out walking with her father. She saw it hunched down in a patch of briers, watching them pass by. He had shoes on that turned up at the toes, knickers, and a torn coat. His face was ugly, his eyes, large and yellow. He scampered from brier to brier, following their path, keeping an eye on them. Anna remembers holding her father's hand tightly and being unable to speak. He didn't look anything like the leprechauns she'd seen in picture books. He had large teeth and claw-like fingers and Anna had wondered, at the time, if leprechauns ate little children. She was sure that they did. The creature finally stopped following them, as her father and she continued down the path. She knew why he had stopped, why he had frozen like a statue. He was protecting his pot of gold, and he would never let himself get too far away from it, ever. That's what having lots of money does to a person Anna had thought. It makes you frozen, little and ugly and willing to eat children.

Anna sat up in her bed, in the institution, and adjusted the pillow behind her back. Everyone, she thought, was looking for their own pot of gold. That's what life was about, finding it and keeping it. To some it was money, others family, love, religion, success at work, or all of the above. Or like the handsome PI sitting across from her, information.

Anna stared at the private investigator. Will Spire was his name. He sat in a stiff wooden chair, smiling. His smile hadn't changed in five minutes. It was as if Anna had paused that TV show he used to be on, while she'd gotten up and made herself some popcorn. It was weird how he could hold it like that. He looked like he was cut out of a magazine. It

244

seemed to her that he should be the one locked up in this place.

He had come back to see her, he had said, because he'd wanted to know more about Maryland. But that was Anna's pot of gold, Anna's secret. The crazy people, who did not believe in God, who didn't believe in the wonder of the world or the afterlife, who had never seen a leprechaun, or a fairy, or even a sprite flittering about in the leaves above, had locked her up in here. They had taken everything away from Anna— her freedom, her youth, her time with others, her life. All Anna had to hold on to, all she had left that was truly hers, were her secrets.

Maryland was her friend. She too had seen creatures others couldn't, when she was young. She had called them her "imaginary friends," but Anna knew they weren't imaginary at all but real. She would never betray Maryland because Maryland had never judged Anna.

But others had. They didn't understand why Anna had killed her family. They acted as if Anna had had some choice in the matter. As if an intelligent girl, like herself, would not recognize the voice of God when He spoke to her and do what He told her to do. The crazy people saw things only on their terms and from their perspective. Their frightened minds could not grasp the fact that the Universe was a much more complex place than their petty riddles and rules implied. Right and wrong was not up to them, but up to God. He was the only one that understood the Master Plan. He was the judge. He was the boss of everyone.

It was not the first time that God had done his bidding, through a young girl, who could hear His voice. Joan of Arc, who was now a Saint, was younger than Anna, when she heard the voice of God. She had led an army to kill thousands for Him. She, like Anna, knew who was boss.

The crazy people didn't like that. They didn't like that they weren't in charge. Anna understood this and so did Maryland. They had talked about this topic for hours, on many occasions. Maryland was very bright. There was nothing she could not conceive of or not understand. Maryland knew that everything came down to a matter of faith.

Faith, Anna once read, was the belief in what you could not understand. The belief that if you stepped out on a limb to do God's work, the limb, though it appeared thin and brittle, would not break, because He would not let it. The crazy people knew nothing of the natural world, of

God's work. They only knew what they wanted to know.

God would always take care of Anna, for she had done His bidding. The crazy people made you pay a high price for this though, at least in this life. They had burned Joan of Arc at the stake, before making her a Saint. That was so them. And they had locked Anna up forever. But she was not alone. He spoke to her every day in many ways. It wasn't that bad, being locked up with God for the rest of your life. And she knew she would have a special place with Him in the next one, for He had told her so. But He knew she was lonely in this place. He knew she was still a young woman with human needs and desires. He knew all. So today He had sent her a visitor.

Anna's eyes moved across the room to the form of the PI. He was very good looking. She seldom was alone with a man. It stirred her. She would not give him what he wanted, her secrets on Maryland. But she liked having him here. Anna got up from her bed and grabbed the back of a stiff wooden chair and dragged it, screeching, across the floor to the corner of the room. She sat down in the chair, across from the PI, her back to the camera that monitored her, mounted on the wall.

Slowly, she spread her legs, giving the PI a good view beneath her gown. She had no panties on, she never did. She put her hand down between her legs and slowly began to touch herself. The PI didn't flinch. He was talking to her, but she didn't hear the words. She was excited and wet and moved her hand faster, her deed hidden from the view of the camera.

She kept her eyes on the PI. It had been so long since she had been with a man. Her excitement built, as she imagined he was touching her, moving within her, taking her right there. The thought aroused her. She wanted to make it last, to have him do to her everything she had never done, to be with him forever. She could feel her desire sweep her away, back to being human, to being a woman, and for a brief moment, she felt free. Free from this place, from its bars and locked doors, its needles and doctors, from her past. She could see everything about him now as she lost herself in his eyes. She had learned, in the institution, to come soft and quiet, but as she did, she heard a deep moan escape her lips, as her legs trembled with the release of her orgasm. Anna gasped for breath as

246

she watched the PI, who had stopped talking. After a moment, her legs stopped quivering and she leaned her head back, the warmth and satisfaction of her climax washing over her.

Finally, she pulled her eyes from his, bringing her gaze to the swaying leaves outside her window. She watched them flicker in the wind, like so many disturbed creatures, before she pressed her gown into the moistness between her legs and closed her eyes.

SIXTY-NINE

I was surprised by Anna's behavior, but not shocked. I had seen a lot in my years as a PI. Behavior targeted to gain control of a situation, to shake, or throw a person off. I had seen people defecate, masturbate, self-mutilate, all in an attempt to deflect questioning or gain the upper hand. Though I had not seen this particular behavior in a woman before, I had seen it. But not this or anything else Anna Burnside wanted to throw at me would deter me from seeking the answers I wanted.

I was drawn back to the institution, after my self-imprisonment at Maryland Sharp's. After recharging my dead cell phone, I had returned Dolen and Dan's hundred plus phone calls, realizing, while I was hunkered under Maryland's bed, that they would be wondering what had happened to me. Dolen had told me of Blue's antics in the desert and the condition of his poor victim. On a hunch, Dolen had convinced Dan to head out onto the main road, farther into the desert, the tracks of Blue's car seeming to lead in that direction.

I told them I had been working a lead, but left out the part of breaking and entering, hiding under the bed, and peeing in the sink. No one with a badge needed to know that. Dolen thought I hadn't called because I'd left my phone at home, and the barrage of obscenities directed at me that followed nearly wore out my newly charged battery. Once he had exhausted himself, I told him that it was nice to know that he cared, in which he replied, "Fuck you, Spire!" and hung up.

After finding the script and having seen the secret door at Maryland's, all, of course, that I'd kept to myself, having discovered them illegally, I had done some quick checking. Maryland, at one point, had been a client of Alfred Green's and he had been responsible for securing her the small

248

role of Marla in the film, "All Gone." As for Shari Canes, she and her wardrobe team had been used on almost all of Bob Bayloff's films. Maryland, herself, was an actress, who had graduated from Boston College and had no police record. Besides that, I had found extremely little information on her. There was even less information on her boyfriend, Mick Carter, but I had been able to secure a copy of his California driver's license photo. He also had no police record. As for the tan van in the driveway, I was still waiting on the DMV report to see if it was registered to him; besides that, nothing. The only other lead I had was that Maryland had been a regular visitor of Anna Burnside in the institution. So here I was. Anna had not answered any of my questions. In fact, the former millionaire debutant had not made a sound, until her breathless moan at the end of her masturbation stunt. Though her behavior was incredibly dysfunctional, it had been less disturbing for me than mutilation or defecation, and perhaps I could use the inappropriate intimacy to my advantage.

"That was nice," I said softly, Anna's eyes gazing out the window. "I could feel you."

Anna brought her eyes slowly from the window to me. Her gaze was penetrating, though she remained silent. I said nothing in return, but held her eyes with mine.

After a long moment, she finally spoke. "Do you think I'm stupid?"

"On the contrary, I think you are incredibly intelligent and beautiful."

"Do you think, because you watched me get off, that I'm going to tell you anything about my friend?"

"I think, because I watched you get off, that I don't care anymore about your friend." I kept my eyes on hers. "Would you like me to visit you again? Perhaps, next time, I could sit with my back to the camera and you could watch."

I could see Anna's chest rise at the thought of this. She shuffled in her seat and pressed her gown down further into her crotch. She lowered her eyes for a long moment and when she raised them, her voice was but a whisper. "Would you do that?"

I nodded slowly, never taking my gaze from hers. "Would you like that?"

I could see her breathing deepen as she nodded her head.

"Then it's a date," I said.

Anna let out a small giggle as she squirmed in her seat. Her giggle turned to a laugh and she bit down on her lip, trying to control herself. "Maryland wouldn't believe it, all this. They always had your show on in the recreation room."

I stopped breathing for a moment. I replied in the most casual way I could. "Did you watch it with her?"

"No, they released her before…" Anna's smile suddenly faded, her eyes darkened. She turned her gaze to the window.

She had slipped up and she knew it. I could feel the hair on my arms rise. Maryland used to be in this institution with Anna, not as a guest, but a patient? I tried to smile my sweetest smile.

"Maryland used to be in here with you?" I asked.

There was no answer from Anna; she kept her eyes on the flickering leaves outside the window. Finally she spoke.

"Do you believe in God?"

"Yes," I replied.

"Have you ever seen a leprechaun?"

"A leprechaun? No. I thought I saw Santa Claus once, but it turned out to be my Uncle Bob."

"You're making fun of me," Anna replied still looking out the window.

"No. I'm sorry. I'm not," I said. "Why? Have you seen a leprechaun?"

"Yes. He was very ugly. I thought he was going to bite me. He thought we were after his pot of gold. But we weren't."

Anna turned toward me. "You know there is nothing worse than stealing someone's pot of gold?"

"No, I didn't know…"

Before I could finish, Anna bolted from her chair and slammed into me. I flew back, my head hitting hard against the tile floor, as Anna punched and clawed at me, while screeching about God and her pot of gold. I tried to defend myself as best I could as I heard an alarm go off. I blocked Anna's blows with my forearms, her hair hanging down wildly

250

across her manic eyes, all semblance of the Rhodes Scholar-debutant gone. Suddenly, the door to Anna's room flew open and three men in white grabbed Anna, as her mouth found my left hand and she bit down hard. I was surprised by my scream as the pain shot up my arm and smashed into by brain. Anna let go as the men in white pulled her away and she laughed hysterically, her blood-stained lips blowing me kisses as they dragged her from the room.

SEVENTY

Blue had to get away from Mick's hole in the ground. He was tired of waiting for him to show up. When Mick finally arrived, he could wait for him. Blue slowed his Mustang down, turning it off the main road that cut through the desert and into the parking lot of a small wooden store with a couple of gas pumps out front. He drove past the pumps and parked the car in front of the Oasis Bar, next door. He stepped out of the car and was immediately met with the heat of the Santa Anas. The dry, hot winds were blowing hard, and it felt to Blue as if he'd just stepped into a blast furnace. He took a puff off the nub of his cigar as he looked around at the nothingness. A hole in the middle of nothing, that's what Mick's cave was. What a perfect place to torture someone, he thought. Someone named Will Spire. To finally get the satisfaction he'd been dreaming about for years.

Blue threw his cigar into the dirt of the parking lot and stepped on it. Though he wasn't a big drinker, he had a hankering for some whiskey. He'd like a little taste before Mick showed up, before he had that twat, Stacey, put a call into Spire. Before the fun and games began. He wanted Mick around when Stacey told Spire where to save her. Which Blue had decided was an old box canyon a couple miles from the cave, after, when Mick's usefulness was done, he'd kill Mick and dump his body down the same mineshaft as Spire's. Then, having kept the two promises he'd made to himself when he got out of Folsom, of getting liquid and killing Spire, he'd cross the border with a bag full of cash and two sweet pieces of pussy to go. The world, like his dad had said, his for the taking.

Blue pulled open the old wood door of the Oasis and stepped inside. He was met with the type of darkness that knew no time, the type that

252

made a man comfortable drinking day or night. Blue bellied up to the bar. The bartender, a big man with a beard and a leather vest marked with the colors of his biker gang, looked at Blue with some distaste. Must be his Armani blazer and dress shirt beneath, thought Blue, or maybe, it was his pretty, clean-shaven face.

"Whiskey, rocks," Blue said.

The big man looked Blue over. "You want a little paper umbrella in that?"

Blue sensed the eyes of the other bikers in the bar on him. He felt like breaking the beer bottle next to him in half and shoving it into the man's throat. Instead, he just smiled and took off his blazer. His sleeves on his dress shirt were rolled up. He locked his fingers together and laid his arms on the bar.

"Yeah," Blue said, "then we could pretend we were on a date."

The bartender's eyes caught the tattoo on Blue's right forearm. It was some good work, though you could still tell it was a prison tattoo. It was the tattoo of the Aryan Brotherhood. The look on the bartender's faced changed. He pulled out a bottle of whisky and poured Blue a glass. He slid the glass across the bar to Blue.

"It's on the house, brother," said the bartender. Blue flashed a fake smile and raised his glass to the man. The bartender nodded at Blue in a show of respect, before he turned and moved away.

Blue took a sip of his free whiskey and spun his stool around eyeing the pool tables nearby. The whiskey had a pleasurable burn and a woody taste to it and Blue liked it. A waitress, slim and built on top with the help of some major technology, moved next to Blue, waiting for her order. She looked over at Blue, which, Blue knew, was why she was really there, and smiled large. Blue flashed his pretty pearly whites right back at her.

"You having a good time?" asked the waitress as she pushed her hair off her forehead.

"Always," Blue replied. "How about you?"

The waitress loaded up her tray with her order. She gave Blue a long look up and down. "Hoping it gets better later," she said, as she gave Blue a wink and moved away.

Blue watched the twitch of the waitress's ass as she walked away and he took another sip of whiskey. Fucking woman, they were all the same. Another time, another place, she'd have a better time all right. She'd be in the trunk of his car before she knew what hit her. But Blue had to be good. He had things to do and he didn't want to attract attention. He had left the sisters back in the cave. They had cleaned themselves up and kept him company while he had waited for Mick. When Mick didn't show, Blue'd stuffed a rag, drenched with chloroform, into their faces and locked them back up, unconscious. He had been tempted to fuck both of them, but he'd reminded himself not to rock the boat. Not with Mick on the way and him needing Stacey's help to get Spire to the box canyon. He had a plan and he had to stick to it. Anyway, there would be plenty of time for that later, he thought, when Mick was out of the way.

Blue would try and make sure Spire came to the canyon alone. Stacey could convince him to do that, come alone, no cops, or he'd find nothing but her body. Spire, the wannabe hero, would do it, his arrogance and affection for his ex putting him right where Blue wanted him. Once there, it would be easy for Blue to nail Spire with a crippling shot, from behind the cover of one of the many large boulders that marked the canyon, and then drag him back to Mick's hole, where the fun could begin.

Blue had grown up hunting with his dad, waiting hours in countless, frozen deer blinds, since the age of six, to get one kill shot. One. It was about the only thing Blue had ever done that put a smile on his dad's face. If Spire was dumb enough to bring the cops, Blue could hit him with a perfectly placed kill shot from over a hundred yards away before slipping out of the canyon. What the fuck, thought Blue, it wouldn't be as much fun as taking his time with Spire, but dead is dead. Either way, he'd have his revenge.

Of course, Stacey would never be in the canyon. Mick wouldn't go for that. But the hook would be set and Spire would show, like all heroes do. Blue had already found his spot, tracked his exit out of the canyon on foot and back underground to the caverns of the mine. He would meet Spire near sunset. If things went south and he had to take Spire out, Blue'd have the cover of darkness on his side. Mick might come in handy too, if the shit hit the fan, but one thing was for sure, Blue was done with him. Mick was out of control, a loose end that had to be tied. He was a time bomb waiting to go off and take Blue with him. One way or the other, Blue knew, he had to kill Mick. As for Maryland, his old friend, Blue would do what the institution and group therapy never could—end Maryland and Mick's twisted relationship for good.

Blue downed the rest of his whiskey as the technology-endowed waitress slid by him again, carrying another order. Christ, he thought, you couldn't jiggle those tits with a jackhammer. Blue sucked the whiskey off the last of his ice cubes and wondered how she ever laid on her stomach without hurting herself. He wished he hadn't been so busy; she looked like a good time. Oh well. Blue pulled his gaze from the waitress and stood up. He moved toward one of the pool tables and a biker he had been watching.

The guy was bent over his cue, lining up his last shot. He unleashed a sweet stroke, banking the 8-ball off the bumpers, twice, before dropping it into the corner pocket. He lifted his head up, eyeing Blue. Blue pulled a hundred-dollar bill out of his gold money clip and laid it on top of a stack of quarters that marked the next game. The shooter stood tall. He leaned on his cue, staring at Blue.

"You up for it?" Blue asked.

The biker didn't seem to like Blue any more than the bartender had. Blue watched as the man pulled out a hundred-dollar bill of his own and laid it on top of Blue's.

"Am I up for it? I'm up as far as you got your head up your ass. Is that up enough?"

Blue let out a loud laugh as he grabbed a cue from the wall and started to chalk it up. "Yeah, but since you brought my ass into it, let's make it two hundred."

Blue laid another hundred on the table as he blew the chalk off the tip of his cue. The biker hesitated, then matched Blue's bill. Blue laughed even louder than before and smiled his million-dollar smile.

SEVENTY-ONE

I sat in the office of Dr. Stewart Jackson, who oversaw the care of Anna, and those like her, in the institution. He had an aristocratic air about him, thick gray hair, and a face that looked like it was formed in a waffle press. Each deep crease, like the lines in the trunk of an old tree, holding the untold story of a year gone by, of the pain and stress that came with running an institution like this for over thirty years. My hand hurt like hell and had required six stitches and a tetanus shot, my non-belief in leprechauns and having tricked Anna into revealing that Maryland Sharp had once been a patient here, having cost me dearly. But it was more than worth it. I was on to something and I knew it. Dr. Jackson, having done some fine work stitching me up, applied a sterile bandage to my hand. He looked up and smiled, pleased with his doctoring. His smile was met with my glare.

"So, you're not going to tell me?" I asked.

"It is not that I'm not going to tell you, Mr. Spire. It is the fact that I am prohibited by law to tell you," he replied. "Maryland Sharp was a patient here, her committal was court-ordered and her records have been sealed by that court, that, I can tell you. As for the primary reason she was committed, as you well know, that is protected by doctor–patient confidentiality. I suggest, that if you want that information for your investigation, you get an order from the court to unseal her records and so order me relieved of that protection, sir."

I hated how doctors talked. They were one flawed gene away from being lawyers. I leaned back in my chair and felt like pulling an Anna on the old guy, biting his hand so hard that he screamed and told me everything I wanted to know.

I remembered that we had gotten, thanks to Frick and Frack, a limited federal warrant for the release of a list of patients that had been in Group with Blue. Maryland Sharp had not been on my radar at the time and I couldn't remember now if her name was on the list of fifty-plus patients. I had last seen that list at the yellow-draped apartment of Kansas, while recovering from the bathroom beating I'd taken from Luke and Tiny Tim. Where was the list now?

The doctor moved from his examination table, where he had stitched me up, and sat down behind his desk in a massive, leather chair.

"Is there any way, Doctor, that you could shed some light on what year Maryland Sharp was here and if that coincided with the time Blue...or should I say... Bud Williams was here?"

"I'm sorry, Mr. Spire, but I have told you all that I can."

"What about group therapy?" I asked.

"What about it?"

"Was that part of her treatment?"

The doctor let out a deep sigh of exasperation as he rocked back and forth in his throne of a chair.

"Without revealing specifics about Ms. Sharp's case, I can say that at one point, ninety percent of our patients participate in Group. I am sorry again about your hand, Mr. Spire. It is the reason all visitors are asked to sign a waiver before being allowed to visit unsupervised. Our patients can be, as you found out, unpredictable. Make sure you take the antibiotics I prescribed and I will be happy to remove the stitches in ten days. Or you can have your primary physician attend to it." Dr. Jackson stood up, motioning politely toward the office door.

I realized, that without a court order, I was getting nothing more from Dr. Jackson. This was not his first rodeo. I stood, said my good-byes, and headed out the doctor's door toward the entrance of the institution.

Out in the sunshine of the L.A. day I felt renewed. This was a big break. The pieces of this puzzle seemed more and more to be glued together around two people, Blue and Maryland. I knew that Maryland had studied at the Miracle Works Playhouse; at the same time, Blue was hanging around posing as a big-time producer, so it was not unlikely that they'd met. How well did Maryland know Blue, if at all, I had no idea.

But if her name popped up on the list of patients that had had group therapy with Blue, or if her time in the institution coincided with his, well, that put a whole different spin on things.

And then there was her boyfriend, Mick Carter, and his secret door. Not to mention the connections I had established, though illegally, between Maryland Sharp, Bob Bayloff, Alfred Green, and Shari Canes, all having had possible contact with each other on the film "All Gone." I had more questions than answers, but I was holding a few strings, tying people and places together. Let's hope the strings could lead me to a place where I could solve this case, before Dolen and Dan found more needle-filled-girls in the desert, or before it was too late for Stacey and Brenda.

I opened the door of my rental car and climbed in. It was time to get my Vette back. If I remembered correctly, the list of patients in Blue's Group was tucked away in a manila folder under the passenger seat of my car. I'm sure, by most people's standards, my filing system was not up to the standards of a good PI. But by using my car as my office, it guaranteed that I would never have to drive anywhere to pick something up, except this time.

I floored the accelerator of my rental car as I pulled onto the 405 Freeway, heading north over the hill to the Valley. The car barely got up enough speed to keep me from getting crushed by a semi-truck, who refused to move over, as my merging lane ran out. Of all the things in L.A. you could hate, this was on the top of my list, driving these fucking freeways. That is, when you could drive them at all and they weren't just parking lots, leaving you only one more intolerable delay away from occupying a room next to Anna.

I was sure, that of all the ways I could die in this city, this is how it would end for me, in a twisted pile of combustible metal slammed against unmovable cement. The ending of my life, marked with little notice, except to piss off a million or so L.A. drivers whose continuing lives were delayed from wherever they were going, and from whatever they wanted to be doing, by my stupid death. How dare he die while I'm trying to get home! What an asshole!

I finally made my way over to the fast lane of the freeway and settled in at an exhilarating 13 miles per hour. I stared at the brake lights of a red

Ferrari in front of me. I knew that car and model. It had a top speed of 225 mph, only 212 mph faster than we were going now. If he lived in L.A., he'd probably never been out of first gear.

I was feeling good, for the first time in a long time. As good as I could feel under the circumstances. Maryland had been in the institution! Ordered by the court! Why? I needed to find out, to call in every contact I had, from the police department to the courts, to find out why. What had she done? Why were her records sealed?

The Ferrari in front of me kicked it up to 26 mph. It's good the driver had his leather racing gloves on, wouldn't want to lose control at this speed. I saw an opening and swerved into the right lane, my rental car blowing over 30 mph and leaving the half million-dollar Ferrari in the dust. And no gloves were needed.

Through the monotony of the never-ending lanes of cars, my mind came back to Stacey. I looked up through the window of the car into the heavens above and silently asked the powers-that-be for a break. To let the threads be sewn together, to form something that I could hold onto, something that could lead me through the darkness of this case to find the killer, before he killed again, and end this ongoing nightmare once and for all.

SEVENTY-TWO

Dolen downed his bottle of root beer and stared at his cell phone. What a piece of shit. Like half the other crap out in the desert it didn't work, no bars, no reception. That's because they were in the middle of no man's land, where no man, thought Dolen, should fucking be. But Blue was close, he could feel it. Dolen leaned his face down toward the blades of a rattling fan, blowing hot air across the floor of the old country store. He guessed the air conditioning in the store was on, the door and windows were shut, but it sure didn't feel like it. It was hot as hell.

Dolen stood up and wiped the sweat from his brow as he looked out the window at Dan. Dan stood by the gas pumps, filling up the car, gazing out into the desert. Dolen knew Dan was about done with their desert adventure, but Dolen wasn't. He tossed his empty root beer bottle into an old crate filled with recyclables and stepped closer to the window. He looked out at the vast desert. Blue was out there, somewhere. He could feel it. He wasn't in L.A., or across the border. He was out there, a needle, hiding in a barren wasteland.

Dan finished filling the car and headed toward the front door of the store. The door swung open with the ring of a little bell.

"We all set?" asked Dolen.

"Let me grab something to drink, cool down for a minute," Dan replied. Dolen nodded his head. He wasn't sure how much longer he could convince Dan to keep going.

Dolen looked at the old-timer behind the counter. His skin was the color of a red pepper and creased over every inch.

"Excuse me, sir, how far 'til the next town, heading east?"

"Sixty miles." The old-timer's right eye seemed to wander off on its

260

own, making Dolen a bit uncomfortable.

"How about south?" asked Dolen.

"About hundred miles, right before you reach the Salton Sea." The old man's eye quickly slipped back the other way. Dolen couldn't help but stare, fascinated.

"Anything, between here and there?" asked Dan.

"Sure there's something between here and there," said the old man, irritated by Dolen's stare.

"What's that?" asked Dolen.

"The fucking desert," said the old-timer, slamming the cash drawer shut.

This seemed to snap Dolen out of his trance.

"Right. Thanks," Dan said, trying to smile.

Dan stepped up to Dolen. "How long are we going to keep this up, Joe? I'm all for playing hunches, but we got nothing, nowhere to look, nowhere to go. I say we pack it in until we have something firm to go on."

"Like another dead body?" Dolen asked.

"God damn, you're a stubborn son-of a-bitch. I'll give you another fifty miles before we turn around. But you're driving!" Dan pressed his finger into Dolen's chest to further his point.

Dolen watched as Dan slung the front door to the store open, crushing the little bell against the wall. He stomped toward their car and climbed into the passenger side of the vehicle before slamming the door shut.

Dan rarely got riled up, but Dolen seemed to have accomplished it this time. But Dolen didn't care. Blue was close and he knew it. Dolen slipped a couple bucks to the old-timer behind the counter and pulled out an ice cream cone from a freezer near the window. He took off the plastic wrapping and took a bite of the vanilla ice cream covered with chocolate and nuts. What they needed was something they hadn't had in a long time, thought Dolen, a fucking break. Dolen stood by the window for another moment, chewing on the chocolate and nuts, thinking about this before he swung the door open and stepped out into the hot wind of the desert.

Dolen licked at his ice cream cone, which had already begun to melt over his fingers, as he walked toward their car. He looked up at the sign of the Oasis bar next door as a large truck backed out of its parking place in front of the bar and pulled away. Dolen took another bite of his ice cream and froze.

Sitting, parked in front of the bar, was a late model, black Shelby Mustang.

SEVENTY-THREE

Blue rolled up the wad of cash he had made from playing pool with the biker and swung the front door of the Oasis Bar open. He put the cash into his pocket as he left the perpetual darkness of the bar and stepped out into the heat and sunshine of the desert. It took a minute for his eyes to adjust to the brightness of the day, and he stopped for a moment on the covered porch of the bar, before taking the final few steps down to the dirt parking lot and his car. Blue reached into his pocket for his keys as he spotted a fat man, with an ice cream cone, standing in the parking lot next door, staring at him. Blue slipped his car key into the lock on the door and pulled it open, when suddenly, he saw the fat man drop his ice cream cone into the dirt. Blue watched as the man's hand went quickly up under his blazer, reappearing holding a snub-nosed revolver, which he proceeded to point at Blue as he screamed, "Stop! Police!"

In a flash, Blue pulled his own gun from his jacket and the two men fired together. Glass shattered, pelting Blue, as the window and side mirror on his car were hit as he stood his ground and returned fire. The fat man dove for cover behind a parked car as a second cop got out of a car near the gas pumps and opened up on Blue. Blue dove inside the Mustang, slamming the driver's door closed. He reached into the back seat, grabbing the assault rifle, which he had stolen from the house in Holmby Hills, before opening the passenger door and dropping out of the car, taking cover behind it.

He then rose up, firing a barrage at the car parked by the gas pumps. Blue's shots, from the assault rifle, riddled the police car sending glass and metal flying as the cop took cover. Blue then swung the rifle quickly toward the fat cop and let off another long burst, the tires of the car the

263

cop was hiding behind exploding, as the car was shot to pieces. Blue quickly lowered the gun, slipping back into driver's seat of the Mustang and starting its engine. He rested the barrel of the gun on top of the driver's door and fired another barrage as he punched the gas and the cars' tires spun backwards in a cloud of dust.

SEVENTY-FOUR

Dolen's heart was racing, his face covered with grease and oil from the shattered engine of the car he was hiding behind. The crack of the assault rifle was deafening as he heard the tires of the Mustang screech through the gunfire. He was getting away, Dolen thought! He was fucking getting away! Dolen raised up, ignoring the bullets hitting all around him. He seemed in another world, slowed down. He saw Blue as clear as anything he'd seen in his life—the sharp angle of his face, the glint of his blue eyes, the flash of the assault rifle firing out the window as the car pulled backwards.

Dolen steadied himself, laying his reloaded revolver on the roof of the car before opening fire. He saw his first three shots hit the front of the car and next two hit near the door. His sixth, and final shot, found its mark, exploding in a burst of red that splashed up onto the car's windshield. Dolen watched as Blue slumped quickly over to the side before slamming the Mustang into gear and peeling out of the driveway in a cloud of dust. The Mustang hit the black pavement of the desert road, its tires screeching, as it tore away with incredible speed.

Dolen turned and watched the Mustang disappear toward the horizon. His arms felt like they were made of lead, his eyes were watering, his mouth was dry with adrenalin and fear, and he felt like he was going to throw up, but he only had one thought running through his brain, like a broken record. I got him...I got him...I got him... Fear suddenly gripped Dolen as he thought of Dan. He looked over toward their shattered police car and saw Dan walking towards him. Thank God. Thank God, Dolen thought.

"You all right, partner?" Dan screamed.

Dolen nodded his head.

"And you?" Dolen yelled.

He saw Dan return his nod as suddenly Dolen's legs gave out and slid down to the ground. Dolen raised his eyes to Dan's, as Dan reached him.

"He's hit."

Dan was taken back for a moment. "He is?" he replied.

Dolen put his hand out and Dan helped him to his feet. Dolen laid his arms on Dan's shoulders, looking him in the eye.

"I put one in him, partner. I saw the scumbag's blood blow onto his windshield. I think I got him good."

"Well, he won't get far then, will he?" Dan replied.

Dolen shook his head. "No."

Dan broke into a huge smile. Dolen rested his forehead on Dan's chest, exhausted, as Dan gave his partner a big hug.

"You son-of-a-bitch!" Dan yelled, "You stubborn, straight shooting son-of a-bitch!"

SEVENTY-FIVE

The bullet had gone right through Blue. He could see it lodged above the CD player, in the dashboard of the car. Blue slumped against the steering wheel in pain. The round had entered his back, above his left shoulder, and exited below his left collarbone. The burning pain of the wound seared through his brain as he tried to control the Mustang and most of all think, think what to do. The bullet was out, but he had no idea what damage it had done. A hospital was out of the question, but he needed to stop the bleeding and dress the wound. More than anything, he needed a place to hide and time to think. Mick's cavern was the perfect place. Mick could help him. He had a first aid kit and pain pills there. Blue could wait it out below ground, in Mick's hole. If he got worse, Mick could drive him to a country doctor, or even a veterinarian, for help. Blue didn't worry about whoever doctored him up alerting the police, because after they helped him, he'd kill them. He wasn't going back to prison.

Blue leaned back into the driver's seat and let out a scream of anger and pain. He didn't fucking believe this. How the fuck did this happen? Blue shook his head; no way he was going to prison. No matter how many people he had to kill. He was never going back. Blue looked down at his white dress shirt and blazer, soaked with blood. Fuck! He had been so close to the end. To completing his plan, to freedom and the border and a bag full of cash and now this, getting shot by some fat, ice-cream-cone-eating cop, in the middle of the fucking desert! What the fuck!

Blue felt light-headed; his eyes were watery and blurry with pain. They would be looking for him. That was for sure. Mick's hole, he had to make it back to Mick's hole. You couldn't see it from the road and there were multiple exits through the old mine shafts and into the desert. According to Mick, hardly anybody knew about the place, including the locals. Blue tried to clear his head through the pain. He just needed a little time. Just a little, to gain some strength, before slipping across the border and never looking back.

Blue pressed on the brake pedal of the Mustang, slowing it down as he saw the turn-off to the mine. It was nothing but a small dirt road, marked by a boulder shaped like a twisted cross. Blue turned the car onto the dirt road, which looked like a hundred others along the highway. He slowed the Mustang to a crawl, not wanting to raise a dust cloud that could be seen from a distance, as the car bounced slowly along, over a hill, and down toward a small valley and the crumpled buildings of the old mine.

Blue parked the Mustang under the roof of an old shed and out of sight. He turned off the car's engine and slumped over the steering wheel. He could not believe how much pain he was in. He closed his eyes, trying to gain some strength. Finally, he opened the car door, and assault rifle in hand, stepped out. He took a deep breath, trying to gather himself as he spotted Maryland's black BMW parked near the entrance of the mine. Thank God, he thought. Maryland would help him, she or Mick. Whoever was there, they could help. Blue took a step toward the mine as he realized his plans for killing Will Spire, and for that matter, Mick, had changed dramatically. No longer could he trifle with getting revenge and satisfaction. He had to think about only one thing, his survival.

Blue stumbled past Maryland's car and down into the mine. He could hear the faint notes of classical music coming from deep within, as he made his way painfully along and across the ladder Mick had placed over the narrow crevasse that separated the mineshaft from the cavern.

Blue entered the dim light of the cavern and stopped. Mick was sitting in one of his leather chairs, reading, his hands covered with latex gloves. He brought his gaze up from the pages of his book to the bloody figure of Blue.

SEVENTY-SIX

Mick looked at Blue, who was covered in blood. His face was pale, his movie star looks, twisted with pain. He held an AR-15 assault rifle limply in his right hand. Blood ran down Blue's arm and off the barrel of the gun, spotting the dirt floor of the cavern.

"You run into some trouble?" asked Mick, his face showing no hint of emotion.

Blue stumbled toward Mick and placed the barrel of the AR-15 against his chest. "Is that supposed to be fucking funny?" Blue gasped through his pain. "I need some pain pills and for you to patch me up."

Mick didn't move. "Well, if you shoot me in the chest, I won't be able to do that, will I?"

Blue lowered the rifle and slumped down into a leather chair across from Mick. He closed his eyes in pain. "Please…" he whispered.

Mick didn't move. He was clear, sharp. He had brought Blue a gift and could feel it in his pocket. He had purchased it for some serious coin across the border. Blue didn't know it, but Mick was going to make him a star. Blue would have top billing, above everyone else, in Mick's production, especially from the men with the tin badges. Mick was smart enough to know that Blue had had his own plan for him, and it had not been a pleasant one. Mick would not patch Blue up and he would certainly not give him any pain pills. He wanted Blue to stay in the moment, to feel, as all good actors do, everything.

Mick knew, having listened to it on the police scanner resting on the table in front of him, that Blue had shot it out with the police, and that police, at this very moment, were looking for him. Mick also knew that it would only be a matter of time before Blue's trail led them to the mine and the very cavern in which they sat. But instead of that being a bad thing, Mick thought it was wonderful and fit in perfectly with his plan.

Blue opened his eyes and saw that Mick had not moved.

"What the fuck are you doing?" Blue screamed as he stood up, once again raising the rifle towards Mick. "Get me the meds and the fucking medical kit!"

Mick had waited a long time for this moment. Justice is rare in the universe. Mick stood up slowly, slipping his gloved hands casually into the pockets of his pants. He stared at Blue.

"You don't look so good, Blue. You threaten me again with that gun and I'll let you die here."

Blue's eyes twitched back and forth, as if his pained brain was trying to figure things out, find an angle.

"Listen, you freak," Blue finally said. "I want to see Maryland. You understand in there, in that demented fucking mind! You pull her out from wherever you fucking keep her and show her to me NOW!" Blue's scream echoed through the cavern.

Mick took a few steps closer to Blue, until the barrel of Blue's gun was once again against his chest.

"Your call, Blue. Lower the gun. Or we both die in here."

Blue slowly lowered the gun. "Maryland...I want to see Maryland..." Blue's voice trailed off in pain.

"Like you saw her the night before you left the institution?"

Blue looked confused. "What..."

"The night you tied her up and shoved a rag into her mouth? The night you raped her until she passed out from the pain and you still kept at her? The night you left her bleeding and unconscious? Is that how you want to see her? Like that?"

Blue tried to process what was happening, but before he could, Mick grabbed Blue's gift from his pocket, a syringe, and plunged its needle deep into Blue's neck. Blue let out a muffled yell as Mick emptied the contents of the syringe into him.

Immediately, Blue dropped the gun and fell straight back, his head slamming against the dirt floor of the cavern and raising a dust cloud around him.

270

Mick stood over Blue, the syringe still stuck in Blue's neck. Blue's eyes, open, stared up at Mick. Yet, he was unable to move. Mick watched as saliva bubbled from Blue's mouth and down his chin. Mick reached down and pulled the syringe from Blue. The only thing that moved on Blue were his eyes.

"I've just injected you with succinylcholine," said Mick, calmly. "It's a neuromuscular blocker that causes paralysis of the muscles while keeping the patient conscious and breathing. It's used along with anesthesia for certain medical procedures. On its own though, the drug allows the patient, you, to feel everything that happens to them, while remaining paralyzed. The drug also dissipates quickly from human tissue and blood and doesn't show up in most toxicology screenings. Fascinating, no?"

Mick brought the heel of his boot down onto Blue's nose, cracking it like a walnut. Blue let out a guttural groan as blood poured from his nose and filled his mouth. Mick bent down near Blue's bloody face.

"I bet you had plans to kill me, didn't you? Raise your right hand if I'm right. Oh, you can't, can you?"

Mick put a straight right fist into Blue's eye, then another and another and two more. Mick, out of breath, looked at Blue's face, which wasn't pretty anymore.

"You still want to see Maryland?" asked Mick.

Mick looked down at Blue as he slowly undid the belt of his pants. "Because she asked me to give you something, something to make you feel all sweet and cozy inside, like she did, that night you came calling."

Mick flipped Blue onto his stomach, pressing his broken nose into the dirt as he yanked off Blue's pants and underwear. And as he climbed on top of Blue for some payback, Mick wondered how many young girls Blue had done the same to. And as Blue's screams echoed through the cavern, Mick grew more violent, trying to rip the man in half, for what he had done to his Maryland.

SEVENTY-SEVEN

Maryland was on the list. She had had been in group therapy with
Blue during his time in the institution. They had definitely known each
other. The list I recovered from my Vette not only held the names of all
the patients who had attended Group during the time Blue was in the
institution, but it was broken down into smaller, subgroups of five that
met once every two weeks. Maryland Sharp's name was listed right under
Blue's, or Bud Williams, as he was known at the time, in Subgroup
number eight.

I sat in my car, parked in the Calabasas hills, not far from my house,
overlooking the Valley. After returning my rental car and picking up my
Vette from the underground parking garage where I had left it, I had come
here, to one of my favorite spots, to make some calls and see if any of my
contacts could tell me why Maryland Sharp had been institutionalized.
They couldn't. The court order was sealed tight. Maryland's life seemed
to have started the day she entered the institution.

I couldn't get the hidden door at Maryland's out of my mind, or the
call sheet from the film "All Gone." The sheet that linked three of the
murder victims, Bob Bayloff, Alfred Green, and Shari Cane, to a singular
place in time with Maryland Sharp, who, it appeared from the call sheet,
had a part in the film and was represented, at the time, by the Alfred
Green Agency. As for the other two victims, Brenda's husband Bill
Benson and my acting coach Mary Higgins, Maryland had studied at the
Miracle Works Playhouse. That left only one victim, Bill Benson, without
a clear tie to her.

But a lot of people in the city had ties to Alfred Green, Bob Bayloff,
and Shari Cane; just about anyone who had worked on one of Bob's films

did. Shari was the wardrobe person on most of Bob's projects and Alfred was his agent. As for Mary Higgins, there was hardly an actor in the business who had not passed across the stage of the Miracle Works Playhouse at one time or another.

And what could Bill's murder and Stacey's and Brenda's abductions possibly have to do with Maryland? Those acts all seemed directed at me, as did the killing of Mary Higgins, my glossy headshot, posed, and staring at her lifeless body upon the stage. Was that a head fake? Something to throw us off, make it seem directed at me, to make it seem that Blue was the killer, when he wasn't?

Then there was the button found under Brenda and Bill's bed. A button covered with Bill's blood and containing Blue's clear and complete fingerprint. That was direct evidence, forensic evidence, connecting Blue to Bill's murder and Brenda's abduction, evidence placing him in their room at the time of the killing. There was absolutely no evidence that Maryland or her boyfriend were ever involved in anything at all. None.

Though they had found Blue's bloody fingerprint at the crime scene, I couldn't shut off my thoughts of Maryland and her boyfriend Mick. It was there, locked in, like whatever was locked behind their secret door.

I looked out at the Valley spreading north, toward the Northridge hills and realized that I didn't want to be here anymore. This was getting me nowhere. I thought about taking a ride up to Maryland's again, but this time, bringing a crowbar with me. Tearing that lock off the door and seeing what there was to see. I picked up my cell phone and dialed Dan's number, then tried Dolen's. Both had the same result, a message saying that the mobile customer I was calling could not be reached at this time.

Dan was convinced Blue was their guy and for good reason, I guess. It made sense, more sense than Maryland and her boyfriend. Dolen and Dan were also worried about me. They took Blue's threats of revenge on my person very seriously, as did I. If this was all about Blue trying to cause me pain, before killing me, why kill Bob Bayloff, the man who stole my wife, or Alfred Greene and Shari Canes, two people I had never even met? To me, that was a big hole in the Blue theory and left the door wide open for other reasons, suspects, and answers. Which brought me right back where I had started, to Maryland.

Suddenly, my cell phone rang, startling me. I raised it to my ear. "Hello?"

"Mr. Spire?"

"Yes?"

"This is Sergeant Warren Stewart of the San Bernardino Sheriff's Department. I've called to relay a message to you from Los Angeles Police Detectives Joe Dolen and Dan Patrick."

"Yes?" I replied.

"They wanted our office to call you and let you know that they have made contact with the escaped felon, Bud Williams, near the town of Willis, in the Mojave Desert. That contact led to an exchange of gunfire between the detectives and the suspect, at which time, it is believed, the suspect was wounded."

I felt my stomach grip my spine. "And the detectives?"

"They sustained no injuries, sir. A manhunt, led by the Sheriff's Department and involving the detectives, is now underway. They wanted you updated on the situation."

I listened to the silence on the other end of the phone, unable to speak for a moment. "Thank you, Sergeant, thank you very much."

"Good day, sir." The Sergeant replied before hanging up.

I lowered the phone from my ear, stunned. Blue was wounded. They had exchanged gunfire. I tried to process it all.

Dolen's hunch had been right. They had found him in the desert. Suddenly, as clear as day I saw Blue's face, at the end of his trial, leaning into the gallery as they pulled him away to serve his sentence and he whispered to me, "You're mine."

I looked down at the phone in my hand and thought to myself that there were moments that were life changing. They came without a warning, with a knock on the door, or a ring of a telephone, and nothing would ever be the same again. In my life, this was such a moment.

Dolen and Dan had wounded Blue and were on his trail, and instead of me being his, soon, with some luck, he would be theirs.

274

SEVENTY-EIGHT

Blue still couldn't move. He lay face down in the cavern, trying to breathe through a broken nose filled with dirt, to think, through a mind filled with pain. It was hard to do either. Mick had come back for more, again and again. Blue had lost count of how many times. Mick pressed Blue's face further into the ground as he finished another session and climbed off of him. Please, Blue thought, begging in his mind, no more, no more. Blue closed his eyes tight, not wanting to believe what was happening to him. A freak was raping him, over and over.

Blue lay on the floor of the cavern, slipping in and out of consciousness, his mind, soft, disconnected. The pain was everywhere and at times he seemed to be floating on it, floating to other places and other times. He had visions, taking him back to his childhood and his father, of peering into his father's workroom, through a crack in the trap door above. He could see his father working, as real as life, sharpening his tools. He could see the blonde woman too, gagged and chained to the dirty mattress. Blue was only eight and he had never seen a naked woman before. He held his baseball mitt and ball in his hand and couldn't pull his eyes from her. He recognized her. It was the same woman his father made him ask directions from, to the candy store.

The woman had taken Blue's hand in hers and led him down the alley, a shortcut to the store. Her hand was smooth and soft and Blue liked her. Blue's mother had disappeared years before and his father never spoke of her, and Blue remembered thinking that the woman, with her sweet perfume and soft skin, was the most beautiful thing he had ever seen and he wouldn't mind it if she were his mother. The woman never made it to the store, though, and Blue never got any candy. His father had seen to that. And as Blue watched his father work throughout the night, he realized that the woman would never make it anywhere else, ever again. He could see it all, so clear and vivid, as if it was happening just now. Of course, Blue knew, it was just a memory. It had to be. His father had been executed ten years ago. Blue desperately tried to move, but couldn't, as his father's words, "Use the world, son, don't let it use you…" echoed in his mind.

Mick reached down and turned Blue onto his back. Blue's gaze, blurry from Mick's beating, stared up at him. Mick pulled up Blue's underwear and pants. He then buckled Blue's belt and dragged him across the floor, placing Blue's back against a large leather chair, next to the table. Blue looked up at Mick, as Mick arranged him carefully against the chair. Blue was weak. He had lost a lot of blood, the pain and drug having clouded his mind. He tried to focus his swollen eyes. The drug was wearing off. He could feel something in his hands and feet.

Blue looked over at the AR-15 lying in the dirt, not far away. If he could buy some time and not let on that the drug was wearing off, he could kill Mick. He could blow a hole right through him. Blue concentrated on his breathing, trying to stay conscious, as Mick turned on the police scanner sitting on the table next to Blue's head. Blue looked down at the tracks across the dirt floor he had made, while Mick was dragging him. Was all that blood his? Blue blinked his eyes. There was a pretty girl standing in the corner of the room. Maryland? No. He recognized her, though. It was Carry Wilkins, the Wilkins girl.

She was standing there naked, just glaring at him. Maybe she could help him, thought Blue. Maybe she could bring him the rifle. But why would she do that? The last time she'd seen him, he'd been tying her to a tree. There were others with her; he could see them in the shadows. So many girls. Did he know them all? He wished they would stop staring.

Blue's breathing was heavy and labored as he watched Mick do a line of cocaine off a gold-rimmed mirror on the table. Mick then stood up, walking over to the rifle and picking it up. He came and stood in front of Blue, the police scanner crackling with distant voices.

Blue kept his eyes on Mick. He just needed a couple more minutes, he thought, to catch his breath, before he stood up. But before he could do anything, Mick kneeled down, placing the butt of the rifle in Blue's lap. Blue was helpless as Mick slipped the barrel of the rifle into Blue's mouth and placed Blue's limp finger on the trigger of the gun.

What was happening, thought Blue? He just needed another minute. The cavern was now filled with girls staring at him. There seemed to be a hundred of them. He saw his Father too, standing in the back, his eyes locked on his son. How strange. And as Blue looked out into the cavern, he thought that he really wasn't a bad guy. That besides the two men in prison he'd poisoned, he'd never really killed anyone, not really, and as he finished that thought, Mick pressed his finger down on the trigger of the gun and blew his head off.

SEVENTY-NINE

The old-timer, at the country store, had called it in, as Dolen's and Dan's cell phones seemed to be useless out in the desert and the radio in their police car was shot to hell. The San Bernardino Sheriff's Department had responded and a full manhunt for the fugitive Bud Williams, better known as Blue, was now underway. A helicopter from the Sheriff's Department had landed in the parking lot of the Oasis Bar, which was now acting as the control center for the investigation, and Dolen and Dan had climbed on board. Dolen looked out the window of the chopper as they searched for any sign of Blue, across the miles of desert landscape, spread out below them. Dolen sat in the front of the helicopter, next to the pilot, with Dan in the back, kept company by a member of the Sheriff's team.

The desert looked nice from the air, thought Dolen, softer, kinder. But that was just an illusion, masking the real hell that lay below, just as Blue's warm smile and movie star looks masked the evil that lay inside. Life was an illusion, thought Dolen, and the women Blue preyed on lived in that illusion, believing that monsters like Blue only existed in books and movies, wore hockey masks, carried butcher knives around, and killed you while you were camping in the woods, or showering on Halloween. They didn't wear three thousand dollar suits, have a smile that made your knees weak, and drive an Aston Martin. They just didn't. But as Dolen knew very well, they did.

As the pilot banked the chopper over the crest of some low lying hills, Dolen wondered how badly he'd hurt Blue? They'd put roadblocks up for over a hundred miles around the Oasis Bar, but Dolen didn't think Blue had left the area, or would be leaving any time soon. Dolen had plugged him pretty good. Blue would need medical attention and a place to hide. He bet Blue was down there right now, hiding, maybe with the help of some locals. He would try and lay low until he gained some strength and was ready to make a run for the border, in darkness and not on the roads. That's what Dolen would do. But hide where, Dolen wondered, as his eyes scanned the desert below him. There was nothing out here, but nothing. But maybe, that's what Blue was counting on.

Dolen suddenly felt a tap on his shoulder. He looked back at Dan, who was pointing out the left window.

"Over there?" Dan's voice crackled through Dolen's headphones. Dolen motioned to the pilot, pointing to a scattering of crumpled structures marking the desert floor. The pilot banked hard. He flew low, about a hundred feet off the ground, toward the setting sun and the structures. The pilot flew over the old wooden buildings, lying in a small valley. It was obvious, by what remained, that the place had at one time been an industry of some sort.

"It's an old silver mine," crackled the pilot's voice as they flew over the buildings.

"Tire tracks," Dan's voice came over the headphones again. "There are tire tracks down there."

Dolen looked out the window as they finished their pass. It was getting dark quickly and becoming hard to see.

"Can you bring us around again, lower?" Dolen asked.

The pilot spun the chopper around, putting it about fifteen feet off the deck as he made another pass. Dolen saw it, as they flew by. They all did. The back end of a shot-up, black Shelby Mustang, pulled underneath a crumbling, wooden shed—Blue's Mustang.

Immediately, the pilot called it in, as Dolen frantically pointed to the ground, signaling for the pilot to land the chopper, which he did, about thirty yards from the Mustang.

Dolen and Dan, armed with shotguns and wearing bulletproof vests, were the first out of the chopper. Followed by the pilot and his fellow officer, both helmeted and vested and armed with automatic rifles. The Sheriff's officers swept the car, which was empty as Dolen and Dan made their way to what looked like the entrance to a mineshaft. Shoe prints and a dried blood trail led into the shaft.

"There are different tire tracks here and more than one set of footprints," Dan said. Dolen, shotgun raised to his shoulder, nodded as he followed the blood trail. Dan shined a flashlight into the shaft. Old iron tracks, once used to get the silver out on rolling cars, sloped down into the mine. The pilot and other officer stepped up next to Dolen and Dan.

"We should wait on S.W.A.T., they're en route," said the pilot.

"We're going in, we're not waiting on anyone," snipped Dolen.

"We have jurisdiction, Detective. Our orders are to stand down until S.W.A.T. arrives, and that means you, too."

"This is our case, our suspect," replied Dan. "You want to back us up, that's fine."

"Or you can shoot us," said Dolen.

And with that, Dolen and Dan stepped into the darkness of the old mineshaft and disappeared, their flashlights raised alongside their shotguns. They followed the iron tracks slowly down the grade of the mine. The shaft smelled of old wood, dirt, and time. Their lights flickered ahead of them, leading them deeper and deeper. It was slow going, down, down. Suddenly, Dolen stopped, grabbing Dan's arm. Dan looked at Dolen as Dolen raised his finger to his ear, in a signal to listen. Dolen listened to the sounds of the shaft and heard it again, static, crackling. They moved slowly, the sound getting clearer, louder, a radio perhaps? Dim light seeped into the darkness up ahead as they rounded a corner and saw it.

It was a cavern, below and at the end of the mineshaft, where the tracks ended. Both men went to their knees and turned off their flashlights. They listened to the crackling static again and realized that the voices they heard were police, talking to each other, that what they were listening to was coming from a police scanner. Dolen rose up, trying to get a good view into the cavern, but he couldn't. Below him was a ladder, laid across a narrow ravine. He motioned to the ladder and Dan nodded, immediately going for it. Dan made it across to the other side easily, with Dolen following, a little slower.

On the other side of the ravine, they moved, one ahead, then one behind, up to the entrance of the cavern. Pressing their backs against the wall of the shaft, they locked eyes. Dolen held his breath, listening to the crackle of the police scanner, before he nodded at Dan, and guns raised, they stepped inside the cavern.

Blue sat on the floor of the cavern, against a leather chair, his head blown off, his assault rifle resting between his legs, the police scanner sitting on a table next to him. Dolen breathed the cool air of the cavern in and out quickly, as he swung the barrel of his shotgun away from Blue, sweeping the rest of the cavern. He listened to the hum of a generator somewhere in the recesses of the cavern as he tried to process the fact of this twisted place, the fact that it even existed, that Blue was dead.

Dolen watched as Dan, gun raised, moved toward a set of red velvet curtains, cutting the cavern in half. Dolen moved with Dan, covering him. Dan reached out to the curtains, making sure Dolen was in place, before ripping them open. Two large, empty beds lay behind the curtains. The beds were covered with satin sheets and more, the more being velvet wristbands and leg bands, connected by chains to the metal posts of the beds. Dolen and Dan swept through the makeshift bedroom to the back of the cavern, finding a washing basin, a portal potty, camping stove, food, water and other supplies. Along with two, large, plywood boxes, with holes drilled into them.

The boxes were side-by-side, one open and vacant, the other one, locked. The boxes were large enough, thought Dolen, to hold a person or two. Or better yet, a girl or two. Dolen knew, almost immediately by the smell, that something human was inside the locked box. Dan raised the butt of his shotgun and brought it down onto the lock, again and again, until it broke away from the box. He then unhinged the door, letting it drop to the ground. Dolen took a step back. There was a body inside the box, wrapped in a sleeping bag from head to toe, only a couple strands of dark hair visible. Dolen bent down and lifted up the corner of the bag revealing the beautiful face of Brenda. Dolen pressed his fingers to her neck, feeling for a pulse.

"She's alive," he said. "She's unconscious, but alive."

"Thank God," Dan replied.

Dan's gaze moved quickly to the empty box next to Brenda's. "But where's her sister, Joe? Where's Stacy?"

EIGHTY

The S.W.A.T. team from the Sheriff's Department had arrived along with other members of law enforcement, representing multiple agencies. With all the manpower at hand, one fact still remained—there was no sign of Stacey. Dolen stood in front of Blue as the police photographers finished up and the forensic boys started in on him. Blue was dead. The douche bag-motherfucker was dead. Dolen could hardly believe it. He sure didn't look like a movie star anymore, thought Dolen, not unless he planned on acting in one of those horror flicks, like the "Night of the Living Dead." The top of his head was gone and most of his face was missing.

Dolen slipped a toothpick into his mouth and gnawed on it. Fuck him, he thought. Blue was gone and Dolen had had a hand in it. Spire was safe. Blue wouldn't have a chance to kill him now. Dolen felt like unzipping his pants and taking a nice, celebratory piss on Blue's body. The scumbag had fueled his life on the pain of innocents, but now he was dead. The FBI boys were kind of an uptight bunch, though, and they might not appreciate a good victory piss, so Dolen kept his prick in his pants and just kept staring at Blue, taking it all in. It was a great night, Dolen thought. The best. If Bobby was here, he'd have him pour him a tall one, because one thing was for sure—Blue would never hurt anyone again.

Dan stepped up next to Dolen. "You got him real good, Joe," Dan said, "From the look of things, he collapsed over there and dragged himself to the chair, too weak to stand."

Dolen looked over to where Dan was pointing. Drag marks on the dirt floor of the cavern, stained with blood, clearly led to Blue's position against the chair.

282

"He was losing a lot of blood," Dan said, motioning to the trail, "Listening to the scanner, he knew we were coming, and he wasn't going back to Folsom, so he took the easy way out."

"They find the cash he took from Holmby Hills?" Dolen asked.

"Some of it. It was in a leather satchel in the trunk of his car," Dan replied.

Dolen watched as one of the forensic boys pulled a gold watch from the pocket of Blue's pants. He bagged it and handed it to Dolen. Dolen examined the ornate pocket watch closely.

"At the murder scene, wasn't Alfred Green's gold pocket watch missing?" asked Dolen as he handed the bag to Dan. Dan looked the watch over.

"That's it," he replied. "We've also found a bottle of sleeping pills that were Bob Bayloff's, an engraved make-up case belonging to Shari Canes, and an imitation Academy Award with Mary Higgins' name on it that she used to keep on her desk."

The forensic boys handed Dolen another evidence bag. It held a silver Zippo lighter, with a Sheriff's star engraved on it.

"And Bill Benson's lighter," Dolen quipped. "It seems douche bag boy liked souvenirs."

Dolen thought about the talk they'd had with Brenda. She had regained consciousness shortly after the arrival of the S.W.A.T. team. She had been extremely dehydrated, disoriented, and foggy from the drugs Blue had given her, but she could speak. She'd held Dan's hand, the man whose life she had helped save, after he was stabbed at Bob Bayloff's funeral, as the paramedics had attended to her. Dan had now returned the favor, having helped save Brenda's life.

Dolen pulled his gaze away from Blue. He took a deep breath and turned to Dan.

"What do you think about what Brenda said?" Dolen asked.

"About hearing a man's voice?" replied Dan.

"About hearing someone pull Stacey from her box while saying, 'It's time to bury you,'" answered Dolen.

"I think, what you think, not good."

"We have to tell Spire," replied Dolen.

"I'll call him," Dan said.

"Tell him we have the dogs searching the desert, in case what Brenda heard was true. Tell him we haven't given up hope that's she's alive."

Dan kicked at the ground, suddenly overwhelmed with emotion. He had known Stacey longer than Will. He brought his eyes up to Dolen's and nodded his head.

EIGHTY-ONE

Maryland sat at the Oasis Bar, pissed. What the hell was she doing here? First, Mick drops her off, for like four hours, while he goes to that hole of his. Then he comes back and splits, leaving her here with these biker assholes and about a hundred cops parked out in the parking lot! Jesus Christ! Maryland took a big sip of her rum and diet and looked at her watch. Mick had given her instructions to wait until after dark and then hit the road, toward the Salton Sea, stopping for the night at the Paradise Motel, off Route 78. Maryland looked over at three cops, huddled by the front door of the bar, and wondered how the hell she was supposed to do that. Apparently, there had been some kind of shootout, like in the movies, the bartender had said, and the police had blocked every road going anywhere, with cars backed up for miles. And where did Mick go, anyway, somewhere with Blue? He was such a dick sometimes!

Maryland looked up as a biker slid in to order a drink next to her. God, she thought, as his eyes wandered all over her body, she wished she hadn't worn this miniskirt. She looked up at the biker, giving him her best "I'll kill you if you don't get away from me" look. She'd already used that look about four hundred times on the bikers and about two hundred times on the cops.

It was dark now. It had been for a while, but Maryland would wait a few more minutes before saying good-bye to this hellhole forever. Secretly, she was hoping she wouldn't have to leave, at least not alone. She was hoping, or more like praying, that Mick would come back and take her away. Maryland watched as more cops came through the door. These guys looked like they were wearing black armor. You couldn't even see their faces. This was the most messed-up thing Mick had ever

285

done to her, by far, and she didn't like the way he'd been acting, either. He kept talking about his "production," and she had no idea what that was, and he seemed almost giddy with joy.

Maryland brought her gaze down to her drink and shook her head. Damn it, Mick better not have had anything to do with that bullshit outside, he and his new buddy Blue. Maryland pushed the thought away. She wasn't going to think of such things. She had been practicing on staying positive lately, on being a positive person. Her acting coach had told her that she held too much hostility inside and that it was poisoning her performance. Maryland thought about her coach's comment for a moment, and then dismissed it. Her teacher was just a bitch.

Maryland closed her eyes, trying to calm herself. She didn't want to be here; she wanted to be at home. Please, Mick. Please come back, she thought. Why was everything in their life so fucked up and different? Why? All she wanted was to be a normal person. She was tired of being in these weird, messed-up situations that Mick put her in. It had gotten really, really bad lately. She couldn't even remember the last time they'd made love or did anything fun. No wonder her acting coach thought she was hostile. She probably went home to a normal life and a normal husband, who went to Costco on the weekends and bought lawn equipment and talked to people about rakes and paint and shit and then came home and watched football. He wasn't out decorating a mineshaft in the middle of the desert with red velvet curtains. Was that normal? Was anything that Mick did normal?

Maryland sipped the rest of her drink down through her straw until it made a gurgling sound. Who was she kidding? She wanted "normal" in her man about as much as she wanted "boring" in her life. If Mick ever went to Costco, she might have to kill him.

Maryland wasn't feeling very good. She was tired and her stomach was tied up in knots. She had a feeling that something really bad had happened. But how could anyone not feel that, when surrounded by a hundred cops? But it was more than that. She felt off, as if her mind was struggling to put things together. She didn't like that cave thing Mick had. It freaked her out. She was scared, that's what it was. She didn't know of what she was scared of, but she was. Only when she was with Mick, did

286

she feel safe. Then there was Blue. He still got to her. She didn't like to see him. Her anger of what he had done to her ran deep, yet at times, she caught herself being drawn to him. How could that be, she asked herself, after what he had done? It was sick. She would have been fine if she had never seen Blue again, after the institution. But Mick had wanted her to contact him. He had some use for Blue that involved that cave.

Maryland's eyes filled slowly with tears. She didn't feel well. No, she didn't. She wanted to go home and never see Blue or that cave ever again. But instead, she had to drive out further into the desert to some shitty motel. What other kind of motel could it be, she thought, but shitty? Everything out here was shitty. She tried to remember what she had always told herself, what had always been the one truth in her life. Mick knew best. He had never let her down. So, if he wanted her to drive to the Paradise Motel in the middle of shitty nowhere, she would.

Still, her stomach was balled into a knot. Was Mick all right? If anything happened to him she didn't think she could go on living. What had Blue gotten him mixed up in? Or was it Mick that had done the mixing? Either way she didn't...

Maryland's thought was cut off as she looked up at the TV above the bar. She stopped breathing, as she stared at Blue's photograph, blown up on the screen, the caption below his photo reading, "Murder Suspect Killed in Desert Hideout." Maryland felt herself leave her body, as if she was floating toward the TV. She watched a pretty, blonde newsgirl, reporting from outside the entrance to Mick's cave, silhouetted against hundreds of flashing lights from emergency vehicles. From that point on, Maryland heard nothing, not the noise of the bar, the policemen, the bikers, or even her breathing. She raised her eyes once again to the TV screen, catching the deep blue of Blue's eyes, staring back at her, before she leaned over and threw up.

EIGHTY-TWO

I got the call from Dan shortly after dinner. I sat on my patio, listening to the sound of wind chimes playing in the warm breeze. I stared out at the blue of my pool as a gust from the Santa Anas ruffled the leaves of the palm trees above, creating a crackling sound. The winds had reached across the desert, where somewhere, my ex-wife was either dead or alive, and had found me at the home we once shared. I raised my glass of whiskey to my lips and thought I heard Stacey's voice in the whispering wind, calling to me, asking where I was, where I had been, and why I hadn't saved her.

Blue was dead. They had found Brenda alive, thank God, but Stacey was gone, perhaps dead and buried somewhere in the desert. The ghosts were back, the ghosts of Stacey and Will, a life lived. I could see them moving about on another plane of existence, in another time, sharing the space with me. I was stunned, numb. My brain was filled with her, us, lost time, false leads, grief, guilt, denial, fading hope. I didn't know where to turn, or who to talk to, so I sat, drinking, falling into myself, searching for something I could do, some way out. I had to think, to be of some use to someone, to myself. I had to believe she was still alive.

Dan had said that Blue's death was an apparent suicide, his wound from Dolen's gunshot having led to his final demise. Blue had taken refuge in the old Sharpsburg Silver Mine that had been closed for nearly a century. He, apparently, had customized a cavern in one of the mineshafts to suit his twisted tastes and pleasures.

Stacey wasn't dead. That's what I had told Dan. I would know if she was. Dan had placated me with, "Of course, Will," but I knew he didn't believe me. I had no scientific evidence to back up my statement that I

288

would "know" if she was dead. But in my heart and soul, where such things where connected to the unknowns of the universe, I felt I would.

I heard my doorbell ring and I stood up, moving inside to answer it. I pulled the front door open and saw Blake standing on the stoop. I had left him a voicemail message after I had gotten off the phone with Dan. He hadn't returned my call, but instead, had made the drive over to the house.

"You got anything to drink?" Blake asked.

"I can scrounge something up," I replied, motioning for Blake to come in. Blake followed me to the bar where I poured him a Jack on the rocks. We took a seat in some comfortable club chairs in my living room, sitting across from each other.

"How you holding up?" Blake asked.

"I'm holding," I replied.

"Any word on Stacey?"

"No," I answered.

"So? Blue turned from a serial rapist to a killer? Is that the theory?" Blake asked. "What does Dan think about that?"

"He believes that he did, that prison must have bent him past rape to murder. He said that besides the multiple tire tracks and footprints outside the mine, all the evidence, including Blue's fingerprints on the victim's belongings, line up with him being the killer. I asked him if Blue could have had a partner, someone who could have taken Stacey."

"And?" asked Blake.

"He hesitated a bit, before saying that they believed Blue had acted alone. Yet, I sensed that he wasn't completely satisfied with that conclusion and neither am I."

Blake nodded, twirling his ice cubes in his glass as I was suddenly overcome with a feeling of deep despair. If Blue said he was going to bury her, then he'd buried her. Who was I kidding? Where else could she be? I closed my eyes and tried to feel Stacey, to see her, to visualize her face, happy and alive, as if the vision could speak to me and answer my question.

"You all right, Will?" Blake asked.

"Something doesn't make sense here, brother," I replied as I opened my eyes.

"Revenge, that's what Dan and Dolen believe this was all about. People who had wronged Blue, either personally or in business, with a special place in his scheme for me. Saving me for last, while setting me up for max pain until then, as I watched those I loved being taken or killed."

"Yeah?" Blake said, trying to follow my train of thought.

"It seems strange to me though, this cave thing," I answered, "How did Blue know about the old mine? A friend, I suppose, or someone he'd served time with could have told him about the mine. Convicts, fantasizing about what a great spot it would be for committing dark deeds and hiding from the law. Footprints and tire tracks? That sounds to me like Blue had some company."

"I take it, you believe Blue had a partner?"

"It makes sense," I answered. "Someone who could have taken Stacey for himself once he saw that things were falling apart? Or she could have been payment from Blue, for the partner's help, while Blue kept Brenda for himself. Dan told me that Brenda had never seen her abductor's face, or the face of her captor."

"So it's possible they were different men, working toward the same criminal purpose," Blake commented, "which would explain the multiple tire tracks and footprints."

"Exactly," I replied.

I grabbed Blake's glass from him and headed to the bar for a refill. "I always come back to Maryland Sharp, who I told you about," I said, "and her painter boyfriend with the secret room. She had known Blue. She had been in the institution with him. How close had they been, I wonder? How close were they, close enough to take a trip out into the desert, to help him?"

I came back from the bar and handed Blake his refill. "You think that's a stretch, that I'm grasping at straws?" I asked.

Blake stared at me. I knew this look; he was about to tell me something important.

"I want to tell you something, Will," Blake said, right on cue. "I did some digging, like you asked, on Maryland Sharp. I pulled in some heavy favors, stuff that could probably get me disbarred if it came to light, which it won't."

Blake hesitated. He then leaned forward, making eye contact with me. "The reason Maryland Sharp's records are sealed, Will, is because she was a minor when she committed the crime that led to her institutionalization. Subsequently, the court sealed any records of crimes she committed as a juvenile. When she became a legal adult, it allowed her to be released back into society, with a new start on life, not hindered by the burdens of any crimes committed as a minor. Though my source gained this information using her current name, there is a good chance that might not have been her name as a juvenile. Name changes are common in these cases."

"What type of crime?" I asked. Blake took a big sip of his drink and leaned back in his chair.

"She killed her father," he answered.

I sat, stunned, not sure I had heard him right. All I could manage, as a response, was, "What?"

"I don't know the specifics," Blake said. "But..."

"Was it a car accident, something like that?" I blurted out.

"No," Blake said. "It was a homicide. It stands to reason that she may have been found not guilty by reason of insanity and that's why she was in the institution and not sent to prison. So maybe your suspicions aren't so far off. Maybe she does have something to do with all of this."

"How did she kill him?" I asked.

"I don't know," Blake, replied. "That's all I know."

Holy shit. My mind was floating on whiskey and shock. Maryland had killed her father and was friends with Anna Burnside, who had killed her whole family, including her father, who she'd stuffed up the chimney on Christmas Day and who was best friends with Blue, the serial rapist. The three murdering Musketeers of the mental institution. Could they all be involved in this? We already knew that Anna had been helping Blue ever since he got out of prison. Had Maryland been doing the same? I looked at Blake, unable to speak.

EIGHTY-THREE

Blake had taken off shortly after delivering his news about Maryland Sharp and the revelation that she had killed her father. He had given me a big piece of the puzzle and reinforced my belief that she was involved with Blue and perhaps the crimes he'd committed. What I was missing was concrete evidence of that involvement. I walked out into the fresh air by the pool and looked up at the stars in the night sky. Maryland had killed her father. The words rolled around my liquored brain. Maryland had killed her father. It was homicide. A gust from the Santa Anas blew hard against me. It came, like a slap from the desert, from Stacey, as if she were saying, "Wake up, Will. Wake up! You're getting close!"

Something else Blake had said had stuck in my mind. "Name changes are common in these cases…" It made sense to me that Maryland would change her name, at least her last name, which was the same as her father, whom she'd killed. It would also explain why in trying to research her past, I had come up with nothing, as if she was born the day she was released from the institution. Which in a way, she was.

Then it hit me. How did Blue know about the silver mine? Could he have learned about the mine from Maryland? Could she have a personal connection to the Sharpsburg mine? Sharpsburg? Sharp? Not far off as last names go. Could Maryland have changed her last name from Sharpsburg to Sharp?

Before I knew it, I was at my computer. I stared down at the screen after looking up the "History of the Sharpsburg Mine." I scrolled through the text and photos of the mine that was opened in 1884 by Greg Sharpsburg and closed, after a very profitable run that made the family wealthy, in 1932. The mine and the property it lay on had been passed

292

down to the male heirs of the family until the death of Ben Sharpsburg, at which time it was tied up for years in a legal dispute between family members. Presently, the owner of record was listed as Ben Sharpsburg's daughter, Maryland Sharpsburg.

I sat back in my chair and took a deep breath, Maryland, the same spelling, like the state, as Maryland Sharp.

I looked down at an old photograph next to the text of the article, showing a smiling Ben Sharpsburg dressed in a tuxedo, his arm wrapped tightly around a young blonde girl of about nine, who was not smiling, her gaze lowered toward the ground. The caption below the photo read "Ben Sharpsburg and his daughter Maryland, at the Brentwood Country Club New Year's Ball." I stared at the young face of Maryland Sharp. I could see the grown woman in the child, the arm of the man she would later kill, wrapped affectionately around her.

I listened to the silence of my home. The ghosts were gone. I was living in the present, in the moment, and that's where I needed to stay. It was Maryland who had told Blue about the old mine, her mine, Maryland Sharpsburg's mine. Tied up for years in a legal dispute between family members? I bet it was. After Maryland killed her father, the other members of her family probably weren't so keen on Maryland inheriting the mine, or for that matter, anything else of Ben Sharpsburg's.

I needed to take a ride back up to Maryland's house. There was a secret door just waiting to be opened there, but how, by breaking and entering again? I could get my ass hung in a sling for that, arrested for sure. I swirled around in my chair. It's funny, I thought, how leads in a case come in. How suddenly after banging your head against the wall, suddenly things can break.

I stopped swirling in my chair and stared down at the latest edition of the L.A. Times lying on my desk, crumpled and disheveled from my morning read. Sticking out from underneath the pile was the caption of an article that read, "Man Found Dead in Hollywood, Police Suspect Foul Play." The photo below the caption showed an old, burned-out Chevy van, sitting in a junkyard. In the photo the license plate of the van was clearly visible, 4JUL178. It was the same van that I had seen parked in Maryland Sharp's driveway.

I pulled the section out from the bottom of the pile and scanned through the article. A known drug dealer, Steve Smith, better known as the "Beaver," 68 years of age, had been found dead in his home of an apparent suicide. The charred van was found to have had counterfeit license plates and registration. The police believed the van was deliberately set on fire and had not ruled out the possibility that the man may have been killed in a drug deal gone bad.

Maryland's boyfriend's van, or at least, the van he was using the day I was trapped under his bed, had been found at a crime scene burned to a crisp, along with an apparent suicide, that could actually be a murder. That was the story. Apparent suicide? Isn't that what Dan had said about Blue's death? I got up from my desk and grabbed my car keys. I was taking a ride, fuck getting arrested. Another gust of wind hit, rattling the chimes outside, and I could swear I heard Stacey's voice whispering with the wind, that I was getting close now, real close.

EIGHTY-FOUR

Dolen recognized her, the girl who had just thrown up on the bar. He had seen her in the institution when they went to visit that crazy debutante who had stuffed her father up the chimney. Dolen stood in the Oasis Bar, by the front door, surrounded by a handful of other cops. He and Dan had just returned to pick up their new car, to what was now the acting control center in the investigation. It was then that Dolen had seen the blonde girl lose it. She had managed to get the bartender and a couple of bikers with her regurgitation, before fleeing to the bathroom in the back.

What the fuck was she doing here? Dolen asked himself. In some desert dive bar, out in the middle of nowhere, dressed in a miniskirt and heels? It was the heels, nice red ones, which had caught Dolen's attention. The forensic boys had told him that a woman wearing heels had made some of the shoe prints at the mine. Dolen hadn't given it much thought at the time, since Stacey had been wearing heels when she'd been abducted, but now this. Dolen twirled his toothpick in his mouth. He'd bet his balls on a crooked horse race that there wasn't a girl within miles of this rat hole that wore shoes like that. Those shoes were pure L.A.

Dolen slid into the corner, behind a wall of cops, and leaned on the jukebox, keeping his eyes on the bathroom. Dan had given Spire the call. Dolen was glad that he hadn't had to do it. It must have been painful. Spire had been working another angle on the case, not convinced that Blue was their guy, and according to Dan, he was still holding out hope that Blue had a partner or two and that Stacey was still alive. Dolen thought she was dead, dead and buried. Some hippy hiker, walking through the endless crap out here smoking his doobie, would probably

295

find her bones years from now. But in Dolen's mind, she was gone.

As for the whole partner thing, well, he might be in Spire's camp on that. Dolen just didn't believe Blue had pulled this thing off by himself. That cave, at the bottom of the mineshaft, just didn't seem like Blue. Blue wouldn't have the patience. Blue wouldn't want to get his hands dirty. He would rather be on Rodeo Drive, spending ten grand on clothes and cruising the clubs for more victims. Would Blue think that the mine was a perfect place to play and be the sick fuck he was? Hell, yes. But would he spend the time and effort it took to put the thing together? No way.

Dolen watched as the door to the bathroom opened and the tall blonde came out. She walked through the bar, her gaze toward the floor. Even so, Dolen could see she'd been crying. Dolen turned toward the jukebox as she passed by, her red heels clicking on the wooden floor of the bar. She stopped for a moment, unable to get past a passel of cops, before moving around them. Dolen looked over toward the bar where Dan was sitting. Dan's eyes found his, knowing something was up. Dolan motioned to the door with his head, and Dan got up off his stool and followed Dolen out.

Dolen and Dan walked through the dirt parking lot toward their new car, a white Chevy.

"What's up?" Dan asked.

"She's up," Dolen answered, motioning with his eyes toward the tall blonde as she climbed inside a black BMW.

"I saw her at the institution, when we were visiting that nut job, Anna Burnside. You know, the same institution Blue was in?"

The engine of the BMW started up. "No, shit…" Dan said. "She's a little overdressed. Wonder what's she doing out here?"

"Exactly," replied Dolen, as he pulled open the passenger door of the Chevy. "Let's find out."

Dolen and Dan followed the BMW out of the parking lot in their new Chevy. They pulled close enough to the back of the car, before it turned onto the main road, for Dolen to jot down its license plate number. He called it in as the BMW made a right turn onto the road. Dan made a left, driving in the opposite direction. Dan drove about fifty yards then turned off the Chevy's headlights and made a U-turn, heading back in the same direction as the BMW, its taillights glowing in the distance. Dan flipped his headlights on again as they passed the parking lot of the Oasis Bar and Dolen's check on the plates came in, crackling over their radio.

"…2014…BMW…registered to a Maryland Sharp…. 2244 Liverpool Lane… Hollywood…no wants or warrants…"

Dolen looked over at Dan. "That's Spire's girl. The one he's been checking out. He thinks she's involved somehow."

"No, shit? That's Will for you," replied Dan. "Pulls a wild card out that nobody thought of and it sticks. The boy's got a sense for things."

Dolen brought his eyes back to the taillights in the distance as he gnawed on his toothpick.

"Maybe he does, partner. Maybe he does."

EIGHTY-FIVE

I wound down Crescent Heights and made a left, heading under the arches of Mt. Olympus and up into the Hollywood Hills toward Maryland's house. What would I do, I wondered, if the bay window in the back was not still cracked open and the entrance into the house was not as easy as before, or worse yet, someone was home? At this point, I was prepared to break the law in a big way, to find out what was behind the secret door of Maryland Sharpsburg, the friend of Blue and Anna and the killer of her own father. I'd never had a stronger feeling that Maryland and her boyfriend were the key to not only finding Stacy alive but to solving this case.

I felt my cell phone vibrate in my pocket as I pulled my Vette over to the side of the road, a couple blocks from Maryland's house. I put the car into park, shut off its engine, and answered my phone.

"Hello?"

"Your girl's in the desert," bellowed the raspy and constantly annoyed voice of Dolen.

"What girl?" I asked.

"Maryland Sharp. We're following her right now. She came all dressed up in her L.A. outfit, to party with the desert prune boys at a shit hole bar called the Oasis, in the middle of fucking nowhere, but only about a mile from Blue's cavern. We been on her for about an hour."

"Is she alone?" I asked as I stared at the darkness of Maryland's home down the street.

"Yeah. We would have called you sooner but we were caught in a no phone, desert vortex. It's fucking weird out here, Spire, Dan swears he saw a UFO, but I told him that's just what happens when you don't have a

298

drink for forty-eight hours. We're following her through the shit, see where it leads us."

"She could be on her way to meet her boyfriend. They live together."

"You got a description?"

"Six feet, dark hair, dark eyes, mustache, glasses, name's Mick Carter. I ran him. Not much there, no wants or warrants. There is one more thing that you should know about Maryland, though," I said.

"What's that?" Dolen asked.

"She killed her father."

"No shit?"

"Her name used to be Maryland Sharpsburg, as in the Sharpsburg mine, where Blue had his little hideout. She is the owner of record. We don't know the specifics, but Blake and I believe she killed her father when she was a minor and must have been found not guilty by reason of insanity and sent to the institution, where she met fellow father killer, Anna Burnside, and our boy Blue."

I could hear the wheels in Dolen's brain spinning.

"You need to get your ass out here, Spire," Dolen barked." You and that candy ass car of yours can be here in two hours."

"I'll be there soon," I said, my eyes still pinned on Maryland's house. "There's just a little something I have to do first."

EIGHTY-SIX

I walked down the sidewalk towards Maryland's house. I had come prepared. I was wearing gloves, with a small crowbar nestled in my jacket pocket, which also held a black beanie that could be pulled down over my face. I was hoping that I wouldn't need such tools and a more subtle approach to entering Maryland's house and the secret room could be applied, but I was ready to do what needed to be done, to enter both.

The street was relatively dark, with only one light overhead and hanging well past Maryland's house. I could still feel the buzz of the whiskey I had had early in the night, making my mind softer than I would have liked for the occasion, but time was of the essence. I needed leads and answers right now, in order to have any chance of finding Stacey.

I moved past the front of the house, walking on the opposite side of the street. The house was dark, with no cars parked in the driveway. I knew where Maryland was, but not her boyfriend, Mick, though I would bet, if she was in the desert, he was somewhere near her. I walked around the block one more time and then crossed the street, making my way down the stone path next to Maryland's house. I ducked under the cover of the orange tree and into Maryland's backyard. I put on the black beanie and pulled it down over my face, leaving just my mouth and eyes visible. If I did run into someone in the house, I didn't want my face seen as I fled.

As luck would have it, the bay window I had used to enter the house before was still cracked open. I reached my gloved hand inside to the handle of the window and cranked it. Before I knew it, I was inside and crawling out from under Mick Carter's desk.

I stood up in the darkness. I pulled a flashlight from my pocket and turned it on. The house was silent. The beam from the light illuminated the interior of the house, which seemed untouched since my last visit. I moved slowly and silently toward the front of the house, stopping at the beginning of the hallway. I turned my flashlight off and listened for any sign of life from the back bedroom. I heard nothing. I inched my way down the hall in darkness, using the wall to guide me. I made it to the end of the hall and could see the form of the tapestry covering the door, to the secret room, hanging on the far wall. Still, I heard no sign of life.

I poked my head slowly around the corner and could see Maryland's vanity and the bedroom beyond. The shades to the window in the bedroom were open, letting the soft moonlight, from the outside, in, and revealing the white comforter of Maryland's bed, a bed which was perfectly made. I moved slowly toward the bedroom and stepped inside. It appeared that I was the only one home.

I walked out of the bedroom and up to the tapestry. I raised its corner and hung it from the hook on the wall, just as I had seen Mick do. I lifted the lock with my gloved hands feeling its weight. I turned my flashlight back on, examining the lock closely. The subtle approach may work, I thought. I reached into my jacket pocket and pulled out a small leather case. A former mentor of mine, in the PI business, had given the case to me when I first went to work for the D.A. It was a lock picking case, containing multiple picks and tools, that when used correctly, could open a variety of locks. The older the lock, the better, and this lock was very old. I held my flashlight in my mouth as I selected the tools I thought I needed from the kit and went to work, inserting them into the lock and trying to engage its tumblers. In my business, very often, lock picking is a must and my mentor had taught me well. Within less than three minutes, the lock clicked open.

I removed the lock from the latch on the door and stood up. A strange feeling suddenly swept over me. I had a sense that I was about to step into a place of deep darkness. I pulled my Beretta free from its holster as I reached for the handle on the door and pulled it open.

The beam of my flashlight was met immediately with red velvet curtains, ruffled on the top, heavy and creased, reaching to the floor. They reminded me of stage curtains or ones that hung across the screens in the movie theaters of old. I slipped open the curtain, my light finding a row of five, old wooden, theater seats, covered in faded red fabric. I stepped into the room, which I realized, at one time, might have been a second bedroom. There was an old 8 mm movie projector set up in front of the row of chairs, pointing toward a movie screen, set on a tripod. The movie screen rested in front of another set of red velvet curtains, closed and tied in the middle

My light found the wall to my right, which was covered with a giant painted mural of the "H" of the Hollywood sign. On top of the "H," in the mural, was the figure of a man, facing out toward the city. Below was a parked a black sedan, its glowing headlights illuminating the H of the Hollywood sign. I swung the beam of my flashlight around to the left wall and moved closer. The wall was covered with some type of makeshift storyboard, marked with a "through line" or a "plot line," as it is known. The line was drawn horizontally across the wall, at about eye level, and had been broken up into three sections, representing the three-act structure of a screenplay. The line was marked along the way, with photographs and index cards, containing scribbled notes tacked to it. I stepped closer; my light finding the first photograph along the plot line marked "1st Act."

I froze, as the photo came into focus. It was of Stacey and me outside Bob's beach house, the day we'd found his body. We were sitting together, on a lawn chair, on the back patio by the beach. Stacey's head was lowered, her eyes closed, my arm wrapped around her. Dolen, who was watching us, was clearly visible in the background.

I moved the beam of light to the next picture on the plot line. It was of Stacey, Dan, and myself at Bob's funeral. The next photo was of Dolen, Dan, Blake, and me, inside the Miracle Works Playhouse, standing by the stage dummy, with my glossy headshot stapled to it. Next, on the plot line, was a photo of Dolen coming out of Frog's, with a wounded and handcuffed Tiny Tim, after I'd shot him. I tried to read the scattered notes on the index cards accompanying the photos, a common practice for writers, developing the plot and structure of a screenplay, but the scribblings were incoherent to me.

I moved the light down the plot line into the 2nd Act, the photos revealing a time line of our investigation. The photographs included at least one of us, either Dan, Dolen, or myself, outside the Miracle Works playhouse, at the Institution, at Brenda's cabin in Big Bear, and so on. The latest and last photo, tacked to the plot line in the beginning of Act 3, was of Dolen and Dan, standing in the parking lot of the Oasis Bar. I followed the empty line past the last photo and across the wall until it ran out, where the inevitable "FADE TO BLACK" was written, signaling the end of the film. Most of the third act of this twisted production, apparently, had yet to be written.

I took a deep breath. There were no photos of the victims along the plot line, formed in the sick mind of either Maryland, her boyfriend Mick, or the both of them. Either way, in terms of breaking the case wide open, I had hit the mother lode. I listened to my breathing in the quiet of the house, my mind spinning. My gaze came to rest on the old 8 mm movie projector. A full reel was loaded in the front of the projector, ready to go. I stepped up to the projector, reached down with my gloved hand and turned it on. The clicking of the old projector broke the silence as the room was lit with the flickering light of the film.

I stared at the screen, as a black slate was held up in front of the camera. It read, "Location Scout, Untitled Project, Director – Mick Carter." The film then started. Silent, it showed the exterior of Bob Bayloff's beach house, the camera, held still. The next shot was of the bench where Alfred Green was killed. The shot was taken from behind the empty bench, the leaves of the tree above moving silently in the breeze, young girls playing kickball on a school blacktop visible in the distance.

Next on the reel was the outside of the Miracle Works Playhouse, again a still shot, with no movement, taken from across the street, cars moving silently by. I knew what was coming next—the exterior of Shari Canes apartment and then Brenda's Big Bear cabin. I watched the camera pick up the sunlight off the frozen lake near the cabin, where Stacey, Brenda, Bill, and I had spent so many wonderful times, and felt sick to my stomach. The next scene was of the exterior of a log cabin, or some type of motel, surrounded by pine trees. It was shot near sunset, the windows glowing with interior light. The last location was of a lone trailer or mobile home. It sat in the distance, alone, on the shores of an expansive lake, a desert lake that looked to me like it could be the Salton Sea.

Next, the black slate came up again, chalked across it, one simple word, "Starring." The slate came down. The next image on the screen was of Bob Bayloff, dead, bloodied, and stuffed grotesquely into his freezer. The following images were all graphic and horrifying—images of Alfred Green, Shari Canes, and my friend, Mary Higgins, taken shortly after they'd been killed.

The slate then reappeared in front of the camera, announcing, "And Playing Himself," followed by the image of the nearly decapitated Sheriff Bill Benson. The room lit up with a bright light as the film came to a sudden end. I stood motionless, staring at the bright white of the screen, the loose end of the film flicking loudly against the projector as it spun round and round. Finally, I reached down and turned the projector off, the room falling once again into darkness.

I sat down in one of the old movie seats, lowering my head. I laid my gun in my lap and closed my eyes. I had found them. The killers. They lived in the Hollywood Hills, had a pink house so clean you could eat off its floors and made love on an antique bed with a white down comforter. But why had they killed? Why had they taken Brenda and Stacey? I thought of Maryland murdering her father, of her institutionalization. Who knew what sickness lay within her. I could feel my hands shaking as I opened my eyes to the darkness. I turned on my flashlight, shining it on the set of curtains behind the movie screen. I walked up to the curtains and untied them, moving through them and into the space beyond.

The beam of my light cut through the darkness, finding a mirrored makeup table against the far wall of the room. I walked up to the mirror, small, round lights outlining its frame. I switched the lights on. The glow from the small bulbs lit the room in a soft light. The space behind the second curtain had been made up as a dressing room, reminiscent of the stars of yesteryear. Besides the vintage makeup table, there were two full-length mirrors and an old, ornate wardrobe closet, a table and chair and a tripod with a 35 mm camera mounted on it. A gold chandelier hung from the ceiling and the walls were covered with framed, black-and-white photographs of old Hollywood.

On the makeup table itself was a variety of stage makeup, brushes, pads and powders, all familiar to me, from my days as an actor. I sat down in front of the makeup table, seeing a photograph wedged into the wooden rim of the mirror. It was of Maryland and Mick, candid and smiling, the backdrop, a beautiful mountain range.

I slid the photo from the mirror, examining it. Mick was as I saw him from under his bed, wearing gold-rimmed glasses. He had dark, short hair, and a mustache to match. His eyes were dark. His teeth, large and white, were visible in a wide smile. His nose was slightly crooked at the bridge, as if it had once been broken, his complexion, muddied. Maryland sat next to Mick, also smiling, her large, blue eyes sparkling in the sunshine and in stark contrast to her alabaster skin, the bangs of her short blonde hair windblown and tousled on her forehead. A happy, normal couple said the picture. Not so much, I thought, anything but normal. As for happy, or what made them so, it seemed like that was built on the suffering of others. Sick was all my overwhelmed mind could come up with.

I was suddenly struck by something in the photo of Maryland and Mick. In the background, there was a small hut perched on a jagged peak behind them. The hut was visible in the distance, over Maryland's right shoulder, and what appeared to be the same hut, was visible over Mick's left shoulder. I looked closer at the contour of the mountains and the woods surrounding the hut and determined that they were the same. It was definitely the same hut. I examined the large boulder Maryland and Mick were sitting on and could see that they were sitting in almost the exact same spot on the boulder, with Mick, just a little bit to the right, therefore, placing the hut over his left shoulder.

I could see clearly now that a photo of the two of them sitting on the boulder together had never been taken. That instead, two separate photos of them sitting alone on the boulder, in nearly the same spot, had been blended, or Photoshopped, into one, so it would appear to the viewer as if they had been sitting together when the photo was taken. But why? Mick's hands were tucked inside his jacket pockets, Maryland's resting politely in her lap, neither touching the other.

I raised my eyes to the old, wooden wardrobe closet. It stood, about six feet tall, on the carved feet of a lion, its once bright, painted colors now faded with time. I moved to it, reaching down to the brass-ringed handle on the right hand side of the closet. I pulled open the right door. Inside the closet were four shelves, each one, holding a Styrofoam head, with a wig on top. Each wig was a different length, cut and color, but obviously, meant to be worn by a man.

Next to each wig, was a selection of mustaches, laid out on red velvet. A variety of eyeglasses were lined up next to the mustaches in perfect order. On the open door of the closet were pinned more than twenty photos of Maryland and Mick together in a variety of locations. I bent down and examined the photos. Some seemed to have been Photoshopped, like the one on the mirror, and in none of them were Maryland or Mick touching each other. No hugs, holding hands, or embracing, the natural behavior of a couple that shared a life and a bed together. I picked up a pair of eyeglasses resting on the red velvet. They were gold, like the ones I'd seen Mick wearing. I raised the lenses to the light of the mirror and saw that they were clear, non-prescription lenses. I placed the eyeglasses back down and opened the door to the other side of the closet.

There were no shelves on the left side of the closet, as there were on the right side, just a number of hooks. Hanging from the hooks were a variety of sex toys. Or in laymen terms, what would be referred to as dildos. To be more specific, strap-ons, in a variety of sizes, all of them, bendable, from limp to erect.

Worn, or "strapped on," by a woman, it would give her the appearance and function of a man, in every sense of the word. But why would Maryland want... I stepped back, my eyes flicking from the wigs and mustaches, to the stage makeup and doctored photos, the truth, firing into my mind like a heated diamond.

Maryland was Mick and Mick was Maryland.

EIGHTY- SEVEN

She was a tall girl, thought Dolen, over six feet. She had a small waist, broad shoulders, her arms were cut and muscular, her tits small. The small tits didn't bother Dolen. He'd never cared about the size of a woman's tits, as long as they had nipples on them. Dolen slipped some Skoal between his cheek and gum as he and Dan watched Maryland Sharp check into the Paradise Motel, off Route 78. They sat in their new Chevy, parked in the parking lot of the motel, having followed Maryland from the Oasis Bar. They could see Maryland through the window of the office. Dolen dug that whole miniskirt and heels thing she had going on, and though it looked like she spent too much time at the gym and could probably kick his ass, he thought she was sexy.

Dolen spit some spittle into a plastic cup as he watched Maryland walk out of the motel office, room key in hand. The motel was a series of separate log cabins, which looked like they were about to fall down.

"If she's meeting her boyfriend here, he must be a real big spender," Dolen said sarcastically. "I wouldn't even stay in this shithole."

"And that's saying something," quipped Dan.

Dolen ignored Dan's comment as he watched Maryland climb back into her car and start it. She drove down the dirt drive toward the far cabin.

"Let's go," Dan said.

Dolen and Dan climbed out of the car and walked casually toward the motel office, then veered off, heading along the back of the cabins. They were in the high desert now and the cabins had the sporadic cover of pine trees, spread across the property. Dolen and Dan made their way along a dry gulch that ran behind the cabins, until they came to the last one,

Maryland's cabin. The light inside was on and the shade to the back bedroom window was open. Dolen could see through the window, which stood about head high, as Maryland brought a suitcase into the bedroom. Dan motioned to Dolen that he was heading around to the other side of the cabin, and Dolen acknowledged him with a nod of his head as he watched Dan vanish into the dark.

Dolen spit his pinch of Skoal out as Maryland moved from the bedroom and into the main part of the cabin and out of Dolen's sight. So Spire thought this girl was involved in the killings, thought Dolen. Well, maybe she was. She had killed her father and spent time in a mental institution with Blue and that nut job, Anna Burnside.

Dolen spun his head around, checking out his cover. He looked up through the branches of the pine tree overhead, the night sky covered with more stars than he had ever seen. As deserts go, Dolen thought, the high part was a little more tolerable than the crap down below, at least it had some trees. Dolen brought his eyes back to the empty bedroom when suddenly a strange feeling, as if he was sinking into a black pool of water, being pulled down, swept over him. He closed his eyes, trying to steady himself. After a moment, he opened them again to the brightness of the bedroom as Maryland walked back in. He watched, as Maryland kicked off her red heels and sat on the bed for a long moment, not moving, her back towards him.

Dolen realized that his hand had slipped under his blazer to the handle of his gun. Maryland didn't move. She just sat there on the bed, eerily still. Dolen slid against the branches of the pine tree, moving closer to the window, wondering what the hell was going on. Maryland's back was straight, her head, lowered, as if she'd been knocked unconscious, her arms lying limply by her side. She sat there, not moving, for what seemed, to Dolen, a very long time. Suddenly, she stood up, grabbing the suitcase off the bed and moving into the bathroom, shutting the door behind her.

Dolen let his hand slip from his gun. He didn't like this. He couldn't shake the bad feeling. He thought about moving around to the other side of the cabin and finding Dan, but dismissed the thought immediately, keeping his gaze pinned on the bathroom door. The heat of the day was gone from the desert and it had gotten downright cold. Dolen could see his breath hanging in the air, as he breathed in and out. After a long while, the door the bathroom opened and Dolen stopped breathing. "What the fuck?" he mumbled softly.

Dolen moved closer to the window as Maryland stepped out of the bathroom. She was naked, sort of. She was wearing a short, dark wig, with a mustache to match, her blue eyes, now the color of coal, her breasts, pressed flat, with the pressure of an ace bandage. Dolen couldn't believe what he was seeing. Dangling between her legs was a cock. Dolen could see, as she moved toward the bed, that a harness, wrapped around her ass, strapped it on to her. She pulled on a pair of men's jeans, adjusting the thing, as if it were real, before buckling her belt up and putting on a sweatshirt. Dolen watched, stunned, as she sat on the bed and laced up a pair of men's work boots. He didn't know what she had done to her face and skin, but as she slipped on a pair of gold eyeglasses, he thought to himself that if he didn't know better, he'd swear, on his grandmother's grave, that that was a man sitting there. The way she moved, even the way she sat, was not like she was pretending to be a man. It was as if she was a man. Maybe in her mind, she was, thought Dolen, the type of fucked-up mind that gets you locked up in an institution.

Suddenly Dolen's cell phone rang. Fuck, he screamed in his mind as fumbled for it. He'd forgotten to turn the thing off! He pulled the phone from his pocket and saw that it was Spire calling and silenced it before it rang again. He brought his eyes back to the bedroom, the bathroom door now closed, the thing that was Maryland, gone.

EIGHTY-EIGHT

Mick stared at himself in the bathroom mirror, as he slipped a tab of Dexedrine under his tongue. He played with it, its taste sweet, like that of his lover. He liked the Paradise Motel, true; it was a little more rundown than it had been when he and Maryland had first visited, years before. They had driven here, on his birthday, and had stayed up all night talking and laughing. Maryland had been in a particularly good mood, since for the first time in her life, she'd been safe. Mick had seen to that, beneath the Hollywood sign.

Earlier that evening, Maryland had thought about killing herself, about jumping off the top of the sign and ending her pain forever. She had called the Bender and told him so and he had come running, but instead of finding Maryland waiting for him, he had found Mick. A seventeen-year-old girl, like Maryland, was no match for the Bender, for his abuse and violence, thought Mick, but he was. Mick stared at his face in the mirror. Killing is strange, he thought. Not something suited for a young girl, but Mick was a man, and men are different. He could still see the round, wet eyes of the Bender fill with fear as he'd stepped into him, the tire iron connecting with a liquid thud, specks of the Bender's blood spotting Mick's face. Mick had watched as the Bender squirmed on the bloody plastic. He had smoked a cigarette, staring out at the lights of Hollywood, celebrating his birthday and remembering all that the Bender had done to his Maryland.

It had started as "little games," as the Bender had called it, played in Maryland's bed, since the age of nine. By the time the Bender met Mick, the "games" had become rape on a regular basis. Mick knew that, as a child, Maryland had tried to hide from the Bender, in the woods, in the

310

recesses of the basement, in the dark closet, filled with the scent of mothballs and the rough touch of wool. But he had always found her. Her small, frail frame was no match for the heft of the man. No match for the size and violence of her father.

Mick had taken his time with the Bender. He'd broken just about every bone in the Bender's body, before crushing his skull with the tire iron. He had driven all the way to the Paradise Motel, still covered with the Bender's blood, Maryland at his side. They said nothing to each other along the way. They didn't need to, their bond, sealed with the Bender's blood. Mick laid a line of cocaine out on the edge of the sink and sniffed it up. His head snapped back as he found his reflection once again in the mirror. "One must learn to love oneself…with a wholesome and healthy love, so that one can bear to be with oneself and not roam." Nietzsche wrote that. It was so true, thought Mick.

After Mick had killed the Bender, Maryland had learned to love herself. Especially during the time Mick was forbidden to see her. There are many benders in life though, those who try and twist you, to bend you to their will, to hurt you. If you are pure, like Maryland, you are never safe. The benders are drawn like a moth to a flame, sensing the goodness, wanting to use it, steal it, or better yet, like what they had done with their own, turn it to bitterness and hate. Maryland had met many benders during her years in Hollywood without Mick, but Mick had returned, and straightened them out.

Even now, so close to the conclusion of Mick's production, to the reunion of three souls, Mick, Maryland, and his lover, there were benders about. Meddling, trying to ruin things, trying to bend them away from each other. In fact, thought Mick, there was one outside the bedroom window right now. Mick did another line off cocaine off the edge of the sink, before turning off the light in the bathroom. He looked out the bathroom window, the full moon casting a soft light upon the desert landscape. He watched the pine trees in the distance, swaying softly in the wind, before quietly sliding the window open and slipping outside.

Mick felt the soft dirt of the high desert beneath his boots as he dropped from the bathroom window. He crouched in the darkness, moving like an apparition, silent, unseen. He kept low as he looked around the corner of the cabin and saw the fat cop, standing under the branches of a pine tree near the bedroom window. The cop had been one of Mick's favorite actors in his production. But Mick had saved his best scene for last, the scene that pulls on the heartstrings of the audience, that makes one a star, the death scene. In a flash, Mick pulled the blade from his pocket and grabbed the fat man from behind. The cop's hand went up, in defense, as Mick ran the blade across his neck and the cop fell straight back to the ground. Mick heard the gurgling sound of the cop, trying to breathe, as he moved calmly toward the front of the cabin. He wiped the blood off the blade of his knife as he thought about how a good director should always have control of his project, control of the final cut, and as he reached into his pocket for the keys to Maryland's BMW, he thought about how he, Mick Carter, was no different.

EIGHTY-NINE

Dolen lay on the ground, looking up at the stars, dying. He had known this was going to happen and now that it had, he was strangely calm. Blood seeped through his fingers, which were wrapped around his throat as he struggled to stay alive for a few more minutes. If he could only tell Dan what he knew, that the killer was a thing, a thing called Maryland.

Suddenly Dan's face came into view, hovering over Dolen.

"Oh, my God, Joe! Oh, my God!" gasped Dan. Dan's face was lit for an instance, with what Dolen could only imagine was a car's headlights.

Dan stood quickly, raising his handgun and opening fire as the sound of a car, peeling away, reached Dolen. Dan kept firing, the flash from his 9 mm lighting up his face. His clip, empty, Dan bent down to Dolen, applying pressure to Dolen's wound.

"Hold on, partner! Hold on! Don't give up on me!"

Dolen's eyes found Dan's, which were filling with tears.

"Keep pressure on it, Joe! Press! Press!"

Dolen did as Dan said, as he heard Dan call it in, "Officer down! Officer down! The Paradise Motel!" but Dolen knew it was no use. He was struggling to breathe and growing weaker. Dolen stared up into the heavens, as Dan's voice faded and the world around him grew soft. He knew what was happening. He was dying, with the useless knowledge of a dead man.

NINETY

Mick had the BMW floored. He was going 125 mph along the dark, desert road and gaining speed. To make matters more thrilling, he was doing it with his headlights off, so that he couldn't be seen, letting the light of the full moon guide his way. He wasn't sure that he'd killed the fat cop. The big man had gotten his hand up at the last minute, partially blocking Mick's blade. Either way, thought Mick, judging by the gurgling sound the cop was making, he wouldn't be meddling in Mick's business anymore.

Mick was glad that he had sent Maryland away, before he had cut the cop. She had done enough, delivering the BMW to him. She had been a wreck when she had arrived at the cabin and Mick had been afraid that she was having another breakdown, as she kept talking about Blue and how the cops had found him dead in Mick's cave, so he had had no choice but to tell her to go. It wasn't her fault. Unlike Mick, she was emotionally frail. He should never have involved her so deeply in his plans, but there had been no getting around it this time. She was not cut out for what Mick did. He knew that; she never had been. She was not Mick.

Mick thought about the cops at the cabin. The blue-eyed one had unloaded on Mick as he'd sped away. Mick didn't like that. He'd heard some of the shots hit the car, but he couldn't stop, not yet. He needed some more distance between him and the cabin. The Beemer was nearing 140 mph now, the full moon hovering over the road. Mick felt as if he was flying through space, heading toward his destiny with his lover. Maryland had finally met her. In a moment of calm, she had told Mick what he had always known she would, that she reminded Maryland of herself. They had a similar past, both having been victims of Bob Bayloff's lies and deceit and hurt by a business filled with benders.

Mick hit a long straightaway and shut his eyes, lifting his hands off the steering wheel, believing the car was alive and driving itself, that destiny had taken hold and was steering for him. He kept the pedal pressed to the floor, with his eyes closed and hands raised, and when he opened them again, he knew he'd been right, the car, flying down the road straight and clean, heading toward the moon and the stars beyond.

It was then that he heard the sound coming from behind him. He recognized it and realized that he couldn't wait any longer to see where the cop's bullets had hit the car. Mick slowly brought the Beemer's speed down and pulled over to the side of the road. Flashlight in hand, he climbed out of the car.

The desert was deathly quiet, the moon lighting the landscape as if it was daylight. He was no longer in the high desert, brush, cactus, and shrubs now marking the empty spaces around him. He breathed in the night air, thinking to himself how he loved the desert. His thoughts were broken, though, by the sounds, once again, coming from behind him. He turned on his flashlight and moved to the back of the car, examining it. There was a hole in the bumper right above the exhaust pipe and another, in the middle of the trunk. Mick stuck his finger into the hole in the trunk, the bullet having passed right through.

"Fuck!" he said aloud.

He pulled out his keys and popped open the trunk, his flashlight finding the open eyes of Stacey, moaning through her gag, her legs and arms bound, her black dress covered in blood.

NINETY-ONE

A bright light blinded Stacey as she felt the bindings on her legs and arms being cut and the gag removed from her mouth. Her eyes adjusted to the darkness as the light was pulled away and she was helped out of the trunk of the car. She leaned on the car for support, trying to focus on the man standing in front of her, the wound to her left shoulder burning like hell. Stacey gasped for breath, her mind clouded by the tranquilizers and chloroform she'd been given back at the cave. The air was fresh and cool and she breathed it in great gulps. She leaned her head back and saw the sky above covered with stars and couldn't remember the last time she had been outside. She couldn't make out the face of the man standing in front of her, but it wasn't Blue.

"Thank you..." she mumbled softly.

The man examined the wound to her shoulder with his flashlight. "We'll have to clean that up, it's bleeding a lot, but it's only a flesh wound," he said to her, his voice quiet and soft.

A flesh wound? How had she been hurt? Stacey couldn't think, couldn't put the pieces together. Everything seemed discombobulated. All she could do was feel the fresh air in her lungs and the breeze blowing through her hair. All she could see were the stars in the sky. She didn't know how long she had been kept in that box in the cave, but Blue had put her there, she and Brenda, after drugging them.

"Where's my sister? Where's Brenda?" Stacey asked the man with the flashlight.

"She's safe.

"Where is she?"

"The police have her."

316

"And Blue?"

"He's dead," said the man. Stacey's eyes filled slowly with tears. She wrapped her arms around herself.

"Dead?"

"Yes."

Stacey broke down and began to sob, her whole body shaking. The man reached out to support her as she brought her hands to her face. "Thank, God...Thank God..." she cried between sobs.

The man brushed the hair from her forehead as he brought a bottle of water towards her lips, his touch soft and gentle.

"Drink, now, drink," he said softly, and Stacey did just that. She lowered the empty bottle, breathing deeply.

"How do you know he's dead?" she asked.

"Because I killed him," the man replied.

A strong wind blew through the desert as Stacey tried to process what the man had said. He'd killed him?

"Blue was not one of us," said the man. "He was not like us."

Stacey listened to the man talk. Though she had never seen his face before, she recognized the voice now. It was the voice of her abductor, the voice that had spoken to her through the metal trunk of the car the day she was taken, the voice that whispered sweet nothings of horror from behind her, the day she stepped off into the ravine. It was the voice of her captor and Blue's partner.

The man turned his face to the light of the full moon; there was something strange about it, thought Stacey. He reached out and took Stacey gently by the arm.

"Now let's get that wound cleaned up," he said. He opened the back door of the car and sat Stacey down on the seat as he pulled a first aid kit from the trunk. He kneeled down in front of Stacey and began attending to her wound. The man seemed to have some twisted affection for her, thought Stacey, so for now, she would play along. She would bide her time because now, it was just her and him, in the middle of nowhere, and she was never going back into a trunk, or a box, or a cave, ever again.

NINETY-TWO

They had airlifted Dolen from the Paradise Motel to the nearest hospital, about thirty-five miles away. I sat in my car, in the parking lot of the Paradise motel, waiting for Dan to finish up. He and a swarm of police detectives and FBI agents were going over Maryland's cabin and the crime scene. Dan had called me about Dolen while I was halfway to the desert and the Oasis Bar, having driven straight from Maryland's house after finding out that Mick was Maryland and Maryland was Mick. I had tried calling both Dolen and Dan to tell them so, but they hadn't picked up their phones. Now, I knew why.

Dolen had been alive but unconscious, Dan said, when they had airlifted him out, and though the blade had missed his carotid artery, he had lost a lot of blood and was in surgery. I had filled Dan in on what I had found and seen at Maryland's house. For now, it was our little secret, as Dan was unable to pass on any of the information, without getting me arrested, to his fellow detectives, because of the illegal way I had obtained it. Now that the word was out, though, about Maryland, a search warrant would be issued for her residence and soon, everyone would know what, for the moment, only Dan and I did.

I saw Dan walking through the dim light toward my car. I had known him a long time and he seemed to have aged ten years since the beginning of this case; maybe we all had. I stepped out of the car and shook Dan's hand as we moved even farther away from the cabin and all of the cops. Dan's eyes found mine with the look of an old friend in pain, one willing to do anything, even beyond his badge, to end this.

"What do you think, Will?" Dan asked.

"I think I know where he might be headed," I said.

"He?" Dan asked, puzzled. "You mean Maryland Sharp?"

"Yes and no," I replied. "I mean Mick Carter. I believe they are two very different people, or I should say, personalities, that operate independently of each other. Yes, it's Maryland and I'll leave the official diagnosis to the doctors, but Mick's the killer. He seems to be on some type of revenge kick and has formulated it into some sick, fantasy film production, with me, you, Dolen, and everyone else, playing a part. We can't forget that they are separate, in the off chance that, if given the opportunity, we may be able to reach Maryland somehow, and shut Mick down."

"Or we can just kill her," replied Dan, "and shut him down that way."

"Or that," I said, "though I'd like the chance to find out what happened to Stacey."

Dan lowered his eyes to the desert and nodded his head.

"He had this thing in the house, this 8 mm film I told you about, titled "location scout." I recognized all of the places, all the crime scenes, but two." Dan raised his eyes to mine.

"And?"

"One was the Paradise Motel, that I now recognize…"

"And the other?" asked Dan.

"It was the Salton Sea. Bombay Beach to be more specific. A broken-down hobble of old trailers and motels, on the shore of what used to be a thriving paradise before the lake turned toxic. I've been there once. It's a perfect place to go, perfect, if you want no one to find you."

A slow smile slipped across Dan's face.

"What are we waiting for then? I'll drive," he said.

The sun was beginning to rise as we pulled out of the parking lot of the Paradise Motel, in the white Chevy. We were both exhausted, but the thought of sleep was far away. I could see the 8 mm film flickering in my head, the heat rising off the Salton Sea, one trailer sitting like a silver dot, parked on the horizon.

"You think he's got Stacey?" asked Dan.

"I hope so," I said, after a long moment, "because if he doesn't, she's dead."

NINETY-THREE

Mick glanced at his lover, Stacey, lying on the back seat of the BMW as he drove. She was deep asleep and would be for a while, thanks to the water Mick had given her earlier in the night, when he had taken her from the trunk of the car. It was better this way, thought Mick, that she was sedated; better for him and for her. He needed some time without disturbance, some time to think, some time to have Maryland join him. Mick looked out at the sun rising in streaks of color above the Salton Sea as he approached its shores. He had picked this place, as a halfway point, for the three of them. A place where they could be reacquainted and let some time pass, away from the probing eyes and ears of the men with the tin badges. A place to recover, before finally heading south across the border to live a life by the sea, a life away from the benders of L.A. and its insidious business, a life with people, pure and simple, like he and Maryland. It had always been Maryland and Mick's dream to live by the Sea of Cortez, in Mexico, and now that dream was about to come true.

But first, there was the matter of time. Time to let things cool down. To let the search for them, on every border crossing from here to Texas, grow tired. Time in a place no one knows and no one goes. A sea turned dead with toxic salt, inhabited by outcasts and eccentrics, living in the rubble, heat, and stench of a once beautiful oasis in the desert.

Mick drove the BMW along a rutted road by the water passing a broken marina. A marina that in the '60s had been filled with boats, ready to be taken out to play on a fresh water haven for water sports. The marina now, like the sea itself, was vacant and lifeless.

Mick pushed a glass "bullet," filled with the Beaver's best coke, up into his nostril and took a hit. He pulled the Beemer off the road and up to

320

an old shack, by the marina, that acted as a general store. A faded sign, advertising "Bait & Tackle For Sale," from decades before, still raised above it.

Mick looked back at Stacey sleeping. She so reminded him of Maryland. He was glad he had saved her from Bob Bayloff, Blue, and the benders of Hollywood, just as he had saved Maryland, both women not deserving of such abuse.

Mick closed his eyes and enjoyed the buzz of the Beaver's coke as he thought about how his production was almost over and had been a rousing success. He felt it would have both critical and commercial staying power and would be remembered for a long time, especially by the men with the tin badges. He wished his escape to the Salton Sea, with his lover, had been cleaner, that Maryland had not led the cops to the Paradise Motel, but unseen events happen on every production and one must improvise. It would not tarnish the brilliance of the final cut.

Mick opened the door to the car and stepped out. He needed some supplies before heading to the trailer. His lover would be hungry when she awoke and he planned on making her a beautiful breakfast. It was time to make up for all the discomfort he had caused her, discomfort that was necessary to save her, but regrettable.

Mick took three steps toward the store and froze in his tracks, his head screaming with sounds, his skin on fire. Mick lowered his gaze to the ground, afraid to look up. It couldn't be, he thought, it just couldn't. It was impossible. But as he raised his eyes slowly to the phone booth, next to the old store, he realized it was true. The Bender had found him again. Sensing how close he and Maryland were to happiness, the Bender had changed forms and tracked him down. Mick stared at the Bender in the phone booth. He thought he could outsmart Mick. He thought if he could get rid of Mick, he could play his "little games" once again with Maryland. He thought by disguising himself as a small, skinny man, with thinning hair and a mustache, that Mick wouldn't recognize him. But he was wrong. Mick watched as the Bender hung up the phone. He turned and looked right at Mick and Mick felt Maryland scream.

The Bender opened the door to the phone booth and stepped outside, moving toward a rusted Ford, parked near the water, his back to Mick. In a flash, Mick closed the distance between him and the Bender. Flipping open his stiletto with a click, he thrust the blade deep into the Bender's head, near the base of his skull. The Bender froze up, like he had been shocked, as Mick pulled the long blade from the back of his head and he fell face down into the dirt.

Mick stared down at the dead Bender. This was getting annoying, he thought. He hoped this was the last time he'd have to kill him, maybe not, though. The Bender was stubborn and would probably keep trying to get to Maryland. Mick searched the Bender's pockets and found the keys to the Ford. He opened the trunk of the car, and without much effort, lifted the skinny Bender into it. He then shut the trunk and threw the keys into the mud of the Salton Sea, before heading inside the store, to buy him and his lover something nice to eat.

NINETY-FOUR

A flood created the Salton Sea in 1905, when water from the Colorado River flowed into the area, creating the largest lake in California. In the '50s and '60s it was deemed "the miracle in the desert," attracting over a half a million visitors a year, including many celebrities from Hollywood, but by the '70s, the lake had begun to die, due to toxic salt levels. Soon, the lakeshore was littered with thousands of dead fish and the stench of rotting algal blooms. Decay in the lake soon followed onshore as people fled, leaving just a few hundred residents to live in the rubble of a broken dream. Who would possibly want to come here? It was a forgotten place, with forgotten people, and as Dan and I approached the lake, I thought that must have been what Mick was hoping for, when he'd decided to hide in a dead miracle, to be forgotten.

Dan pulled the white Chevy up to an old Bait and Tackle store, which after driving along the lake for miles, seemed to be the only sign of life. It had been a long night and morning, and as the sun headed toward afternoon, we both needed a strong cup of coffee and something to eat. We smelled the stench of the lake before we even climbed out of the car. I stretched my arms over my head as I looked past a rusted Ford to the mud of the lake and a broken-down marina.

"Holy shit," Dan said, getting a whiff of the lake. "You said you've been here before? Why the hell did you do that?"

"Stacey and I drove through once, right after we were married. We both wanted see it. It's an environmental freak," I said.

"Like your Mick and Maryland," Dan replied. "Only difference is the lake is dead and they're not."

Dan brushed passed me and opened the door to the store. I knew he was upset about Dolen, tired and sick of the case, as was I. It didn't help that we'd gotten a call about Dolen's condition. He was out of surgery and on life support, but it was too early to tell if he would make it. The doctors put the odds at fifty-fifty.

I followed Dan into the store. It was a cluttered general store with just about everything, but my favorite part was its air conditioning. There was a kid behind the counter, a teenager. As Dan searched for something to eat, I walked up to the kid and pulled out a photo of Mick and Maryland I had taken from their wardrobe closet. I slid the photo across the counter toward the kid, who looked up from his cell phone like I was the most annoying thing in the world.

"By any chance, have you seen either one of these people?"

The boy looked quickly from the picture to me. I showed him my credentials. "I'm a private investigator."

The boy pointed to my ID. "How do I know that's real?" he said with some attitude. Dan walked up to the counter carrying some sandwiches and drinks. He laid his Gold Shield down.

"This is real," he said. He then opened up his blazer, giving the kid a good look at his gun. "So is this."

The kid seemed to turn pale as he looked at Dan's gun and glare. He pointed to Mick in the photo. "This guy was in here this morning...buying some breakfast stuff."

"Was he alone?" I asked. The kid nodded.

"Anything strike you as strange about him?" asked Dan.

"Like what?" the kid replied.

"His appearance? Did he seem like...a normal...man to you...or did something seem off?"

I looked at Dan, surprised by his question. I guess he was having a hard time swallowing what I told him about Maryland.

"Yeah..."

"Yeah, something seemed off?"

"Yeah..."

"Like what?" Dan said, getting frustrated with the kid. The boy looked from Dan to me.

"He looked like he wanted to kick my ass, that's what. He looked

324

fucking crazy…" blurted the kid almost breaking into tears. "My dad was here and he thought the same thing, only he'd spoken to the guy on the phone a couple months ago when the guy bought a trailer my dad was selling, out past Bombay Beach. It was Mr. Wilson's trailer, one of the nicest ones here, but he passed away and this guy saw it online and my dad sold it to him. That's all I know…I swear…I swear…"

The kid looked like he was going to pass out from anxiety. Dan laid his hand on the kid's shoulder. "That's really good, really good. What's your name, son?"

"Johnny, Johnny Roberts."

"Well, Johnny," Dan said, with the warmest smile he could muster on no sleep, "we only have one more question for you. Could you tell us how to get to that trailer your dad sold?"

"That's easy," said the kid, looking relieved. "You just stay on this road, out past everything. It's the last trailer on the lake, right across from the Sands Motel."

Dan and I walked out into heat and the stench of the miracle in the desert. It amazed me that anyone still lived here. Dan made his way to the car as I passed the rusty old Ford, a scraggly dog licking at the ground near its rear. I stopped as I saw a thick, red liquid drip from the trunk of the car to the dusty ground below.

"Hey, Dan!" I called out, just as Dan was climbing into the Chevy. "Come here a minute."

Dan moved beside me. I pointed at the dripping trunk. Dan moved closer, kneeling down toward the trunk and the dirt. He reached into the breast pocket of his blazer and pulled out a pair of latex gloves, snapping them on. He rubbed one of the drops between the fingers of his gloves. He stood up and looked back at me as I moved next to him.

Dan pressed a rusted button in the middle of the trunk and lifted up its lid. Inside was a small, skinny man, with thinning hair and a mustache. The man lay face down in the trunk, in a pool of blood, dripping from a hole in the back of his head. Dan raised his eyes to mine.

"We better call the boys for some backup. Tell them what we know, before this gets more out of hand."

"You call it in," I said, "but we're not waiting. We're still heading out

325

to the trailer, right?

Dan nodded his head. "You bet we are, partner." Dan closed the trunk of the car. "Right fucking now."

NINETY-FIVE

Stacey woke up to the smell of bacon cooking. She was lying on a bed, in one of the two cabins of a mobile home. Her right wrist, secured by a handcuff, connected to a long chain locked around a bar above the bathroom sink, used for hanging towels. She had opened her eyes and seen her captor cooking when she smelled the bacon, having a clear view of him, through the open door to her room. He was a tall, spooky looking thing, she thought. Even the way he cooked looked threatening. He spoke to himself in soft mumbles and Stacey had no doubt that he was insane. He had left her dressed and covered with a light blanket, a new, silk pillow beneath her head. When he was done cooking, he had set two plates across from each other on the galley table, a vase of fresh flowers in the middle, as if he was preparing for a date.

It was then that Stacey had closed her eyes and pretended that she was still asleep. He had walked into the cabin, gently shaking her, trying to wake her up, calling her "lover," and telling her that breakfast was ready and that it was time for a "new beginning," but she had kept her eyes closed tight and soon he had moved away. That had been two hours ago.

Stacey didn't know how long she could pretend that she was still sedated from the drugs he had given her the night before. Soon, she thought, he would find out that she was faking. So, she did the only thing in her power. She waited, watching him through the flickering light of her eyelashes, waiting for a chance to do something, making a plan in her mind. That chance came near noon. Stacey watched, as her captor did three lines of cocaine off a gold-rimmed mirror in the salon. He then stood up and grabbed the keys to his car. Stacey shut her eyes as she saw him approach the front door of the trailer. She heard it open, then shut, his

327

footsteps banging on the metal stairs leading to the ground.

Stacey stood up immediately, looking out the window of her cabin as the man walked toward his car. Quickly, she lay down on the bathroom floor, grabbing the chain that bound her with both hands. She placed her feet on the wall beneath the towel holder she was chained to and pulled as hard as she could against it, using her legs as leverage. Stacey arched her back as the bar began to pull slowly away from the thin wall of the trailer. She gave one last yank with all her strength and the bar pulled free from the wall.

Stacey lay still for a second, listening to the silence before she grabbed the metal bar and stood up, looking once again out the window. The man was walking back from his car, having retrieved a bottle of liquor. Stacey moved quickly out of the bedroom and behind the front door. She could feel her heart racing as she heard him climb the three steps to the trailer door. Stacey held the bar like a baseball bat and waited. The man opened the door and stepped inside and Stacey swung the bar as hard as she could.

The THUNK of the bar against the man's head hung in the air as he stumbled into the far wall and to the floor. Stacey's eyes found his, open and staring at her, before she dove out the door, tripping on the metal stairs and landing hard on the ground below. She stood up and ran like hell toward the main road. She looked back and saw her captor stumbling down the stairs, handgun in hand. She screamed at the top of her lungs for help, but there was nobody there to hear her. There was nothing around at all, but an old motel. Stacey ran across the road to the dilapidated motel, trying to find cover, squeezing through the rotted boards that blocked its front door.

Stacey entered the darkness of the motel, halls leading away to the left and the right, two sets of stairs, on each side, heading up to a second level. Light trickled in through the decay and partially boarded windows. She held onto the towel pole tightly, knowing full well that it was no match for a gun and that her only chance was to hide. She bolted down the hall to her left, entering one of the last rooms in the hallway. She moved through the rubble of the room and opened the door to an old, crumbling closet and moved inside. She pulled the door closed, hiding within the closet's darkness. She tried to calm her breathing as she heard the sound of boards breaking near the front of the motel and she knew he was near. There were many rooms in the motel, she thought. He would have to pick the right one to find her. She closed her eyes and thought that she would get away, or die trying. Those were the only two things she would allow to happen. She felt herself relax, as she realized that one way or another, today, it would end.

Stacey heard footsteps coming down the hall. She listened as doors opened and then closed one after another, the footsteps getting closer until they entered her room. No, Stacey thought, her eyes closed tight, no. She tried not to breathe, not to make a sound. Then, there it was, a slow scratching sound on the door of the closet, just like the day she been taken and held in the trunk. He was trying to torment her once again. But she was not the same woman. Stacey raised the point of the metal bar toward the closet door. When he opened the door, she would put it right through his eye. Yet, the door didn't open. Instead, she heard the man's soft voice whispering through the wood of the closet, "I love you, I love you, I love you," then the sound of the man's footsteps leaving the room and heading back down the hall.

Stacey didn't move as she listened to the silence. He was gone, she thought. He had left. She held her breath, listening. Yet, all she heard was her heart beating. Why did he leave? He knew she was in the closet. Was he letting her go? Had that been his plan all along? Is that what he meant by "a new beginning"? She wrapped herself in the silence. He was definitely gone.

Suddenly, Stacey realized how weak she was. Her body ached and she burned with thirst and hunger. The heat and dust of the closet were overwhelming and she wasn't sure how much longer she could take it. Stacey rested her head against the closet door for what seemed like an eternity, listening for any sound, but she heard nothing. Slowly she slid the door to the closet open and stepped out into the room. She looked between the cracks of the boarded-up window and could see the trailer sitting across the street. Had he gone back there, she wondered? She didn't want to find out. She would make her way out through the back of the motel and follow the road until she reached something or someone.

Stacey moved slowly out into the hall and back toward the direction of the front door. She passed each door to the various rooms with caution until she saw a sign that read "POOL" with an arrow leading toward the rear of the motel. Perfect, Stacey thought. She approached the hall and turned the corner, and he was there.

Before Stacey could react, he jabbed his right hand out, the blue spark of the stun gun connecting to her chest in a crackling jolt that lifted her off her feet and to the floor. Stacey lay on her back, unable to move, her body twitching from the shock. He stood over her, shaking his head.

"Why would you do this to me, lover?" he asked, in a voice so soft and calm it chilled her. Stacey concentrated on her breathing, her head fuzzy and filled with pain.

"I know you have been among the benders for too long. But the three of us, Maryland, myself, and you, are connected by destiny. Once you've shed the bender's shackles, you'll remember that. But for now, you are like a horse that needs to be broken, before finding its true path."

The man reached down and yanked Stacey easily to her feet, smiling at her. "So that's just what I intend to do."

The man then dragged Stacey toward the front door of the motel, the boards once covering the entrance, gone. She tried to move her feet, but they just slipped along the floor. Suddenly, he stopped.

Stacey raised her eyes to the entrance of the motel, seeing a white Chevy parked in front of the trailer across the street. There were two men there, one standing, one kneeling, looking down at the ground. The man kneeling stood up and pointed toward the motel as they started to walk toward it.

Suddenly, Stacey's heart felt like it would leave her chest as she watched the man on the left begin to cross the street. Her eyes flooded with tears. It was Will! The man, holding Stacey, quickly pulled his gun, raising it toward the two men as Stacey screamed, "GET DOWN! WILL!"

NINETY-SIX

I heard the scream at the same time as the shot and hit the dirt. I knew, before my chest hit the ground, that the scream had been Stacey's. Dan returned fire as I yelled at him "IT'S STACEY! HOLD YOUR FIRE!" Dan looked over to me as I got up, sprinting toward the old motel sign for cover; Dan right on my heels. I slammed my back against the cement of the sign, Dan landing beside me.

"You think that was Stacey?"

"I know it was!" I said. The shooting from the motel had stopped. I raised my head above the sign, the entrance to the motel clear. I stood up and ran toward the front of the motel with Dan. We reached the motel, pressing our backs against its wall. We slid towards the entrance, entering it, guns raised.

I swept the lobby of the dark motel with the barrel of my gun. Light trickled in through the half-boarded windows. I looked down the halls in both directions and up the stairs. There were a lot of rooms.

"You take the right side, I'll clear the left," Dan said. I looked over at Dan, wondering about the wisdom of splitting up.

"He's in here, Will. We need to flush him out. He's got nowhere else to go."

I nodded as Dan disappeared down the hallway to the left and I moved down the hallway to the right, listening for any sound at all. I swung my gun from room to room as I moved by their open doors.

I saw a sign, marking the entrance to the motel bar, off to the left. I moved inside the rubble of the bar, a dilapidated pool table sitting in the middle of the room. What must have been, at one point, a nice, wooden bar, ran along the wall past a rack of old pool cues. I moved through the darkness of the bar, past the dust-covered tables toward the back and the form of a small stage there.

I stopped, gun raised, trying to let my eyes adjust to the darkness. It's then that I saw her. Stacey was on stage, tied to a pole. A metal chain, cuffed to her wrist, was wrapped around the pole and her neck. Stacey had a rag stuffed into her mouth. Her eyes, opened wide, were on me. She shook her head as I moved toward her. She screamed through her gag, when suddenly, the crackling spark of a stun gun lit up the darkness, it's jolt electrifying my body and lifting me off my feet.

I landed hard on my back, my gun tumbling from my hand and across the floor. I saw Mick step from the darkness, stun gun in hand. I tried to move, but couldn't. I tried to scream for Dan, but all that came out was a gurgling sound. I saw my gun lying on the floor a few feet away. I turned slowly onto my side, feebly reaching for it with my hand. Mick grabbed an old pool cue from the rack on the wall, and as I reached out for my gun, he brought it down with a CRACK onto my head. The force of the blow broke the pool cue in half, and put me on my back again.

I looked up, through eyes blurry with pain, as Mick stood over me. He pulled his gun from the waistband of his pants and sat on my chest, slipping its barrel into my mouth.

"When I take this gun from your mouth, you're going to call, nice and sweet, to your blue-eyed friend and get him in here. If you don't I'm going to blow your head off. Understand?" Mick removed the gun from my mouth, putting it against my head. "Call to him," he said.

"So you can kill him? No way…" I replied. I stared up at Mick. Even this close, I could see no Maryland within him. Mick removed the gun from my head and brought its metal to my jaw with a crunch. I felt a tooth loosen as blood filled my mouth.

"You are an actor, take your direction."

I spit out a bloody breath as Mick placed the gun once again to my temple.

"You've seen my work," he said calmly. "You know what I'm capable of. Though you are not a bender, you are interfering with our destiny and my production. Call to him, or the shot through your head will bring him here."

Suddenly there was gunfire, a round taking a chunk out of the bar near Mick. Mick returned fire as he grabbed me and yanked me to my feet, using me as a human shield. I saw Dan, near the door to the bar, taking cover as Mick kept firing, pulling me back through a set of swinging doors and into the kitchen of the motel. I tried to move my feet, but they were like Jell-O, as Mick pulled me across the kitchen floor, our bodies slamming against the metal bar of the back door, which opened with a bang.

Outside, my eyes tried to adjust to the blinding sunshine as Mick slid a piece of rusted junk through the handle of the kitchen door. I could hear Dan pushing on the door from the other side, trying to get out as Mick yanked me toward the street as he screamed, "Move!"

Suddenly, Mick stopped, his arm around my neck, his gun to my head. He was staring, as was I, at his trailer across the street, two police cars parked in front, one, a K-9 unit. I watched as the officers exited the trailer, one holding the leash of a German Shepherd. Mick spun me around, his gun to the back of my head. "Run!" he screamed as he grabbed me by the collar and pushed me forward.

I ran as best I could across the open field, an old water tower, the only thing in sight. My head was on fire, my legs were weak, and I was spitting blood. I glanced back at the trailer as the officers released the German Shepherd. He ran, at full speed, straight towards us.

I could hear the barking of the dog get closer and closer as we approached the old water tower. A metal ladder ran from the ground to its top. Mick pushed me along, faster, and I almost fell. I felt I had no control of my body. My head was soft and foggy, my vision blurred. We reached the water tower and Mick shoved me against the ladder.

"There is no way out," I said, spitting blood. "Give up…"

"Climb or die," Mick said calmly. I looked over his shoulder, the police dog closing fast. I wasn't sure if he was headed for Mick or me. I started to climb.

The dog reached the tower just as Mick's feet left the ground. He jumped, barking and biting at Mick, unable to reach him as I continued to climb, Mick close behind me.

Suddenly there was a tremendous WOOSH as a Sheriff's helicopter flew over our heads. It turned, banking around the water tower as we reached the top. Mick immediately grabbed me, putting his gun to the back of my head as the chopper flew around the water tower, a megaphone crackling from it, telling Mick to "DROP YOUR WEAPON! PUT YOUR HANDS IN THE AIR!"

The helicopter circled at eye level, a sniper visible in its open door, his telescopic sight trained on us. Mick held me in front of him for cover, slowly turning us, tracking the helicopter's path.

Mick pushed me to the edge of the tower, his body pressed to mine. A shot to him would kill me, too. I looked down at the forty-foot drop. There were three police cars sitting below, sirens in the distance, signaling more on the way. I saw Dan moving across the open field toward the tower, his arm wrapped tightly around Stacey. The chopper's blades cut through the air, around and around, in a dizzying pattern. She was alive, I thought, Stacey was alive and finally safe.

"Maryland!" I screamed above the sound of the chopper. "Don't let them kill you!"

"Maryland isn't here, my friend," said the soft voice behind me. "It's just the two of us."

Mick inched both of us closer to the edge and I realized that he was going to end this thing on his terms and most likely take me with him. He was ready to die, to stay in control. I saw Stacey looking up at me and remembered what I had always told her about not being a victim. With that, I brought my head straight back into Mick's nose and heard it CRUNCH.

Mick stumbled back as his grip loosened and I spun around grabbing the gun, struggling for control. The gun went off as I swung my right leg to his feet, taking them out from underneath him and putting him onto his back. I bent his wrist back with both hands and he dropped the gun, which slid down the sloped top of the water tower, coming to rest near its edge. Mick quickly brought his knee up into my groin and I let out a guttural grown as he slid out from underneath me.

He dove toward the gun and I grabbed one of his legs, trying to keep him from it. I tried to pull him back as the chopper hovered overhead. Mick placed a kick to my pained face, and I lost my grip on him. I saw him reach the gun and raise it toward me as a shot rang out from above and Mick's shoulder exploded in a burst of red, the power of the sniper's shot sending him over the edge.

I got up and moved to the edge of the tower. Mick was hanging from a bar, just below the rim, holding on with one hand, looking up at me. I reached my hand down.

"Grab hold! Take my hand!" I screamed. He slowly lifted his free hand, covered in blood, up toward mine.

NINETY-SEVEN

Mick grabbed the hand of the actor and smiled. They thought they had him now, but he had them. It was Mick's production. He would have the last say in how it ended and whom it starred. He saw his lover far below his dangling feet, looking up at him. Even now, he could feel her. He could sense the rediscovery he had placed within her soul, the knowledge of their eternity. He knew, deep down, that she was proud of him for all he had done, for saving her from the benders, as was Maryland. The bullhorn, from the chopper blared, but Mick did not listen. He was in charge.

The actor tried to pull Mick up to the top of the tower, but Mick knew it was too late. Mick had been so preoccupied that he had failed to see that the Bender had returned and changed forms once again. Mick saw him clearly now, sitting in the rear of the hovering helicopter, his telescopic sight trained on Mick's head. The next shot from the Bender would kill Mick. But for now, the actor was in the way. The actor was yelling at him and calling him Maryland for some reason and begging Mick to pull himself up, but Mick would not give the Bender a clean shot. He would not give him the satisfaction of ending his life, in this world, as Mick had ended his. Mick thought of how much he loved Maryland and all that he had done for her.

"Whatever is done for love always occurs beyond good and evil." Nietzsche wrote that, thought Mick. It was so true.

The actor understood this. He loved, as Mick did, forever. That's why he was here. Though Mick had tried to kill the actor, looking up at him now, he was glad he hadn't. Mick had always known his destiny, known how his production would end. It was he, who was the real star.

336

Immortality, Mick thought, was but forty feet away. Like Marilyn and James Dean, he would never be forgotten. Real artists live forever, and as he let go of the actor's hand and fell toward the desert, he hoped that Maryland would understand this too, understand him, but then again, he thought, she always did.

NINETY-EIGHT

Mick's body hit the ground with a sickening crunch. I could still feel his grip on my hand, dangling over the edge of the tower. He had smiled at me and then let go. I stood up and moved to the ladder. I grabbed its metal rungs and climbed, faster than I should have, down, down, toward the desert floor, one hand below the other, quickly. I was almost there. I reached the bottom and moved toward Mick, pushing my way through the cops surrounding him. I heard an officer call for an ambulance as I reached him. Mick lay on his back, blood seeping from the back of his head, his gaze toward the sky. I stood over him. He blinked, his eyes finding mine. He raised his hand feebly and I kneeled down beside him as he tried to speak. I took his hand in mine as a breathless voice came from him, pained and pleading.

"Don't hurt Maryland," he gasped.

And with that, Mick Carter was gone. I stared at him, unable to pull myself away. I reached down and gently slid the dark contact from Mick's right eye, revealing the lifeless, blue eye of Maryland Sharp, staring up at me.

I felt Dan's hand on my shoulder as I heard his voice from above.

"It's over, Will," he whispered, "it's over."

NINETY-NINE

"Don't hurt Maryland." Mick's last words echoed in my mind. It's what the whole case had been about. It had been two weeks since the death of Maryland and Mick, and I had learned a lot. From Maryland's own writings found in her home, we were able to piece together the grievances, Mick believed, the victims had perpetrated on Maryland.

Shari Canes was guilty of openly questioning Maryland's sanity to the producers of the film "All Gone," saying it was impossible to work with her and that she had been told, by a close friend, that Maryland had spent time in a mental institution. This accusation spread quickly, in the rumor mill that is Hollywood, and led to Maryland being fired, over the protests of Bob Bayloff, by the studio, the day before filming began. The studio stating that they did not want the risk, or publicity, of an "institutionalized actress" on set. Shortly after, Bob Bayloff kicked Maryland out of his house and his life, and Alfred Green dropped her as a client, sighting her "unstable nature" to other agents, in essence, blackballing her from the business.

Seeking refuge, Maryland sought out her old acting coach, Mary Higgins, for support. But Mary had apparently gotten the "memo," and not wanting to be associated with failure, the worst sin in Hollywood, refused to work with Maryland, or see her for any casting sessions, stating to industry insiders that, "...except for her lack of talent, she barely remembered the girl..."

Shortly thereafter, Mick returned to Maryland's life.

My ex-brother-in-law, Bill Benson, was simply in the wrong place at the wrong time. By then, Mick's resurrection was in full swing, and his twisted, fantasy film production was well underway. It starred all of us, but only a lucky few, myself included, would make it out alive. Blue would not. Though he and Mick had formed a twisted alliance, his violent violation of Maryland, when they had been in the institution, coupled with his premature parole, put him right on top of Mick's payback list for those who had "hurt Maryland."

Dolen, though, had survived. He was still in the hospital, but was recovering nicely, evident, Dan said, by his ever-increasing grumpiness. Dan had tried to cheer Dolen up by showing him his picture on the front page of the L.A. Times and by notifying Dolen that he was to be decorated with the Police Department's highest Medal of Valor, as would Dan, for their shootout with Blue. Dolen's only response was to quip that maybe now, he could get laid.

With Maryland dead, her files had been unsealed, confirming what Blake and I had suspected, that she had been found not guilty, by reason of insanity, for the killing of her father, the night before her eighteenth birthday. Which, according to Dr. Stewart Jackson, who had overseen her care at the institution, was the night "Mick" was born.

The clinical term for Maryland's condition was "Dissociative Identity Disorder," formally known as "Multiple Personality Disorder." According to Dr. Jackson, Dissociative Identity Disorder is a "coping mechanism," thought to be an effect of severe trauma during childhood, usually from extreme, repetitive physical, emotional, or sexual abuse. Maryland had experienced all of these, at the hands of her father, having been sexually molested since the age of nine. That is, until Mick arrived.

The disorder is characterized by the presence of one or more "distinct" identities or personalities that have power over the person's behavior. The change is called "switching" and can take from seconds, to minutes, to days. The "alters," as they are known, or different identities, have their own race, age, and sex, along with their own gestures, posture, way of walking, talking, and distinct memory variations. Other symptoms can include auditory and visual hallucinations, flashbacks in reaction to certain "triggers," drug abuse, suicidal tendencies, amnesia, lost time, out of body experiences, trances, and violence. All of which, the doctor said, Maryland suffered when she first arrived at the institution. But with treatment and time, Maryland healed her damaged psyche and purged her violent "alter," Mick, from her life. She went on to be healthy and productive, graduating from college and even earning a master's degree in literature, before returning to Hollywood to pursue acting, where, after experiencing pain, failure, and humiliation at the hands of those within the "business," her disorder and Mick returned with a vengeance.

The doctor believed that Mick's obsession with Stacey was Maryland's subconscious seeing the two of them as fellow victims. This obsession manifested itself in her "alter," Mick, as a belief that they were long lost lovers and soul mates destined to be reunited.

After recovering for a time in L.A., Stacey had gone up to Big Bear to stay with her sister, Brenda, both women having suffered great trauma and loss, and judging from what Stacey had said, the move could be permanent.

Stacey and I had spent an emotional few days together at my house, before she left to see her sister. My love, as hers, was still there for the Stacey and Will we used to be. In some ways, it had grown stronger. I loved her and always would. But things were different now. She was different. I was different, in a way, both for the better. Our friendship and bond had been strengthened by the ordeal we had gone through, and I would always be there for her, as she would for me. But the future did not hold a place for the Will and Stacey we had once been. How could it? They no longer existed. And as Stacey kissed me good-bye and smiled, we both seemed to understand that love had many shades. It wasn't black or white and that, sometimes, the true test of real love was letting go.

As for me, the fame and notoriety of the case seemed to have made me temporarily famous for a second time in my life. Though I was grateful for the endless parade of cases that could employ me for the next twenty years, for the moment, I wanted none of it, so I had returned to the desert.

As I looked out at the sparkling blue of the pool from the shade of my misted cabana at the Ritz-Carlton, in Palm Springs, I thought to myself that this was not the desert that Dolen so famously hated; even he could be happy here. I took a sip of my Jack and Coke as I watched a beautiful girl, in a blue bikini, step from the pool. To my amazement, the young woman headed right for me, the moisture glistening on her skin. She looked like a silken creature from another world as she slipped into the chair beside me and laid her head upon my chest. I smiled at Kansas and gave the beautiful creature a kiss.

I closed my eyes and listened to the silence in my head, to the peace and the calm within. I had found the "monster" and Mick had been a monster. But he had not been born from the evil fires of Hell, but from the damaged mind of a young girl. A fragile, human mind, which I knew very well, is where all real monsters were born.

I felt the breath of Kansas upon my chest and gave thanks, to the powers that be, that I was alive, that Stacey, Dan, and Dolen were in the land of the living. I didn't know what the future would bring—none of us ever do—but I knew that I had put the past where it belonged, behind me. I was trying to live in the moment, and as I felt the warm winds of the Santa Anas and the form of Kansas against my body, I knew that living in the moment is exactly where I wanted to be.

51649581R00194

Made in the USA
San Bernardino, CA
29 July 2017